EX LIBRIS

VINTAGE **CLASSICS**

CLASSIC GHOST STORIES

CLASSIC GHOST STORIES

E.F. Benson, Mary Elizabeth Braddon,
Francis Marion Crawford, Charles Dickens,
Arthur Conan Doyle, Elizabeth Gaskell,
Lafcadio Hearn, O. Henry, Henry James,
M.R. James, Rudyard Kipling, Perceval Landon,
Joseph Sheridan Le Fanu, Edith Nesbit,
Margaret Oliphant, Arthur Quiller-Couch,
Catherine Wells, H.G. Wells, Edith Wharton

VINTAGE

7 9 10 8

Vintage Classics is part of the Penguin Random House group of companies
whose addresses can be found at global.penguinrandomhouse.com.

Penguin
Random House
UK

Title page illustration copyright © Andrew Davis 2022
Interior illustrations copyright © Ed Kluz 2017
Story compilation © Vintage Classics 2017, an imprint of
The Random House Group Limited

This collection first published by Vintage Classics in 2017
This paperback first published in Vintage Classics in 2022

penguin.co.uk/vintage-classics

A CIP catalogue record for this book is available from the British Library

ISBN 9781784877835

Typset in 12.5/15 pt Fournier MT by Jouve (UK), Milton Keynes
Printed and bound in Great Britain by Clays Ltd, Elcograf S.p.A.

The authorised representative in the EEA is Penguin Random House Ireland,
Morrison Chambers, 32 Nassau Street, Dublin D02 YH68

Penguin Random House is committed to a sustainable future
for our business, our readers and our planet. This book is made
from Forest Stewardship Council® certified paper.

MIX
Paper from
responsible sources
FSC
www.fsc.org   FSC® C018179

CONTENTS

THE SIGNALMAN
BY CHARLES DICKENS

Charles Dickens was born in Hampshire on 7 February 1812. His father was a clerk in the navy pay office, who was well paid but often ended up in financial troubles. When Dickens was twelve years old he was sent to work in a shoe polish factory because his family had been taken to the debtors' prison. His career as a writer of fiction started in 1833 when his short stories and essays began to appear in periodicals. *The Pickwick Papers*, his first commercial success, was published in 1836. In the same year he married the daughter of his friend George Hogarth, Catherine Hogarth. *Oliver Twist* and many other novels followed. *The Old Curiosity Shop* brought Dickens international fame and he became a celebrity in America as well as Britain. He separated from his wife in 1858. Charles Dickens died on 9 June 1870, leaving his last novel, *The Mystery of Edwin Drood*, unfinished. He is buried in Westminster Abbey.

'HALLOA! BELOW there!'

When he heard a voice thus calling to him, he was standing at the door of his box, with a flag in his hand, furled round its short pole. One would have thought, considering the nature of the ground, that he could not have doubted from what quarter the voice came; but instead of looking up to where I stood on the top of the steep cutting nearly over his head, he turned himself about, and looked down the line. There was something remarkable in his manner of doing so, though I could not have said for my life what. But I know it was remarkable enough to attract my notice, even though his figure was fore-shortened and shadowed, down in the deep trench, and mine was high above him, so steeped in the glow of an angry sunset that I had shaded my eyes with my hand before I saw him at all.

'Halloa! Below!'

From looking down the line, he turned himself about again, and raising his eyes, saw my figure high above him.

'Is there any path by which I can come down and speak to you?'

He looked up at me without replying, and I looked down at him without pressing him too soon with a repetition of my idle question. Just then there came a vague vibration in the earth and air, quickly changing into a violent pulsation, and an oncoming rush that caused me to start back, as though it had force to draw me down. When such vapour as rose to my height from this rapid train had passed me, and was skimming away over the landscape, I looked down again, and saw him refurling the flag he had shown while the train went by.

I repeated my enquiry. After a pause, during which he seemed to regard me with fixed attention, he motioned with his rolled-up flag towards a point on my level, some two or three hundred yards distant. I called down to him, 'All right!' and made for that point. There, by dint of looking closely about me, I found a rough zigzag descending path notched out, which I followed.

The cutting was extremely deep, and unusually precipitate. It was made through a clammy stone, that became oozier and wetter as I went down. For these reasons, I found the way long enough to give me time to recall a singular air of reluctance or compulsion with which he had pointed out the path.

When I came down low enough upon the zigzag descent to see him again, I saw that he was standing between the rails on the way by which the train had lately passed, in an attitude as if he were waiting for me to appear. He had his left hand at his chin, and that left elbow rested on his right hand, crossed over his breast. His attitude was one of such expectation and watchfulness that I stopped a moment, wondering at it.

I resumed my downward way, and stepping out upon the level of the railroad, and drawing nearer to him, saw that he was a dark sallow man, with a dark beard and rather heavy eyebrows. His post was in as solitary and dismal a place as ever I saw. On either side, a dripping-wet wall of jagged stone, excluding all view but a strip of sky; the perspective one way only a crooked prolongation of this great dungeon; the shorter perspective in the other direction terminating in a gloomy red light, and the gloomier entrance to a black tunnel, in whose massive architecture there was a barbarous, depressing and forbidding air. So little sunlight ever found its way to this spot, that it had an earthy, deadly smell; and so much cold wind rushed through it, that it struck chill to me, as if I had left the natural world.

Before he stirred, I was near enough to him to have touched him. Not even then removing his eyes from mine, he stepped back one step, and lifted his hand.

This was a lonesome post to occupy (I said), and it had riveted my attention when I looked down from up yonder. A visitor was a rarity, I should suppose; not an unwelcome rarity, I hoped? In me, he merely saw a man who had been shut up within narrow limits all his life, and who, being at last set free, had a newly-awakened interest in these great works. To such purpose I spoke to him; but I am far from sure of the terms I used; for, besides that I am not happy in opening any conversation, there was something in the man that daunted me.

He directed a most curious look towards the red light near the tunnel's mouth, and looked all about it, as if something were missing from it, and then looked at me.

That light was part of his charge? Was it not?

He answered in a low voice, 'Don't you know it is?'

The monstrous thought came into my mind, as I perused the fixed eyes and the saturnine face, that this was a spirit, not a man. I have speculated since, whether there may have been infection in his mind.

In my turn, I stepped back. But in making the action, I detected in his eyes some latent fear of me. This put the monstrous thought to flight.

'You look at me,' I said, forcing a smile, 'as if you had a dread of me.'

'I was doubtful,' he returned, 'whether I had seen you before.'
'Where?'

He pointed to the red light he had looked at.

'There?' I said.

Intently watchful of me, he replied (but without sound), 'Yes.'

'My good fellow, what should I do there? However, be that as it may, I never was there, you may swear.'

'I think I may,' he rejoined. 'Yes; I am sure I may.'

His manner cleared, like my own. He replied to my remarks with readiness, and in well-chosen words. Had he much to do there? Yes; that was to say, he had enough responsibility to bear; but exactness and watchfulness were what was required of him, and of actual work — manual labour — he had next to none. To change that signal, to trim those lights, and to turn this iron handle now and then, was all he had to do under that head. Regarding those many long and lonely hours of which I seemed to make so much, he could only say that the routine of his life had shaped itself into that form, and he had grown used to it. He had taught himself a language down here, if only to know it by sight, and to have formed his own crude ideas of its pronunciation, could be called learning it. He had also worked at fractions and decimals, and tried a little algebra; but he was, and had been as a boy, a poor hand at figures. Was it necessary for him when on duty always to remain in that channel of damp air, and could he never rise into the sunshine between those high stone walls? Why, that depended upon times and circumstances. Under some conditions there would be less upon the line than under others, and the same held good as to certain hours of the day and night. In bright weather, he did choose occasions for getting a little above these lower shadows; but, being at all times liable to be called by his electric bell, and at such times listening for it with redoubled anxiety, the relief was less than I would suppose.

He took me into his box, where there was a fire, a desk for an official book in which he had to make certain entries, a telegraphic instrument with its dial, face and needles, and the little bell of which he had spoken. On my trusting that he would excuse the remark that he had been well educated, and (I hoped I might say without offence) perhaps educated above that station, he observed that instances of slight incongruity in such wise would rarely be found wanting among large bodies of men; that he had heard it was so in workhouses, in the police force, even in that last desperate resource, the army; and that he knew it was so, more or less, in any great railway staff. He had been, when young (if I could believe it, sitting in that hut – he scarcely could), a student of natural philosophy, and had attended lectures; but he had run wild, misused his opportunities, gone down and never risen again. He had no complaint to offer about that. He had made his bed, and he lay upon it. It was far too late to make another.

All that I have here condensed he said in a quiet manner, with his grave dark regards divided between me and the fire. He threw in the word 'sir' from time to time, and especially when he referred to his youth, as though to request me to understand that he claimed to be nothing but what I found him. He was several times interrupted by the little bell, and had to read off messages, and send replies. Once he had to stand without the door, and display a flag as a train passed, and make some verbal communication to the driver. In the discharge of his duties, I observed him to be remarkably exact and vigilant, breaking off his discourse at a syllable, and remaining silent until what he had to do was done.

In a word, I should have set this man down as one of the safest of men to be employed in that capacity, but for the circumstance that while he was speaking to me he twice broke off with a fallen colour, turned his face towards the little bell when it did not ring, opened the door of the hut (which was kept shut to exclude the unhealthy damp), and looked out towards the red light near the mouth of the tunnel On both of those occasions, he came back to the fire with the inexplicable air upon him which I had remarked, without being able to define, when we were so far asunder.

Said I, when I rose to leave him, 'You almost make me think that I have met with a contented man.'

(I am afraid I must acknowledge that I said it to lead him on.)

'I believe I used to be so,' he rejoined, in the low voice in which he had first spoken; 'but I am troubled, sir, I am troubled.'

He would have recalled the words if he could. He had said them, however, and I took them up quickly.

'With what? What is your trouble?'

'It is very difficult to impart, sir. It is very, very difficult to speak of. If ever you make me another visit, I will try to tell you.'

'But I expressly intend to make you another visit. Say, when shall it be?'

'I go off early in the morning, and I shall be on again at ten tomorrow night, sir.'

'I will come at eleven.'

He thanked me, and went out at the door with me. 'I'll show my white light, sir,' he said, in his peculiar low voice, 'till you have found the way up. When you have found it, don't call out! And when you are at the top, don't call out!'

His manner seemed to make the place strike colder to me, but I said no more than, 'Very well.'

'And when you come down tomorrow night, don't call out! Let me ask you a parting question. What made you cry, "Halloa! Below there!" tonight?'

'Heaven knows,' said I. 'I cried something to that effect –'

'Not to that effect, sir. Those were the very words. I know them well.'

'I admit those were the very words. I said them, no doubt, because I saw you below.'

'For no other reason?'

'What other reason could I possibly have?'

'You had no feeling that they were conveyed to you in any supernatural way?'

'No.'

He wished me good-night, and held up his light. I walked by the side of the down line of rails (with a very disagreeable sensation of a train coming behind me) until I found the path. It was easier to mount than to descend, and I got back to my inn without any adventure.

Punctual to my appointment, I placed my foot on the first notch of the zigzag next night, as the distant clocks were striking eleven. He was waiting for me at the bottom, with his white light on. 'I have not called out,' I said, when we came close together; 'may I speak now?' 'By all means, sir.' 'Good-night, then, and here's my hand.' 'Good-night, sir, and here's mine.' With that we walked side by side to his box, entered it, closed the door, and sat down by the fire.

'I have made up my mind, sir,' he began, bending forward as soon as we were seated, and speaking in a tone but a little above a whisper, 'that you shall not have to ask me twice what troubles me. I took you for someone else yesterday evening. That troubles me.'

'That mistake?'

'No. That someone else.'

'Who is it?'

'I don't know.'

'Like me?'

'I don't know. I never saw the face. The left arm is across the face, and the right arm is waved – violently waved. This way.'

I followed his action with my eyes, and it was the action of an arm gesticulating, with the utmost passion and vehemence, 'For God's sake, clear the way!'

'One moonlight night,' said the man, 'I was sitting here, when I heard a voice cry, "Halloa! Below there!" I started up, looked from that door, and saw this someone else standing by the red light near the tunnel, waving as I just now showed you. The voice seemed hoarse with shouting, and it cried, "Look out! Look out!" And then again, "Halloa! Below there! Look out!" I caught up my lamp, turned it on red, and ran towards the figure, calling, "What's wrong? What has happened? Where?" It stood just outside the blackness of the tunnel. I advanced so close upon it that I wondered at its keeping the sleeve across its eyes. I ran right up at it, and had my hand stretched out to pull the sleeve away, when it was gone.'

'Into the tunnel?' said I.

'No. I ran on into the tunnel, five hundred yards. I stopped, and held my lamp above my head, and saw the figures of the measured distance, and saw the wet stains stealing down the walls and trickling through the arch. I ran out again faster than I had run in (for I had a mortal abhorrence of the place upon me), and I looked all round the red light with my own red light, and I went up the iron ladder to the gallery atop of it, and I came down again, and ran back here. I telegraphed both ways, "An alarm has been given is anything wrong?" The answer came back, both ways, "All well."'

Resisting the slow touch of a frozen finger tracing out my spine, I showed him how that this figure must be a deception of his sense of sight; and how that figures, originating in disease of the delicate nerves that minister to the functions of the eye, were known to have often troubled patients, some of whom had become conscious of the nature of their affliction, and had even proved it by experiments upon themselves. 'As to an imaginary cry,' said I, 'do but listen for a moment to the wind in this unnatural valley while we speak so low, and to the wild harp it makes of the telegraph wires.'

That was all very well, he returned, after we had sat listening for a while, and he ought to know something of the wind and the wires – he who so often passed long winter nights there, alone and watching. But he would beg to remark that he had not finished.

I asked his pardon, and he slowly added these words, touching my arm, 'Within six hours after the appearance, the memorable accident on this line happened, and within ten hours the dead and wounded were brought along through the tunnel over the spot where the figure had stood.'

A disagreeable shudder crept over me, but I did my best against it. It was not to be denied, I rejoined, that this was a remarkable coincidence, calculated deeply to impress his mind. But it was unquestionable that remarkable coincidences did continually occur, and they must be taken into account in dealing with such a subject. Though to be sure I must admit, I added (for I thought I saw that he was going to bring the objection to bear upon me), men of common sense did not allow much for coincidences in making the ordinary calculations of life.

He again begged to remark that he had not finished.

I again begged his pardon for being betrayed into interruptions.

'This,' he said, again laying his hand upon my arm, and glancing over his shoulder with hollow eyes, 'was just a year ago. Six or seven months passed, and I had recovered from the surprise

and shock, when one morning, as the day was breaking, I standing at the door, looked towards the red light and saw the spectre
again.' He stopped, with a fixed look at me.

'Did it cry out?'

'No. It was silent.'

'Did it wave its arm?'

'No. It leaned against the shaft of the light, with both hands
before the face. Like this.'

Once more I followed his action with my eyes. It was an
action of mourning. I have seen such an attitude in stone figures
on tombs.

'Did you go up to it?'

'I came in and sat down, partly to collect my thoughts, partly
because it had turned me faint. When I went to the door again,
daylight was above, and the ghost was gone.'

'But nothing followed? Nothing came of this?'

He touched me on the arm with his forefinger twice or thrice,
giving a ghastly nod each time: 'That very day, as a train came
out of the tunnel, I noticed, at a carriage window on my side,
what looked like a confusion of hands and heads, and something
waved. I saw it just in time to signal the driver, Stop! He shut off,
and put his brake on, but the train drifted past here a hundred
and fifty yards or more. I ran after it, and, as I went along, heard
terrible screams and cries. A beautiful young lady had died
instantaneously in one of the compartments, and was brought in
here, and laid down on this floor between us.'

Involuntarily I pushed my chair back, as I looked from the
boards at which he pointed to himself.

'True, sir, True. Precisely as it happened, so I tell it you.'

I could think of nothing to say to any purpose, and my mouth
was very dry. The wind and the wires took up the story with a
long lamenting wail.

He resumed. 'Now, sir, mark this, and judge how my mind is troubled. The spectre came back a week ago. Ever since, it has been there, now and again, by fits and starts.'

'At the light?'

'At the danger-light.'

'What does it seem to do?'

He repeated, if possible with increased passion and vehemence, that former gesticulation of, 'For God's sake, clear the way!'

Then he went on. 'I have no peace or rest from it. It calls to me, for many minutes together, in an agonised manner, "Below there! Look out! Look out!" It stands waving to me. It rings my little bell –'

I caught at that. 'Did it ring your bell yesterday evening when I was here, and you went to the door?'

'Twice.'

'Why, see,' said I, 'how your imagination misleads you. My eyes were on the bell, and my ears were open to the bell, and if I am a living man, it did *not* ring at those times. No, nor at any other time, except when it was rung in the natural course of physical things by the station communicating with you.'

He shook his head. 'I have never made a mistake as to that yet, sir. I have never confused the spectre's ring with the man's. The ghost's ring is a strange vibration in the bell that it derives from nothing else, and I have not asserted that the bell stirs to the eye. I don't wonder that you failed to hear it. But I heard it.'

'And did the spectre seem to be there, when you looked out?'

'It *was* there.'

'Both times?'

He repeated firmly, 'Both times.'

'Will you come to the door with me, and look for it now?'

He bit his underlip as though he were somewhat unwilling,

but arose. I opened the door, and stood on the step, while he stood in the doorway. There was the danger-light. There was the dismal mouth of the tunnel. There were the high, wet stone walls of the cutting. There were the stars above them.

'Do you see it?' I asked him, taking particular note of his face. His eyes were prominent and strained, but not very much more so, perhaps, than my own had been when I had directed them earnestly towards the same spot.

'No,' he answered, 'it is not there.'

'Agreed,' said I.

We went in again, shut the door, and resumed our seats. I was thinking how best to improve this advantage, if it might be called one, when he took up the conversation in such a matter-of-course way, so assuming that there could be no serious question of fact between us, that I felt myself placed in the weakest of positions.

'By this time you will fully understand, sir,' he said, 'that what troubles me so dreadfully is the question, What does the spectre mean?'

I was not sure, I told him, that I did fully understand.

'What is its warning against?' he said, ruminating, with his eyes on the fire, and only by times turning them on me. 'What is the danger? Where is the danger? There is danger overhanging somewhere on the line. Some dreadful calamity will happen. It is not to be doubted this third time, after what has gone before. But surely this is a cruel haunting of *me*. What can I do?'

He pulled out his handkerchief, and wiped the drops from his heated forehead.

'If I telegraphed danger on either side of me, or on both, I can give no reason for it,' he went on, wiping the palms of his hands. 'I should get into trouble, and do no good. They would think I was mad. This is the way it would work: Message — "Danger!

Take care!" Answer – "What danger? Where?" Message – "Don't know. But, for God's sake, take care!" They would displace me. What else could they do?'

His pain of mind was most pitiable to see. It was the mental torture of a conscientious man, oppressed beyond endurance by an unintelligible responsibility involving life.

'When it first stood under the danger-light,' he went on, putting his dark hair back from his head, and drawing his hands outward across and across his temples in an extremity of feverish distress, 'why not tell me where that accident was to happen – if it must happen? Why not tell me how it could be averted – if it could have been averted? When on its second coming it hid its face, why not tell me, instead, "She is going to die. Let them keep her at home"? If it came, on those two occasions, only to show me that its warnings were true, and so to prepare me for the third, why not warn me plainly now? And I, Lord help me! A mere poor signalman on this solitary station! Why not go to somebody with credit to be believed, and power to act?'

When I saw him in this state, I saw that for the poor man's sake, as well as for the public safety, what I had to do for the time was to compose his mind. Therefore, setting aside all question of reality or unreality between us, I represented to him that whoever thoroughly discharged his duty must do well, and that at least it was his comfort that he understood his duty, though he did not understand these confounding appearances. In this effort I succeeded far better than in the attempt to reason him out of his conviction. He became calm; the occupations incidental to his post as the night advanced began to make larger demands on his attention: and I left him at two in the morning. I had offered to stay through the night, but he would not hear of it.

That I more than once looked back at the red light as I ascended the pathway, that I did not like the red light, and that

I should have slept but poorly if my bed had been under it, I see no reason to conceal. Nor did I like the two sequences of the accident and the dead girl. I see no reason to conceal that either.

But what ran most in my thoughts was the consideration how ought I to act, having become the recipient of this disclosure? I had proved the man to be intelligent, vigilant, painstaking and exact; but how long might he remain so, in his state of mind? Though in a subordinate position, still he held a most important trust, and would I (for instance) like to stake my own life on the chances of his continuing to execute it with precision?

Unable to overcome a feeling that there would be something treacherous in my communicating what he had told me to his superiors in the company, without first being plain with himself and proposing a middle course to him, I ultimately resolved to offer to accompany him (otherwise keeping his secret for the present) to the wisest medical practitioner we could hear of in those parts, and to take his opinion. A change in his time of duty would come round next night, he had apprised me, and he would be off an hour or two after sunrise, and on again soon after sunset. I had appointed to return accordingly.

Next evening was a lovely evening, and I walked out early to enjoy it. The sun was not yet quite down when I traversed the field path near the top of the deep cutting. I would extend my walk for an hour, I said to myself, half an hour on and half an hour back, and it would then be time to go to my signalman's box.

Before pursuing my stroll, I stepped to the brink and mechanically looked down, from the point from which I had first seen him. I cannot describe the thrill that seized upon me when, close at the mouth of the tunnel, I saw the appearance of a man, with his left sleeve across his eyes, passionately waving his right arm.

The nameless horror that oppressed me passed in a moment, for in a moment I saw that this appearance of a man was a man indeed, and that there was a little group of other men, standing at a short distance, to whom he seemed to be rehearsing the gesture he made. The danger light was not yet lighted. Against its shaft, a little low hut, entirely new to me, had been made of some wooden supports and tarpaulin. It looked no bigger than a bed.

With an irresistible sense that something was wrong, with a flashing self-reproachful fear that fatal mischief had come of my leaving the man there, and causing no one to be sent to overlook or correct what he did, I descended the notched path with all the speed I could make.

'What is the matter?' I asked the men.

'Signalman killed this morning, sir.'

'Not the man belonging to that box?'

'Yes, sir.'

'Not the man I know?'

'You will recognise him, sir, if you knew him,' said the man who spoke for the others, solemnly uncovering his own head and raising the end of the tarpaulin, 'for his face is quite composed.'

'Oh, how did this happen, how did this happen?' I asked, turning from one to another as the hut closed in again.

'He was cut down by an engine, sir. No man in England knew his work better. But somehow he was not clear of the outer rail. It was just at broad day. He had struck the light, and had the lamp in his hand. As the engine came out of the tunnel, his back was towards her, and she cut him down. That man drove her, and was showing how it happened. Show the gentleman, Tom.'

The man, who wore rough dark dress, stepped back to his former place at the mouth of the tunnel.

'Coming round the curve in the tunnel, sir,' he said, 'I saw him at the end, like as if I saw him down a perspective-glass. There was no time to check speed, and I knew him to be very careful. As he didn't seem to take heed of the whistle, I shut it off when we were running down upon him, and called to him as loud as I could call.'

'What did you say?'

'I said, "Below there! Look out! Look out! For God's sake, clear the way!"'

I started.

'Ah! it was a dreadful time, sir. I never left off calling to him. I put this arm before my eyes not to see, and I waved this arm to the last; but it was no use.'

Without prolonging the narrative to dwell on any one of its curious circumstances more than on any other, I may, in closing it, point out the coincidence that the warning of the engine-driver included, not only the words which the unfortunate signalman had repeated to me as haunting him, but also the words which I myself – not he – had attached, and that only in my own mind, to the gesticulation he had imitated.

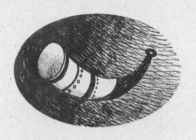

AT CHRIGHTON ABBEY
BY MARY ELIZABETH BRADDON

Mary Elizabeth Braddon was born in London in 1835. She was briefly an actress, and published poems and stories in various periodicals before the publication of *Lady Audley's Secret* (1862) won her great fame and popularity. She went on to write seventy-four books, mainly 'sensation fiction' and supernatural tales, and she edited several successful magazines. She married a publisher in 1874 and had six children. Mary Elizabeth Braddon died in Richmond in 1915.

THE CHRIGHTONS were very great people in that part of the country where my childhood and youth were spent. To speak of Squire Chrighton was to speak of a power in that remote western region of England. Chrighton Abbey had belonged to the family ever since the reign of Stephen, and there was a curious old wing and a cloistered quadrangle still remaining of the original edifice, and in excellent preservation. The rooms at this end of the house were low, and somewhat darksome and gloomy, it is true; but, though rarely used, they were perfectly habitable, and were of service on great occasions when the Abbey was crowded with guests.

The central portion of the Abbey had been rebuilt in the reign of Elizabeth, and was of noble and palatial proportions. The southern wing, and a long music-room with eight tall narrow windows added on to it, were as modern as the time of Anne. Altogether, the Abbey was a very splendid mansion, and one of the chief glories of our country.

All the land in Chrighton parish, and for a long way beyond its boundaries, belonged to the great Squire. The parish church was within the park walls, and the living in the Squire's gift – not a very valuable benefice, but a useful thing to bestow upon a younger son's younger son, once in a way, or sometimes on a tutor or dependant of the wealthy house.

I was a Chrighton, and my father, a distant cousin of the reigning Squire, had been rector of Chrighton parish. His death left me utterly unprovided for, and I was fain to go out into the bleak unknown world, and earn my living in a position of dependence – a dreadful thing for a Chrighton to be obliged to do.

Out of respect for the traditions and prejudices of my race, I made it my business to seek employment abroad, where the degradation of one solitary Chrighton was not so likely to inflict shame upon the ancient house to which I belonged. Happily for myself, I had been carefully educated, and had industriously cultivated the usual modern accomplishments in the calm retirement of the Vicarage. I was so fortunate as to obtain a situation at Vienna, in a German family of high rank; and here I remained seven years, laying aside year by year a considerable portion of my liberal salary. When my pupils had grown up, my kind mistress procured me a still more profitable position at St Petersburg, where I remained five more years, at the end of which time I yielded to a yearning that had been long growing upon me – an ardent desire to see my dear old country home once more.

I had no very near relations in England. My mother had died some years before my father; my only brother was far away, in the Indian Civil Service; sister I had none. But I was a Chrighton, and I loved the soil from which I had sprung. I was sure, moreover, of a warm welcome from friends who had loved and honoured my father and mother, and I was still further encouraged to treat myself to this holiday by the very cordial letters I had from time to time received from the Squire's wife, a noble warm-hearted woman, who fully approved the independent course I had taken, and who had ever shown herself my friend.

In all her letters for some time past Mrs Chrighton begged that, whenever I felt myself justified in coming home, I would pay a long visit to the Abbey.

'I wish you could come at Christmas,' she wrote, in the autumn of the year of which I am speaking. 'We shall be very gay, and I expect all kinds of pleasant people at the Abbey. Edward is to be married early in the spring – much to his father's satisfaction, for the match is a good and appropriate one. His *fiancée* is to be among our guests. She is a very beautiful girl; perhaps I should say handsome rather than beautiful. Julia Tremaine, one of the Tremaines of Old Court, near Hayswell – a very old family, as I daresay you remember. She had several brothers and sisters, and will have little, perhaps nothing, from her father; but she has a considerable fortune left her by an aunt, and is thought quite an heiress in the country – not, of course, that this latter fact had any influence with Edward. He fell in love with her at an assize ball in his usual impulsive fashion, and proposed to her in something less than a fortnight. It is, I hope and believe, a thorough love-match on both sides.'

After this followed a cordial repetition of the invitation to myself. I was to go straight to the Abbey when I went to England, and was to take up my abode there as long as ever I pleased.

This letter decided me. The wish to look on the dear scenes of my happy childhood had grown almost into a pain. I was free to take a holiday, without detriment to my prospects. So, early in December, regardless of the bleak dreary weather, I turned my face homewards, and made the long journey from St Petersburg to London, under the kind escort of Major Manson, a Queen's Messenger, who was a friend of my late employer, the Baron Fruydorff, and whose courtesy had been enlisted for me by that gentleman.

I was three-and-thirty years of age. Youth was quite gone;

beauty I had never possessed; and I was content to think of myself as a confirmed old maid, a quiet spectator of life's great drama, disturbed by no feverish desire for an active part in the play. I had a disposition to which this kind of passive existence is easy. There was no wasting fire in my veins. Simple duties, rare and simple pleasures, filled up my sum of life. The dear ones who had given a special charm and brightness to my existence were gone. Nothing could recall *them*, and without them actual happiness seemed impossible to me. Everything had a subdued and neutral tint; life at its best was calm and colourless, like a grey sunless day in early autumn, serene but joyless.

The old Abbey was in its glory when I arrived there, at about nine o'clock on a clear starlit night. A light frost whitened the broad sweep of grass that stretched away from the long stone terrace in front of the house to a semicircle of grand old oaks and beeches. From the music-room at the end of the southern wing, to the heavily framed Gothic windows of the old rooms on the north, there shone one blaze of light. The scene reminded me of some weird palace in a German legend; and I half expected to see the lights fade out all in a moment, and the long stone façade wrapped in sudden darkness.

The old butler, whom I remembered from my very infancy, and who did not seem to have grown a day older during my twelve years' exile, came out of the dining-room as the footman opened the hall-door for me, and gave me cordial welcome, nay insisted upon helping to bring in my portmanteau with his own hands, an act of unusual condescension, the full force of which was felt by his subordinates.

'It's a real treat to see your pleasant face once more, Miss Sarah,' said this faithful retainer, as he assisted me to take off my travelling-cloak, and took my dressing-bag from my hand. 'You look a trifle older than when you used to live at the Vicarage twelve year ago, but you're looking uncommon well for all that; and, Lord love your heart, miss, how pleased they all will be to see you! Missus told me with her own lips about your coming. You'd like to take off your bonnet before you go to the drawing-room, I daresay. The house is full of company. Call Mrs Marjorum, James, will you?'

The footman disappeared into the back regions, and presently reappeared with Mrs Marjorum, a portly dame, who, like Truefold the butler, had been a fixture at the Abbey in the time of the present Squire's father. From her I received the same cordial greeting, and by her I was led off up staircases and along corridors, till I wondered where I was being taken.

We arrived at last at a very comfortable room – a square tapes-tried chamber, with a low ceiling supported by a great oaken beam. The room looked cheery enough, with a bright fire roaring in the wide chimney; but it had a somewhat ancient aspect, which the superstitiously inclined might have associated with possible ghosts.

I was fortunately of a matter-of-fact disposition, utterly sceptical upon the ghost subject; and the old-fashioned appearance of the room took my fancy.

'We are in King Stephen's wing, are we not, Mrs Marjorum?' I asked; 'this room seems quite strange to me. I doubt if I have ever been in it before.'

'Very likely not, miss. Yes, this is the old wing. Your window looks out into the old stable-yard, where the kennel used to be in the time of our Squire's grandfather, when the Abbey was even a finer place than it is now, I've heard say. We are so full of company this winter, you see, miss, that we are obliged to make use of all these rooms. You'll have no need to feel lonesome. There's Captain and Mrs Cranwick in the next room to this, and the two Miss Newports in the blue room opposite.'

'My dear good Marjorum, I like my quarters excessively; and I quite enjoy the idea of sleeping in a room that was extant in the time of Stephen, when the Abbey really was an abbey. I daresay some grave old monk has worn these boards with his devout knees.'

The old woman stared dubiously, with the air of a person who had small sympathy with monkish times, and begged to be excused for leaving me, she had so much on her hands just now.

There was coffee to be sent in; and she doubted if the still-room maid would manage matters properly, if she, Mrs Marjorum, were not at hand to see that things were right.

'You've only to ring your bell, miss, and Susan will attend to you. She's used to help waiting on our young ladies sometimes, and she's very handy. Missus has given particular orders that she should be always at your service.'

'Mrs Chrighton is very kind; but I assure you, Marjorum, I don't require the help of a maid once in a month. I am accustomed to do everything for myself. There, run along, Mrs Marjorum, and see after your coffee; and I'll be down in the drawing-room in ten minutes. Are there many people there, by the bye?'

'A good many. There's Miss Tremaine, and her mamma and younger sister; of course you've heard all about the marriage – such a handsome young lady – rather too proud for my liking; but the Tremaines always were a proud family, and this one's an heiress. Mr Edward is so fond of her – thinks the ground is scarcely good enough for her to walk upon, I do believe; and somehow I can't help wishing he'd chosen someone else – someone who would have thought more of him, and who would not take all his attentions in such a cool offhand way. But of course it isn't my business to say such things, and I wouldn't venture upon it to any one but you, Miss Sarah.'

She told me that I would find dinner ready for me in the breakfast-room, and then bustled off, leaving me to my toilet.

This ceremony I performed as rapidly as I could, admiring the perfect comfort of my chamber as I dressed. Every modern appliance had been added to the sombre and ponderous furniture of an age gone by, and the combination produced a very pleasant effect. Perfume-bottles of ruby-coloured Bohemian glass, china brush-trays and ring-stands brightened the massive oak dressing-table; a low luxurious chintz-covered easy-chair of the Victorian era stood before the hearth; a dear little writing-table of polished maple was placed conveniently near it; and in the background the tapestried walls loomed duskily, as they had done hundreds of years before my time.

I had no leisure for dreamy musings on the past, however, provocative though the chamber might be of such thoughts. I arranged my hair in its usual simple fashion, and put on a dark-grey silk dress, trimmed with some fine old black lace that had been given to me by the Baroness – an unobtrusive demi-toilette, adapted to any occasion. I tied a massive gold cross, an ornament that had belonged to my dear mother, round my neck with a scarlet ribbon; and my costume was complete. One glance at the looking-glass convinced me that there was nothing dowdy in my appearance; and then I hurried along the corridor and down the staircase to the hall, where Truefold received me and conducted me to the breakfast-room, in which an excellent dinner awaited me.

I did not waste much time over this repast, although I had eaten nothing all day; for I was anxious to make my way to the drawing-room. Just as I had finished, the door opened, and Mrs Chrighton sailed in, looking superb in a dark-green velvet dress richly trimmed with old point lace. She had been a beauty in her youth, and, as a matron, was still remarkably handsome. She had, above all, a charm of expression which to me was rarer and more delightful than her beauty of feature and complexion.

She put her arms round me, and kissed me affectionately.

'I have only this moment been told of your arrival, my dear Sarah,' she said; 'and I find you have been in the house half an hour. What must you have thought of me!'

'What can I think of you, except that you are all goodness, my dear Fanny? I did not expect you to leave your guests to receive me, and am really sorry that you have done so. I need no ceremony to convince me of your kindness.'

'But, my dear child, it is not a question of ceremony. I have been looking forward so anxiously to your coming, and I should not have liked to see you for the first time before all those people. Give me another kiss, that's a darling. Welcome to Chrighton. Remember, Sarah, this house is always to be your home, whenever you have need of one.'

'My dear kind cousin! And you are not ashamed of me, who have eaten the bread of strangers?'

'Ashamed of you! No, my love; I admire your industry and spirit. And now come to the drawing-room. The girls will be so pleased to see you.'

'And I to see them. They were quite little things when I went away, romping in the hayfields in their short white frocks; and now, I suppose, they are handsome young women.'

'They are very nice-looking; not as handsome as their brother. Edward is really a magnificent young man. I do not think my maternal pride is guilty of any gross exaggeration when I say that.'

'And Miss Tremaine?' I said. 'I am very curious to see her.'

I fancied a faint shadow came over my cousin's face as I mentioned this name.

'Miss Tremaine – yes – you cannot fail to admire her,' she said, rather thoughtfully.

She drew my hand through her arm and led me to the drawing-room: a very large room, with a fireplace at each end, brilliantly lighted tonight, and containing about twenty people, scattered about in little groups, and all seeming to be talking and laughing merrily. Mrs Chrighton took me straight to one of the fireplaces, beside which two girls were sitting on a low sofa, while a young man of something more than six feet high stood near them, with his arm resting on the broad marble slab of the mantelpiece. A glance told me that this young man with the dark eyes and crisp waving brown hair was Edward Chrighton. His likeness to his mother was in itself enough to tell me who he was; but I remembered the boyish face and bright eyes which had so often looked up to mine in the days when the heir of the Abbey was one of the most juvenile scholars at Eton.

The lady seated nearest Edward Chrighton attracted my chief attention; for I felt sure that this lady was Miss Tremaine. She was tall and slim, and carried her head and neck with a stately air, which struck me more than anything in that first glance. Yes, she was handsome, undeniably handsome; and my cousin had been right when she said I could not fail to admire her; but to me the dazzlingly fair face with its perfect features, the marked aquiline nose, the short upper lip expressive of unmitigated pride, the full cold blue eyes, pencilled brows, and aureole of pale golden hair, were the very reverse of sympathetic. That Miss Tremaine must needs be universally admired, it was impossible to doubt; but I could not understand how any man could fall in love with such a woman.

She was dressed in white muslin, and her only ornament was a superb diamond locket, heart-shaped, tied round her long white throat with a broad black ribbon. Her hair, of which she seemed to have a great quantity, was arranged in a massive coronet of plaits, which surmounted the small head as proudly as an imperial crown.

To this young lady Mrs Chrighton introduced me.

'I have another cousin to present to you, Julia,' she said smiling –
'Miss Sarah Chrighton, just arrived from St Petersburg.'

'From St Petersburg? What an awful journey! How do you
do, Miss Chrighton? It was really very courageous of you to
come so far. Did you travel alone?'

'No; I had a companion as far as London, and a very kind
one. I came on to the Abbey by myself.'

The young lady had given me her hand with rather a languid
air, I thought. I saw the cold blue eyes surveying me curiously
from head to foot, and it seemed to me as if I could read the con-
demnatory summing-up – 'A frump, and a poor relation' – in
Miss Tremaine's face.

I had not much time to think about her just now; for Edward
Chrighton suddenly seized both my hands, and gave me so
hearty and loving a welcome, that he almost brought the tears
'up from my heart into my eyes'.

Two pretty girls in blue crape came running forward from
different parts of the room, and gaily saluted me as 'Cousin
Sarah'; and the three surrounded me in a little cluster, and
assailed me with a string of questions – whether I remembered
this, and whether I had forgotten that, the battle in the hayfield,
the charity-school tea-party in the vicarage orchard, our picnics
in Hawsley Combe, our botanical and entomological excursions
on Chorwell-common, and all the simple pleasures of their
childhood and my youth. While this catechism was going on,
Miss Tremaine watched us with a disdainful expression, which
she evidently did not care to hide.

'I should not have thought you capable of such Arcadian simplicity, Mr Chrighton,' she said at last. 'Pray continue your
recollections. These juvenile experiences are most interesting.'

'I don't expect you to be interested in them, Julia,' Edward answered, with a tone that sounded rather too bitter for a lover. 'I know what a contempt you have for trifling rustic pleasures. Were you ever a child yourself, I wonder, by the way? I don't believe you ever ran after a butterfly in your life.'

Her speech put an end to our talk of the past, somehow. I saw that Edward was vexed, and that all the pleasant memories of his boyhood had fled before that cold scornful face. A young lady in pink, who had been sitting next Julia Tremaine, vacated the sofa, and Edward slipped into her place, and devoted himself for the rest of the evening to his betrothed. I glanced at his bright expressive face now and then as he talked to her, and could not help wondering what charm he could discover in one who seemed to me so unworthy of him.

It was midnight when I went back to my room in the north wing, thoroughly happy in the cordial welcome that had been given me. I rose early next morning – for early rising had long been habitual to me – and, drawing back the damask-curtain that sheltered my window, looked out at the scene below.

I saw a stable-yard, a spacious quadrangle, surrounded by the closed doors of stables and dog-kennels: low massive buildings of grey stone, with the ivy creeping over them here and there, and with an ancient moss-grown look, that gave them a weird kind of interest in my eyes. This range of stabling must have been disused for a long time, I fancied. The stables now in use were a pile of handsome red-brick buildings at the other extremity of the house, to the rear of the music-room, and forming a striking feature in the back view of the Abbey.

I had often heard how the present Squire's grandfather had kept a pack of hounds, which had been sold immediately after his death; and I knew that my cousin, the present Mr Chrighton, had been more than once requested to follow his ancestor's good example; for there were no hounds now within twenty miles of the Abbey, though it was a fine country for fox-hunting.

George Chrighton, however — the reigning lord of the Abbey — was not a hunting man. He had, indeed, a secret horror of the sport; for more than one scion of the house had perished untimely in the hunting-field. The family had not been altogether a lucky one, in spite of its wealth and prosperity. It was not often that the goodly heritage had descended to the eldest son. Death in some form or other — on too many occasions a violent death — had come between the heir and his inheritance. And when I pondered on the dark pages in the story of the house, I used to wonder whether my cousin Fanny was ever troubled by morbid forebodings about her only and fondly loved son.

Was there a ghost at Chrighton — that spectral visitant without which the state and splendour of a grand old house seem scarcely complete? Yes, I had heard vague hints of some shadowy presence that had been seen on rare occasions within the precincts of the Abbey; but I had never been able to ascertain what shape it bore.

Those whom I questioned were prompt to assure me that they had seen nothing. They had heard stories of the past — foolish legends, most likely, not worth listening to. Once, when I had spoken of the subject to my cousin George, he told me angrily never again to let him hear any allusion to *that* folly from my lips.

That December passed merrily. The old house was full of really pleasant people, and the brief winter days were spent in one unbroken round of amusement and gaiety. To me the old familiar English country-house life was a perpetual delight — to feel myself amongst kindred an unceasing pleasure. I could not have believed myself capable of being so completely happy.

I saw a great deal of my cousin Edward, and I think he

contrived to make Miss Tremaine understand that, to please him, she must be gracious to me. She certainly took some pains to make herself agreeable to me; and I discovered that, in spite of that proud disdainful temper, which she so rarely took the trouble to conceal, she was really anxious to gratify her lover.

Their courtship was not altogether a halcyon period. They had frequent quarrels, the details of which Edward's sisters Sophy and Agnes delighted to discuss with me. It was the struggle of two proud spirits for mastery; but my cousin Edward's pride was of the nobler kind – the lofty scorn of all things mean – a pride that does not ill-become a generous nature. To me he seemed all that was admirable, and I was never tired of hearing his mother praise him. I think my cousin Fanny knew this, and that she used to confide in me as fully as if I had been her sister.

'I daresay you can see I am not quite so fond as I should wish to be of Julia Tremaine,' she said to me one day; 'but I am very glad that my son is going to marry. My husband's has not been a fortunate family, you know, Sarah. The eldest sons have been wild and unlucky for generations past; and when Edward was a boy I used to have many a bitter hour, dreading what the future might bring forth. Thank God he has been, and is, all that I can wish. He has never given me an hour's anxiety by any act of his. Yet I am not the less glad of his marriage. The heirs of Chrighton who have come to an untimely end have all died unmarried. There was Hugh Chrighton, in the reign of George the Second, who was killed in a duel; John, who broke his back in the hunting-field thirty years later; Theodore, shot accidentally by a schoolfellow at Eton; Jasper, whose yacht went down in the Mediterranean forty years ago. An awful list, is it not, Sarah? I shall feel as if my son were safer somehow when he is married. It will seem as if he has escaped the ban that has fallen on so many of our house. He will have greater reason to be careful of his life when he is a married man.'

I agreed with Mrs Chrighton; but could not help wishing that Edward had chosen any other woman than the cold handsome Julia. I could not fancy his future life happy with such a mate.

Christmas came by and by – a real old English Christmas – frost and snow without, warmth and revelry within; skating on the great pond in the park, and sledging on the ice-bound high-roads, by day; private theatricals, charades, and amateur concerts, by night. I was surprised to find that Miss Tremaine refused to take any active part in these evening amusements. She preferred to sit among the elders as a spectator, and had the air and bearing of a princess for whose diversion all our entertainments had been planned. She seemed to think that she fulfilled her mission by sitting still and looking handsome. No desire to show off appeared to enter her mind. Her intense pride left no room for vanity. Yet I knew that she could have distinguished herself as a musician if she had chosen to do so; for I had heard her sing and play in Mrs Chrighton's morning-room, when only Edward, his sisters, and myself were present; and I knew that both as a vocalist and a pianist she excelled all our guests.

The two girls and I had many a happy morning and afternoon, going from cottage to cottage in a pony-carriage laden with Mrs Chrighton's gifts to the poor of her parish. There was no public formal distribution of blanketing and coals, but the wants of all were amply provided for in a quiet friendly way. Agnes and Sophy, aided by an indefatigable maid, the Rector's daughter, and one or two other young ladies, had been at work for the last three months making smart warm frocks and useful under-garments for the children of the cottagers; so that on Christmas morning every child in the parish was arrayed in a complete set of new garments. Mrs Chrighton had an admirable faculty of knowing precisely what was most wanted in every household; and our pony-carriage used to convey a varied collection of goods, every parcel directed in the firm free hand of the châtelaine of the Abbey.

Edward used sometimes to drive us on these expeditions, and I found that he was eminently popular among the poor of Chrighton parish. He had such an airy pleasant way of talking to them, a manner which set them at their ease at once. He never forgot their names or relationships, or wants or ailments; had a packet of exactly the kind of tobacco each man liked best always ready in his coat-pockets; and was full of jokes, which may not have been particularly witty, but which used to make the small low-roofed chambers ring with hearty laughter.

Miss Tremaine coolly declined any share in these pleasant duties.

'I don't like poor people,' she said. 'I daresay it sounds very dreadful, but it's just as well to confess my iniquity at once. I never can get on with them, or they with me. I am not *simpatica*, I suppose. And then I cannot endure their stifling rooms. The close faint odour of their houses gives me a fever. And again, what is the use of visiting them? It is only an inducement to them to become hypocrites. Surely it is better to arrange on a sheet of paper what it is just and fair for them to have – blankets, and coals, and groceries, and money, and wine, and so on – and let them receive the things from some trustworthy servant. In that case, there need be no cringing on one side, and no endurance on the other.'

'But, you see, Julia, there are some kinds of people to whom that sort of thing is not a question of endurance,' Edward answered, his face flushing indignantly. 'People who like to share in the pleasure they give – who like to see the poor careworn faces lighted up with sudden joy – who like to make these sons of the soil feel that there is some friendly link between themselves and their masters – some point of union between the cottage and the great house. There is my mother, for instance: all these duties which you think so tiresome are to her an unfailing delight. There will be a change, I'm afraid, Julia, when you are mistress of the Abbey.'

'You have not made me that yet,' she answered; 'and there is plenty of time for you to change your mind, if you do not think me suited for the position. I do not pretend to be like your mother. It is better that I should not affect any feminine virtues which I do not possess.'

After this Edward insisted on driving our pony-carriage almost every day, leaving Miss Tremaine to find her own amusement; and I think this conversation was the beginning of an estrangement between them, which became more serious than any of their previous quarrels had been.

Miss Tremaine did not care for sledging, or skating, or billiard-playing. She had none of the 'fast' tendencies which have become so common lately. She used to sit in one particular bow-window of the drawing-room all the morning, working a screen in berlin-wool and beads, assisted and attended by her younger sister Laura, who was a kind of slave to her – a very colourless young lady in mind, capable of no such thing as an original opinion, and in person a pale replica of her sister.

Had there been less company in the house, the breach between Edward Chrighton and his betrothed must have become notorious; but with a house so full of people, all bent on enjoying themselves, I doubt if it was noticed. On all public occasions my cousin showed himself attentive and apparently devoted to Miss Tremaine. It was only I and his sisters who knew the real state of affairs.

I was surprised, after the young lady's total repudiation of all benevolent sentiments, when she beckoned me aside one morning, and slipped a little purse of gold – twenty sovereigns – into my hand.

'I shall be very much obliged if you will distribute that among your cottagers today, Miss Chrighton,' she said. 'Of course I should like to give them something; it's only the trouble of talking to them that I shrink from; and you are just the person for an almoner. Don't mention my little commission to any one, please.'

'Of course I may tell Edward,' I said; for I was anxious that he should know his betrothed was not as hard-hearted as she had appeared.

'To him least of all,' she answered eagerly. 'You know that our ideas vary on that point. He would think I gave the money to please him. Not a word, pray, Miss Chrighton.' I submitted, and distributed my sovereigns quietly, with the most careful exercise of my judgement.

So Christmas came and passed. It was the day after the great anniversary – a very quiet day for the guests and family at the Abbey, but a grand occasion for the servants, who were to have their annual ball in the evening – a ball to which all the humbler class of tenantry were invited. The frost had broken up suddenly, and it was a thorough wet day – a depressing kind of day for any one whose spirits are liable to be affected by the weather, as mine are. I felt out of spirits for the first time since my arrival at the Abbey.

No one else appeared to feel the same influence. The elder ladies sat in a wide semicircle round one of the fireplaces in the drawing-room; a group of merry girls and dashing young men chatted gaily before the other. From the billiard-room there came the frequent clash of balls, and cheery peals of stentorian laughter. I sat in one of the deep windows, half hidden by the curtains, reading a novel – one of a boxful that came from town every month.

If the picture within was bright and cheerful, the prospect was dreary enough without. The fairy forest of snow-wreathed trees, the white valleys and undulating banks of snow, had vanished, and the rain dripped slowly and sullenly upon a darksome expanse of sodden grass, and a dismal background of leafless timber. The merry sound of the sledge-bells no longer enlivened the air; all was silence and gloom.

Edward Chrighton was not amongst the billiard-players; he was pacing the drawing-room to and fro from end to end, with an air that was at once moody and restless.

'Thank heaven, the frost has broken up at last!' he exclaimed, stopping in front of the window where I sat.

He had spoken to himself, quite unaware of my close neighbourhood. Unpromising as his aspect was just then, I ventured to accost him.

'What bad taste, to prefer such weather as this to frost and snow!' I answered. 'The park looked enchanting yesterday – a real scene from fairyland. And only look at it today!'

'O yes, of course, from an artistic point of view, the snow was better. The place does look something like the great dismal swamp today; but I am thinking of hunting, and that confounded frost made a day's sport impossible. We are in for a spell of mild weather now, I think.'

'But you are not going to hunt, are you, Edward?'

'Indeed I am, my gentle cousin, in spite of that frightened look in your amiable countenance.'

'I thought there were no hounds hereabouts.'

'Nor are there; but there is as fine a pack as any in the country – the Daleborough hounds – five-and-twenty miles away.'

'And you are going five-and-twenty miles for the sake of a day's run?'

'I would travel forty, fifty, a hundred miles for that same diversion. But I am not going for a single day this time; I am going over to Sir Francis Wycherly's place – young Frank Wycherly and I were sworn chums at Christchurch – for three or four days. I am due today, but I scarcely cared to travel by cross-country roads in such rain as this. However, if the flood-gates of the sky are loosened for a new deluge, I must go tomorrow.'

'What a headstrong young man!' I exclaimed. 'And what will Miss Tremaine say to this desertion?' I asked in a lower voice.

'Miss Tremaine can say whatever she pleases. She had it in her power to make me forget the pleasures of the chase, if she had chosen, though we had been in the heart of the shires, and the welkin ringing with the baying of hounds.'

'O, I begin to understand. This hunting engagement is not of long standing.'

'No; I began to find myself bored here a few days ago, and wrote to Frank to offer myself for two or three days at Wycherly. I received a most cordial answer by return, and am booked till the end of this week.'

'You have not forgotten the ball on the first?'

'O, no; to do that would be to vex my mother, and to offer a slight to our guests. I shall be here for the first, come what may.'

Come what may! so lightly spoken. The time came when I had bitter occasion to remember those words.

'I'm afraid you will vex your mother by going at all,' I said. 'You know what a horror both she and your father have of hunting.'

'A most un-country-gentleman-like aversion on my father's part. But he is a dear old book-worm, seldom happy out of his library. Yes, I admit they both have a dislike to hunting in the abstract; but they know I am a pretty good rider, and that it would need a bigger country than I shall find about Wycherly to floor me. You need not feel nervous, my dear Sarah; I am not going to give papa and mamma the smallest ground for uneasiness.'

'You will take your own horses, I suppose?'

'That goes without saying. No man who has cattle of his own cares to mount another man's horses. I shall take Pepperbox and the Druid.'

'Pepperbox has a queer temper, I have heard your sisters say.'

'My sisters expect a horse to be a kind of overgrown baa-lamb. Everything splendid in horseflesh and womankind is prone to that slight defect, an ugly temper. There is Miss Tremaine, for instance.'

'I shall take Miss Tremaine's part. I believe it is you who are in the wrong in the matter of this estrangement, Edward.'

'Do you? Well, wrong or right, my cousin, until the fair Julia comes to me with sweet looks and gentle words, we can never be what we have been.'

'You will return from your hunting expedition in a softer mood,' I answered; 'that is to say, if you persist in going. But I hope and believe you will change your mind.'

'Such a change is not within the limits of possibility, Sarah. I am fixed as Fate.'

He strolled away, humming some gay hunting-song as he went. I was alone with Mrs Chrighton later in the afternoon, and she spoke to me about this intended visit to Wycherly.

'Edward has set his heart upon it evidently,' she said regretfully, 'and his father and I have always made a point of avoiding anything that could seem like domestic tyranny. Our dear boy is such a good son, that it would be very hard if we came between

him and his pleasures. You know what a morbid horror my husband has of the dangers of the hunting-field, and perhaps I
am almost as weak-minded. But in spite of this we have never
interfered with Edward's enjoyment of a sport which he is passionately fond of; and hitherto, thank God! he has escaped
without a scratch. Yet I have had many a bitter hour, I can assure
you, my dear, when my son has been away in Leicestershire
hunting four days a week.'

'He rides well, I suppose.'

'Superbly. He has a great reputation among the sportsmen of
our neighbourhood. I daresay when he is master of the Abbey
he will start a pack of hounds, and revive the old days of his
great-grandfather, Meredith Chrighton.'

'I fancy the hounds were kenneled in the stable-yard below
my bedroom window in those days, were they not, Fanny?'

'Yes,' Mrs Chrighton answered gravely; and I wondered at
the sudden shadow that fell upon her face.

I went up to my room earlier than usual that afternoon, and I
had a clear hour to spare before it would be time to dress for the
seven o'clock dinner. This leisure hour I intended to devote to
letter-writing; but on arriving in my room I found myself in a
very idle frame of mind, and instead of opening my desk, I
seated myself in the low easy-chair before the fire, and fell into a
reverie.

How long I had been sitting there I scarcely know; I had been
half meditating, half dozing, mixing broken snatches of thought
with brief glimpses of dreaming, when I was startled into wakefulness by a sound that was strange to me.

It was a huntsman's horn — a few low plaintive notes on a
huntsman's horn — notes which had a strange far-away sound,
that was more unearthly than anything my ears had ever heard.
I thought of the music in *Der Freischutz*; but the weirdest snatch

of melody Weber ever wrote had not so ghastly a sound as these few simple notes conveyed to my ear.

I stood transfixed, listening to that awful music. It had grown dusk, my fire was almost out, and the room in shadow. As I listened, a light flashed suddenly on the wall before me. The light was as unearthly as the sound – a light that never shone from earth or sky.

I ran to the window; for this ghastly shimmer flashed through the window upon the opposite wall. The great gates of the stable-yard were open, and men in scarlet coats were riding in, a pack of hounds crowding in before them, obedient to the huntsman's whip. The whole scene was dimly visible by the declining light of the winter evening and the weird gleams of a lantern carried by one of the men. It was this lantern which had shone upon the tapestried wall. I saw the stable-doors opened one after another; gentlemen and grooms alighting from their horses; the dogs driven into their kennel; the helpers hurrying to and fro; and that strange wan lantern-light glimmering here and there in the gathering dusk. But there was no sound of horse's hoof or of human voices – not one yelp or cry from the hounds. Since those faint far-away sounds of the horn had died out in the distance, the ghastly silence had been unbroken.

I stood at my window quite calmly, and watched while the group of men and animals in the yard below noiselessly dispersed. There was nothing supernatural in the manner of their disappearance. The figures did not vanish or melt into empty air. One by one I saw the horses led into their separate quarters; one by one the redcoats strolled out of the gates, and the grooms departed, some one way, some another. The scene, but for its noiselessness, was natural enough; and had I been a stranger in the house, I might have fancied that those figures were real – those stables in full occupation.

But I knew that stable-yard and all its range of buildings to have been disused for more than half a century. Could I believe that, without an hour's warning, the long-deserted quadrangle could be filled – the empty stalls tenanted?

Had some hunting-party from the neighbourhood sought shelter here, glad to escape the pitiless rain? That was not impossible, I thought. I was an utter unbeliever in all ghostly things – ready to credit any possibility rather than suppose that I had been looking upon shadows. And yet the noiselessness, the awful sound of that horn – the strange unearthly gleam of that lantern! Little superstitious as I might be, a cold sweat stood out upon my forehead, and I trembled in every limb.

For some minutes I stood by the window, statue-like, staring blankly into the empty quadrangle. Then I roused myself suddenly, and ran softly downstairs by a back staircase leading to the servants' quarters, determined to solve the mystery somehow or other. The way to Mrs Marjorum's room was familiar to me from old experience, and it was thither that I bent my steps, determined to ask the housekeeper the meaning of what I had seen. I had a lurking conviction that it would be well for me not to mention that scene to any member of the family till I had taken counsel with some one who knew the secrets of Chrighton Abbey.

I heard the sound of merry voices and laughter as I passed the kitchen and servants' hall. Men and maids were all busy in the pleasant labour of decorating their rooms for the evening's festival. They were putting the last touches to garlands of holly and laurel, ivy and fir, as I passed the open doors; and in both rooms I saw tables laid for a substantial tea. The housekeeper's room was in a retired nook at the end of a long passage – a charming old room, panelled with dark oak, and full of capacious cupboards, which in my childhood I had looked upon as storehouses of inexhaustible treasures in the way of preserves and other confectionery. It was a shady old room, with a wide old-fashioned fireplace, cool in summer, when the hearth was adorned with a great jar of roses and lavender; and warm in winter, when the logs burnt merrily all day long.

I opened the door softly, and went in. Mrs Marjorum was dozing in a high-backed arm-chair by the glowing hearth, dressed in her state gown of grey watered silk, and with a cap that was a perfect garden of roses. She opened her eyes as I approached her, and stared at me with a puzzled look for the first moment or so.

'Why, is that you, Miss Sarah?' she exclaimed; 'and looking as pale as a ghost, I can see, even by this firelight! Let me just light a candle, and then I'll get you some sal volatile. Sit down in my armchair, miss; why, I declare you're all of a tremble!'

She put me into her easy-chair before I could resist, and lighted the two candles which stood ready upon her table, while I was trying to speak. My lips were dry, and it seemed at first as if my voice was gone.

'Never mind the sal volatile, Marjorum,' I said at last. 'I am not ill; I've been startled, that's all; and I've come to ask you for an explanation of the business that frightened me.'

'What business, Miss Sarah?'

'You must have heard something of it yourself, surely. Didn't you hear a horn just now, a huntsman's horn?'

'A horn! Lord no, Miss Sarah. What ever could have put such a fancy into your head?'

I saw that Mrs Marjorum's ruddy cheeks had suddenly lost their colour, that she was now almost as pale as I could have been myself.

'It was no fancy,' I said; 'I heard the sound, and saw the people. A hunting-party has just taken shelter in the north quad-rangle. Dogs and horses, and gentlemen and servants.'

'What were they like, Miss Sarah?' the housekeeper asked in a strange voice.

'I can hardly tell you that. I could see that they wore red coats; and I could scarcely see more than that. Yes, I did get a glimpse of one of the gentlemen by the light of the lantern. A tall man, with grey hair and whiskers, and a stoop in his shoulders. I noticed that he wore a short-waisted coat with a very high collar – a coat that looked a hundred years old.'

'The old Squire!' muttered Mrs Marjorum under her breath; and then turning to me, she said with a cheery resolute air, 'You've been dreaming, Miss Sarah, that's just what it is. You've dropped off in your chair before the fire, and had a dream, that's it.'

'No, Marjorum, it was no dream. The horn woke me, and I stood at my window and saw the dogs and huntsmen come in.'

'Do you know, Miss Sarah, that the gates of the north quadrangle have been locked and barred for the last forty years, and that no one ever goes in there except through the house?'

'The gates may have been opened this evening to give shelter to strangers,' I said.

'Not when the only keys that will open them hang yonder in my cupboard, miss,' said the housekeeper, pointing to a corner of the room.

'But I tell you, Marjorum, these people came into the quadrangle; the horses and dogs are in the stables and kennels at this moment. I'll go and ask Mr Chrighton, or my cousin Fanny, or Edward, all about it, since you won't tell me the truth.'

I said this with a purpose, and it answered. Mrs Marjorum caught me eagerly by the wrist.

'No, miss, don't do that; for pity's sake don't do that; don't breathe a word to missus or master.'

'But why not?'

'Because you've seen that which always brings misfortune and sorrow to this house, Miss Sarah. You've seen the dead.'

'What do you mean?' I gasped, awed in spite of myself.

'I daresay you've heard say that there's been *something* seen at times at the Abbey – many years apart, thank God; for it never came that trouble didn't come after it.'

'Yes,' I answered hurriedly; 'but I could never get any one to tell me what it was that haunted this place.'

'No, miss. Those that know have kept the secret. But you have seen it all tonight. There's no use in trying to hide it from you any longer. You have seen the old Squire, Meredith Chrighton, whose eldest son was killed by a fall in the hunting-field, brought home dead one December night, an hour after his father and the rest of the party had come safe home to the Abbey. The old gentleman had missed his son in the field, but had thought nothing of that, fancying that master John had had enough of the day's sport, and had turned his horse's head homewards. He was found by a labouring-man, poor lad, lying in a ditch with his back broken, and his horse beside him staked. The old Squire never held his head up after that day, and never rode to hounds again, though he was passionately fond of hunting. Dogs and horses were sold, and the north quadrangle has been empty from that day.'

'How long is it since this kind of thing has been seen?'

'A long time, miss. I was a slip of a girl when it last happened. It was in the winter-time – this very night – the night Squire Meredith's son was killed; and the house was full of company, just as it is now. There was a wild young Oxford gentleman sleeping in your room at that time, and he saw the hunting-party come into the quadrangle; and what did he do but throw his window wide open, and give them the view-hallo as loud as ever he could. He had only arrived the day before, and knew nothing about the neighbourhood; so at dinner he began to ask where were his friends the sportsmen, and to hope he should be allowed to have a run with the Abbey hounds next day. It was in the time of our master's father; and his lady at the head of the table turned as white as a sheet when she heard this talk. She had good reason, poor soul. Before the week was out her husband was lying dead. He was struck with a fit of apoplexy, and never spoke or knew any one afterwards.'

'An awful coincidence,' I said; 'but it may have been only a coincidence.'

'I've heard other stories, miss – heard them from those that wouldn't deceive – all proving the same thing: that the appearance of the old Squire and his pack is a warning of death to this house.'

'I cannot believe these things,' I exclaimed; 'I *cannot* believe them. Does Mr Edward know anything about this?'

'No, miss. His father and mother have been most careful that it should be kept from him.'

'I think he is too strong-minded to be much affected by the fact,' I said.

'And you'll not say anything about what you've seen to my master or my mistress, will you, Miss Sarah?' pleaded the faithful old servant. 'The knowledge of it would be sure to make them nervous and unhappy. And if evil is to come upon this house, it isn't in human power to prevent its coming.'

'God forbid that there is any evil at hand!' I answered. 'I am no believer in visions or omens. After all, I would sooner fancy that I was dreaming – dreaming with my eyes open as I stood at the window – than that I beheld the shadows of the dead.'

Mrs Marjorum sighed, and said nothing. I could see that she believed firmly in the phantom hunt.

I went back to my room to dress for dinner. However

rationally I might try to think of what I had seen, its effect upon my mind and nerves was not the less powerful. I could think of nothing else; and a strange morbid dread of coming misery weighted me down like an actual burden.

There was a very cheerful party in the drawing-room when I went downstairs, and at dinner the talk and laughter were unceasing; but I could see that my cousin Fanny's face was a little graver than usual, and I had no doubt she was thinking of her son's intended visit to Wycherly.

At the thought of this a sudden terror flashed upon me. How if the shadows I had seen that evening were ominous of danger to him – to Edward, the heir and only son of the house? My heart grew cold as I thought of this, and yet in the next moment I despised myself for such weakness.

'It is natural enough for an old servant to believe in such things,' I said to myself; 'but for me – an educated woman of the world – preposterous folly.'

And yet from that moment I began to puzzle myself in the endeavour to devise some means by which Edward's journey might be prevented. Of my own influence I knew that I was powerless to hinder his departure by so much as an hour; but I fancied that Julia Tremaine could persuade him to any sacrifice of his inclination, if she could only humble her pride so far as to entreat it. I determined to appeal to her in the course of the evening.

We were very merry all that evening. The servants and their guests danced in the great hall, while we sat in the gallery above, and in little groups upon the staircase, watching their diversions. I think this arrangement afforded excellent opportunities for flirtation, and that the younger members of our party made good use of their chances – with one exception: Edward Chrighton and his affianced contrived to keep far away from each other all the evening.

While all was going on noisily in the hall below, I managed to get Miss Tremaine apart from the others in the embrasure of a painted window on the stairs, where there was a wide oaken seat. Seated here side by side, I described to her, under a promise of secrecy, the scene which I had witnessed that afternoon, and my conversation with Mrs Marjorum.

'But, good gracious me, Miss Chrighton!' the young lady exclaimed, lifting her pencilled eyebrows with unconcealed disdain, 'you don't mean to tell me that you believe in such nonsense – ghosts and omens, and old woman's folly like that!'

'I assure you, Miss Tremaine, it is most difficult for me to believe in the supernatural,' I answered earnestly; 'but that which I saw this evening was something more than human. The thought of it has made me very unhappy; and I cannot help connecting it somehow with my cousin Edward's visit to Wycherly. If I had the power to prevent his going, I would do it at any cost; but I have not. You alone have influence enough for that. For heaven's sake use it! do anything to hinder his hunting with the Daleborough hounds.'

'You would have me humiliate myself by asking him to forgo his pleasure, and that after his conduct to me during the last week?'

'I confess that he has done much to offend you. But you love him, Miss Tremaine, though you are too proud to let your love be seen: I am certain that you do love him. For pity's sake speak to him; do not let him hazard his life, when a few words from you may prevent the danger.'

'I don't believe he would give up this visit to please me,' she answered; 'and I shall certainly not put it in his power to humiliate me by a refusal. Besides, all this fear of yours is such utter nonsense. As if nobody had ever hunted before. My brothers hunt four times a week every winter, and not one of them has ever been the worse for it yet.'

I did not give up the attempt lightly. I pleaded with this proud obstinate girl for a long time, as long as I could induce her to listen to me; but it was all in vain. She stuck to her text — no one should persuade her to degrade herself by asking a favour of Edward Chrighton. He had chosen to hold himself aloof from her, and she would show him that she could live without him. When she left Chrighton Abbey, they would part as strangers.

So the night closed, and at breakfast next morning I heard that Edward had started for Wycherly soon after daybreak. His absence made, for me at least, a sad blank in our circle. For one other also, I think; for Miss Tremaine's fair proud face was very pale, though she tried to seem gayer than usual, and exerted herself in quite an unaccustomed manner in her endeavour to be agreeable to everyone.

The days passed slowly for me after my cousin's departure. There was a weight upon my mind, a vague anxiety, which I struggled in vain to shake off. The house, full as it was of pleasant people, seemed to me to have become dull and dreary now that Edward was gone. The place where he had sat appeared always vacant to my eyes, though another filled it, and there was no gap on either side of the long dinner-table. Lighthearted young men still made the billiard-room resonant with their laughter; merry girls flirted as gaily as ever, undisturbed in the smallest degree by the absence of the heir of the house. Yet for me all was changed. A morbid fancy had taken complete possession of me. I found myself continually brooding over the housekeeper's words; those words which had told me that the shadows I had seen boded death and sorrow to the house of Chrighton.

My cousins, Sophy and Agnes, were no more concerned about their brother's welfare than were their guests. They were full of excitement about the New-Year's ball, which was to be a very grand affair. Every one of importance within fifty miles was to be present, every nook and corner of the Abbey would be filled with visitors coming from a great distance, while others were to be billeted upon the better class of tenantry round about. Altogether the organisation of this affair was no small business; and Mrs Chrighton's mornings were broken by discussions with the housekeeper, messages from the cook, interviews with the head-gardener on the subject of floral decorations, and other details, which all alike demanded the attention of the châtelaine herself. With these duties, and with the claims of her numerous guests, my cousin Fanny's time was so fully occupied, that she had little leisure to indulge in anxious feelings about her son, whatever secret uneasiness may have been lurking in her maternal heart. As for the master of the Abbey, he spent so much of his time in the library, where, under the pretext of business with his bailiff, he read Greek, that it was not easy for any one to discover what he did feel. Once, and once only, I heard him speak of his son, in a tone that betrayed an intense eagerness for his return.

The girls were to have new dresses from a French milliner in Wigmore Street; and as the great event drew near, bulky packages of millinery were continually arriving, and feminine consultations and expositions of finery were being held all day long in bedrooms and dressing-rooms with closed doors. Thus, with a mind always troubled by the same dark shapeless foreboding, I was perpetually being called upon to give an opinion about pink tulle and lilies of the valley, or maize silk and apple-blossoms.

New-Year's morning came at last, after an interval of abnormal length, as it seemed to me. It was a bright clear day, an almost springlike sunshine lighting up the leafless landscape. The great dining-room was noisy with congratulations and good wishes as we assembled for breakfast on this first morning of a new year, after having seen the old one out cheerily the night before; but Edward had not yet returned, and I missed him sadly. Some touch of sympathy drew me to the side of Julia Tremaine on this particular morning. I had watched her very often during the last few days, and I had seen that her cheek grew paler every day. Today her eyes had the dull heavy look that betokens a sleepless night. Yes, I was sure that she was unhappy – that the proud relentless nature suffered bitterly.

'He must be home today,' I said to her in a low voice, as she sat in stately silence before an untasted breakfast.

'Who must?' she answered, turning towards me with a cold distant look.

'My cousin Edward. You know he promised to be back in time for the ball.'

'I know nothing of Mr Chrighton's intended movements,' she said in her haughtiest tone; 'but of course it is only natural that he should be here tonight. He would scarcely care to insult half the county by his absence, however little he may value those now staying in his father's house.'

'But you know that there is one here whom he does value better than any one else in the world, Miss Tremaine,' I answered, anxious to soothe this proud girl.

'I know nothing of the kind. But why do you speak so solemnly about his return? He will come, of course. There is no reason he should not come.'

She spoke in a rapid manner that was strange to her, and looked at me with a sharp enquiring glance, that touched me somehow, it was so unlike herself – it revealed to me so keen an anxiety.

'No, there is no reasonable cause for anything like uneasiness,' I said; 'but you remember what I told you the other night.

That has preyed upon my mind, and it will be an unspeakable relief to me when I see my cousin safe at home.'

'I am sorry that you should indulge in such weakness, Miss Chrighton.'

That was all she said; but when I saw her in the drawing-room after breakfast, she had established herself in a window that commanded a view of the long winding drive leading to the front of the Abbey. From this point she could not fail to see anyone approaching the house. She sat there all day; everyone else was more or less busy with arrangements for the evening, or at any rate occupied with an appearance of business; but Julia Tremaine kept her place by the window, pleading a headache as an excuse for sitting still, with a book in her hand, all day, yet obstinately refusing to go to her room and lie down, when her mother entreated her to do so.

'You will be fit for nothing tonight, Julia,' Mrs Tremaine said, almost angrily; 'you have been looking ill for ever so long, and today you are as pale as a ghost.'

I knew that she was watching for *him*; and I pitied her with all my heart, as the day wore itself out, and he did not come.

We dined earlier than usual, played a game or two of billiards after dinner, made a tour of inspection through the bright rooms, lit with wax-candles only, and odorous with exotics; and then came a long interregnum devoted to the arts and mysteries of the toilet; while maids flitted to and fro laden with frilled muslin petticoats from the laundry, and a faint smell of singed hair pervaded the corridors. At ten o'clock the band were tuning their violins, and pretty girls and elegant-looking men were coming slowly down the broad oak staircase, as the roll of fast-coming wheels sounded louder without, and stentorian voices announced the best people in the county.

I have no need to dwell long upon the details of that evening's festival. It was very much like other balls – a brilliant success, a night of splendour and enchantment for those whose hearts were light and happy, and who could abandon themselves utterly to the pleasure of the moment; a far-away picture of fair faces and bright-hued dresses, a wearisome kaleidoscopic procession of form and colour for those whose minds were weighed down with the burden of a hidden care.

For me the music had no melody, the dazzling scene no charm. Hour after hour went by; supper was over, and the waltzers were enjoying those latest dances which always seem the most delightful, and yet Edward Chrighton had not appeared amongst us.

There had been innumerable enquiries about him, and Mrs Chrighton had apologised for his absence as best she might. Poor soul, I well knew that his non-return was now a source of poignant anxiety to her, although she greeted all her guests with the same gracious smile, and was able to talk gaily and well upon every subject. Once, when she was sitting alone for a few minutes, watching the dancers, I saw the smile fade from her face, and a look of anguish come over it. I ventured to approach her at this moment, and never shall I forget the look which she turned towards me.

'My son, Sarah!' she said in a low voice – 'something has happened to my son!'

I did my best to comfort her; but my own heart was growing heavier and heavier, and my attempt was a very poor one.

Julia Tremaine had danced a little at the beginning of the evening, to keep up appearances, I believe, in order that no one might suppose that she was distressed by her lover's absence; but after the first two or three dances she pronounced herself tired, and withdrew to a seat amongst the matrons. She was looking very lovely in spite of her extreme pallor, dressed in white tulle, a perfect cloud of airy puffings, and with a wreath of ivy-leaves and diamonds crowning her pale golden hair.

The night waned, the dancers were revolving in the last waltz, when I happened to look towards the doorway at the end of the room. I was startled by seeing a man standing there, with his hat in his hand, not in evening costume; a man with a pale anxious-looking face, peering cautiously into the room. My first thought was of evil; but in the next moment the man had disappeared, and I saw no more of him.

I lingered by my cousin Fanny's side till the rooms were empty. Even Sophy and Aggy had gone off to their own apartments, their airy dresses sadly dilapidated by a night's vigorous dancing. There were only Mr and Mrs Chrighton and myself in the long suite of rooms, where the flowers were drooping and the wax-lights dying out one by one in the silver sconces against the walls.

'I think the evening went off very well,' Fanny said, looking rather anxiously at her husband, who was stretching himself and yawning with an air of intense relief.

'Yes, the affair went off well enough. But Edward has committed a terrible breach of manners by not being here. Upon my word, the young men of the present day think of nothing but their own pleasures. I suppose that something especially attractive was going on at Wycherly today, and he couldn't tear himself away.'

'It is so unlike him to break his word,' Mrs Chrighton answered. 'You are not alarmed, Frederick? You don't think that anything has happened – any accident?'

'What should happen? Ned is one of the best riders in the county. I don't think there's any fear of his coming to grief.'

'He might be ill.'

'Not he. He's a young Hercules. And if it were possible for

him to be ill – which it is not – we should have had a message from Wycherly.'

The words were scarcely spoken when Truefold the old butler stood by his master's side, with a solemn anxious face.

'There is a – a person who wishes to see you, sir,' he said in a low voice, 'alone.'

Low as the words were, both Fanny and myself heard them.

'Someone from Wycherly?' she exclaimed. 'Let him come here.'

'But, madam, the person most particularly wished to see master alone. Shall I show him into the library, sir? The lights are not out there.'

'Then it *is* someone from Wycherly,' said my cousin, seizing my wrist with a hand that was icy cold. 'Didn't I tell you so, Sarah? Something has happened to my son. Let the person come here, Truefold, here; I insist upon it.'

The tone of command was quite strange in a wife who was always deferential to her husband, in a mistress who was ever gentle to her servants.

'Let it be so, Truefold,' said Mr Chrighton. 'Whatever ill news has come to us we will hear together.'

He put his arm round his wife's waist. Both were pale as marble, both stood in stony stillness waiting for the blow that was to fall upon them.

The stranger, the man I had seen in the doorway, came in. He was curate of Wycherly church, and chaplain to Sir Francis Wycherly; a grave middle-aged man. He told what he had to tell with all kindness, with all the usual forms of consolation which Christianity and an experience of sorrow could suggest. Vain words, wasted trouble. The blow must fall, and earthly consolation was unable to lighten it by a feather's weight.

There had been a steeplechase at Wycherly – an amateur

affair with gentlemen riders – on that bright New-Year's day, and Edward Chrighton had been persuaded to ride his favourite hunter Pepperbox. There would be plenty of time for him to return to Chrighton after the races. He had consented; and his horse was winning easily, when, at the last fence, a double one, with water beyond, Pepperbox baulked his leap, and went over head-foremost, flinging his rider over a hedge into a field close beside the course, where there was a heavy stone roller. Upon this stone roller Edward Chrighton had fallen, his head receiving the full force of the concussion. All was told. It was while the curate was relating the fatal catastrophe that I looked round suddenly, and saw Julia Tremaine standing a little way behind the speaker. She had heard all; she uttered no cry, she showed no signs of fainting, but stood calm and motionless, waiting for the end.

I know not how that night ended: there seemed an awful calm upon us all. A carriage was got ready, and Mr and Mrs Chrighton started for Wycherly to look upon their dead son. He had died while they were carrying him from the course to Sir Francis's house. I went with Julia Tremaine to her room, and sat with her while the winter morning dawned slowly upon us – a bitter dawning.

I have little more to tell. Life goes on, though hearts are broken. Upon Chrighton Abbey there came a dreary time of desolation. The master of the house lived in his library, shut from the outer world, buried almost as completely as a hermit in his cell. I have heard that Julia Tremaine was never known to smile after that day. She is still unmarried, and lives entirely at her father's country house; proud and reserved in her conduct to her equals, but a very angel of mercy and compassion amongst the poor of the neighbourhood. Yes; this haughty girl, who once declared herself unable to endure the hovels of the poor, is now a Sister of Charity in all but the robe. So does a great sorrow change the current of a woman's life.

I have seen my cousin Fanny many times since that awful New-Year's night; for I have always the same welcome at the Abbey. I have seen her calm and cheerful, doing her duty, smiling upon her daughter's children, the honoured mistress of a great household; but I know that the mainspring of life is broken, that for her there hath passed a glory from the earth, and that upon all the pleasures and joys of this world she looks with the solemn calm of one for whom all things are dark with the shadow of a great sorrow.

THE TRIUMPH OF NIGHT
BY EDITH WHARTON

Edith Wharton was born on 24 January 1862 in New York. She was educated in both America and Europe. In 1899 she published her first work, a collection of stories called *The Greater Inclination*, followed by her first novel, *The Touchstone*. She wrote many other works including home decoration manuals, short stories and her famous novels *The House of Mirth* (1905), *Ethan Frome* (1911), *The Custom of the Country* (1913) and *The Age of Innocence* (1920). She lived in France from 1907 and was made a Chevalier of the Legion of Honour in 1916 for her work helping refugees during the war. Edith Wharton died on 11 August 1937.

I T WAS clear that the sleigh from Weymore had not come; and the shivering young traveller from Boston, who had counted on jumping into it when he left the train at Northridge Junction, found himself standing alone on the open platform, exposed to the full assault of nightfall and winter.

The blast that swept him came off New Hampshire snowfields and ice-hung forests. It seemed to have traversed interminable leagues of frozen silence, filling them with the same cold roar and sharpening its edge against the same bitter black-and-white landscape. Dark, searching and sword-like, it alternately muffled and harried its victim, like a bullfighter now whirling his cloak and now planting his darts. This analogy brought home to the young man the fact that he himself had no cloak, and that the overcoat in which he had faced the relatively temperate air of Boston seemed no thicker than a sheet of paper on the bleak heights of Northridge. George Faxon said to himself that the place was uncommonly well named. It clung to an exposed ledge over the valley from which the train had lifted him, and the wind combed it with teeth of steel that he seemed actually to hear scraping against the wooden sides of the station. Other building there was none: the village lay far down the road, and thither – since the Weymore sleigh had not come – Faxon saw himself under the necessity of plodding through several feet of snow.

He understood well enough what had happened: his hostess had forgotten that he was coming. Young as Faxon was, this sad lucidity of soul had been acquired as the result of long experience, and he knew that the visitors who can least afford to hire a carriage are almost always those whom their hosts forget to send for. Yet to say that Mrs Culme had forgotten him was too crude a way of putting it. Similar incidents led him to think that she had probably told her maid to tell the butler to telephone the coachman to tell one of the grooms (if no one else needed him) to drive over to Northridge to fetch the new secretary; but on a night like this, what groom who respected his rights would fail to forget the order?

Faxon's obvious course was to struggle through the drifts to the village, and there rout out a sleigh to convey him to Weymore; but what if, on his arrival at Mrs Culme's, no one remembered to ask him what this devotion to duty had cost? That, again, was one of the contingencies he had expensively learned to look out for, and the perspicacity so acquired told him it would be cheaper to spend the night at the Northridge inn, and advise Mrs Culme of his presence there by telephone. He had reached this decision, and was about to entrust his luggage to a vague man with a lantern, when his hopes were raised by the sound of bells.

Two sleighs were just dashing up to the station, and from the foremost there sprang a young man muffled in furs.

'Weymore? – No, these are not the Weymore sleighs.'

The voice was that of the youth who had jumped to the platform – a voice so agreeable that, in spite of the words, it fell consolingly on Faxon's ears. At the same moment the wandering station-lantern, casting a transient light on the speaker, showed his features to be in the pleasantest harmony with his voice. He was very fair and very young – hardly in the twenties, Faxon thought – but his face, though full of a morning freshness, was a trifle too thin and fine-drawn, as though a vivid spirit contended in him with a strain of physical weakness. Faxon was perhaps the quicker to notice such delicacies of balance because his own temperament hung on lightly quivering nerves, which yet, as he believed, would never quite swing him beyond a normal sensibility.

'You expected a sleigh from Weymore?' the newcomer continued, standing beside Faxon like a slender column of fur.

Mrs Culme's secretary explained his difficulty, and the other brushed it aside with a contemptuous 'Oh, *Mrs Culme!*' that carried both speakers a long way toward reciprocal understanding.

'But then you must be –' The youth broke off with a smile of interrogation.

'The new secretary? Yes. But apparently there are no notes to be answered this evening.' Faxon's laugh deepened the sense of solidarity which had so promptly established itself between the two.

His friend laughed also. 'Mrs Culme,' he explained, 'was lunching at my uncle's today, and she said you were due this evening. But seven hours is a long time for Mrs Culme to remember anything.'

'Well,' said Faxon philosophically, 'I suppose that's one of the reasons why she needs a secretary. And I've always the inn at Northridge,' he concluded.

'Oh, but you haven't, though! It burned down last week.'

'The deuce it did!' said Faxon; but the humour of the situation struck him before its inconvenience. His life, for years past, had been mainly a succession of resigned adaptations, and he had learned, before dealing practically with his embarrassments, to extract from most of them a small tribute of amusement.

'Oh, well, there's sure to be somebody in the place who can put me up.'

'No one *you* could put up with. Besides, Northridge is three miles off, and our place — in the opposite direction — is a little nearer.' Through the darkness, Faxon saw his friend sketch a gesture of self-introduction. 'My name's Frank Rainer, and I'm staying with my uncle at Overdale. I've driven over to meet two friends of his, who are due in a few minutes from New York. If you don't mind waiting till they arrive I'm sure Overdale can do you better than Northridge. We're only down from town for a few days, but the house is always ready for a lot of people.'

'But your uncle —?' Faxon could only object, with the odd sense, through his embarrassment, that it would be magically dispelled by his invisible friend's next words.

'Oh, my uncle — you'll see! I answer for *him*! I dare say you've heard of him — John Lavington?'

John Lavington! There was a certain irony in asking if one had heard of John Lavington! Even from a post of observation as obscure as that of Mrs Culme's secretary the rumour of John Lavington's money, of his pictures, his politics, his charities and his hospitality, was as difficult to escape as the roar of a cataract in a mountain solitude. It might almost have been said that the one place in which one would not have expected to come upon him was in just such a solitude as now surrounded the speakers — at least in this deepest hour of its desertedness. But it was just like Lavington's brilliant ubiquity to put one in the wrong even there.

'Oh, yes, I've heard of your uncle.'

'Then you *will* come, won't you? We've only five minutes to wait,' young Rainer urged, in the tone that dispels scruples by ignoring them; and Faxon found himself accepting the invitation as simply as it was offered.

A delay in the arrival of the New York train lengthened their five minutes to fifteen; and as they paced the icy platform Faxon began to see why it had seemed the most natural thing in the world to accede to his new acquaintance's suggestion. It was because Frank Rainer was one of the privileged beings who simplify human intercourse by the atmosphere of confidence and good humour they diffuse. He produced this effect, Faxon noted, by the exercise of no gift but his youth, and of no art but his sincerity; and these qualities were revealed in a smile of such sweetness that Faxon felt, as never before, what Nature can achieve when she deigns to match the face with the mind.

He learned that the young man was the ward, and the only nephew, of John Lavington, with whom he had made his home since the death of his mother, the great man's sister. Mr Lavington, Rainer said, had been 'a regular brick' to him — 'But then he is to everyone, you know' — and the young fellow's situation seemed in fact to be perfectly in keeping with his person. Apparently the only shade that had ever rested on him was cast by the physical weakness which Faxon had already detected. Young Rainer had been threatened with tuberculosis, and the disease was so far advanced that, according to the highest authorities, banishment to Arizona or New Mexico was inevitable. 'But luckily my uncle didn't pack me off, as most people would have done, without getting another opinion. Whose? Oh, an awfully clever chap, a young doctor with a lot of new ideas, who simply laughed at my being sent away, and said I'd do perfectly well in New York if I didn't dine out too much, and if I dashed off occasionally to Northridge for a little fresh air. So it's really my uncle's doing that I'm not in exile — and I feel no end better since the new chap told me I needn't bother.' Young Rainer went on to confess that he was extremely fond of dining out, dancing and similar distractions; and Faxon, listening to him, was inclined to think that the physician who had refused to cut him off altogether from these pleasures was probably a better psychologist than his seniors.

'All the same you ought to be careful, you know.' The sense of elder-brotherly concern that forced the words from Faxon made him, as he spoke, slip his arm through Frank Rainer's.

The latter met the movement with a responsive pressure. 'Oh, I *am*: awfully, awfully. And then my uncle has such an eye on me!'

'But if your uncle has such an eye on you, what does he say to your swallowing knives out here in this Siberian wild?'

Rainer raised his fur collar with a careless gesture. 'It's not that that does it – the cold's good for me.'

'And it's not the dinners and dances? What is it, then?' Faxon good-humouredly insisted; to which his companion answered with a laugh: 'Well, my uncle says it's being bored; and I rather think he's right!'

His laugh ended in a spasm of coughing and a struggle for breath that made Faxon, still holding his arm, guide him hastily into the shelter of the fireless waiting-room.

Young Rainer had dropped down on the bench against the wall and pulled off one of his fur gloves to grope for a handkerchief. He tossed aside his cap and drew the handkerchief across his forehead, which was intensely white, and beaded with moisture, though his face retained a healthy glow. But Faxon's gaze remained fastened to the hand he had uncovered: it was so long, so colourless, so wasted, so much older than the brow he passed it over.

'It's queer – a healthy face but dying hands,' the secretary mused: he somehow wished young Rainer had kept on his glove.

The whistle of the express drew the young men to their feet, and the next moment two heavily-furred gentlemen had descended to the platform and were breasting the rigour of the night. Frank Rainer introduced them as Mr Grisben and Mr Balch, and Faxon, while their luggage was being lifted into the second sleigh, discerned them, by the roving lantern-gleam, to be an elderly grey-headed pair, of the average prosperous business cut.

They saluted their host's nephew with friendly familiarity, and Mr Grisben, who seemed the spokesman of the two, ended his greeting with a genial – 'and many many more of them, dear boy!' which suggested to Faxon that their arrival coincided with an anniversary. But he could not press the enquiry, for the seat allotted him was at the coachman's side, while Frank Rainer joined his uncle's guests inside the sleigh.

A swift flight (behind such horses as one could be sure of John Lavington's having) brought them to tall gateposts, an illuminated lodge, and an avenue on which the snow had been levelled to the smoothness of marble. At the end of the avenue the long house loomed up, its principal bulk dark, but one wing sending out a ray of welcome; and the next moment Faxon was receiving a violent impression of warmth and light, of hot-house plants, hurrying servants, a vast spectacular oak hall like a stage-setting, and, in its unreal middle distance, a small figure, correctly dressed, conventionally featured, and utterly unlike his rather florid conception of the great John Lavington.

The surprise of the contrast remained with him through his hurried dressing in the large luxurious bedroom to which he had been shown. 'I don't see where he comes in,' was the only way he could put it, so difficult was it to fit the exuberance of Lavington's public personality into his host's contracted frame and manner. Mr Lavington, to whom Faxon's case had been rapidly explained by young Rainer, had welcomed him with a sort of dry and stilted cordiality that exactly matched his narrow face, his stiff hand, and the whiff of scent on his evening handkerchief. 'Make yourself at home – at home!' he had repeated, in a tone that suggested, on his own part, a complete inability to perform the feat he urged on his visitor. 'Any friend of Frank's . . . delighted . . . make yourself thoroughly at home!'

II

IN SPITE of the balmy temperature and complicated conveniences of Faxon's bedroom, the injunction was not easy to obey. It was wonderful luck to have found a night's shelter under the opulent roof of Overdale, and he tasted the physical satisfaction to the full. But the place, for all its ingenuities of comfort, was oddly cold and unwelcoming. He couldn't have said why, and could only suppose that Mr Lavington's intense personality – intensely negative, but intense all the same – must, in some occult way, have penetrated every corner of his dwelling. Perhaps, though, it was merely that Faxon himself was tired and hungry, more deeply chilled than he had known till he came in from the cold, and unutterably sick of all strange houses, and of the prospect of perpetually treading other people's stairs.

'I hope you're not famished?' Rainer's slim figure was in the doorway. 'My uncle has a little business to attend to with Mr Grisben, and we don't dine for half an hour. Shall I fetch you, or can you find your way down? Come straight to the dining-room—the second door on the left of the long gallery.'

He disappeared, leaving a ray of warmth behind him, and Faxon, relieved, lit a cigarette and sat down by the fire.

Looking about with less haste, he was struck by a detail that had escaped him. The room was full of flowers – a mere 'bachelor's room', in the wing of a house opened only for a few days, in the dead middle of a New Hampshire winter! Flowers were everywhere, not in senseless profusion, but placed with the same conscious art that he had remarked in the grouping of the blossoming shrubs in the hall. A vase of arums stood on the writing-table, a cluster of strange-hued carnations on the stand at his elbow, and from bowls of glass and porcelain clumps of freesia-bulbs diffused their melting fragrance. The fact implied acres of glass – but that was the least interesting part of it. The flowers themselves, their quality, selection and arrangement, attested on someone's part – and on whose but John Lavington's? – a solicitous and sensitive passion for that particular form of beauty. Well, it simply made the man, as he had appeared to Faxon, all the harder to understand!

The half-hour elapsed, and Faxon, rejoicing at the prospect of food, set out to make his way to the dining-room. He had not noticed the direction he had followed in going to his room, and was puzzled, when he left it, to find that two staircases, of apparently equal importance, invited him. He chose the one to his right, and reached, at its foot, a long gallery such as Rainer had described. The gallery was empty, the doors down its length were closed; but Rainer had said: 'The second to the left,' and Faxon, after pausing for some chance enlightenment which did not come, laid his hand on the second knob to the left.

The room he entered was square, with dusky picture-hung walls. In its centre, about a table lit by veiled lamps, he fancied

Mr Lavington and his guests to be already seated at dinner; then he perceived that the table was covered not with viands but with papers, and that he had blundered into what seemed to be his host's study. As he paused Frank Rainer looked up.

'Oh, here's Mr Faxon. Why not ask him –?'

Mr Lavington, from the end of the table, reflected his nephew's smile in a glance of impartial benevolence.

'Certainly. Come in, Mr Faxon. If you won't think it a liberty –'

Mr Grisben, who sat opposite his host, turned his head toward the door. 'Of course Mr Faxon's an American citizen?'

Frank Rainer laughed. 'That's all right! . . . Oh, no, not one of your pin-pointed pens, Uncle Jack! Haven't you got a quill somewhere?'

Mr Balch, who spoke slowly and as if reluctantly, in a muffled voice of which there seemed to be very little left, raised his hand to say: 'One moment: you acknowledge this to be –?'

'My last will and testament?' Rainer's laugh redoubled. 'Well, I won't answer for the "last". It's the first, anyway.'

'It's a mere formula,' Mr Balch explained.

'Well, here goes.' Rainer dipped his quill in the inkstand his uncle had pushed in his direction, and dashed a gallant signature across the document.

Faxon, understanding what was expected of him, and conjecturing that the young man was signing his will on the attainment of his majority, had placed himself behind Mr Grisben, and stood awaiting his turn to affix his name to the instrument. Rainer, having signed, was about to push the paper across the table to Mr Balch; but the latter, again raising his hand, said in his sad imprisoned voice: 'The seal –?'

'Oh, does there have to be a seal?'

Faxon, looking over Mr Grisben at John Lavington, saw

a faint frown between his impassive eyes. 'Really, Frank!' He seemed, Faxon thought, slightly irritated by his nephew's frivolity.

'Who's got a seal?' Frank Rainer continued, glancing about the table. 'There doesn't seem to be one here.'

Mr Grisben interposed. 'A wafer will do. Lavington, you have a wafer?'

Mr Lavington had recovered his serenity. 'There must be some in one of the drawers. But I'm ashamed to say I don't know where my secretary keeps these things. He ought to have seen to it that a wafer was sent with the document.'

'Oh, hang it –' Frank Rainer pushed the paper aside: 'It's the hand of God – and I'm as hungry as a wolf. Let's dine first, Uncle Jack.'

'I think I've a seal upstairs,' said Faxon.

Mr Lavington sent him a barely perceptible smile. 'So sorry to give you the trouble –'

'Oh, I say, don't send him after it now. Let's wait till after dinner!'

Mr Lavington continued to smile on *his* guest, and the latter, as if under the faint coercion of the smile, turned from the room and ran upstairs. Having taken the seal from his writing-case he came down again, and once more opened the door of the study. No one was speaking when he entered – they were evidently awaiting his return with the mute impatience of hunger, and he put the seal in Rainer's reach, and stood watching while Mr Grisben struck a match and held it to one of the candles flanking the inkstand. As the wax descended on the paper Faxon remarked again the strange emaciation, the premature physical weariness, of the hand that held it: he wondered if Mr Lavington had ever noticed his nephew's hand, and if it were not poignantly visible to him now.

With this thought in his mind, Faxon raised his eyes to look at Mr Lavington. The great man's gaze rested on Frank Rainer with an expression of untroubled benevolence; and at the same instant Faxon's attention was attracted by the presence in the room of another person, who must have joined the group while he was upstairs searching for the seal. The newcomer was a man of about Mr Lavington's age and figure, who stood just behind his chair, and who, at the moment when Faxon first saw him, was gazing at young Rainer with an equal intensity of attention. The likeness between the two men – perhaps increased by the fact that the hooded lamps on the table left the figure behind the chair in shadow – struck Faxon the more because of the contrast in their expression. John Lavington, during his nephew's clumsy attempt to drop the wax and apply the seal, continued to fasten on him a look of half-amused affection; while the man behind the chair, so oddly reduplicating the lines of his features and figure, turned on the boy a face of pale hostility.

The impression was so startling that Faxon forgot what was going on about him. He was just dimly aware of young Rainer's exclaiming; 'Your turn, Mr Grisben!' of Mr Grisben's protesting: 'No – no; Mr Faxon first', and of the pen's being thereupon transferred to his own hand. He received it with a deadly sense of being unable to move, or even to understand what was expected of him, till he became conscious of Mr Grisben's paternally pointing out the precise spot on which he was to leave his autograph. The effort to fix his attention and steady his hand prolonged the process of signing, and when he stood up – a strange weight of fatigue on all his limbs – the figure behind Mr Lavington's chair was gone.

Faxon felt an immediate sense of relief. It was puzzling that the man's exit should have been so rapid and noiseless, but the door behind Mr Lavington was screened by a tapestry hanging, and Faxon concluded that the unknown looker-on had merely had to raise it to pass out. At any rate he was gone, and with his withdrawal the strange weight was lifted. Young Rainer was lighting a cigarette, Mr Balch inscribing his name at the foot of the document, Mr Lavington — his eyes no longer on his nephew — examining a strange white-winged orchid in the vase at his elbow. Every thing suddenly seemed to have grown natural and simple again, and Faxon found himself responding with a smile to the affable gesture with which his host declared: 'And now, Mr Faxon, we'll dine.'

III

'I WONDER how I blundered into the wrong room just now; I thought you told me to take the second door to the left,' Faxon said to Frank Rainer as they followed the older men down the gallery.

'So I did; but I probably forgot to tell you which staircase to take. Coming from your bedroom, I ought to have said the fourth door to the right. It's a puzzling house, because my uncle keeps adding to it from year to year. He built this room last summer for his modern pictures.'

Young Rainer, pausing to open another door, touched an electric button which sent a circle of light about the walls of a long room hung with canvases of the French impressionist school.

Faxon advanced, attracted by a shimmering Monet, but Rainer laid a hand on his arm.

'He bought that last week. But come along – I'll show you all this after dinner. Or *he* will, rather – he loves it.'

'Does he really love things?'

Rainer stared, clearly perplexed at the question. 'Rather! Flowers and pictures especially! Haven't you noticed the flowers? I suppose you think his manner's cold; it seems so at first; but he's really awfully keen about things.'

Faxon looked quickly at the speaker. 'Has your uncle a brother?'

'Brother? No – never had. He and my mother were the only ones.'

'Or any relation who – who looks like him? Who might be mistaken for him?'

'Not that I ever heard of. Does he remind you of someone?'

'Yes.'

'That's queer. We'll ask him if he's got a double. Come on!'

But another picture had arrested Faxon, and some minutes elapsed before he and his young host reached the dining-room. It was a large room, with the same conventionally handsome furniture and delicately grouped flowers; and Faxon's first glance showed him that only three men were seated about the dining-table. The man who had stood behind Mr Lavington's chair was not present, and no seat awaited him.

When the young men entered, Mr Grisben was speaking, and his host, who faced the door, sat looking down at his untouched soup-plate and turning the spoon about in his small dry hand.

'It's pretty late to call them rumours – they were devilish close to facts when we left town this morning,' Mr Grisben was saying, with an unexpected incisiveness of tone.

Mr Lavington laid down his spoon and smiled interrogatively. 'Oh, facts – what *are* facts? Just the way a thing happens to look at a given minute . . .'

'You haven't heard anything from town?' Mr Grisben persisted.

'Not a syllable. So you see . . . Balch, a little more of that *petite marmite*. Mr Faxon . . . between Frank and Mr Grisben, please.'

The dinner progressed through a series of complicated courses, ceremoniously dispensed by a prelatical butler attended by three tall footmen, and it was evident that Mr Lavington took a certain satisfaction in the pageant. That, Faxon reflected, was probably the joint in his armour – that and the flowers. He had changed the subject – not abruptly but firmly – when the young men entered, but Faxon perceived that it still possessed the thoughts of the two elderly visitors, and Mr Balch presently observed, in a voice that seemed to come from the last survivor down a mine-shaft: 'If it *does* come, it will be the biggest crash since '93.'

Mr Lavington looked bored but polite. 'Wall Street can stand crashes better than it could then. It's got a robuster constitution.'

'Yes; but –'

'Speaking of constitutions,' Mr Grisben intervened: 'Frank, are you taking care of yourself?'

A flush rose to young Rainer's cheeks.

'Why, of course! Isn't that what I'm here for?'

'You're here about three days in the month, aren't you? And the rest of the time it's crowded restaurants and hot ballrooms in town. I thought you were to be shipped off to New Mexico?'

'Oh, I've got a new man who says that's rot.'

'Well, you don't look as if your new man were right,' said Mr Grisben bluntly.

Faxon saw the lad's colour fade, and the rings of shadow deepen under his gay eyes. At the same moment his uncle turned to him with a renewed intensity of attention. There was such solicitude in Mr Lavington's gaze that it seemed almost to fling a shield between his nephew and Mr Grisben's tactless scrutiny.

'We think Frank's a good deal better,' he began; 'this new doctor —'

The butler, coming up, bent to whisper a word in his ear, and the communication caused a sudden change in Mr Lavington's expression. His face was naturally so colourless that it seemed not so much to pale as to fade, to dwindle and recede into something blurred and blotted-out. He half rose, sat down again and sent a rigid smile about the table.

'Will you excuse me? The telephone. Peters, go on with the dinner.' With small precise steps he walked out of the door which one of the footmen had thrown open.

A momentary silence fell on the group; then Mr Grisben once more addressed himself to Rainer. 'You ought to have gone, my boy; you ought to have gone.'

The anxious look returned to the youth's eyes. 'My uncle doesn't think so, really.'

'You're not a baby, to be always governed by your uncle's opinion. You came of age today, didn't you? Your uncle spoils you . . . that's what's the matter . . .'

The thrust evidently went home, for Rainer laughed and looked down with a slight accession of colour.

'But the doctor —'

'Use your common sense, Frank! You had to try twenty doctors to find one to tell you what you wanted to be told.'

A look of apprehension overshadowed Rainer's, gaiety. 'Oh, come — I say! . . . What would *you* do?' he stammered.

'Pack up and jump on the first train.' Mr Grisben leaned forward and laid his hand kindly on the young man's arm. 'Look here: my nephew Jim Grisben is out there ranching on a big scale. He'll take you in and be glad to have you. You say your new doctor thinks it won't do you any good; but he doesn't pretend to say it will do you harm, does he? Well, then – give it a trial. It'll take you out of hot theatres and night restaurants, anyhow . . . And all the rest of it . . . Eh, Balch?'

'Go!' said Mr Balch hollowly. 'Go *at once*,' he added, as if a closer look at the youth's face had impressed on him the need of backing up his friend.

Young Rainer had turned ashy-pale. He tried to stiffen his mouth into a smile. 'Do I look as bad as all that?'

Mr Grisben was helping himself to terrapin. 'You look like the day after an earthquake,' he said.

The terrapin had encircled the table, and been deliberately enjoyed by Mr Lavington's three visitors (Rainer, Faxon noticed, left his plate untouched) before the door was thrown open to re-admit their host. Mr Lavington advanced with an air of recovered composure. He seated himself, picked up his napkin and consulted the gold-monogrammed menu. 'No, don't bring back the filet . . . Some terrapin; yes . . .' He looked affably about the table. 'Sorry to have deserted you, but the storm has played the deuce with the wires, and I had to wait a long time before I could get a good connection. It must be blowing up for a blizzard.'

'Uncle Jack,' young Rainer broke out, 'Mr Grisben's been lecturing me.'

Mr Lavington was helping himself to terrapin. 'Ah – what about?'

'He thinks I ought to have given New Mexico a show.'

'I want him to go straight out to my nephew at Santa Paz and stay there till his next birthday.' Mr Lavington signed to the butler to hand the terrapin to Mr Grisben, who, as he took a second helping, addressed himself again to Rainer. 'Jim's in New York now, and going back the day after tomorrow in Olyphant's private car. I'll ask Olyphant to squeeze you in if you'll go. And when you've been out there a week or two, in the saddle all day and sleeping nine hours a night, I suspect you won't think much of the doctor who prescribed New York.'

Faxon spoke up, he knew not why. 'I was out there once: it's a splendid life. I saw a fellow – oh, a really *bad* case – who'd been simply made over by it.'

'It *does* sound jolly,' Rainer laughed, a sudden eagerness in his tone.

His uncle looked at him gently. 'Perhaps Grisben's right. It's an opportunity –'

Faxon glanced up with a start: the figure dimly perceived in the study was now more visibly and tangibly planted behind Mr Lavington's chair.

'That's right, Frank: you see your uncle approves. And the trip out there with Olyphant isn't a thing to be missed. So drop a few dozen dinners and be at the Grand Central the day after tomorrow at five.'

Mr Grisben's pleasant grey eye sought corroboration of his host, and Faxon, in a cold anguish of suspense, continued to watch him as he turned his glance on Mr Lavington. One could not look at Lavington without seeing the presence at his back, and it was clear that, the next minute, some change in Mr Grisben's expression must give his watcher a clue.

But Mr Grisben's expression did not change: the gaze he fixed on his host remained unperturbed, and the clue he gave was the startling one of not seeming to see the other figure.

Faxon's first impulse was to look away, to look anywhere else, to resort again to the champagne glass the watchful butler had already brimmed; but some fatal attraction, at war in him with an overwhelming physical resistance, held his eyes upon the spot they feared.

The figure was still standing, more distinctly, and therefore more resemblingly, at Mr Lavington's back; and while the latter continued to gaze affectionately at his nephew, his counterpart, as before, fixed young Rainer with eyes of deadly menace.

Faxon, with what felt like an actual wrench of the muscles, dragged his own eyes from the sight to scan the other countenances about the table; but not one revealed the least consciousness of what he saw, and a sense of mortal isolation sank upon him.

'It's worth considering, certainly –' he heard Mr Lavington continue; and as Rainer's face lit up, the face behind his uncle's chair seemed to gather into its look all the fierce weariness of old unsatisfied hates. That was the thing that, as the minutes laboured by, Faxon was becoming most conscious of. The watcher behind the chair was no longer merely malevolent: he had grown suddenly, unutterably tired. His hatred seemed to well up out of the very depths of baulked effort and thwarted hopes, and the fact made him more pitiable, and yet more dire.

Faxon's look reverted to Mr Lavington, as if to surprise in him a corresponding change. At first none was visible: his pinched smile was screwed to his blank face like a gas-light to a white-washed wall. Then the fixity of the smile became ominous: Faxon saw that its wearer was afraid to let it go. It was evident that Mr Lavington was unutterably tired too, and the discovery sent a colder current through Faxon's veins. Looking down at his untouched plate, he caught the soliciting twinkle of the champagne glass; but the sight of the wine turned him sick.

'Well, we'll go into the details presently,' he heard Mr Lavington say, still on the question of his nephew's future. 'Let's have a cigar first. No – not here, Peters.' He turned his smile on Faxon. 'When we've had coffee I want to show you my pictures.'

'Oh, by the way, Uncle Jack — Mr Faxon wants to know if you've got a double?'

'A double?' Mr Lavington, still smiling, continued to address himself to his guest. 'Not that I know of. Have you seen one, Mr Faxon?'

Faxon thought: 'My God, if I look up now they'll *both* be looking at me!' To avoid raising his eyes he made as though to lift the glass to his lips; but his hand sank inert, and he looked up. Mr Lavington's glance was politely bent on him, but with a loosening of the strain about his heart he saw that the figure behind the chair still kept its gaze on Rainer.

'Do you think you've seen my double, Mr Faxon?'

Would the other face turn if he said yes? Faxon felt a dryness in his throat. 'No,' he answered.

'Ah? It's possible I've a dozen. I believe I'm extremely usual-looking,' Mr Lavington went on conversationally; and still the other face watched Rainer.

'It was . . . a mistake . . . a confusion of memory . . .' Faxon heard himself stammer. Mr Lavington pushed back his chair, and as he did so Mr Grisben suddenly leaned forward.

'Lavington! What have we been thinking of? We haven't drunk Frank's health!'

Mr Lavington reseated himself. 'My dear boy! . . . Peters, another bottle . . .' He turned to his nephew. 'After such a sin of omission I don't presume to propose the toast myself . . . but Frank knows . . . Go ahead, Grisben!'

The boy shone on his uncle. 'No, no, Uncle Jack! Mr Grisben won't mind. Nobody but *you* — today!'

The butler was replenishing the glasses. He filled Mr Lavington's last, and Mr Lavington put out his small hand to raise it . . . As he did so, Faxon looked away.

'Well, then — All the good I've wished you in all the past

years . . . I put it into the prayer that the coming ones may be healthy and happy and many . . . and *many*, dear boy!'

Faxon saw the hands about him reach out for their glasses. Automatically, he reached for his. His eyes were still on the table, and he repeated to himself with a trembling vehemence: 'I won't look up! I won't . . . I won't . . .'

His fingers clasped the glass and raised it to the level of his lips. He saw the other hands making the same motion. He heard Mr Grisben's genial 'Hear! Hear!' and Mr Batch's hollow echo. He said to himself, as the rim of the glass touched his lips: 'I won't look up! I swear I won't! –' and he looked.

The glass was so full that it required an extraordinary effort to hold it there, brimming and suspended, during the awful interval before he could trust his hand to lower it again, untouched, to the table. It was this merciful preoccupation which saved him, kept him from crying out, from losing his hold, from slipping down into the bottomless blackness that gaped for him. As long as the problem of the glass engaged him he felt able to keep his seat, manage his muscles, fit unnoticeably into the group; but as the glass touched the table his last link with safety snapped. He stood up and dashed out of the room.

IV

IN THE gallery, the instinct of self-preservation helped him to turn back and sign to young Rainer not to follow. He stammered out something about a touch of dizziness, and joining them presently; and the boy nodded sympathetically and drew back.

At the foot of the stairs Faxon ran against a servant. 'I should like to telephone to Weymore,' he said with dry lips.

'Sorry, sir; wires all down. We've been trying the last hour to get New York again for Mr Lavington.'

Faxon shot on to his room, burst into it, and bolted the door. The lamplight lay on furniture, flowers, books; in the ashes a log still glimmered. He dropped down on the sofa and hid his face. The room was profoundly silent, the whole house was still: nothing about him gave a hint of what was going on, darkly and dumbly, in the room he had flown from, and with the covering of his eyes oblivion and reassurance seemed to fall on him. But they fell for a moment only; then his lids opened again to the monstrous vision. There it was, stamped on his pupils, a part of him forever, an indelible horror burnt into his body and brain. But why into his – just his? Why had he alone been chosen to see what he had seen? What business was it of *his*, in God's name? Any one of the others, thus enlightened, might have exposed the horror and defeated it; but *he*, the one weaponless and defenceless spectator, the one whom none of the others would believe or understand if he attempted to reveal what he knew – *he* alone had been singled out as the victim of this dreadful initiation!

Suddenly he sat up, listening: he had heard a step on the stairs. Someone, no doubt, was coming to see how he was – to urge him, if he felt better, to go down and join the smokers. Cautiously he opened his door; yes, it was young Rainer's step. Faxon looked down the passage, remembered the other stairway and darted to it. All he wanted was to get out of the house. Not another instant would he breathe its abominable air! What business was it of *his*, in God's name?

He reached the opposite end of the lower gallery, and beyond it saw the hall by which he had entered. It was empty, and on a long table he recognised his coat and cap. He got into his coat, unbolted the door, and plunged into the purifying night.

The darkness was deep, and the cold so intense that for an instant it stopped his breathing. Then he perceived that only a thin snow was falling, and resolutely he set his face for flight. The trees along the avenue marked his way as he hastened with long strides over the beaten snow. Gradually, while he walked, the tumult in his brain subsided. The impulse to fly still drove him forward, but he began feel that he was flying from a terror of his own creating, and that the most urgent reason for escape was the need of hiding his state, of shunning other eyes till he should regain his balance.

He had spent the long hours in the train in fruitless broodings on a discouraging situation, and he remembered how his bitterness had turned to exasperation when he found that the Weymore sleigh was not awaiting him. It was absurd, of course; but, though he had joked with Rainer over Mrs Culme's forgetfulness, to confess it had cost a pang. That was what his rootless life had brought him to: for lack of a personal stake in things his sensibility was at the mercy of such trifles . . . Yes; that, and the cold and fatigue, the absence of hope and the haunting sense of starved aptitudes, all these had brought him to the perilous verge over which, once or twice before, his terrified brain had hung.

Why else, in the name of any imaginable logic, human or devilish, should he, a stranger, be singled out for this experience? What could it mean to him, how was he related to it, what bearing had it on his case? . . . Unless, indeed, it was just because he was a stranger – a stranger everywhere – because he had no personal life, no warm screen of private egotisms to shield him from exposure, that he had developed this abnormal sensitiveness to the vicissitudes of others. The thought pulled him up with a shudder. No! Such a fate was too abominable; all that was strong and sound in him rejected it. A thousand times better regard himself as ill, disorganised, deluded, than as the predestined victim of such warnings!

He reached the gates and paused before the darkened lodge. The wind had risen and was sweeping the snow into his race. The cold had him in its grasp again, and he stood uncertain. Should he put his sanity to the test and go back? He turned and looked down the dark drive to the house. A single ray shone through the trees, evoking a picture of the lights, the flowers, the faces grouped about that fatal room. He turned and plunged out into the road . . .

He remembered that, about a mile from Overdale, the coachman had pointed out the road to Northridge; and he began to walk in that direction. Once in the road he had the gale in his face, and the wet snow on his moustache and eyelashes instantly hardened to ice. The same ice seemed to be driving a million blades into his throat and lungs, but he pushed on, the vision of the warm room pursuing him.

The snow in the road was deep and uneven. He stumbled across ruts and sank into drifts, and the wind drove against him like a granite cliff. Now and then he stopped, gasping, as if an invisible hand had tightened an iron band about his body; then he started again, stiffening himself against the stealthy penetration of the cold. The snow continued to descend out of a pall of inscrutable darkness, and once or twice he paused, fearing he had missed the road to Northridge; but, seeing no sign of a turn, he ploughed on.

At last, feeling sure that he had walked for more than a mile, he halted and looked back. The act of turning brought immediate relief, first because it put his back to the wind, and then because, far down the road, it showed him the gleam of a lantern. A sleigh was coming – a sleigh that might perhaps give him a lift to the village! Fortified by the hope, he began to walk back toward the light. It came forward very slowly, with unaccountable zigzags and waverings; and even when he was within a few yards of it he could catch no sound of sleigh-bells. Then it paused and became stationary by the roadside, as though carried by a pedestrian who had stopped, exhausted by the cold. The thought made Faxon hasten on, and a moment later he was stooping over a motionless figure huddled against the snow-bank. The lantern had dropped from its bearer's hand, and Faxon, fearfully raising it, threw its light into the face of Frank Rainer.

'Rainer! What on earth are you doing here?'

The boy smiled back through his pallor. 'What are *you*, I'd like to know?' he retorted; and, scrambling to his feet with a clutch on Faxon's arm, he added gaily: 'Well, I've run you down!'

Faxon stood confounded, his heart sinking. The lad's face was grey.

'What madness –' he began.

'Yes, it *is*. What on earth did you do it for?'

'I? Do what? . . . Why I . . . I was just taking a walk . . . I often walk at night . . .'

Frank Rainer burst into a laugh. 'On such nights? Then you hadn't bolted?'

'Bolted?'

'Because I'd done something to offend you? My uncle thought you had.'

Faxon grasped his arm. 'Did your uncle send you after me?'

'Well, he gave me an awful rowing for not going up to your room with you when you said you were ill. And when we found you'd gone we were frightened – and he was awfully upset – so I said I'd catch you . . . You're *not* ill, are you?'

'Ill? No. Never better.' Faxon picked up the lantern. 'Come; let's go back. It was awfully hot in that dining-room.'

'Yes; I hoped it was only that.'

They trudged on in silence for a few minutes; then Faxon questioned: 'You're not too done up?'

'Oh, no. It's a lot easier with the wind behind us.'

'All right. Don't talk any more.'

They pushed ahead, walking, in spite of the light that guided them, more slowly than Faxon had walked alone into the gale. The fact of his companion's stumbling against a drift gave Faxon a pretext for saying: 'Take hold of my arm,' and Rainer obeying, gasped out: 'I'm blown!'

'So am I. Who wouldn't be?'

'What a dance you led me! If it hadn't been for one of the servants happening to see you —'

'Yes; all right. And now, won't you kindly shut up?'

Rainer laughed and hung on him. 'Oh, the cold doesn't hurt me . . .'

For the first few minutes after Rainer had overtaken him, anxiety for the lad had been Faxon's only thought. But as each labouring step carried them nearer to the spot he had been fleeing, the reasons for his flight grew more ominous and more insistent. No, he was not ill, he was not distraught and deluded — he was the instrument singled out to warn and save; and here he was, irresistibly driven, dragging the victim back to his doom!

The intensity of the conviction had almost checked his steps. But what could he do or say? At all costs he must get Rainer out of the cold, into the house and into his bed. After that he would act.

The snowfall was thickening, and as they reached a stretch of the road between open fields the wind took them at an angle, lashing their faces with barbed thongs. Rainer stopped to take breath, and Faxon felt the heavier pressure of his arm.

'When we get to the lodge, can't we telephone to the stable for a sleigh?'

'If they're not all asleep at the lodge.'

'Oh, I'll manage. Don't talk!' Faxon ordered; and they plodded on . . .

At length the lantern ray showed ruts that curved away from the road under tree-darkness.

Faxon's spirits rose. 'There's the gate! We'll be there in five minutes.'

As he spoke he caught, above the boundary hedge, the gleam of a light at the farther end of the dark avenue. It was the same light that had shone on the scene of which every detail was burnt into his brain; and he felt again its overpowering reality. No – he couldn't let the boy go back!

They were at the lodge at last, and Faxon was hammering on the door. He said to himself: 'I'll get him inside first, and make them give him a hot drink. Then I'll see – I'll find an argument . . .'

There was no answer to his knocking, and after an interval Rainer said: 'Look here – we'd better go on.'

'No!'

'I can, perfectly –'

'You shan't go to the house, I say!' Faxon redoubled his blows, and at length steps sounded on the stairs. Rainer was leaning against the lintel, and as the door opened the light from the hall flashed on his pale face and fixed eyes. Faxon caught him by the arm and drew him in.

'It *was* cold out there.' he sighed; and then, abruptly, as if invisible shears at a single stroke had cut every muscle in his body, he swerved, drooped on Faxon's arm, and seemed to sink into nothing at his feet.

The lodge-keeper and Faxon bent over him, and somehow, between them, lifted him into the kitchen and laid him on a sofa by the stove.

The lodge-keeper, stammering 'I'll ring up the house', dashed out of the room. But Faxon heard the words without heeding them: omens mattered nothing now, beside this woe fulfilled. He knelt down to undo the fur collar about Rainer's throat, and as he did so he felt a warm moisture on his hands. He held them up, and they were red . . .

V

THE PALMS threaded their endless line along the yellow river. The little steamer lay at the wharf, and George Faxon, sitting in the verandah of the wooden hotel, idly watched the coolies carrying the freight across the gang-plank.

He had been looking at such scenes for two months. Nearly five had elapsed since he had descended from the train at North-ridge and strained his eyes for the sleigh that was to take him to Weymore: Weymore, which he was never to behold! . . . Part of the interval — the first part — was still a great grey blur. Even now he could not be quite sure how he had got back to Boston, reached the house of a cousin, and been thence transferred to a quiet room looking out on snow under bare trees. He looked out a long time at the same scene, and finally one day a man he had known at Harvard came to see him and invited him to go out on a business trip to the Malay Peninsula.

'You've had a bad shake-up, and it'll do you no end of good to get away from things.'

When the doctor came the next day it turned out that he knew of the plan and approved it. 'You ought to be quiet for a year. Just loaf and look at the landscape,' he advised.

Faxon felt the first faint stirrings of curiosity.

'What's been the matter with me, anyway?'

'Well, overwork, I suppose. You must have been bottling up for a bad breakdown before you started for New Hampshire last December. And the shock of that poor boy's death did the rest.'

Ah, yes – Rainer had died. He remembered . . .

He started for the East, and gradually, by imperceptible degrees, life crept back into his weary bones and leaden brain. His friend was patient and considerate, and they travelled slowly and talked little. At first Faxon had felt a great shrinking from whatever touched on familiar things. He seldom looked at a newspaper and he never opened a letter without a contraction of the heart. It was not that he had any special cause for apprehension, but merely that a great trail of darkness lay on everything. He had looked too deep down into the abyss . . . But little by little health and energy returned to him, and with them the common promptings of curiosity. He was beginning to wonder how the world was going, and when, presently, the hotel-keeper told him there were no letters for him in the steamer's mailbag, he felt a distinct sense of disappointment. His friend had gone into the jungle on a long excursion, and he was lonely, unoccupied and wholesomely bored. He got up and strolled into the stuffy reading-room.

There he found a game of dominoes, a mutilated picture-puzzle, some copies of *Zion's Herald* and a pile of New York and London newspapers.

He began to glance through the papers, and was disappointed

to find that they were less recent than he had hoped. Evidently the last numbers had been carried off by luckier travellers. He continued to turn them over, picking out the American ones first. These, as it happened, were the oldest: they dated back to December and January. To Faxon, however, they had all the flavour of novelty, since they covered the precise period during which he had virtually ceased to exist. It had never before occurred to him to wonder what had happened in the world during that interval of obliteration; but now he felt a sudden desire to know.

To prolong the pleasure, he began by sorting the papers chronologically, and as he found and spread out the earliest number, the date at the top of the page entered into his consciousness like a key slipping into a lock. It was the seventeenth of December: the date of the day after his arrival at Northridge. He glanced at the first page and read in blazing characters: 'Reported Failure of Opal Cement Company. Lavington's name involved. Gigantic Exposure of Corruption Shakes Wall Street to Its Foundations.'

He read on, and when he had finished the first paper he turned to the next. There was a gap of three days, but the Opal Cement 'Investigation' still held the centre of the stage. From its complex revelations of greed and ruin his eye wandered to the death notices, and he read: 'Rainer. Suddenly, at Northridge, New Hampshire, Francis John, only son of the late . . .'

His eyes clouded, and he dropped the newspaper and sat for a long time with his face in his hands. When he looked up again he noticed that his gesture had pushed the other papers from the table and scattered them at his feet. The uppermost lay spread out before him, and heavily his eyes began their search again. 'John Lavington comes forward with plan for reconstructing Company. Offers to put in ten millions of his own – The proposal under consideration by the District Attorney.'

Ten millions . . . ten millions of his own. But if John Lavington was ruined? . . . Faxon stood up with a cry. That was it, then – that was what the warning meant! And if he had not fled from it, dashed wildly away from it into the night, he might have broken the spell of iniquity, the powers of darkness might not have prevailed! He caught up the pile of newspapers and began to glance through each in turn for the headline: 'Wills Admitted to Probate'. In the last of all he found the paragraph he sought, and it stared up at him as if with Rainer's dying eyes.

That – *that* was what he had done! The powers of pity had singled him out to warn and save, and he had closed his ears to their call, and washed his hands of it, and fled. Washed his hands of it! That was the word. It caught him back to the dreadful moment in the lodge when, raising himself up from Rainer's side, he had looked at his hands and seen that they were red . . .

IN THE DARK *BY* EDITH NESBIT

Edith Nesbit was born in 1858. Her father died when she was only three and her impoverished family moved continually all over England. As a young married woman with small children, she sold stories and poems to supplement the family income. Her first children's book, *The Treasure Seekers*, was published in 1899. She also wrote *Five Children and It* but her most famous story, *The Railway Children*, was first published in 1905 and has never been out of print. Edith Nesbit died in 1924.

I T MAY have been a form of madness. Or it may be that he really was what is called haunted. Or it may – though I don't pretend to understand how – have been the development, through intense suffering, of a sixth sense in a very nervous, highly-strung nature. Something certainly led him where They were. And to him They were all one.

He told me the first part of the story, and the last part of it I saw with my own eyes.

I

H ALDANE AND I were friends even in our school-days. What first brought us together was our common hatred of Visger, who came from our part of the country. His people knew our people at home, so he was put on to us when he came. He was the most intolerable person, boy and man, that I have ever known. He would not tell a lie. And that was all right. But he didn't stop at that. If he were asked whether any other chap had done anything – been out of bounds, or up to any sort of lark – he would always say, 'I don't know, sir, but I believe so.' He never did know – we took care of that. But what he believed was always right. I remember Haldane twisting his arm to say how he knew about that cherry tree business, and he only said, 'I don't know – I just feel sure. And I was right, you see.' What can you do with a boy like that?

We grew up to be men. At least Haldane and I did. Visger grew up to be a prig. He was a vegetarian and a teetotaller, and an all-wooler and Christian Scientist, and all the things that prigs are – but he wasn't a common prig. He knew all sorts of things that he oughtn't to have known, that he *couldn't* have known in any ordinary decent way. It wasn't that he found things out. He just knew them. Once, when I was very unhappy, he came into my rooms – we were all in our last year at Oxford – and talked about things I hardly knew myself. That was really why I went to India that winter. It was bad enough to be unhappy, without having that beast knowing all about it.

I was away over a year. Coming back, I thought a lot about how jolly it would be to see old Haldane again. If I thought about Visger at all, I wished he was dead. But I didn't think about him much.

I did want to see Haldane. He was always such a jolly chap – gay, and kindly, and simple, honourable, upright, and full of practical sympathies. I longed to see him, to see the smile in his jolly blue eyes, looking out from the net of wrinkles that laughing had made round them, to hear his jolly laugh, and feel the good grip of his big hand. I went straight from the docks to his chambers in Grey's Inn, and I found him cold, pale, anaemic, with dull eyes and a limp hand, and pale lips that smiled without mirth, and uttered a welcome without gladness.

He was surrounded by a litter of disordered furniture and personal effects half packed. Some big boxes stood corded, and there were cases of books, filled and waiting for the enclosing boards to be nailed on.

'Yes, I'm moving,' he said. 'I can't stand these rooms. There's something rum about them – something devilish rum. I clear out tomorrow.'

The autumn dusk was filling the corners with shadows. 'You got the furs,' I said, just for something to say, for I saw the big case that held them lying corded among the others.

'Furs?' he said. 'Oh yes. Thanks awfully. Yes. I forgot about the furs.' He laughed, out of politeness, I suppose, for there was no joke about the furs. They were many and fine – the best I could get for money, and I had seen them packed and sent off when my heart was very sore. He stood looking at me, and saying nothing.

'Come out and have a bit of dinner,' I said as cheerfully as I could.

'Too busy,' he answered, after the slightest possible pause, and a glance round the room – 'look here – I'm awfully glad to see you – If you'd just slip over and order in dinner – I'd go myself – only – Well, you see how it is.'

I went. And when I came back, he had cleared a space near the fire, and moved his big gate-table into it. We dined there by candle light. I tried to be amusing. He, I am sure, tried to be amused. We did not succeed, either of us. And his haggard eyes watched me all the time, save in those fleeting moments when, without turning his head, he glanced back over his shoulder into the shadows that crowded round the little lighted place where we sat.

When we had dined and the man had come and taken away the dishes, I looked at Haldane very steadily, so that he stopped in a pointless anecdote, and looked interrogation at me.

'Well?' I said.

'You're not listening,' he said petulantly. 'What's the matter?'

'That's what you'd better tell me,' I said.

He was silent, gave one of those furtive glances at the shadows, and stooped to stir the fire to – I knew it – a blaze that must light every corner of the room.

'You're all to pieces,' I said cheerfully. 'What have you been up to? Wine? Cards? Speculation? A woman? If you won't tell me, you'll have to tell your doctor. Why, my dear chap, you're a wreck.'

'You're a comfortable friend to have about the place,' he said, and smiled a mechanical smile not at all pleasant to see.

'I'm the friend you want, I think,' said I. 'Do you suppose I'm blind? Something's gone wrong and you've taken to something. Morphia, perhaps? And you've brooded over the thing till you've lost all sense of proportion. Out with it, old chap. I bet you a dollar it's not so bad as you think it.'

'If I could tell you – or tell anyone,' he said slowly, 'it wouldn't be so bad as it is. If I could tell anyone, I'd tell you. And even as it is, I've told you more than I've told anyone else.'

I could get nothing more out of him. But he pressed me to stay – would have given me his bed and made himself a shake-down, he said. But I had engaged my room at the Victoria, and I was expecting letters. So I left him, quite late – and he stood on the stairs, holding a candle over the banisters to light me down.

When I went back next morning, he was gone. Men were moving his furniture into a big van with somebody's Pantech-nicon painted on it in big letters.

He had left no address with the porter, and had driven off in a hansom with two portmanteaux – to Waterloo, the porter thought.

Well, a man has a right to the monopoly of his own troubles, if he chooses to have it. And I had troubles of my own that kept me busy.

II

IT WAS more than a year later that I saw Haldane again. I had got rooms in the Albany by this time, and he turned up there one morning, very early indeed – before breakfast in fact. And if he looked ghastly before, he now looked almost ghostly. His face looked as though it had worn thin, like an oyster shell that has for years been cast up twice a day by the sea on a shore all pebbly. His hands were thin as bird's claws, and they trembled like caught butterflies.

I welcomed him with enthusiastic cordiality and pressed breakfast on him. This time, I decided, I would ask no questions. For I saw that none were needed. He would tell me. He intended to tell me. He had come here to tell me, and for nothing else.

I lit the spirit lamp – I made coffee and small talk for him, and I ate and drank, and waited for him to begin. And it was like this that he began: 'I am going,' he said, 'to kill myself – oh, don't be alarmed' – I suppose I had said or looked something – 'I shan't do it here, or now. I shall do it when I have to – when I can't bear it any longer. And I want someone to know why. I don't want to feel that I'm the only living creature who does know. And I can trust you, can't I?'

I murmured something reassuring.

'I should like you, if you don't mind, to give me your word, that you won't tell a soul what I'm going to tell you, as long as I'm alive. Afterwards . . . you can tell whom you please.'

I gave him my word.

He sat silent looking at the fire. Then he shrugged his shoulders.

'It's extraordinary how difficult it is to say it,' he said, and smiled. 'The fact is – you know that beast, George Visger.'

'Yes,' I said. 'I haven't seen him since I came back. Someone told me he'd gone to some island or other to preach vegetarianism to cannibals. Anyhow, he's out of the way, bad luck to him.'

'Yes,' said Haldane, 'he's out of the way. But he's not preaching anything. In point of fact, he's dead.'

'Dead?' was all I could think of to say.

'Yes,' said he; 'it's not generally known, but he is.'

'What did he die of?' I asked, not that I cared. The bare fact was good enough for me.

'You know what an interfering chap he always was. Always knew everything. Heart to heart talks – and have everything open and above board. Well, he interfered between me and someone else – told her a pack of lies.'

'Lies?'

'Well, the *things* were true, but he made lies of them the way he told them – *you* know.' I did. I nodded. 'And she threw me over. And she died. And we weren't even friends. And I couldn't see her – before – I couldn't even . . . Oh, my God . . . But I went to the funeral. He was there. They'd asked *him*. And then I came back to my rooms. And I was sitting there, thinking. And he came up.'

'He would do. It's just what he would do. The beast! I hope you kicked him out.'

'No, I didn't. I listened to what he'd got to say. He came to say, No doubt it was all for the best. And he hadn't known the things he told her. He'd only guessed. He'd guessed right, damn him. What right had he to guess right? And he said it was all for the best, because, besides that, there was madness in my family. He'd found that out too –'

'And is there?'

'If there is, I didn't know it. And that was why it was all for the best. So then I said, "There wasn't any madness in my family before, but there is now," and I got hold of his throat. I am not sure whether I meant to kill him; I ought to have meant to kill him. Anyhow, I did kill him. What did you say?'

I had said nothing. It is not easy to think at once of the tactful and suitable thing to say, when your oldest friend tells you that he is a murderer.

'When I could get my hands out of his throat – it was as difficult as it is to drop the handles of a galvanic battery – he fell in a lump on the hearth-rug. And I saw what I'd done. How is it that murderers ever get found out?'

'They're careless, I suppose,' I found myself saying, 'they lose their nerve.'

'I didn't,' he said. 'I never was calmer, I sat down in the big chair and looked at him, and thought it all out. He was just off to that island – I knew that. He'd said goodbye to everyone. He'd told me that. There was no blood to get rid of – or only a touch at the corner of his slack mouth. He wasn't going to travel in his own name because of interviewers. Mr Somebody Something's luggage would be unclaimed and his cabin empty. No one would guess that Mr Somebody Something was Sir George Visger, FRS. It was all as plain as plain. There was nothing to get rid of, but the man. No weapon, no blood – and I got rid of him all right.'

'How?'

He smiled cunningly.

'No, no,' he said; 'that's where I draw the line. It's not that I doubt your word, but if you talked in your sleep, or had a fever or anything. No, no. As long as you don't know where the body is, don't you see, I'm all right. Even if you could prove that I've said all this – which you can't – it's only the wanderings of my poor unhinged brain. See?'

I saw. And I was sorry for him. And I did not believe that he had killed Visger. He was not the sort of man who kills people. So I said: 'Yes, old chap, I see. Now look here. Let's go away together, you and I – travel a bit and see the world, and forget all about that beastly chap.'

His eyes lighted up at that. 'Why,' he said, 'you understand. You don't hate me and shrink from me. I wish I'd told you before – you know – when you came and I was packing all my sticks. But it's too late now.'

'Too late? Not a bit of it,' I said. 'Come, we'll pack our traps and be off tonight – out into the unknown, don't you know.'

'That's where *I'm* going,' he said. 'You wait. When you've heard what's been happening to me, you won't be so keen to go travelling about with me.'

'But you've told me what's been happening to you,' I said, and the more I thought about what he had told me, the less I believed it.

'No,' he said, slowly, 'no – I've told you what happened to *him*. What happened to me is quite different. Did I tell you what his last words were? Just when I was coming at him. Before I'd got his throat, you know. He said, "Look out. You'll never be able to get rid of the body – Besides, anger's sinful." You know that way he had, like a tract on its hind legs. So afterwards I got thinking of that. But I didn't think of it for a year. Because I did get rid of his body all right. And then I was sitting in that comfortable chair, and I thought, "Hullo, it must be about a year now, since that —" and I pulled out my pocket-book and went to the window to look at a little almanack I carry about — it was getting dusk — and sure enough it was a year, to the day. And then I remembered what he'd said. And I said to myself, "Not much trouble about getting rid of *your* body, you brute." And then I looked at the hearth-rug and — Ah!' he screamed suddenly and very loud — 'I can't tell you — no, I can't.'

My man opened the door — he wore a smooth face over his wriggling curiosity. 'Did you call, sir?'

'Yes,' I lied. 'I want you to take a note to the bank, and wait for an answer.'

When he was got rid of, Haldane said: 'Where was I? —'

'You were just telling me what happened after you looked at the almanack. What was it?'

'Nothing much,' he said, laughing softly, 'oh, nothing much — only that I glanced at the hearth-rug — and there *he* was — the man I'd killed a year before. Don't try to explain, or I shall lose my temper. The door was shut. The windows were shut. He hadn't been there a minute before. And he was there then. That's all.'

Hallucination was one of the words I stumbled among.

'Exactly what I thought,' he said triumphantly, 'but — I touched it. It was quite real. Heavy, you know, and harder than live people are somehow, to the touch — more like a stone thing covered with kid the hands were, and the arms like a marble statue in a blue serge suit. Don't you hate men who wear blue serge suits?'

'There are hallucinations of touch too,' I found myself saying.

'Exactly what I thought,' said Haldane more triumphant than ever, 'but there are limits, you know – limits. So then I thought someone had got him out – the real him – and stuck him there to frighten me – while my back was turned, and I went to the place where I'd hidden him, and he was there – ah! – just as I'd left him. Only . . . it was a year ago. There are two of him there now.'

'My dear chap,' I said, 'this is simply comic.'

'Yes,' he said, 'it is amusing. I find it so myself. Especially in the night when I wake up and think of it. I hope I shan't die in the dark, Winston. That's one of the reasons why I think I shall have to kill myself. I could be sure then of not dying in the dark.'

'Is *that* all?' I asked, feeling sure that it must be.

'No,' said Haldane at once. 'That's *not* all. He's come back to me again. In a railway carriage it was. I'd been asleep. When I woke up, there he was lying on the seat opposite me. Looked just the same. I pitched him out on the line in Red Hill tunnel. And if I see him again, I'm going out myself. I can't stand it. It's too much. I'd sooner go. Whatever the next world's like, there aren't things in it like that. We leave them here, in graves and boxes and . . . You think I'm mad. But I'm not. You can't help me – no one can help me. He *knew*, you see. He said I shouldn't be able to get rid of the body. And I can't get rid of it. I can't. I can't. He knew. He always did know things that he *couldn't* know. But I'll cut his game short. After all, I've got the ace of trumps, and I play it on his next trick. I give you my word of honour, Winston, that I'm not mad.'

'My dear old man,' I said, 'I don't think you're mad. But I do think your nerves are very much upset. Mine are a bit, too. Do you know why I went to India? It was because of you and her. I couldn't stay and see it, though I wished for your happiness and all that; you know I did. And when I came back, she . . . and you . . . Let's see it out together,' I said. 'You won't keep fancy-ing things if you've got me to talk to. And I always said you weren't half a bad old duffer.'

'She liked you,' he said.

'Oh, yes,' I said, 'she liked me.'

III

THAT WAS how we came to go abroad together. I was full of hope for him. He'd always been such a splendid chap – so sane and strong. I couldn't believe that he was gone mad, gone for ever, I mean, so that he'd never come right again. Perhaps my own trouble made it easy for me to see things not quite straight. Anyway, I took him away to recover his mind's health, exactly as I should have taken him away to get strong after a fever. And the madness seemed to pass away, and in a month or two we were perfectly jolly, and I thought I had cured him. And I was very glad because of that old friendship of ours, and because she had loved him and liked me.

We never spoke of Visger. I thought he had forgotten all about him. I thought I understood how his mind, over-strained by sorrow and anger, had fixed on the man he hated, and woven a nightmare web of horror round that detestable personality. And I had got the whip hand of my own trouble. And we were as jolly as sandboys together all those months.

And we came to Bruges at last in our travels, and Bruges was very full, because of the Exhibition. We could only get one room and one bed. So we tossed for the bed, and the one who lost the toss was to make the best of the night in the armchair. And the bed-clothes we were to share equitably.

We spent the evening at a *café chantant* and finished at a beer hall, and it was late and sleepy when we got back to the Grande Vigne. I took our key from its nail in the concierge's room, and we went up. We talked awhile, I remember, of the town, and the belfry, and the Venetian aspect of the canals by moonlight, and then Haldane got into bed, and I made a chrysalis of myself with my share of the blankets and fitted the tight roll into the armchair. I was not at all comfortable, but I was compensatingly tired, and I was nearly asleep when Haldane roused me up to tell me about his will.

'I've left everything to you, old man,' he said. 'I know I can trust you to see to everything.'

'Quite so,' said I, 'and if you don't mind, we'll talk about it in the morning.'

He tried to go on about it, and about what a friend I'd been, and all that, but I shut him up and told him to go to sleep. But no. He wasn't comfortable, he said. And he'd got a thirst like a lime kiln. And he'd noticed that there was no water-bottle in the room. 'And the water in the jug's like pale soup,' he said.

'Oh, all right,' said I. 'Light your candle and go and get some water, then, in Heaven's name, and let me get to sleep.'

But he said, 'No – you light it. I don't want to get out of bed in the dark. I might – I might step on something, mightn't I – or walk into something that wasn't there when I got into bed.'

'Rot,' I said, 'walk into your grandmother.' But I lit the candle all the same. He sat up in bed and looked at me – very pale – with his hair all tumbled from the pillow, and his eyes blinking and shining.

'That's better,' he said. And then, 'I say – look here.

Oh – yes – I see. It's all right. Queer how they mark the sheets here. Blest if I didn't think it was blood, just for the minute.'

The sheet was marked, not at the corner, as sheets are marked at home, but right in the middle where it turns down, with big, red, cross-stitching.

'Yes, I see,' I said, 'it is a queer place to mark it.'

'It's queer letters to have on it,' he said. 'G. V.'

'Grande Vigne,' I said. 'What letters do you expect them to mark things with? Hurry up.'

'You come too,' he said. 'Yes, it does stand for Grande Vigne, of course. I wish you'd come down too, Winston.'

'I'll *go* down,' I said and turned with the candle in my hand.

He was out of bed and close to me in a flash.

'No,' said he, 'I don't want to stay alone in the dark.'

He said it just as a frightened child might have done.

'All right then, come along,' I said. And we went. I tried to make some joke, I remember, about the length of his hair, and the cut of his pyjamas – but I was sick with disappointment. For it was almost quite plain to me, even then, that all my time and trouble had been thrown away, and that he wasn't cured after all. We went down as quietly as we could, and got a carafe of water from the long bare dining table in the *salle-à-manger*. He got hold of my arm at first, and then he got the candle away from me, and went very slowly, shading the light with his hand, and looking very carefully all about, as though he expected to see something that he wanted very desperately not to see. And of course, I knew what that something was. I didn't like the way he was going on. I can't at all express how deeply I didn't like it. And he looked over his shoulder every now and then, just as he did that first evening after I came back from India.

The thing got on my nerves so that I could hardly find the way back to our room. And when we got there, I give you my word, I more than half expected to see what *he* had expected to see – that, or something like that, on the hearth-rug. But of course there was nothing.

I blew out the light and tightened my blankets round me – I'd been trailing them after me in our expedition. And I was settled in my chair when Haldane spoke.

'You've got all the blankets,' he said.

'No, I haven't,' said I, 'only what I've always had.'

'I can't find mine then,' he said and I could hear his teeth chattering. 'And I'm cold. I'm . . . For God's sake, light the candle. Light it. Light it. Something horrible . . .'

And I couldn't find the matches.

'Light the candle, light the candle,' he said, and his voice broke, as a boy's does sometimes in chapel. 'If you don't he'll come to me. It is so easy to come at anyone in the dark. Oh Winston, light the candle, for the love of God! I can't die in the dark.'

'I am lighting it,' I said savagely, and I was feeling for the matches on the marble-topped chest of drawers, on the mantelpiece – everywhere but on the round centre table where I'd put them. 'You're not going to die. Don't be a fool,' I said. 'It's all right. I'll get a light in a second.'

He said, 'It's cold. It's cold. It's cold,' like that, three times. And then he screamed aloud, like a woman – like a child – like a hare when the dogs have got it. I had heard him scream like that once before.

'What is it?' I cried, hardly less loud. 'For God's sake, hold your noise. What is it?'

There was an empty silence. Then, very slowly: 'It's Visger,' he said. And he spoke thickly, as through some stifling veil.

'Nonsense. Where?' I asked, and my hand closed on the matches as he spoke.

'Here,' he screamed sharply, as though he had torn the veil away, 'here, beside me. In the bed.'

I got the candle alight. I got across to him.

He was crushed in a heap at the edge of the bed. Stretched on the bed beyond him was a dead man, white and very cold.

Haldane had died in the dark.

It was all so simple.

We had come to the wrong room. The man the room belonged to was there, on the bed he had engaged and paid for before he died of heart disease, earlier in the day. A French *commis-voyageur* representing soap and perfumery; his name, Felix Leblanc.

Later, in England, I made cautious enquiries. The body of a man had been found in the Red Hill tunnel – a haberdasher man named Simmons, who had drunk spirits of salts, owing to the depression of trade. The bottle was clutched in his dead hand.

For reasons that I had, I took care to have a police inspector with me when I opened the boxes that came to me by Haldane's will. One of them was the big box, metal lined, in which I had sent him the skins from India – for a wedding present, God help us all!

It was closely soldered.

Inside were the skins of beasts? No. The bodies of two men. One was identified, after some trouble, as that of a hawker of pens in city offices – subject to fits. He had died in one, it seemed. The other body was Visger's, right enough.

Explain it as you like. I offered you, if you remember, a choice of explanations before I began the story. I have not yet found the explanation that can satisfy me.

A WARNING TO THE CURIOUS
BY M.R. JAMES

Montague Rhodes James was born on 1 August 1862 near Bury St Edmunds. He studied at Eton and King's College, Cambridge, where he was eventually elected Fellow. In 1918 he became Provost of Eton. He was a renowned medievalist and biblical scholar, and published works on palaeography, antiquarianism, bibliography and history. However, he remains best known for his ghost stories, which were published in several collections, including *Ghost Stories of an Antiquary* (1904), *A Thin Ghost and Other Stories* (1919), *A Warning to the Curious* (1925) and a collected edition in 1931. M.R. James never married and died on 12 June 1936.

THE PLACE on the east coast which the reader is asked to consider is Seaburgh. It is not very different now from what I remember it to have been when I was a child. Marshes intersected by dykes to the south, recalling the early chapters of *Great Expectations*; flat fields to the north, merging into heath; heath, fir woods, and, above all, gorse, inland. A long sea-front and a street: behind that a spacious church of flint, with a broad, solid western tower and a peal of six bells. How well I remember their sound on a hot Sunday in August, as our party went slowly up the white, dusty slope of road towards them, for the church stands at the top of a short, steep incline. They rang with a flat clacking sort of sound on those hot days, but when the air was softer they were mellower too. The railway ran down to its little terminus farther along the same road. There was a gay white windmill just before you came to the station, and another down near the shingle at the south end of the town, and yet others on higher ground to the north. There were cottages of bright red brick with slate roofs . . . but why do I encumber you with these commonplace details? The fact is that they come crowding to the point of the pencil when it begins to write of Seaburgh.

I should like to be sure that I had allowed the right ones to get on to the paper. But I forgot. I have not quite done with the word-painting business yet.

Walk away from the sea and the town, pass the station, and turn up the road on the right. It is a sandy road, parallel with the railway, and if you follow it, it climbs to somewhat higher ground. On your left (you are now going northward) is heath, on your right (the side towards the sea) is a belt of old firs, wind-beaten, thick at the top, with the slope that old seaside trees have; seen on the skyline from the train they would tell you in an instant, if you did not know it, that you were approaching a windy coast. Well, at the top of my little hill, a line of these firs strikes out and runs towards the sea, for there is a ridge that goes that way; and the ridge ends in a rather well-defined mound commanding the level fields of rough grass, and a little knot of fir trees crowns it. And here you may sit on a hot spring day, very well content to look at blue sea, white windmills, red cottages, bright green grass, church tower, and distant martello tower on the south.

As I have said, I began to know Seaburgh as a child; but a gap of a good many years separates my early knowledge from that which is more recent. Still it keeps its place in my affections, and any tales of it that I pick up have an interest for me. One such tale is this: it came to me in a place very remote from Seaburgh, and quite accidentally, from a man whom I had been able to oblige – enough in his opinion to justify his making me his confidant to this extent.

I know all that country more or less (he said). I used to go to Seaburgh pretty regularly for golf in the spring. I generally put up at the 'Bear', with a friend – Henry Long it was, you knew him perhaps – ('Slightly,' I said) and we used to take a sitting-room and be very happy there. Since he died I haven't cared to go there. And I don't know that I should anyhow after the particular thing that happened on our last visit.

It was in April, 19 – , we were there, and by some chance we were almost the only people in the hotel. So the ordinary public rooms were practically empty, and we were the more surprised when, after dinner, our sitting-room door opened, and a young man put his head in. We were aware of this young man. He was rather a rabbity anaemic subject – light hair and light eyes – but not unpleasing. So when he said: 'I beg your pardon, is this a private room?' we did not growl and say: 'Yes, it is,' but Long said, or I did – no matter which: 'Please come in.' 'Oh, may I?' he said, and seemed relieved. Of course it was obvious that he wanted company; and as he was a reasonable kind of person – not the sort to bestow his whole family history on you – we urged him to make himself at home. 'I dare say you find the other rooms rather bleak,' I said. Yes, he did: but it was really too good of us, and so on. That being got over, he made some pretence of reading a book. Long was playing Patience, I was writing. It became plain to me after a few minutes that this visitor of ours was in rather a state of fidgets or nerves, which communicated itself to me, and so I put away my writing and turned to at engaging him in talk.

After some remarks, which I forget, he became rather confidential. 'You'll think it very odd of me' (this was the sort of way he began), 'but the fact is I've had something of a shock.' Well, I recommended a drink of some cheering kind, and we had it. The waiter coming in made an interruption (and I thought our young man seemed very jumpy when the door opened), but after a while he got back to his woes again. There was nobody he knew in the place, and he did happen to know who we both were (it turned out there was some common acquaintance in town), and really he did want a word of advice, if we didn't mind. Of course we both said: 'By all means,' or 'Not at all,' and Long put away his cards. And we settled down to hear what his difficulty was.

'It began,' he said, 'more than a week ago, when I bicycled over to Froston, only about five or six miles, to see the church; I'm very much interested in architecture, and it's got one of those pretty porches with niches and shields. I took a photograph of it, and then an old man who was tidying up in the churchyard came and asked if I'd care to look into the church. I said yes, and he produced a key and let me in. There wasn't much inside, but I told him it was a nice little church, and he kept it very clean. "But," I said, "the porch is the best part of it." We were just outside the porch then, and he said, "Ah, yes, that is a nice porch; and do you know, sir, what's the meanin' of that coat of arms there?"

'It was the one with the three crowns, and though I'm not much of a herald, I was able to say yes, I thought it was the old arms of the kingdom of East Anglia.

' "That's right, sir," he said, "and do you know the meanin' of them three crowns that's on it?"

'I said I'd no doubt it was known, but I couldn't recollect to have heard it myself.

' "Well, then," he said, "for all you're a scholard, I can tell you something you don't know. Them's the three 'oly crowns what was buried in the ground near by the coast to keep the Germans from landing – ah, I can see you don't believe that. But I tell you, if it hadn't have been for one of them 'oly crowns bein' there still, them Germans would a landed here time and again, they would. Landed with their ships, and killed man, woman and child in their beds. Now then, that's the truth what I'm telling you, that is; and if you don't believe me, you ast the rector. There he comes: you ast him, I says."

'I looked round, and there was the rector, a nice-looking old man, coming up the path; and before I could begin assuring my old man, who was getting quite excited, that I didn't disbelieve him, the rector struck in, and said: "What's all this about, John? Good day to you, sir. Have you been looking at our little church?"

'So then there was a little talk which allowed the old man to calm down, and then the rector asked him again what was the matter.

' "Oh," he said, "it warn't nothink, only I was telling this gentleman he'd ought to ast you about them 'oly crowns."

' "Ah, yes, to be sure," said the rector, "that's a very curious matter, isn't it? But I don't know whether the gentleman is interested in our old stories, eh?"

' "Oh, he'll be interested fast enough," says the old man, "he'll put his confidence in what you tells him, sir; why, you known William Ager yourself, father and son too."

Then I put in a word to say how much I should like to hear all about it, and before many minutes I was walking up the village street with the rector, who had one or two words to say to parishioners, and then to the rectory, where he took me into his study. He had made out, on the way, that I really was capable of taking an intelligent interest in a piece of folklore, and not quite the ordinary tripper. So he was very willing to talk, and it is rather surprising to me that the particular legend he told me has not made its way into print before. His account of it was this: "There has always been a belief in these parts in the three holy crowns. The old people say they were buried in different places near the coast to keep off the Danes or the French or the Germans. And they say that one of the three was dug up a long time ago, and another has disappeared by the enroaching of the sea, and one's still left doing its work, keeping off invaders. Well, now, if you have read the ordinary guides and histories of this county, you will remember perhaps that in 1687 a crown, which was said to be the crown of Redwald, King of the East Angles, was dug up at Rendlesham, and alas! alas! melted down before it was even properly described or drawn. Well, Rendlesham isn't on the coast, but it isn't so very far inland, and it's on a very important line of access. And I believe that is the crown which the people mean when they say that one has been dug up. Then on the south you don't want me to tell you where there was a Saxon royal palace which is now under the sea, eh? Well, there was the second crown, I take it. And up beyond these two, they say, lies the third."

' "Do they say where it is?" of course I asked.

'He said, "Yes, indeed, they do, but they don't tell," and his manner did not encourage me to put the obvious question. Instead of that I waited a moment, and said: "What did the old man mean when he said you knew William Ager, as if that had something to do with the crowns?"

' "To be sure," he said, "now that's another curious story. These Agers — it's a very old name in these parts, but I can't find that they were ever people of quality or big owners — these Agers say, or said, that their branch of the family were the guardians of the last crown. A certain old Nathaniel Ager was the first one I knew — I was born and brought up quite near here — and he, I believe, camped out at the place during the whole of the war of 1870. William, his son, did the same, I know, during the South African War. And young William, *his* son, who has only died fairly recently, took lodgings at the cottage nearest the spot, and I've no doubt hastened his end, for he was a consumptive, by exposure and night watching. And he was the last of that branch. It was a dreadful grief to him to think that he was the last, but he could do nothing, the only relations at all near to him were in the colonies. I wrote letters for him to them imploring them to come over on business very important to the family, but there has been no answer. So the last of the holy crowns, if it's there, has no guardian now."

'That was what the rector told me, and you can fancy how interesting I found it. The only thing I could think of when I left him was how to hit upon the spot where the crown was supposed to be. I wish I'd left it alone.

'But there was a sort of fate in it, for as I bicycled back past the churchyard wall my eye caught a fairly new gravestone, and on it was the name of William Ager. Of course I got off and read it. It said "of this parish, died at Seaburgh, 19 – , aged 28." There it was, you see. A little judicious questioning in the right place, and I should at least find the cottage nearest the spot. Only I didn't quite know what was the right place to begin my questioning at. Again there was fate: it took me to the curiosity-shop down that way – you know – and I turned over some old books, and, if you please, one was a prayer-book of 1740 odd, in a rather handsome binding – I'll just go and get it, it's in my room.'

He left us in a state of some surprise, but we had hardly time to exchange any remarks when he was back, panting, and handed us the book opened at the fly-leaf, on which was, in a straggly hand:

'Nathaniel Ager is my name and England is my nation,
Seaburgh is my dwelling-place and Christ is my Salvation,
When I am dead and in my Grave, and all my bones are
    rotton,
I hope the Lord will think on me when I am quite
    forgotton.'

This poem was dated 1754, and there were many more entries of Agers, Nathaniel, Frederick, William, and so on, ending with William, 19 –.

'You see,' he said, 'anybody would call it the greatest bit of luck. *I* did, but I don't now. Of course I asked the shopman about William Ager, and of course he happened to remember that he lodged in a cottage in the North Field and died there. This was just chalking the road for me. I knew which the cottage must be: there is only one sizable one about there. The next thing was to scrape some sort of acquaintance with the people, and I took a walk that way at once. A dog did the business for me: he made at me so fiercely that they had to run out and beat him off, and then naturally begged my pardon, and we got into talk. I had only to bring up Ager's name, and pretend I knew, or thought I knew something of him, and then the woman said how sad it was him dying so young, and she was sure it came of him spending the night out of doors in the cold weather. Then I had to say: "Did he go out on the sea at night?" and she said: "Oh, no, it was on the hillock yonder with the trees on it." And there I was.

'I know something about digging in these barrows: I've opened many of them in the down country. But that was with owner's leave, and in broad daylight and with men to help. I had to prospect very carefully here before I put a spade in: I couldn't trench across the mound, and with those old firs growing there I knew there would be awkward tree roots. Still the soil was very light and sandy and easy, and there was a rabbit hole or so that might be developed into a sort of tunnel. The going out and coming back at odd hours to the hotel was going to be the awkward part. When I made up my mind about the way to excavate I told the people that I was called away for a night, and I spent it out there. I made my tunnel: I won't bore you with the details of how I supported it and filled it in when I'd done, but the main thing is that I got the crown.'

Naturally we both broke out into exclamations of surprise and interest. I for one had long known about the finding of the crown at Rendlesham and had often lamented its fate. No one has ever seen an Anglo-Saxon crown – at least no one had. But our man gazed at us with a rueful eye. 'Yes,' he said, 'and the worst of it is I don't know how to put it back.'

'Put it back?' we cried out. 'Why, my dear sir, you've made one of the most exciting finds ever heard of in this country. Of course it ought to go to the Jewel House at the Tower. What's your difficulty? If you're thinking about the owner of the land, and treasure-trove, and all that, we can certainly help you through. Nobody's going to make a fuss about technicalities in a case of this kind.'

Probably more was said, but all he did was to put his face in his hands, and mutter: 'I don't know how to put it back.'

At last Long said: 'You'll forgive me, I hope, if I seem impertinent, but are you *quite* sure you've got it?' I was wanting to ask much the same question myself, for of course the story did seem a lunatic's dream when one thought over it. But I hadn't quite dared to say what might hurt the poor young man's feelings. However, he took it quite calmly – really, with the calm of despair, you might say. He sat up and said: 'Oh, yes, there's no doubt of that: I have it here, in my room, locked up in my bag. You can come and look at it if you like: I won't offer to bring it here.'

We were not likely to let the chance slip. We went with him; his room was only a few doors off. The boots was just collecting shoes in the passage: or so we thought: afterwards we were not sure. Our visitor – his name was Paxton – was in a worse state of shivers than before, and went hurriedly into the room, and beckoned us after him, turned on the light, and shut the door carefully. Then he unlocked his kit-bag, and produced a bundle of clean pocket-handkerchiefs in which something was wrapped, laid it on the bed, and undid it. I can now say I *have* seen an actual Anglo-Saxon crown. It was of silver – as the Rendlesham one is always said to have been – it was set with some gems, mostly antique intaglios and cameos, and was of rather plain, almost rough workmanship. In fact, it was like those you see on the coins and in the manuscripts. I found no reason to think it was later than the ninth century. I was intensely interested, of course, and I wanted to turn it over in my hands, but Paxton prevented me. 'Don't *you* touch it,' he said, 'I'll do that.' And with a sigh that was, I declare to you, dreadful to hear, he took it up and turned it about so that we could see every part of it. 'Seen enough?' he said at last, and we nodded. He wrapped it up and locked it in his bag, and stood looking at us dumbly. 'Come back to our room,' Long said, 'and tell us what the trouble is.' He thanked us, and said: 'Will you go first and see if – if the coast is clear?' That wasn't very intelligible, for our proceedings hadn't been, after all, very suspicious, and the hotel, as I said, was practically empty. However, we were beginning to have inklings of – we didn't know what, and anyhow nerves are infectious. So we did go, first peering out as we opened the door, and fancying (I found we both had the fancy) that a shadow, or more than a shadow – but it made no sound – passed from before us to one side as we came out into the passage. 'It's all right,' we whispered to Paxton – whispering seemed the proper tone – and we went, with him between us, back to our sitting-room. I was preparing, when we got there, to be ecstatic about the unique interest of what we had seen, but when I looked at Paxton I saw that would be terribly out of place, and I left it to him to begin.

'What *is* to be done?' was his opening. Long thought it right (as he explained to me afterwards) to be obtuse, and said: 'Why not find out who the owner of the land is, and inform –' 'Oh, no, no!' Paxton broke in impatiently, 'I beg your pardon: you've been very kind, but don't you see it's *got* to go back, and I daren't be there at night, and daytime's impossible. Perhaps, though, you don't see: well, then, the truth is that I've never been alone since I touched it.' I was beginning some fairly stupid comment, but Long caught my eye, and I stopped. Long said: 'I think I do see, perhaps: but wouldn't it be — a relief — to tell us a little more clearly what the situation is?'

Then it all came out: Paxton looked over his shoulder and beckoned to us to come nearer to him, and began speaking in a low voice: we listened most intently, of course, and compared notes afterwards, and I wrote down our version, so I am confident I have what he told us almost word for word. He said: 'It began when I was first prospecting, and put me off again and again. There was always somebody — a man — standing by one of the firs. This was in daylight, you know. He was never in front of me. I always saw him with the tail of my eye on the left or the right, and he was never there when I looked straight for him. I would lie down for quite a long time and take careful observations, and make sure there was no one, and then when I got up and began prospecting again, there he was. And he began to give me hints, besides; for wherever I put that prayer-book — short of locking it up, which I did at last — when I came back to my room it was always out on my table open at the fly-leaf where the names are, and one of my razors across it to keep it open. I'm sure he just can't open my bag, or something more would have happened. You see, he's light and weak, but all the same I daren't face him. Well, then, when I was making the tunnel, of course it was worse, and if I hadn't been so keen I should have dropped the whole thing and run. It was like someone scraping at my back all the time: I thought for a long time it was only soil dropping on me, but as I got nearer the — the crown, it was unmistakable. And when I actually laid it bare and got my fingers into the ring of it and pulled it out, there came a sort of cry

behind me – oh, I can't tell you how desolate it was! And horribly threatening too. It spoilt all my pleasure in my find – cut it
off that moment. And if I hadn't been the wretched fool I am, I
should have put the thing back and left it. But I didn't. The rest
of the time was just awful. I had hours to get through before I
could decently come back to the hotel. First I spent time filling
up my tunnel and covering my tracks, and all the while he was
there trying to thwart me. Sometimes, you know, you see him,
and sometimes you don't, just as he pleases, I think: he's there,
but he has some power over your eyes. Well, I wasn't off the spot
very long before sunrise, and then I had to get to the junction for
Seaburgh, and take a train back. And though it was daylight
fairly soon, I don't know if that made it much better. There were
always hedges, or gorse-bushes, or park fences along the road –
some sort of cover, I mean – and I was never easy for a second.
And then when I began to meet people going to work, they
always looked behind me very strangely: it might have been that
they were surprised at seeing anyone so early; but I didn't think
it was only that, and I don't now: they didn't look exactly at *me*.
And the porter at the train was like that too. And the guard held
open the door after I'd got into the carriage – just as he would if
there was somebody else coming, you know. Oh, you may be
very sure it isn't my fancy,' he said with a dull sort of laugh.
Then he went on: 'And even if I do get it put back, he won't
forgive me: I can tell that. And I was so happy a fortnight ago.'
He dropped into a chair, and I believe he began to cry.

We didn't know what to say, but we felt we must come to the
rescue somehow, and so – it really seemed the only thing – we
said if he was so set on putting the crown back in its place,
we would help him. And I must say that after what we had heard
it did seem the right thing. If these horrid consequences had
come on this poor man, might there not really be something in

the original idea of the crown having some curious power bound up with it, to guard the coast? At least, that was my feeling, and I think it was Long's too. Our offer was very welcome to Paxton, anyhow. When could we do it? It was nearing half-past ten. Could we contrive to make a late walk plausible to the hotel people that very night? We looked out of the window: there was a brilliant full moon — the Paschal moon. Long undertook to tackle the boots and propitiate him. He was to say that we should not be much over the hour, and if we did find it so pleasant that we stopped out a bit longer we would see that he didn't lose by sitting up. Well, we were pretty regular customers of the hotel, and did not give much trouble, and were considered by the servants to be not under the mark in the way of tips; and so the boots *was* propitiated, and let us out on to the sea-front, and remained, as we heard later, looking after us. Paxton had a large coat over his arm, under which was the wrapped-up crown.

So we were off on this strange errand before we had time to think how very much out of the way it was. I have told this part quite shortly on purpose, for it really does represent the haste with which we settled our plan and took action. 'The shortest way is up the hill and through the churchyard,' Paxton said, as we stood a moment before the hotel looking up and down the front. There was nobody about — nobody at all. Seaburgh out of the season is an early, quiet place. 'We can't go along the dyke by the cottage, because of the dog,' Paxton also said, when I pointed to what I thought a shorter way along the front and across two fields. The reason he gave was good enough. We went up the road to the church, and turned in at the churchyard gate. I confess to having thought that there might be some lying there who might be conscious of our business: but if it was so, they were also conscious that one who was on their side, so to say, had us under surveillance, and we saw no sign of them. But under observation we felt we were, as have never felt it at another time. Specially was it so when we passed out of the churchyard into a narrow path with close high hedges, through which we hurried as Christian did through that Valley; and so got out into open fields. Then along hedges, though I would sooner have been in the open, where I could see if anyone was visible behind me; over a gate or two, and then a swerve to the left, taking us up on to the ridge which ended in that mound.

As we neared it, Henry Long felt, and I felt too, that there were what I can only call dim presences waiting for us, as well as a far more actual one attending us. Of Paxton's agitation all this time I can give you no adequate picture: he breathed like a hunted beast, and we could not either of us look at his face. How he would manage when we got to the very place we had not troubled to think: he had seemed so sure that that would not be difficult. Nor was it. I never saw anything like the dash with which he flung himself at a particular spot in the side of the mound, and tore at it, so that in a very few minutes the greater part of his body was out of sight. We stood holding the coat and that bundle of handkerchiefs, and looking, very fearfully, I must admit, about us. There was nothing to be seen: a line of dark firs behind us made one skyline, more trees and the church tower half a mile off on the right, cottages and a windmill on the horizon on the left, calm sea dead in front, faint barking of a dog at a cottage on a gleaming dyke between us and it: full moon making that path we know across the sea: the eternal whisper of the Scotch firs just above us, and of the sea in front. Yet, in all this quiet, an acute, an acrid consciousness of a restrained hostility very near us, like a dog on a leash that might be let go at any moment.

Paxton pulled himself out of the hole, and stretched a hand back to us. 'Give it to me,' he whispered, 'unwrapped.' We pulled off the handkerchiefs, and he took the crown. The moonlight just fell on it as he snatched it. We had not ourselves touched that bit of metal, and I have thought since that it was just as well. In another moment Paxton was out of the hole again and busy shovelling back the soil with hands that were already bleeding. He would have none of our help, though. It was much the longest part of the job to get the place to look undisturbed: yet – I don't know how – he made a wonderful success of it. At last he was satisfied, and we turned back.

We were a couple of hundred yards from the hill when Long suddenly said to him: 'I say, you've left your coat there. That won't do. See?' And I certainly did see it – the long dark overcoat lying where the tunnel had been. Paxton had not stopped, however: he only shook his head, and held up the coat on his arm. And when we joined him, he said, without any excitement, but as if nothing mattered any more: 'That wasn't my coat.' And, indeed, when we looked back again, that dark thing was not to be seen.

Well, we got out on to the road, and came rapidly back that way. It was well before twelve when we got in, trying to put a good face on it, and saying – Long and I – what a lovely night it was for a walk. The boots was on the look-out for us, and we made remarks like that for his edification as we entered the hotel. He gave another look up and down the sea-front before he locked the front door, and said: 'You didn't meet many people about, I s'pose, sir?' 'No, indeed, not a soul,' I said; at which I remember Paxton looked oddly at me. 'Only I thought I see someone turn up the station road after you gentlemen,' said the boots. 'Still, you was three together, and I don't suppose he meant mischief.' I didn't know what to say; Long merely said 'Good night,' and we went off upstairs, promising to turn out all lights, and to go to bed in a few minutes.

Back in our room, we did our very best to make Paxton take a cheerful view. 'There's the crown safe back,' we said; 'very likely you'd have done better not to touch it' (and he heavily assented to that), 'but no real harm has been done, and we shall never give this away to anyone who would be so mad as to go near it. Besides, don't you feel better yourself? I don't mind confessing,' I said, 'that on the way there I was very much inclined to take your view about – well, about being followed; but going back, it wasn't at all the same thing, was it?' No, it wouldn't do: '*You've* nothing to trouble yourselves about,' he said, 'but I'm not forgiven. I've got to pay for that miserable sacrilege still. I know what you are going to say. The Church might help. Yes, but it's the body that has to suffer. It's true I'm not feeling that he's waiting outside for me just now. But –' Then he stopped. Then he turned to thanking us, and we put him off as soon as we could. And naturally we pressed him to use our sitting-room next day, and said we should be glad to go out with him. Or did he play golf, perhaps? Yes, he did, but he didn't think he should care about that tomorrow. Well, we recommended him to get up late and sit in our room in the morning while we were playing, and we would have a walk later in the day. He was very submissive and *piano* about it all: ready to do just what we thought best, but clearly quite certain in his own mind that what was coming could not be averted or palliated. You'll wonder why we didn't insist on accompanying him to his home and seeing him safe into the care of brothers or someone. The fact was he had nobody. He had had a flat in town, but lately he had made up his mind to settle for a time in Sweden, and he had dismantled his flat and shipped off his belongings, and was whiling away a fortnight or three weeks before he made a start. Anyhow, we didn't see what we could do better than sleep on it – or not sleep very much, as was my case – and see what we felt like tomorrow morning.

We felt very different, Long and I, on as beautiful an April morning as you could desire; and Paxton also looked very different when we saw him at breakfast. 'The first approach to a decent night I seem ever to have had,' was what he said. But he was going to do as we had settled: stay in probably all the morning, and come out with us later. We went to the links; we met some other men and played with them in the morning, and had lunch there rather early, so as not to be late back. All the same, the snares of death overtook him.

Whether it could have been prevented, I don't know. I think he would have been got at somehow, do what we might. Anyhow, this is what happened.

We went straight up to our room. Paxton was there, reading quite peaceably. 'Ready to come out shortly?' said Long. 'Say in half an hour's time?' 'Certainly,' he said: and I said we would change first, and perhaps have baths, and call for him in half an hour. I had my bath first, and went and lay down on my bed, and slept for about ten minutes. We came out of our rooms at the same time, and went together to the sitting-room. Paxton wasn't there – only his book. Nor was he in his room, nor in the downstair rooms. We shouted for him. A servant came out and said: 'Why, I thought you gentlemen was gone out already, and so did the other gentleman. He heard you a-calling from the path there, and run out in a hurry, and I looked out of the coffee-room window, but I didn't see you. 'Owever, he run off down the beach that way.'

Without a word we ran that way too – it was the opposite direction to that of last night's expedition. It wasn't quite four o'clock, and the day was fair, though not so fair as it had been, so there was really no reason, you'd say, for anxiety: with people about, surely a man couldn't come to much harm.

But something in our look as we ran out must have struck the servant, for she came out on the steps, and pointed, and said, 'Yes, that's the way he went.' We ran on as far as the top of the shingle bank, and there pulled up. There was a choice of ways: past the houses on the sea-front, or along the sand at the bottom of the beach, which, the tide being now out, was fairly broad. Or of course we might keep along the shingle between these two tracks and have some view of both of them; only that was heavy going. We chose the sand, for that was the loneliest, and some-one *might* come to harm there without being seen from the public path.

Long said he saw Paxton some distance ahead, running and waving his stick, as if he wanted to signal to people who were on ahead of him. I couldn't be sure: one of these sea-mists was com-ing up very quickly from the south. There was someone, that's all I could say. And there were tracks on the sand as of someone running who wore shoes; and there were other tracks made before those – for the shoes sometimes trod in them and inter-fered with them – of someone not in shoes. Oh, of course, it's only my word you've got to take for all this: Long's dead, we'd no time or means to make sketches or take casts, and the next tide washed everything away. All we could do was to notice these marks as we hurried on. But there they were over and over again, and we had no doubt whatever that what we saw was the track of a bare foot, and one that showed more bones than flesh.

The notion of Paxton running after – after anything like this, and supposing it to be the friends he was looking for, was very dreadful to us. You can guess what we fancied: how the thing he was following might stop suddenly and turn round on him, and what sort of face it would show, half-seen at first in the mist – which all the while was getting thicker and thicker. And as I ran on wondering how the poor wretch could have been lured into mistaking that other thing for us, I remembered his saying, 'He has some power over your eyes.' And then I wondered what the end would be, for I had no hope now that the end could be averted, and — well, there is no need to tell all the dismal and horrid thoughts that flitted through my head as we ran on into the mist. It was uncanny, too, that the sun should still be bright in the sky and we could see nothing. We could only tell that we were now past the houses and had reached that gap there is between them and the old martello tower. When you are past the tower, you know, there is nothing but shingle for a long way — not a house, not a human creature, just that spit of land, or rather shingle, with the river on your right and the sea on your left.

But just before that, just by the martello tower, you remember there is the old battery, close to the sea. I believe there are only a few blocks of concrete left now: the rest has all been washed away, but at this time there was a lot more, though the place was a ruin. Well, when we got there, we clambered to the top as quick as we could to take breath and look over the shingle in front if by chance the mist would let us see anything. But a moment's rest we must have. We had run a mile at least. Nothing whatever was visible ahead of us, and we were just turning by common consent to get down and run hopelessly on, when we heard what I can only call a laugh: and if you can understand what I mean by a breathless, a lungless laugh, you have it: but I don't suppose you can. It came from below, and swerved away into the mist. That was enough. We bent over the wall. Paxton was there at the bottom.

You don't need to be told that he was dead. His tracks showed that he had run along the side of the battery, had turned sharp round the corner of it, and, small doubt of it, must have dashed straight into the open arms of someone who was waiting there. His mouth was full of sand and stones, and his teeth and jaws were broken to bits. I only glanced once at his face.

At the same moment, just as we were scrambling down from the battery to get to the body, we heard a shout, and saw a man running down the bank of the martello tower. He was the caretaker stationed there, and his keen old eyes had managed to descry through the mist that something was wrong. He had seen Paxton fall, and had seen us a moment after, running up – fortunate this, for otherwise we could hardly have escaped suspicion of being concerned in the dreadful business. Had he, we asked, caught sight of anybody attacking our friend? He could not be sure.

We sent him off for help, and stayed by the dead man till they came with the stretcher. It was then that we traced out how he had come, on the narrow fringe of sand under the battery wall. The rest was shingle, and it was hopelessly impossible to tell whither the other had gone.

What were we to say at the inquest? It was a duty, we felt, not to give up, there and then, the secret of the crown, to be published in every paper. I don't know how much you would have told; but what we did agree upon was this: to say that we had only made acquaintance with Paxton the day before, and that he had told us he was under some apprehension of danger at the hands of a man called William Ager. Also that we had seen some other tracks besides Paxton's when we followed him along the beach. But of course by that time everything was gone from the sands.

No one had any knowledge, fortunately, of any William Ager living in the district. The evidence of the man at the martello tower freed us from all suspicion. All that could be done was to return a verdict of wilful murder by some person or persons unknown.

Paxton was so totally without connections that all the inquiries that were subsequently made ended in a No Thoroughfare. And I have never been at Seaburgh, or even near it, since.

THE FACE *BY* E.F. BENSON

Edward Frederic Benson was born on 24 July 1867 in Berkshire, the son of a future Archbishop of Canterbury, and one of six children. He studied at King's College, Cambridge and at the British School of Archaeology in Athens. Benson's first book, *Dodo*, was published to popular acclaim in 1893 and was followed by over a hundred books, including novels, histories, biographies and ghost stories. In 1920 Benson became a full-time tenant of Lamb House in Rye, which had once been home to the novelist Henry James. Rye provided the setting for the *Mapp and Lucia* stories and their author served three terms as mayor of Rye in the late 1930s. E.F. Benson died on 29 February 1940.

H ESTER WARD, sitting by the open window on this hot afternoon in June, began seriously to argue with herself about the cloud of foreboding and depression which had encompassed her all day, and, very sensibly, she enumerated to herself the manifold causes for happiness in the fortunate circumstances of her life. She was young, she was extremely good-looking, she was well-off, she enjoyed excellent health, and above all, she had an adorable husband and two small, adorable children. There was no break, indeed, anywhere in the circle of prosperity which surrounded her, and had the wishing-cap been handed to her that moment by some beneficent fairy, she would have hesitated to put it on her head, for there was positively nothing that she could think of which would have been worthy of such solemnity. Moreover, she could not accuse herself of a want of appreciation of her blessings; she appreciated enormously, she enjoyed enormously, and she thoroughly wanted all those who so munificently contributed to her happiness to share in it.

She made a very deliberate review of these things, for she was really anxious, more anxious, indeed, than she admitted to herself, to find anything tangible which could possibly warrant this ominous feeling of approaching disaster. Then there was the weather to consider; for the last week London had been stiflingly hot, but if that was the cause, why had she not felt it before? Perhaps the effect of these broiling, airless days had been cumulative. That was an idea, but, frankly, it did not seem a very good one, for, as a matter of fact, she loved the heat; Dick, who hated it, said that it was odd he should have fallen in love with a salamander.

She shifted her position, sitting up straight in this low window-seat, for she was intending to make a call on her courage. She had known from the moment she awoke this morning what it was that lay so heavy on her, and now, having done her best to shift the reason of her depression on to anything else, and having completely failed, she meant to look the thing in the face. She was ashamed of doing so, for the cause of this leaden mood of fear which held her in its grip, was so trivial, so fantastic, so excessively silly.

'Yes, there never was anything so silly,' she said to herself. 'I must look at it straight, and convince myself how silly it is.' She paused a moment, clenching her hands.

'Now for it,' she said.

She had had a dream the previous night, which, years ago, used to be familiar to her, for again and again when she was a child she had dreamed it. In itself the dream was nothing, but in those childish days, whenever she had this dream which had visited her last night, it was followed on the next night by another which contained the source and the core of the horror, and she would awake screaming and struggling in the grip of overwhelming nightmare. For some ten years now she had not experienced it, and would have said that, though she remembered it, it had become dim and distant to her. But last night she had had that warning dream, which used to herald the visitation of the nightmare, and now that whole store-house of memory crammed as it was with bright things and beautiful contained nothing so vivid.

The warning dream, the curtain that was drawn up on the succeeding night, and disclosed the vision she dreaded, was simple and harmless enough in itself. She seemed to be walking on a high sandy cliff covered with short down-grass; twenty yards to the left came the edge of this cliff, which sloped steeply down to the sea that lay at its foot. The path she followed led through fields bounded by low hedges, and mounted gradually upwards. She went through some half-dozen of these, climbing over the wooden stiles that gave communication; sheep grazed there, but she never saw another human being, and always it was dusk, as if evening was falling, and she had to hurry on, because some-one (she knew not whom) was waiting for her, and had been waiting not a few minutes only, but for many years. Presently, as she mounted this slope, she saw in front of her a copse of stunted trees, growing crookedly under the continual pressure of the wind that blew from the sea, and when she saw those she knew her journey was nearly done, and that the nameless one, who had been waiting for her so long, was somewhere close at hand. The path she followed was cut through this wood and the slanting boughs of the trees on the seaward side almost roofed it in; it was like walking through a tunnel. Soon the trees in front began to grow thin, and she saw through them the grey tower of a lonely church. It stood in a graveyard, apparently long disused, and the body of the church, which lay between the tower and the edge of the cliff, was in ruins, roofless, and with gaping windows, round which ivy grew thickly.

At that point this prefatory dream always stopped. It was a troubled, uneasy dream, for there was over it the sense of dusk and of the man who had been waiting for her so long, but it was not of the order of nightmare. Many times in childhood had she experienced it, and perhaps it was the subconscious knowledge of the night that so surely followed it, which gave it its disquiet. And now last night it had come again, identical in every particular but one. For last night it seemed to her that in the course of these ten years which had intervened since last it had visited her, the glimpse of the church and churchyard was changed. The edge of the cliff had come nearer to the tower, so that it now was within a yard or two of it, and the ruined body of the church, but for one broken arch that remained, had vanished. The sea had encroached, and for ten years had been busily eating at the cliff.

Hester knew well that it was this dream and this alone which had darkened the day for her, by reason of the nightmares that used to follow it, and, like a sensible woman, having looked it once in the face, she refused to admit into her mind any conscious calling-up of the sequel. If she let herself contemplate that, as likely or not the very thinking about it would be sufficient to ensure its return, and of one thing she was very certain, namely, that she didn't at all want it to do so. It was not like the confused jumble and jangle of ordinary nightmare, it was very simple, and she felt it concerned the nameless one who waited for her . . . But she must not think of it; her whole will and intention was set on not thinking of it, and to aid her resolution, there was the rattle of Dick's latch-key in the front-door, and his voice calling her.

She went out into the little square front hall; there he was, strong and large, and wonderfully undreamlike.

'This heat's a scandal, it's an outrage, it's an abomination of desolation,' he cried, vigorously mopping. 'What have we done that Providence should place us in this frying-pan? Let us thwart him, Hester! Let us drive out of this inferno and have our dinner at – I'll whisper it so that he shan't overhear – at Hampton Court!'

She laughed: this plan suited her excellently. They would return late, after the distraction of a fresh scene; and dining out at night was both delicious and stupefying.

'The very thing,' she said, 'and I'm sure Providence didn't hear. Let's start now!'

'Rather. Any letters for me?'

He walked to the table where there were a few rather uninteresting-looking envelopes with half penny stamps.

'Ah, receipted bill,' he said. 'Just a reminder of one's folly in paying it. Circular . . . unasked advice to invest in German marks. . . . Circular begging letter, beginning "Dear Sir or Madam." Such impertinence to ask one to subscribe to something without ascertaining one's sex. . . . Private view, portraits at the Walton Gallery. . . . Can't go: business meetings all day. You might like to have a look in, Hester. Some one told me there were some fine Vandycks. That's all: let's be off.'

Hester spent a thoroughly reassuring evening, and though she thought of telling Dick about the dream that had so deeply imprinted itself on her consciousness all day, in order to hear the great laugh he would have given her for being such a goose, she refrained from doing so, since nothing that he could say would be so tonic to these fantastic fears as his general robustness. Besides, she would have to account for its disturbing effect, tell him that it was once familiar to her, and recount the sequel of the nightmares that followed. She would neither think of them, nor mention them: it was wiser by far just to soak herself in his extraordinary sanity, and wrap herself in his affection. . . . They dined out-of-doors at a riverside restaurant and strolled about afterwards, and it was very nearly midnight when, soothed with coolness and fresh air, and the vigour of his strong companionship, she let herself into the house, while he took the car back to the garage. And now she marvelled at the mood which had beset her all day, so distant and unreal had it become. She felt as if she had dreamed of shipwreck, and had awoke to find herself in some secure and sheltered garden where no tempest raged nor waves beat. But was there, ever so remotely, ever so dimly, the noise of far-off breakers somewhere?

He slept in the dressing-room which communicated with her bedroom, the door of which was left open for the sake of air and coolness, and she fell asleep almost as soon as her light was out, and while his was still burning. And immediately she began to dream.

She was standing on the sea-shore; the tide was out, for level sands strewn with stranded jetsam glimmered in a dusk that was deepening into night. Though she had never seen the place it was awfully familiar to her. At the head of the beach there was a steep cliff of sand, and perched on the edge of it was a grey church tower. The sea must have encroached and undermined the body of the church, for tumbled blocks of masonry lay close to her at the bottom of the cliff, and there were gravestones there, while others still in place were silhouetted whitely against the sky. To the right of the church tower there was a wood of stunted trees, combed sideways by the prevalent sea-wind, and she knew that along the top of the cliff a few yards inland there lay a path through fields, with wooden stiles to climb, which led through a tunnel of trees and so out into the churchyard. All this she saw in a glance, and waited, looking at the sand-cliff crowned by the church tower, for the terror that was going to reveal itself. Already she knew what it was, and, as so many times before, she tried to run away. But the catalepsy of nightmare was already on her; frantically she strove to move, but her utmost endeavour could not raise a foot from the sand. Frantically she tried to look away from the sand-cliffs close in front of her, where in a moment now the horror would be manifested. . . .

It came. There formed a pale oval light, the size of a man's face, dimly luminous in front of her and a few inches above the level of her eyes. It outlined itself, short reddish hair grew low on the forehead, below were two grey eyes, set very close together, which steadily and fixedly regarded her. On each side the ears stood noticeably away from the head, and the lines of the jaw met in a short pointed chin. The nose was straight and rather long, below it came a hairless lip, and last of all the mouth took shape and colour, and there lay the crowning terror. One side of it, soft-curved and beautiful, trembled into a smile, the other side, thick and gathered together as by some physical deformity, sneered and lusted.

The whole face, dim at first, gradually focused itself into clear outline: it was pale and rather lean, the face of a young man. And then the lower lip dropped a little, showing the glint of teeth, and there was the sound of speech. 'I shall soon come for you now,' it said, and on the words it drew a little nearer to her, and the smile broadened. At that the full hot blast of nightmare poured in upon her. Again she tried to run, again she tried to scream, and now she could feel the breath of that terrible mouth upon her. Then with a crash and a rending like the tearing asunder of soul and body she broke the spell, and heard her own voice yelling, and felt with her fingers for the switch of her light. And then she saw that the room was not dark, for Dick's door was open, and the next moment, not yet undressed, he was with her.

'My darling, what is it?' he said. 'What's the matter?'

She clung desperately to him, still distraught with terror.

'Ah, he has been here again,' she cried. 'He says he will soon come to me. Keep him away, Dick.'

For one moment her fear infected him, and he found himself glancing round the room.

'But what do you mean?' he said. 'No one has been here.'

She raised her head from his shoulder.

'No, it was just a dream,' she said. 'But it was the old dream, and I was terrified. Why, you've not undressed yet. What time is it?'

'You haven't been in bed ten minutes, dear,' he said. 'You had hardly put out your light when I heard you screaming.'

She shuddered.

'Ah, it's awful,' she said. 'And he will come again. . . .'

He sat down by her.

'Now tell me all about it,' he said.

She shook her head.

'No, it will never do to talk about it,' she said, 'it will only make it more real. I suppose the children are all right, are they?'

'Of course they are. I looked in on my way upstairs.'

'That's good. But I'm better now, Dick. A dream hasn't anything real about it, has it? It doesn't mean anything?'

He was quite reassuring on this point, and soon she quieted down. Before he went to bed he looked in again on her, and she was asleep.

Hester had a stern interview with herself when Dick had gone down to his office next morning. She told herself that what she was afraid of was nothing more than her own fear. How many times had that ill-omened face come to her in dreams, and what significance had it ever proved to possess? Absolutely none at all, except to make her afraid. She was afraid where no fear was: she was guarded, sheltered, prosperous, and what if a nightmare of childhood returned? It had no more meaning now than it had then, and all those visitations of her childhood had passed away without trace. . . . And then, despite herself, she began thinking over that vision again. It was grimly identical with all its previous occurrences, except . . . And then, with a sudden shrinking of the heart, she remembered that in earlier years those terrible lips had said: 'I shall come for you when you are older,' and last night they had said: 'I shall soon come for you now.' She remembered, too, that in the warning dream the sea had encroached, and it had now demolished the body of the church. There was an awful consistency about these two changes in the otherwise identical visions. The years had brought their change to them for in the one the encroaching sea had brought down the body of the church, in the other the time was now near. . . .

It was no use to scold or reprimand herself, for to bring her mind to the contemplation of the vision meant merely that the grip of terror closed on her again; it was far wiser to occupy herself, and starve her fear out by refusing to bring it the sustenance of thought. So she went about her household duties, she took the children out for their airing in the park, and then, determined to leave no moment unoccupied, set off with the card of invitation to see the pictures in the private view at the Walton Gallery. After that her day was full enough, she was lunching out, and going on to a matinée, and by the time she got home Dick would have returned, and they would drive down to his little house at Rye for the week-end. All Saturday and Sunday she would be playing golf, and she felt that fresh air and physical fatigue would exorcise the dread of these dreaming fantasies.

The gallery was crowded when she got there; there were friends among the sightseers, and the inspection of the pictures was diversified by cheerful conversation. There were two or three fine Raeburns, a couple of Sir Joshuas, but the gems, so she gathered, were three Vandycks that hung in a small room by themselves. Presently she strolled in there, looking at her catalogue. The first of them, she saw, was a portrait of Sir Roger

Wyburn. Still chatting to her friend she raised her eye and saw it. . . .

Her heart hammered in her throat, and then seemed to stand still altogether. A qualm, as of some mental sickness of the soul overcame her, for there in front of her was he who would soon come for her. There was the reddish hair, the projecting ears, the greedy eyes set close together, and the mouth smiling on one side, and on the other gathered up into the sneering menace that she knew so well. It might have been her own nightmare rather than a living model which had sat to the painter for that face.

'Ah, what a portrait, and what a brute!' said her companion. 'Look, Hester, isn't that marvellous?'

She recovered herself with an effort To give way to this ever-mastering dread would have been to allow nightmare to invade her waking life, and there, for sure, madness lay. She forced herself to look at it again, but there were the steady and eager eyes regarding her; she could almost fancy the mouth began to move. All round her the crowd bustled and chattered, but to her own sense she was alone there with Roger Wyburn.

And yet, so she reasoned with herself, this picture of him for it was he and no other – should have reassured her. Roger Wyburn, to have been painted by Vandyck, must have been dead near on two hundred years; how could he be a menace to her? Had she seen that portrait by some chance as a child; had it made some dreadful impression on her, since overscored by other memories, but still alive in the mysterious subconsciousness, which flows eternally, like some dark underground river, beneath the surface of human life? Psychologists taught that these early impressions fester or poison the mind like some hidden abscess. That might account for this dread of one, nameless no longer, who waited for her.

That night down at Rye there came again to her the prefatory dream, followed by the nightmare, and clinging to her husband as the terror began to subside, she told him what she had resolved to keep to herself. Just to tell it brought a measure of comfort, for it was so outrageously fantastic, and his robust common sense upheld her. But when on their return to London there was a recurrence of these visions, he made short work of her demur and took her straight to her doctor.

'Tell him all, darling,' he said. 'Unless you promise to do that, I will. I can't have you worried like this. It's all nonsense, you know, and doctors are wonderful people for curing nonsense.'

She turned to him.

'Dick, you're frightened,' she said quietly.

He laughed.

'I'm nothing of the kind,' he said, 'but I don't like being awakened by your screaming. Not my idea of a peaceful night. Here we are.'

The medical report was decisive and peremptory. There was nothing whatever to be alarmed about; in brain and body she was perfectly healthy, but she was run down. These disturbing dreams were, as likely as not, an effect, a symptom of her condition, rather than the cause of it, and Dr Baring unhesitatingly recommended a complete change to some bracing place. The wise thing would be to send her out of this stuffy furnace to some quiet place to where she had never been. Complete change; quite so. For the same reason her husband had better not go with her; he must pack her off to, let us say, the East coast. Sea-air and coolness and complete idleness. No long walks; no long bathings; a dip, and a deck-chair on the sands. A lazy, soporific life. How about Rushton? He had no doubt that Rushton would set her up again. After a week or so, perhaps, her husband might go down and see her. Plenty of sleep – never mind the nightmares – plenty of fresh air.

Hester, rather to her husband's surprise, fell in with this suggestion at once, and the following evening saw her installed in solitude and tranquillity. The little hotel was still almost empty, for the rush of summer tourists had not yet begun, and all day she sat out on the beach with the sense of a struggle over. She need not fight the terror any more; dimly it seemed to her that its malignancy had been relaxed. Had she in some way yielded to it and done its secret bidding? At any rate no return of its nightly visitations had occurred, and she slept long and dreamlessly, and woke to another day of quiet. Every morning there was a line for her from Dick, with good news of himself and the children, but he and they alike seemed somehow remote, like memories of a very distant time. Something had driven in between her and them, and she saw them as if through glass. But equally did the memory of the face of Roger Wyburn, as seen on the master's canvas or hanging close in front of her against the crumbling sand-cliff, become blurred and indistinct, and no return of her nightly terrors visited her. This truce from all emotion reacted not on her mind alone, lulling her with a sense of soothed security, but on her body also, and she began to weary of this day-long inactivity.

The village lay on the lip of a stretch of land reclaimed from the sea. To the north the level marsh, now beginning to glow with the pale bloom of the sea-lavender, stretched away featureless till it lost itself in distance, but to the south a spur of hill came down to the shore ending in a wooded promontory. Gradually, as her physical health increased, she began to wonder what lay beyond this ridge which cut short the view, and one afternoon she walked across the intervening level and strolled up its wooded slopes. The day was close and windless, the invigorating sea-breeze which till now had spiced the hate with freshness had died, and she looked forward to finding a current of air stirring when she had topped the hill. To the south a mass of dark cloud lay along the horizon, but there was no imminent threat of storm. The slope was easily surmounted, and presently she stood at the top and found herself on the edge of a tableland of wooded pasture, and following the path, which ran not far from the edge of the cliff, she came out into more open country. Empty fields, where a few sheep were grazing, mounted gradually upwards. Wooden stiles made a communication in the hedges that bounded them. And there, not a mile in front of her, she saw a wood, with trees growing slantingly away from the push of the prevalent sea winds, crowning the upward slope, and over the top of it peered a grey church tower.

For the moment, as the awful and familiar scene identified itself, Hester's heart stood still: the next a wave of courage and resolution poured in upon her. Here, at last was the scene of that prefatory dream, and here was she presented with the opportunity of fathoming and dispelling it. Instantly her mind was made up, and under the strange twilight of the shrouded sky, she walked swiftly on through the fields she had so often traversed in sleep, and up to the wood, beyond which he was waiting for her. She closed her ears against the clanging bell of terror, which now she could silence for ever, and unfalteringly entered that dark tunnel of wood. Soon in front of her the trees began to thin, and through them, now close at hand, she saw the church tower. In a few yards farther she came out of the belt of trees, and round her were the monuments of a graveyard long disused. The cliff was broken off close to the church tower: between it and the edge there was no more of the body of the church than a broken arch, thick hung with ivy. Round this she passed and saw below the ruin of fallen masonry, and the level sands strewn with head-stones and disjected rubble, and at the edge of the cliff were graves already cracked and toppling. But there was no one here, none waited for her, and the churchyard where she had so often pictured him was as empty as the fields she had just traversed.

A huge elation filled her; her courage had been rewarded, and all the terrors of the past became to her meaningless phantoms. But there was no time to linger, for now the storm threatened, and on the horizon a blink of lightning was followed by a crackling peal. Just as she turned to go her eye fell on a tombstone that was balanced on the very edge of the cliff, and she read on it that here lay the body of Roger Wyburn.

Fear, the catalepsy of nightmare, rooted her for the moment to the spot; she stared in stricken amazement at the moss-grown letters; almost she expected to see that fell terror of a face rise and hover over his resting-place. Then the fear which had frozen her lent her wings, and with hurrying feet she sped through the arched pathway in the wood and out into the fields. Not one backward glance did she give till she had come to the edge of the ridge above the village, and, turning, saw the pastures she had traversed empty of any living presence. None had followed; but the sheep, apprehensive of the coming storm, had ceased to feed, and were huddling under shelter of the stunted hedges.

Her first idea, in the panic of her mind, was to leave the place at once, but the last train for London had left an hour before, and besides, where was the use of flight if it was the spirit of a man long dead from which she fled? The distance from the place where his bones lay did not afford her safety; that must be sought for within. But she longed for Dick's sheltering and confident presence; he was arriving in any case tomorrow, but there were long dark hours before tomorrow, and who could say what the perils and dangers of the coming night might be? If he started this evening instead of tomorrow morning, he could motor down here in four hours, and would be with her by ten o'clock or eleven. She wrote an urgent telegram: 'Come at once,' she said. 'Don't delay.'

The storm which had flickered on the south now came quickly up, and soon after it burst in appalling violence. For preface there were but a few large drops that splashed and dried on the roadway as she came back from the post-office, and just as she reached the hotel again the roar of the approaching rain sounded, and the sluices of heaven were opened. Through the deluge flared the fire of the lightning, the thunder crashed and echoed overhead, and presently the street of the village was a torrent of sandy turbulent water, and sitting there in the dark one picture leapt floating before her eyes, that of the tombstone of Roger Wyburn, already tottering to its fall at the edge of the cliff of the church tower. In such rains as these, acres of the cliffs were loosened; she seemed to hear the whisper of the sliding sand that would precipitate those perished sepulchres and what lay within to the beach below.

By eight o'clock the storm was subsiding, and as she dined she was handed a telegram from Dick, saying that he had already started and sent this off *en route*. By half-past ten, therefore, if all was well, he would be here, and somehow he would stand between her and her fear. Strange how a few days ago both it and the thought of him had become distant and dim to her; now the one was as vivid as the other, and she counted the minutes to his arrival. Soon the rain ceased altogether, and looking out of the curtained window of her sitting-room where she sat watching the slow circle of the hands of the clock, she saw a tawny moon rising over the sea. Before it had climbed to the zenith, before her clock had twice told the hour again, Dick would be with her.

It had just struck ten when there came a knock at her door, and the page-boy entered with the message that a gentleman had come for her. Her heart leaped at the news; she had not expected

Dick for half an hour yet, and now the lonely vigil was over. She ran downstairs, and there was the figure standing on the step outside. His face was turned away from her; no doubt he was giving some order to his chauffeur. He was outlined against the white moonlight, and in contrast with that, the gas-jet in the entrance just above his head gave his hair a warm, reddish tinge.

She ran across the hall to him.

'Ah, my darling, you've come,' she said. 'It was good of you. How quick you've been!' Just as she laid her hand on his shoulder he turned. His arm was thrown out round her, and she looked into a face with eyes close set, and a mouth smiling on one side, the other, thick and gathered together as by some physical deformity, sneered and lusted.

The nightmare was on her; she could neither run nor scream, and supporting her dragging steps, he went forth with her into the night.

Half an hour later Dick arrived. To his amazement he heard that a man had called for his wife not long before, and that she had gone out with him. He seemed to be a stranger here, for the boy who had taken his message to her had never seen him before, and presently surprise began to deepen into alarm; enquiries were made outside the hotel, and it appeared that a witness or two had seen the lady whom they knew to be staying there walking, hatless, along the top of the beach with a man whose arm was linked in hers. Neither of them knew him, but one had seen his face and could describe it.

The direction of the search thus became narrowed down, and though with a lantern to supplement the moonlight they came upon footprints which might have been hers, there were no marks of any who walked beside her. But they followed these until they came to an end, a mile away, in a great landslide of sand, which had fallen from the old churchyard on the cliff, and had brought down with it half the tower and a gravestone, with the body that had lain below.

The gravestone was that of Roger Wyburn, and his body lay by it, untouched by corruption or decay, though two hundred years had elapsed since it was interred there. For a week afterwards the work of searching the landslide went on, assisted by the high tides that gradually washed it away. But no further discovery was made.

THE CAPTAIN OF THE *POLESTAR*
BY ARTHUR CONAN DOYLE

Arthur Conan Doyle was born on 22 May 1859 in Edinburgh. He studied medicine at the University of Edinburgh and began to write stories while he was a student. Over his life he produced more than thirty books, 150 short stories, poems, plays and essays across a wide range of genres. His most famous creation is the detective Sherlock Holmes, who he introduced in his first novel *A Study in Scarlet* (1887). In 1893 Conan Doyle published 'The Final Problem' in which he killed off his famous detective so that he could turn his attention more towards historical fiction. However, Holmes was so popular that Conan Doyle eventually relented and published a further Holmes adventure, *The Hound of the Baskervilles*, in 1901. The detective was finally retired in 1927 and Arthur Conan Doyle died on 7 July 1930.

Being an extract from the singular journal of
JOHN MCALISTER RAY, *student of medicine*

SEPTEMBER 11 – Lat. 81° 40' N; long. 2° E. Still lying-to amid enormous ice-fields. The one which stretches away to the north of us, and to which our ice-anchor is attached, cannot be smaller than an English county. To the right and left unbroken sheets extend to the horizon. This morning the mate reported that there were signs of pack ice to the southward. Should this form of sufficient thickness to bar our return, we shall be in a position of danger, as the food, I hear, is already running somewhat short. It is late in the season, and the nights are beginning to reappear. This morning I saw a star twinkling just over the fore-yard, the first since the beginning of May. There is considerable discontent among the crew, many of whom are anxious to get back home to be in time for the herring season, when labour always commands a high price upon the Scotch coast. As yet their displeasure is only signified by sullen countenances and black looks, but I heard from the second mate this afternoon that they contemplated sending a deputation to the captain to explain their grievance. I much doubt how he will receive it, as he is a man of fierce temper and very sensitive about anything approaching an infringement of his rights. I shall venture after dinner to say a few words to him upon the subject. I have always found that he will tolerate from me what he would resent from any other member of the crew. Amsterdam Island, at the north-west corner of Spitzbergen, is visible upon our starboard quarter – a rugged line of volcanic rocks, intersected by white seams, which represent glaciers. It is curious to think that at the present moment there is probably no human being nearer to us than the Danish settlements in the south of Greenland – a good nine hundred miles as the crow flies. A captain takes a great responsibility upon himself when he risks his vessel under such circumstances. No whaler has ever remained in these latitudes till so advanced a period of the year.

9.00 p.m. – I have spoken to Captain Craigie, and though the result has been hardly satisfactory, I am bound to say that he listened to what I had to say very quietly and even deferentially. When I had finished he put on that air of iron determination which I have frequently observed upon his face, and paced rapidly backwards and forwards across the narrow cabin for some minutes. At first I feared that I had seriously offended him, but he dispelled the idea by sitting down again and putting his hand upon my arm with a gesture which almost amounted to a caress. There was a depth of tenderness too in his wild dark eyes which surprised me considerably. 'Look here, doctor,' he said, 'I'm sorry I ever took you – I am indeed – and I would give fifty pounds this minute to see you standing safe upon the Dundee quay. It's hit or miss with me this time. There are fish to the north of us. How dare you shake your head, sir, when I tell you I saw them blowing from the masthead?' – this in a sudden burst of fury, though I was not conscious of having shown any signs of doubt. 'Two-and-twenty fish in as many minutes as I am a living man, and not one under ten foot.* Now, doctor, do you think I can leave the country when there is only one infernal strip of ice between me and my fortune? If it came on to blow from the north tomorrow we could fill the ship and be away before the frost could catch us. If it came on to blow from the south – well, I suppose the men are paid for risking their lives, and as for myself it matters but little to me, for I have more to bind me to the other world than to this one. I confess that I am sorry for *you*, though. I wish I had old Angus Tait who was with me last voyage, for he was a man that would never be missed, and you – you said once that you were engaged, did you not?'

'Yes,' I answered, snapping the spring of the locket which hung from my watch-chain, and holding up the little vignette of Flora.

'Curse you!' he yelled, springing out of his seat, with his very beard bristling with passion. 'What is your happiness to me? What have I to do with her that you must dangle her photograph before my eyes?' I almost thought that he was about to strike me in the frenzy of his rage, but with another imprecation he dashed open the door of the cabin and rushed out upon deck, leaving me considerably astonished at his extraordinary violence. It is the first time that he has ever shown me anything but courtesy and kindness. I can hear him pacing excitedly up and down overhead as I write these lines.

I should like to give a sketch of the character of this man, but it seems presumptuous to attempt such a thing upon paper, when the idea in my own mind is at best a vague and uncertain one.

* A whale is measured among whalers not by the length of its body, but by the length of its whalebone.

Several times I have thought that I grasped the clue which might explain it, only to be disappointed by his presenting himself in some new light which would upset all my conclusions. It may be that no human eye but my own shall ever rest upon these lines, yet as a psychological study I shall attempt to leave some record of Captain Nicholas Craigie.

A man's outer case generally gives some indication of the soul within. The captain is tall and well formed, with a dark, handsome face and a curious way of twitching his limbs, which may arise from nervousness or be simply an outcome of his excessive energy. His jaw and whole cast of countenance is manly and resolute, but the eyes are the distinctive feature of his face. They are of the very darkest hazel, bright and eager, with a singular mixture of recklessness in their expression, and of something else which I have sometimes thought was more allied with horror than any other emotion. Generally the former predominated, but on occasions, and more particularly when he was thoughtfully inclined, the look of fear would spread and deepen until it imparted a new character to his whole countenance. It is at these times that he is most subject to tempestuous fits of anger, and he seems to be aware of it, for I have known him lock himself up so that no one might approach him until his dark hour was passed. He sleeps badly, and I have heard him shouting during the night, but his cabin is some little distance from mine and I could never distinguish the words which he said.

This is one phase of his character, and the most disagreeable one. It is only through my close association with him, thrown together as we are day after day, that I have observed it. Otherwise he is an agreeable companion, well read and entertaining, and as gallant a seaman as ever trod a deck. I shall not easily forget the way in which he handled the ship when we were caught by a gale among the loose ice at the beginning of April. I have never seen him so cheerful, and even hilarious, as he was that night, as he paced backwards and forwards upon the bridge amid the flashing of the lightning and the howling of the wind. He has told me several times that the thought of death was a pleasant one to him, which is a sad thing for a young man to say; he cannot be much more than thirty, though his hair and moustache are already slightly grizzled. Some great sorrow must have overtaken him and blighted his whole life. Perhaps I should be the same if I lost my Flora – God knows! I think if it were not for her that I should care very little whether the wind blew from the north or the south tomorrow. There, I hear him come down the companion, and he has locked himself up in his room, which shows that he is still in an unamiable mood. And so to bed, as old Pepys would say, for the candle is burning down (we have to use them now since the nights are closing in) and the steward has turned in, so there are no hopes of another one.

September 12 – Calm, clear day, and still lying in the same position. What wind there is comes from the south-east, but it is very slight. Captain is in a better humour, and apologised to me at breakfast for his rudeness. He still looks somewhat distrait, however, and retains that wild look in his eyes which in a Highlander would mean that he was 'fey' – at least so our chief engineer remarked to me, and he has some reputation among the Celtic portion of our crew as a seer and expounder of omens.

It is strange that superstition should have obtained such mastery over this hard-headed and practical race. I could not have believed to what an extent it is carried had I not observed it for myself. We have had a perfect epidemic of it this voyage, until I have felt inclined to serve out rations of sedatives and nerve-tonics with the Saturday allowance of grog. The first symptom of it was that shortly after leaving Shetland the men at the wheel used to complain that they heard plaintive cries and screams in the wake of the ship, as if something were following it and were unable to overtake it. This fiction has been kept up during the whole voyage, and on dark nights at the beginning of the seal-fishing it was only with great difficulty that men could be induced to do their spell. No doubt what they heard was either the creaking of the rudder-chains or the cry of some passing sea-bird. I have been fetched out of bed several times to listen to it, but I need hardly say that I was never able to distinguish anything unnatural. The men, however, are so absurdly positive upon the subject that it is hopeless to argue with them. I mentioned the matter to the captain once, but to my surprise he took it very gravely, and indeed appeared to be considerably disturbed by what I told him. I should have thought that he at least would have been above such vulgar delusions.

All this disquisition upon superstition leads me up to the fact that Mr Manson, our second mate, saw a ghost last night – or, at least, says that he did, which of course is the same thing. It is quite refreshing to have some new topic of conversation after the eternal routine of bears and whales which has served us for so many months. Manson swears the ship is haunted; and that he would not stay in her a day if he had any other place to go to. Indeed the fellow is honestly frightened, and I had to give him some chloral and bromide of potassium this morning to steady him down. He seemed quite indignant when I suggested that he had been having an extra glass the night before, and I was obliged to pacify him by keeping as grave a countenance as possible during his story, which he certainly narrated in a very straightforward and matter-of-fact way.

'I was on the bridge,' he said, 'about four bells in the middle watch, just when the night was at its darkest. There was a bit of a moon, but the clouds were blowing across it so that you couldn't see far from the ship. John McLeod, the harpooner, came aft from the fo'c'sle-head and reported a strange noise on the starboard bow. I went forward and we both heard it, sometimes like a bairn crying and sometimes like a wench in pain. I've been seventeen years to the country and I never heard seal, old or young, make a sound like that. As we were standing there on the fo'c'sle-head the moon came out from behind a cloud, and we both saw a sort of white figure moving across the ice-field in the same direction that we had heard the cries. We lost sight of it for a while, but it came back on the port bow, and we could just make it out like a shadow on the ice. I sent a hand aft for the rifles, and McLeod and I went down on to the pack, thinking that maybe it might be a bear. When we got on the ice I lost sight of McLeod, but I pushed on in the direction where I could still hear the cries. I followed them for a mile or maybe more, and then running round a hummock I came right on to the top of it, standing and waiting for me seemingly. I don't know what it was. It wasn't a bear, anyway. It was tall and white and straight, and if it wasn't a man nor a woman, I'll stake my davy it was something worse. I made for the ship as hard as I could run, and precious glad I was to find myself aboard. I signed articles to do my duty by the ship, and on the ship I'll stay, but you don't catch me on the ice again after sundown.'

That is his story, given as far as I can in his own words. I fancy what he saw must, in spite of his denial, have been a young bear erect upon its hind legs, an attitude which they often assume when alarmed. In the uncertain light this would bear a resemblance to a human figure, especially to a man whose nerves were already somewhat shaken. Whatever it may have been, the occurrence is unfortunate, for it has produced a most unpleasant effect upon the crew. Their looks are more sullen than before, and their discontent more open. The double grievance of being debarred from the herring fishing and of being detained in what they choose to call a haunted vessel, may lead them to do something rash. Even the harpooners, who are the oldest and steadiest among them, are joining in the general agitation.

Apart from this absurd outbreak of superstition, things are looking rather more cheerful. The pack which was forming to the south of us has partly cleared away, and the water is so warm as to lead me to believe that we are lying in one of those branches of the Gulf Stream which run up between Greenland and Spitzbergen. There are numerous small medusae and sea-lemons about the ship, with abundance of shrimps, so that there is every possibility of 'fish' being sighted. Indeed one was seen blowing about dinner-time, but in such a position that it was impossible for the boats to follow it.

September 13 — Had an interesting conversation with the chief mate, Mr Milne, upon the bridge. It seems that our captain is as great an enigma to the seamen, and even to the owners of the vessel, as he has been to me. Mr Milne tells me that when the ship is paid off, upon returning from a voyage, Captain Craigie disappears and is not seen again until the approach of another season, when he walks quietly into the office of the company and asks whether his services will be required. He has no friend in Dundee, nor does anyone pretend to be acquainted with his early history. His position depends entirely upon his skill as a seaman, and the name for courage and coolness which he had earned in the capacity of mate, before being entrusted with a separate command. The unanimous opinion seems to be that he is not a Scotchman, and that his name is an assumed one. Mr Milne thinks that he has devoted himself to whaling simply for the reason that it is the most dangerous occupation which he could select, and that he courts death in every possible manner.

He mentioned several instances of this, one of which is rather curious, if true. It seems that on one occasion he did not put in an appearance at the office, and a substitute had to be selected in his place. That was at the time of the last Russian and Turkish War. When he turned up again next spring he had a puckered wound in the side of his neck which he used to endeavour to conceal with his cravat. Whether the mate's inference that he had been engaged in the war is true or not I cannot say. It was certainly a strange coincidence.

The wind is veering round in an easterly direction, but is still very slight. I think the ice is lying closer than it did yesterday. As far as the eye can reach on every side there is one wide expanse of spotless white, only broken by an occasional rift or the dark shadow of a hummock. To the south there is the narrow lane of blue water which is our sole means of escape, and which is closing up every day. The captain is taking a heavy responsibility upon himself. I hear that the tank of potatoes has been finished, and even the biscuits are running short, but he preserves the same impassable countenance, and spends the greater part of the day at the crow's nest, sweeping the horizon with his glass. His manner is very variable, and he seems to avoid my society, but there has been no repetition of the violence which he showed the other night.

7.30 p.m. – My deliberate opinion is that we are commanded by a madman. Nothing else can account for the extraordinary vagaries of Captain Craigie. It is fortunate that I have kept this journal of our voyage, as it will serve to justify us in case we have to put him under any sort of restraint, a step which I should only consent to as a last resource. Curiously enough it was he himself who suggested lunacy and not mere eccentricity as the secret of his strange conduct. He was standing upon the bridge about an hour ago, peering as usual through his glass, while I was walking up and down the quarter-deck. The majority of the men were below at their tea, for the watches have not been regularly kept of late. Tired of walking, I leaned against the bulwarks, and admired the mellow glow cast by the sinking sun upon the great ice-fields which surround us. I was suddenly aroused from the reverie into which I had fallen by a hoarse voice at my elbow, and starting round I found that the captain had descended and was standing by my side. He was staring out over the ice with an expression in which horror, surprise and something approaching to joy were contending for the mastery. In spite of the cold, great drops of perspiration were coursing down his forehead, and he was evidently fearfully excited. His limbs twitched like those of a man upon the verge of an epileptic fit, and the lines about his mouth were drawn and hard.

'Look!' he gasped, seizing me by the wrist, but still keeping his eyes upon the distant ice and moving his head slowly in a horizontal direction, as if following some object which was moving across the field of vision. 'Look! There, man, there! Between the hummocks! Now coming out from behind the far one! You see her – you *must* see her! There still! Flying from me, by God, flying from me – and gone!'

He uttered the last two words in a whisper of concentrated agony which shall never fade from my remembrance. Clinging to the ratlines he endeavoured to climb up upon the top of the bulwarks as if in the hope of obtaining a last glance at the departing object. His strength was not equal to the attempt, however, and he staggered back against the saloon skylights, where he leaned panting and exhausted. His face was so livid that I expected him to become unconscious, so I lost no time in leading him down the companion and stretching him upon one of the sofas in the cabin. I then poured him out some brandy, which I held to his lips, and which had a wonderful effect upon him, bringing the blood back into his white face and steadying his poor shaking limbs. He raised himself up upon his elbow, and looking round to see that we were alone, he beckoned to me to come and sit beside him.

'You saw it, didn't you?' he asked, still in the same subdued awesome tone so foreign to the nature of the man.

'No, I saw nothing.'

His head sank back again upon the cushions. 'No, he wouldn't without the glass,' he murmured. 'He couldn't. It was the glass that showed her to me, and then the eyes of love – the eyes of love. I say, doc, don't let the steward in! He'll think I'm mad. Just bolt the door, will you!'

I rose and did what he had commanded.

He lay quiet for a while, lost in thought apparently, and then raised himself up upon his elbow again, and asked for some more brandy.

'You don't think I am, do you, doc?' he asked, as I was putting the bottle back into the after-locker. 'Tell me now, as man to man, do you think that I am mad?'

'I think you have something on your mind,' I answered, 'which is exciting you and doing you a good deal of harm.'

'Right there, lad!' he cried, his eyes sparkling from the effects of the brandy. 'Plenty on my mind – plenty! But I can work out the latitude and the longitude, and I can handle my sextant and manage my logarithms. You couldn't prove me mad in a court of law, could you, now?' It was curious to hear the man lying back and coolly arguing out the question of his own sanity.

'Perhaps not,' I said; 'but still I think you would be wise to get home as soon as you can, and settle down to a quiet life for a while.'

'Get home, eh?' he muttered, with a sneer upon his face. 'One word for me and two for yourself, lad. Settle down with Flora – pretty little Flora. Are bad dreams signs of madness?'

'Sometimes,' I answered.

'What else? What would be the first symptoms?'

'Pains in the head, noises in the ears, flashes before the eyes, delusions –'

'Ah! what about them?' he interrupted. 'What would you call a delusion?'

'Seeing a thing which is not there is a delusion –'

'But she was there!' he groaned to himself. 'She *was* there!' and rising, he unbolted the door and walked with slow and uncertain steps to his own cabin, where I have no doubt that he will remain until tomorrow morning. His system seems to have received a terrible shock, whatever it may have been that he imagined himself to have seen. The man becomes a greater mystery every day, though I fear that the solution which he has himself suggested is the correct one, and that his reason is affected. I do not think that a guilty conscience has anything to do with his behaviour. The idea is a popular one among the officers and, I believe, the crew; but I have seen nothing to support it. He has not the air of a guilty man, but of one who has had terrible usage at the hands of fortune, and who should be regarded as a martyr rather than a criminal.

The wind is veering round to the south tonight. God help us if it blocks that narrow pass which is our only road to safety! Situated as we are on the edge of the main Arctic pack, or the 'barrier' as it is called by the whalers, any wind from the north has the effect of shredding out the ice around us and allowing our escape, while a wind from the south blows up all the loose ice behind us, and hems us in between two packs. God help us, I say again!

*

September 14 – Sunday, and a day of rest. My fears have been confirmed, and the thin strip of blue water has disappeared from the southward. Nothing but the great motionless ice-fields around us, with their weird hummocks and fantastic pinnacles. There is a deathly silence over their wide expanse which is horrible. No lapping of the waves now, no cries of seagulls or straining of sails, but one deep universal silence in which the murmurs of the seamen and the creak of their boots upon the white shining deck seem discordant and out of place. Our only visitor was an Arctic fox, a rare animal upon the pack, though common enough upon the land. He did not come near the ship, however, but after surveying us from a distance fled rapidly across the ice. This was curious conduct, as they generally know nothing of man, and being of an inquisitive nature, become so familiar that they are easily captured. Incredible as it may seem, even this little incident produced a bad effect upon the crew. 'Yon puir beastie kens mair, ay, an' sees mair nor you nor me!' was the comment of one of the leading harpooners, and the others nodded their acquiescence. It is vain to attempt to argue against such puerile superstition. They have made up their minds that there is a curse upon the ship, and nothing will ever persuade them to the contrary.

The captain remained in seclusion all day except for about half an hour in the afternoon, when he came out upon the quarter-deck. I observed that he kept his eye fixed upon the spot where the vision of yesterday had appeared, and was quite prepared for another outburst, but none such came. He did not seem to see me, although I was standing close beside him. Divine service was read as usual by the chief engineer. It is a curious thing that in whaling vessels the Church of England Prayer Book is always employed, although there is never a member of that church among either officers or crew. Our men are all Roman

Catholics or Presbyterians, the former predominating. Since a ritual is used which is foreign to both, neither can complain that the other is preferred to them, and they listen with all attention and devotion, so that the system has something to recommend it.

A glorious sunset, which made the great fields of ice look like a lake of blood. I have never seen a finer and at the same time more weird effect. Wind is veering round. If it will blow twenty-four hours from the north all will yet be well.

September 15 — Today is Flora's birthday. Dear lass! it is well that she cannot see her boy, as she used to call me, shut up among the ice-fields with a crazy captain and a few weeks' provisions. No doubt she scans the shipping list in the *Scotsman* every morning to see if we are reported from Shetland. I have to set an example to the men and look cheery and unconcerned; but God knows, my heart is very heavy at times.

The thermometer is at nineteen Fahrenheit today. There is but little wind, and what there is comes from an unfavourable quarter. Captain is in an excellent humour; I think he imagines he has seen some other omen or vision, poor fellow, during the night, for he came into my room early in the morning and, stooping down over my bunk, whispered, 'It wasn't a delusion, doc; it's all right!' After breakfast he asked me to find out how much food was left, which the second mate and I proceeded to do. It is even less than we had expected. Forward they have half a tank full of biscuits, three barrels of salt meat, and a very limited supply of coffee beans and sugar. In the after-hold and lockers there are a good many luxuries, such as tinned salmon, soups, haricot mutton, etc., but they will go a very short way among a crew of fifty men. There are two barrels of flour in the store-room, and an unlimited supply of tobacco. Altogether there is about enough to keep the men on half rations for eighteen or twenty days – certainly not more. When we reported the state of things to the captain, he ordered all hands to be piped and addressed them from the quarter-deck. I never saw him to better advantage. With his tall, well-knit figure and dark animated face, he seemed a man born to command, and he discussed the situation in a cool sailor-like way which showed that while appreciating the danger he had an eye for every loophole of escape.

'My lads,' he said, 'no doubt you think I brought you into this fix, if it is a fix, and maybe some of you feel bitter against me on account of it. But you must remember that for many a season no ship that comes to the country has brought in as much oil-money as the old *Polestar*, and every one of you has had his share of it. You can leave your wives behind you in comfort, while other poor fellows come back to find their lassies on the parish. If you have to thank me for the one you have to thank me for the other, and we may call it quits. We've tried a bold venture before this and succeeded, so now that we've tried one and failed we've no cause to cry out about it. If the worst comes to the worst, we can make the land across the ice, and lay in a stock of seals which will keep us alive until the spring. It won't come to that, though, for you'll see the Scotch coast again before three weeks are out. At present every man must go on half rations, share and share alike, and no favour to any. Keep up your hearts and you'll pull through this as you've pulled through many a danger before.' These few simple words of his had a wonderful effect upon the crew. His former unpopularity was forgotten, and the old harpooner, whom I have already mentioned for his superstition, led off three cheers, which were heartily joined in by all hands.

September 16 – The wind has veered round to the north during the night, and the ice shows some symptoms of opening out.

The men are in a good humour in spite of the short allowance upon which they have been placed. Steam is kept up in the engine-room, that there may be no delay should an opportunity for escape present itself. The captain is in exuberant spirits, though he still retains that wild 'fey' expression which I have already remarked upon. This burst of cheerfulness puzzles me more than his former gloom. I cannot understand it. I think I mentioned in an early part of this journal that one of his oddities is that he never permits any person to enter his cabin, but insists upon making his own bed, such as it is, and performing every other office for himself. To my surprise he handed me the key today and requested me to go down there and take the time by his chronometer while he measured the altitude of the sun at noon. It is a bare little room, containing a washing-stand and a few books, but little else in the way of luxury, except some pictures upon the walls. The majority of these are small cheap oleographs, but there was one watercolour sketch of the head of a young lady which arrested my attention. It was evidently a portrait, and not one of those fancy types of female beauty which sailors particularly affect. No artist could have evolved from his own mind such a curious mixture of character and weakness. The languid, dreamy eyes, with their drooping lashes, and the broad, low brow, unruffled by thought or care, were in strong contrast with the clean-cut, prominent jaw and the resolute set of the lower lip. Underneath it in one of the corners was written, *M. B., aet. 19.* That anyone in the short space of nineteen years of existence could develop such strength of will as was stamped upon her face seemed to me at the time to be well-nigh incredible. She must have been an extraordinary woman. Her features have thrown such a glamour over me that, though I had but a fleeting glance at them, I could, were I a draughtsman, reproduce them line for line upon this page of the journal. I wonder what part she has played in our captain's life. He has hung her picture at the end of his berth, so that his eyes continually rest upon it. Were he a less reserved man I should make some remark upon the subject. Of the other things in his cabin there was nothing worthy of mention – uniform coats, a camp-stool, small looking-glass, tobacco-box and numerous pipes, including an oriental hookah – which, by the by, gives some colour to Mr Milne's story about his participation in the war, though the connection may seem rather a distant one.

11.20 p.m. – Captain just gone to bed after a long and interesting conversation on general topics. When he chooses he can be a most fascinating companion, being remarkably well read, and having the power of expressing his opinion forcibly without appearing to be dogmatic. I hate to have my intellectual toes trod upon. He spoke about the nature of the soul, and sketched out the views of Aristotle and Plato upon the subject in a masterly manner. He seems to have a leaning for metempsychosis and the doctrines of Pythagoras. In discussing them we touched upon modern spiritualism, and I made some joking allusion to the impostures of Slade, upon which, to my surprise, he warned me most impressively against confusing the innocent with the guilty, and argued that it would be as logical to brand Christianity as an error because Judas, who professed that religion, was a villain. He shortly afterwards bade me good-night and retired to his room.

The wind is freshening up, and blows steadily from the north. The nights are as dark now as they are in England. I hope tomorrow may set us free from our frozen fetters.

September 17 – The Bogie again. Thank heaven that I have strong nerves! The superstition of these poor fellows, and the circumstantial accounts which they give, with the utmost earnestness and self-conviction, would horrify any man not accustomed to their ways. There are many versions of the matter, but the sum-total of them all is that something uncanny has been flitting round the ship all night, and that Sandie McDonald of Peterhead and 'lang' Peter Williamson of Shetland saw it, as also did Mr Milne on the bridge – so, having three witnesses, they can make a better case of it than the second mate did. I spoke to Milne after breakfast, and told him that he should be above such nonsense, and that as an officer he ought to set the men a better example. He shook his weatherbeaten head ominously, but answered with characteristic caution, 'Mebbe, aye, mebbe na, doctor,' he said, 'I didna ca' it a ghaist. I canna' say I preen my faith in sea-bogles an' the like, though there's a mony as claims to ha' seen a' that and waur. I'm no easy feared, but maybe your ain bluid would run a bit cauld, mun, if instead o' speerin' aboot it in daylicht ye were wi' me last night, an' seed an awfu' like shape, white an' gruesome, whiles here, whiles there, an' it greetin' and ca'ing in the darkness like a bit lambie that hae lost its mither. Ye would na' be sae ready to put it a' doon to auld wives' clavers then, I'm thinkin'.' I saw it was hopeless to reason with him, so contented myself with begging him as a personal favour to call me up the next time the spectre appeared – a request to which he acceded with many ejaculations expressive of his hopes that such an opportunity might never arise.

As I had hoped, the white desert behind us has become broken by many thin streaks of water which intersect it in all directions. Our latitude today was 80° 52' N, which shows that there is a strong southerly drift upon the pack. Should the wind continue favourable it will break up as rapidly as it formed. At present we can do nothing but smoke and wait and hope for the best. I am rapidly becoming a fatalist. When dealing with such uncertain factors as wind and ice a man can be nothing else. Perhaps it was the wind and sand of the Arabian deserts which gave the minds of the original followers of Mahomet their tendency to bow to kismet.

These spectral alarms have a very bad effect upon the captain. I feared that it might excite his sensitive mind, and endeavoured to conceal the absurd story from him, but unfortunately he overheard one of the men making an allusion to it and insisted upon being informed about it. As I had expected, it brought out all his latent lunacy in an exaggerated form. I can hardly believe that this is the same man who discoursed philosophy last night with the most critical acumen and coolest judgement. He is pacing backwards and forwards upon the quarter-deck like a caged tiger, stopping now and again to throw out his hands with a yearning gesture, and stare impatiently out over the ice. He keeps up a continual mutter to himself, and once he called out, 'But a little time, love – but a little time!' Poor fellow, it is sad to see a gallant seaman and accomplished gentleman reduced to such a pass and to think that imagination and delusion can cow a mind to which real danger was but the salt of life. Was ever a man in such a position as I, between a demented captain and a ghost-seeing mate? I sometimes think I am the only really sane man aboard the vessel – except perhaps the second engineer, who is a kind of ruminant, and would care nothing for all the fiends in the Red Sea so long as they would leave him alone and not disarrange his tools.

The ice is still opening rapidly, and there is every probability of our being able to make a start tomorrow morning. They will think I am inventing when I tell them at home all the strange things that have befallen me.

12.00 p.m. – I have been a good deal startled, though I feel steadier now, thanks to a stiff glass of brandy. I am hardly myself yet, however, as this handwriting will testify. The fact is, that I have gone through a very strange experience and am beginning to doubt whether I was justified in branding everyone on board as madmen because they professed to have seen things which did not seem reasonable to my understanding. Pshaw! I am a fool to let such a trifle unnerve me; and yet, coming as it does after all these alarms, it has an additional significance, for I cannot doubt either Mr Manson's story or that of the mate, now that I have experienced that which I used formerly to scoff at.

After all it was nothing very alarming – a mere sound, and that was all. I cannot expect that anyone reading this, if anyone ever should read it, will sympathise with my feelings or realise the effect which it produced upon me at the time. Supper was over, and I had gone on deck to have a quiet pipe before turning in. The night was very dark – so dark that, standing under the quarter-boat, I was unable to see the officer upon the bridge. I think I have already mentioned the extraordinary silence which prevails in these frozen seas. In other parts of the world, be they ever so barren, there is some slight vibration of the air – some faint hum, be it from the distant haunts of men, or from the leaves of the trees, or the wings of the birds, or even the faint rustle of the grass that covers the ground. One may not actively perceive the sound, and yet if it were withdrawn it would be missed. It is only here in these Arctic seas that stark, unfathomable stillness obtrudes itself upon you all in its gruesome reality. You find your tympanum straining to catch some little murmur, and dwelling eagerly upon every accidental sound within the vessel. In this state I was leaning against the bulwarks when there arose from the ice almost directly underneath me a cry, sharp and shrill, upon the silent air of the night, beginning, as it seemed to me, at a note such as prima donna never reached, and mounting from that ever higher and higher until it culminated in a long wail of agony, which might have been the last cry of a lost soul. The ghastly scream is still ringing in my ears. Grief, unutterable grief, seemed to be expressed in it, and a great longing, and yet through it all there was an occasional wild note of exultation. It shrilled out from close beside me, and yet as I glared into the darkness I could discern nothing. I waited some little time but without hearing any repetition of the sound, so I came below, more shaken than I have ever been in my life before. As I came down the companion I met Mr Milne coming up to relieve the watch. 'Weel, doctor,' he said, 'maybe that's auld wives' clavers tae? Did ye no hear it skirling? Maybe that's a supersteetion? What d'ye think o't noo?' I was obliged to apologise to the honest fellow, and acknowledge that I was as puzzled by it as he was. Perhaps tomorrow things may look different. At present I dare hardly write all that I think. Reading it again in days to come, when I have shaken off all these associations, I should despise myself for having been so weak.

September 18 — Passed a restless and uneasy night, still haunted by that strange sound. The captain does not look as if he had had much repose either, for his face is haggard and his eyes bloodshot. I have not told him of my adventure of last night, nor shall I. He is already restless and excited, standing up, sitting down, and apparently utterly unable to keep still.

A fine lead appeared in the pack this morning, as I had expected, and we were able to cast off our ice-anchor and steam about twelve miles in a west-sou'-westerly direction. We were then brought to a halt by a great floe as massive as any which we have left behind us. It bars our progress completely, so we can do nothing but anchor again and wait until it breaks up, which it will probably do within twenty-four hours, if the wind holds. Several bladder-nosed seals were seen swimming in the water, and one was shot, an immense creature more than eleven feet long. They are fierce, pugnacious animals, and are said to be more than a match for a bear. Fortunately they are slow and clumsy in their movements, so that there is little danger in attacking them upon the ice.

The captain evidently does not think we have seen the last of our troubles, though why he should take a gloomy view of the situation is more than I can fathom since everyone else on board considers that we have had a miraculous escape and are sure now to reach the open sea.

'I suppose you think it's all right now, doctor?' he said, as we sat together after dinner.

'I hope so,' I answered.

'We mustn't be too sure — and yet no doubt you are right. We'll all be in the arms of our own true loves before long, lad, won't we? But we mustn't be too sure — we mustn't be too sure.'

He sat silent a little, swinging his leg thoughtfully backwards and forwards. 'Look here,' he continued; 'it's a dangerous place this, even at its best — a treacherous, dangerous place. I have known men cut off very suddenly in a land like this. A slip would do it sometimes — a single slip, and down you go through a crack, and only a bubble on the green water to show where it was that you sank. It's a queer thing,' he continued with a nervous laugh, 'but all the years I've been in this country I never once thought of making a will — not that I have anything to leave in particular, but still when a man is exposed to danger he should have everything arranged and ready — don't you think so?'

'Certainly,' I answered, wondering what on earth he was driving at.

'He feels better for knowing it's all settled,' he went on. 'Now if anything should ever befall me, I hope that you will look after things for me. There is very little in the cabin, but such as it is I should like it to be sold, and the money divided in the same proportion as the oil-money among the crew. The chronometer I wish you to keep yourself as some slight remembrance of our voyage. Of course all this is a mere precaution, but I thought I would take the opportunity of speaking to you about it. I suppose I might rely upon you if there were any necessity?'

'Most assuredly,' I answered; 'and since you are taking this step, I may as well —'

'You! you!' he interrupted. '*You're* all right. What the devil is the matter with *you?* There, I didn't mean to be peppery, but I don't like to hear a young fellow, that has hardly begun life, speculating about death. Go up on deck and get some fresh air into your lungs instead of talking nonsense in the cabin, and encouraging me to do the same.'

The more I think of this conversation of ours the less do I like it. Why should the man be settling his affairs at the very time when we seem to be emerging from all danger? There must be some method in his madness. Can it be that he contemplates suicide? I remember that upon one occasion he spoke in a deeply reverent manner of the heinousness of the crime of self-destruction. I shall keep my eye upon him, however, and though I cannot obtrude upon the privacy of his cabin, I shall at least make a point of remaining on deck as long as he stays up.

Mr Milne pooh-poohs my fears, and says it is only the 'skipper's little way'. He himself takes a very rosy view of the situation. According to him we shall be out of the ice by the day after tomorrow, pass Jan Meyen two days after that, and sight Shetland in little more than a week. I hope he may not be too sanguine. His opinion may be fairly balanced against the gloomy precautions of the captain, for he is an old and experienced seaman and weighs his words well before uttering them.

*

The long-impending catastrophe has come at last. I hardly know what to write about it. The captain is gone. He may come back to us again alive, but I fear me — I fear me. It is now seven o'clock of the morning of the 19th of September. I have spent the whole night traversing the great ice-floe in front of us with a party of seamen in the hope of coming upon some trace of him, but in vain. I shall try to give some account of the circumstances which attended upon his disappearance. Should anyone ever chance to read the words which I put down, I trust they will remember that I do not write from conjecture or from hearsay, but that I, a sane and educated man, am describing accurately what actually occurred before my very eyes. My inferences are my own, but I shall be answerable for the facts.

The captain remained in excellent spirits after the conversation which I have recorded. He appeared to be nervous and impatient, however, frequently changing his position, and moving his limbs in an aimless choreic way which is characteristic of him at times. In a quarter of an hour he went upon deck seven times, only to descend after a few hurried paces. I followed him each time, for there was something about his face which confirmed my resolution of not letting him out of my sight. He seemed to observe the effect which his movements had produced, for he endeavoured by an overdone hilarity, laughing boisterously at the very smallest of jokes, to quiet my apprehensions.

After supper he went on to the poop once more, and I with him. The night was dark and very still, save for the melancholy soughing of the wind among the spars. A thick cloud was coming up from the north-west, and the ragged tentacles which it threw out in front of it were drifting across the face of the moon, which only shone now and again through a rift in the wrack. The captain paced rapidly backwards and forwards, and then seeing me still dogging him, he came across and hinted that he thought I should be better below – which, I need hardly say, had the effect of strengthening my resolution to remain on deck.

I think he forgot about my presence after this, for he stood silently leaning over the taffrail and peering out across the great desert of snow, part of which lay in shadow while part glittered mistily in the moonlight. Several times I could see by his movements that he was referring to his watch, and once he muttered a short sentence, of which I could only catch the one word 'ready'. I confess to having felt an eerie feeling creeping over me as I watched the loom of his tall figure through the darkness and noted how completely he fulfilled the idea of a man who is keeping a tryst. A tryst with whom? Some vague perception began to dawn upon me as I pieced one fact with another, but I was utterly unprepared for the sequel.

By the sudden intensity of his attitude I felt that he saw something. I crept up behind him. He was staring with an eager questioning gaze at what seemed to be a wreath of mist, blown swiftly in a line with the ship. It was a dim nebulous body, devoid of shape, sometimes more, sometimes less apparent, as the light fell on it. The moon was dimmed in its brilliancy at the moment by a canopy of thinnest cloud, like the coating of an anemone.

'Coming, lass, coming,' cried the skipper, in a voice of unfathomable tenderness and compassion, like one who soothes a beloved one by some favour long looked for, and as pleasant to bestow as to receive.

What followed happened in an instant. I had no power to interfere. He gave one spring to the top of the bulwarks and another which took him on to the ice, almost to the feet of the pale misty figure. He held out his hands as if to clasp it, and so ran into the darkness with outstretched arms and loving words. I still stood rigid and motionless, straining my eyes after his retreating form, until his voice died away in the distance. I never thought to see him again, but at that moment the moon shone out brilliantly through a chink in the cloudy heaven and illuminated the great field of ice. Then I saw his dark figure already a very long way off, running with prodigious speed across the frozen plain. That was the last glimpse which we caught of him – perhaps the last we ever shall. A party was organised to follow him, and I accompanied them, but the men's hearts were not in the work and nothing was found. Another will be formed within a few hours. I can hardly believe I have not been dreaming or suffering from some hideous nightmare as I write these things down.

7.30 p.m. – Just returned dead beat and utterly tired out from a second unsuccessful search for the captain. The floe is of enormous extent, for though we have traversed at least twenty miles of its surface, there has been no sign of its coming to an end. The frost has been so severe of late that the overlying snow is frozen as hard as granite, otherwise we might have had the footsteps to guide us. The crew are anxious that we should cast off and steam round the floe and so to the southward, for the ice has opened up during the night, and the sea is visible upon the horizon. They argue that Captain Craigie is certainly dead, and that we are all risking our lives to no purpose by remaining when we have an opportunity of escape. Mr Milne and I have had the greatest difficulty in persuading them to wait until tomorrow night, and have been compelled to promise that we will not under any circumstances delay our departure longer than that. We propose therefore to take a few hours' sleep and then to start upon a final search.

September 20, evening – I crossed the ice this morning with a party of men exploring the southern part of the floe, while Mr

Milne went off in a northerly direction. We pushed on for ten or twelve miles without seeing a trace of any living thing, except a single bird, which fluttered a great way over our heads, and which by its flight I should judge to have been a falcon. The southern extremity of the ice-field tapered away into a long narrow spit which projected out into the sea. When we came to the base of this promontory, the men halted, but I begged them to continue to the extreme end of it, that we might have the satisfaction of knowing that no possible chance had been neglected.

We had hardly gone a hundred yards before McDonald of Peterhead cried out that he saw something in front of us and began to run. We all got a glimpse of it and ran too. At first it was only a vague darkness against the white ice, but as we raced along together it took the shape of a man, and eventually of the man of whom we were in search. He was lying face downwards upon a frozen bank. Many little crystals of ice and feathers of snow had drifted on to him as he lay, and sparkled upon his dark seaman's jacket. As we came up some wandering puff of wind caught these tiny flakes in its vortex, and they whirled up into the air, partially descended again, and then, caught once more in the current, sped rapidly away in the direction of the sea. To my eyes it seemed but a snowdrift, but many of my companions averred that it started up in the shape of a woman, stooped over the corpse and kissed it, and then hurried away across the floe. I have learned never to ridicule any man's opinion, however strange it may seem. Sure it is that Captain Nicholas Craigie had met with no painful end, for there was a bright smile upon his blue pinched features, and his hands were still outstretched as though grasping at the strange visitor which had summoned him away into the dim world that lies beyond the grave.

We buried him the same afternoon with the ship's ensign around him and a thirty-two-pound shot at his feet. I read the burial service, while the rough sailors wept like children, for there were many who owed much to his kind heart and who showed now the affection which his strange ways had repelled during his lifetime. He went off the grating with a dull, sullen, splash, and as I looked into the green water I saw him go down, down, down until he was but a little flickering patch of white hanging upon the outskirts of eternal darkness. Then even that faded away and he was gone. There he shall lie, with his secret and his sorrows and his mystery all still buried in his breast, until that great day when the sea shall give up its dead and Nicholas Craigie come out from among the ice with the smile upon his face and his stiffened arms outstretched in greeting. I pray that his lot may be a happier one in that life than it has been in this.

I shall not continue my journal. Our road to home lies plain and clear before us and the great ice-field will soon be but a remembrance of the past. It will be some time before I get over the shock produced by recent events. When I began this record of our voyage I little thought of how I should be compelled to finish it. I am writing these final words in the lonely cabin, still starting at times and fancying I hear the quick nervous step of the dead man upon the deck above me. I entered his cabin tonight, as was my duty, to make a list of his effects in order that they might be entered in the official log. All was as it had been upon my previous visit, save that the picture which I have described as having hung at the end of his bed had been cut out of its frame, as with a knife, and was gone. With this last link in a strange chain of evidence I close my diary of the voyage of the *Polestar*.

Note by DR JOHN MCALISTER RAY *senior* – I have read over the strange events connected with the death of the captain of the

Polestar as narrated in the journal of my son. That everything occurred exactly as he describes it I have the fullest confidence, and, indeed, the most positive certainty, for I know him to be a strong-nerved and unimaginative man with the strictest regard for veracity. Still, the story is, on the face of it, so vague and so improbable that I was long opposed to its publication. Within the last few days, however, I have had independent testimony upon the subject which throws a new light upon it. I had run down to Edinburgh to attend a meeting of the British Medical Association, when I chanced to come across Dr P –, an old college chum of mine, now practising at Saltash, in Devonshire. Upon my telling him of this experience of my son's, he declared to me that he was familiar with the captain, and proceeded, to my no small surprise, to give me a description of him which tallied remarkably well with that given in the journal, except that he depicted him as a younger man. According to his account, he had been engaged to a young lady of singular beauty residing upon the Cornish coast. During his absence at sea his betrothed had died under circumstances of peculiar horror.

THE FURNISHED ROOM *BY* O. HENRY

William Sydney Porter was born in North Carolina on 11 September 1862. He left school at fifteen and moved to Texas several years later, where he married and worked as a journalist. In 1897 he was convicted of embezzling money, and he began a five-year sentence at Columbus, Ohio the following year. He began to write short stories while in prison, to raise money to support his family. Porter changed his name to O. Henry on his release from prison in 1901 and continued to write. His first collection of stories, *Cabbages and Kings*, was published three years later, followed by another nine collections and over six hundred stories. O. Henry died of cirrhosis of the liver on 5 June 1910 in New York.

R ESTLESS, ALWAYS moving, forever passing like time itself, are most of the people who live in those old red houses. This is on New York's West Side.

The people are homeless, yet they have a hundred homes. They go from furnished room to furnished room. They are transients, transients forever — transients in living place, transients in heart and mind. They sing the song, 'Home, Sweet Home,' but they sing it without feeling what it means. They can carry everything they own in one small box. They know nothing of gardens. To them, flowers and leaves are something to put on a woman's hat.

The houses of this part of the city have had a thousand people living in them. Therefore each house should have a thousand stories to tell. Perhaps most of these stories would not be interesting. But it would be strange if you did not feel, in some of these houses, that you were among people you could not see. The spirits of some who had lived and suffered there must surely remain, though their bodies had gone.

One evening a young man appeared, going from one to another of these big old houses, ringing the doorbell. At the twelfth house, he put down the bag he carried. He cleaned the dust from his face. Then he touched the bell. It sounded far, far away, as if it were ringing deep underground.

The woman who owned the house came to the door. The young man looked at her. He thought that she was like some fat, colourless, legless thing that had come up from a hole in the ground, hungrily hoping for something, or someone, to eat.

He asked if there was a room that he could have for the night.

'Come in,' said the woman. Her voice was soft, but for some reason he did not like it. 'I have the back room on the third floor. Do you wish to look at it?'

The young man followed her up. There was little light in the halls. He could not see where that light came from. The covering on the floor was old and ragged. There were places in the walls made, perhaps, to hold flowering plants. If this were true, the plants had died long before this evening. The air was bad; no flowers could have lived in it for long.

'This is the room,' said the woman in her soft, thick voice. 'It's a nice room. Someone is usually living in it. I had some very nice people in it last summer. I had no trouble with them. They paid on time. The water is at the end of the hall. Sprowls and Mooney had the room for three months. You know them? Theatre people. The gas is here. You see there is plenty of space to hang your clothes. It's a room everyone likes. If you don't take it, someone else will take it soon.'

'Do you have many theatre people living here?' asked the young man.

'They come and go. Many of my people work in the theatre. Yes, sir, this is the part of the city where theatre people live. They never stay long any place. They live in all the houses near here. They come and they go.'

The young man paid for the room for a week. He was going to stay there, he said, and rest. He counted out the money.

The room was all ready, she said. He would find everything that he needed. As she moved away he asked his question. He had asked it already a thousand times. It was always there, waiting to be asked again.

'A young girl – Eloise Vashner – do you remember her? Has she ever been in this house? She would be singing in the theatre, probably. A girl of middle height, thin, with red-gold hair and a small dark spot on her face near her left eye.'

'No, I don't remember the name. Theatre people change names as often as they change their rooms. They come and they go. No, I don't remember that one.'

No. Always no. He had asked his question for five months, and the answer was always no.

Every day he questioned men who knew theatre people. Had she gone to them to ask for work?

Every evening he went to the theatres. He went to good theatres and to bad ones. Some were so bad that he was afraid to find her there. Yet he went to them, hoping.

He who had loved her best had tried to find her. She had suddenly gone from her home. He was sure that this great city, this island, held her. But everything in the city was moving, restless. What was on top today, was lost at the bottom tomorrow.

The furnished room received the young man with a certain warmth. Or it seemed to receive him warmly. It seemed to promise that here he could rest. There was a bed and there were two chairs with ragged covers. Between the two windows there was a looking-glass about twelve inches wide. There were pictures on the walls.

The young man sat down in a chair, while the room tried to tell him its history. The words it used were strange, not easy to understand, as if they were words of many distant foreign countries.

There was a floor covering of many colours, like an island of flowers in the middle of the room. Dust lay all around it.

There was bright wallpaper on the wall. There was a fireplace. On the wall above it, some bright pieces of cloth were hanging. Perhaps they had been put there to add beauty to the room. This they did not do. And the pictures on the walls were pictures the young man had seen a hundred times before in other furnished rooms.

Here and there around the room were small objects forgotten by others who had used the room. There were pictures of theatre people, something to hold flowers, but nothing valuable.

One by one the little signs grew clear. They showed the young man the others who had lived there before him.

In front of the looking-glass there was a thin spot in the floor covering. That told him that women had been in the room.

Small fingermarks on the wall told of children, trying to feel their way to sun and air.

A larger spot on the wall made him think of someone, in anger, throwing something there.

Across the looking-glass, some person had written the name, 'Marie.'

It seemed to him that those who had lived in the furnished room had been angry with it, and had done all they could to hurt it. Perhaps their anger had been caused by the room's brightness and its coldness. For there was no true warmth in the room.

There were cuts and holes in the chairs and in the walls. The bed was half broken. The floor cried out as if in pain when it was walked on.

People for a time had called this room 'home,' and yet they had hurt it. This was a fact not easy to believe. But perhaps it was, strangely, a deep love of home that was the cause. The people who had lived in the room perhaps never knew what a real home was. But they knew that this room was not a home. Therefore their deep anger rose up and made them strike out.

The young man in the chair allowed these thoughts to move one by one, softly, through his mind.

At the same time, sounds and smells from other furnished rooms came into his room. He heard someone laughing, laughing in a manner that was neither happy nor pleasant. From other rooms he heard a woman talking too loudly; and he heard people playing games for money; and he heard a woman singing to a baby, and he heard someone weeping. Above him there was music. Doors opened and closed. The trains outside rushed noisily past. Some animal cried out in the night outside.

And the young man felt the breath of the house. It had a smell that was more than bad; it seemed cold and sick and old and dying.

Then suddenly, as he rested there, the room was filled with the strong, sweet smell of a flower, small and white, named mignonette. The smell came so surely and so strongly that it almost seemed like a living person entering the room. And the man cried aloud: 'What, dear?' as if he had been called.

He jumped up and turned around. The rich smell was near, and all around him. He opened his arms for it. For a moment he did not know where he was or what he was doing.

How could anyone be called by a smell? Surely it must have been a sound. But could a sound have touched him?

'She has been in this room,' he cried, and he began to seek some sign of her. He knew that if he found any small thing that had belonged to her, he would know that it was hers. If she had only touched it, he would know it. This smell of flowers that was all around him – she had loved it and had made it her own. Where did it come from?

The room had been carelessly cleaned. He found many small things that women had left. Something to hold their hair in place. Something to wear in the hair to make it more beautiful. A piece of cloth that smelled of another flower. A book. Nothing that had been hers.

And he began to walk around the room like a dog hunting a wild animal. He looked in corners. He got down on his hands and knees to look at the floor.

He wanted something that he could see. He could not realise that she was there beside, around, against, within, above him, near to him, calling him.

Then once again he felt the call. Once again he answered loudly: 'Yes, dear!' and turned, wild-eyed, to look at nothing. For he could not yet see the form and colour and love and reaching arms that were there in the smell of white flowers. Oh, God! Where did the smell of flowers come from? Since when has a smell had a voice to call? So he wondered, and went on seeking.

He found many small things, left by many who had used the room. But of her, who may have been there, whose spirit seemed to be there, he found no sign.

And then he thought of the owner.

He ran from the room, with its smell of flowers, going down and to a door where he could see a light.

She came out.

He tried to speak quietly. 'Will you tell me,' he asked her, 'who was in my room before I came here?'

'Yes, sir. I can tell you again. It was Sprowls and Mooney, as I said. It was really Mr and Mrs Mooney, but she used her own name. Theatre people do that.'

'Tell me about Mrs Mooney. What did she look like?'

'Black-haired, short and fat. They left here a week ago.'

'And before they were here?'

'There was a gentleman. Not in the theatre business. He didn't pay. Before him was Mrs Crowder and her two children. They stayed four months. And before them was old Mr Doyle. His sons paid for him. He had the room six months. That is a year, and further I do not remember.'

He thanked her and went slowly back to his room.

The room was dead. The smell of flowers had made it alive, but the smell of flowers was gone. In its place was the smell of the house.

His hope was gone. He sat looking at the yellow gaslight. Soon he walked to the bed and took the covers. He began to tear them into pieces. He pushed the pieces into every open space around windows and door. No air, now, would be able to enter the room. When all was as he wished it, he put out the burning gaslight. Then, in the dark, he started the gas again, and he lay down thankfully on the bed.

It was Mrs McCool's night to go and get them something cold to drink. So she went and came back, and sat with Mrs Purdy in one of those rooms underground where the women who own these old houses meet and talk.

'I have a young man in my third floor back room this evening,' said Mrs Purdy, taking a drink. 'He went up to bed two hours ago.'

'Is that true, Mrs Purdy?' said Mrs McCool. It was easy to see that she thought this was a fine and surprising thing. 'You always find someone to take a room like that. I don't know how you do it. Did you tell him about it?'

'Rooms,' said Mrs Purdy, in her soft thick voice, 'are furnished to be used by those that need them. I did not tell him, Mrs McCool.'

'You are right, Mrs Purdy. It's the money we get for the rooms that keeps us alive. You have the real feeling for business. There are many people who wouldn't take a room like that if they knew. If you told them that someone had died in the bed, and died by their own hand, they wouldn't enter the room.'

'As you say, we have our living to think of,' said Mrs Purdy.

'Yes, it is true. Only one week ago I helped you there in the third floor back room. She was a pretty little girl. And to kill herself with the gas! She had a sweet little face, Mrs Purdy.'

'She would have been called beautiful, as you say,' said Mrs Purdy, 'except for that dark spot she had growing by her left eye. Do fill up your glass again, Mrs McCool.'

THE FRIENDS OF THE FRIENDS
BY HENRY JAMES

Henry James was born on 15 April 1843 in New York to a wealthy and intellectual family and as a youth travelled widely and studied in Europe. He briefly studied law at Harvard before he took up writing full-time. His first novel, *Watch and Ward*, was published in 1871 and many followed including *Portrait of a Lady* (1881), *The Wings of the Dove* (1902), *The Ambassadors* (1903) and *The Golden Bowl* (1904). He also wrote short stories, reviews, biographies, plays and travel books. After a brief period in Paris, James moved to London. He later settled in Rye in Sussex and became a British citizen in 1915. Henry James died on 28 February 1916.

I FIND, as you prophesied, much that's interesting, but little that helps the delicate question – the possibility of publication. Her diaries are less systematic than I hoped; she only had a blessed habit of noting and narrating. She summarised, she saved; she appears seldom indeed to have let a good story pass without catching it on the wing. I allude of course not so much to things she heard as to things she saw and felt. She writes sometimes of herself, sometimes of others, sometimes of the combination. It's under this last rubric that she's usually most vivid. But it's not, you'll understand, when she's most vivid that she's always most publishable. To tell the truth she's fearfully indiscreet, or has at least all the material for making *me* so. Take as an instance the fragment I send you after dividing it for your convenience into several small chapters. It's the contents of a thin blank-book which I've had copied out and which has the merit of being nearly enough a rounded thing, an intelligible whole. These pages evidently date from years ago. I've read with the liveliest wonder the statement they so circumstantially make and done my best to swallow the prodigy they leave to be inferred. These things would be striking, wouldn't they? to any reader; but can you imagine for a moment my placing such a document before the world, even though, as if she herself had desired the world should have the benefit of it, she has given her friends neither name nor initials? Have you any sort of clue to their identity? I leave her the floor.

I

I KNOW perfectly of course that I brought it upon myself; but that doesn't make it any better. I was the first to speak of her to him — he had never even heard her mentioned. Even if I had happened not to speak someone else would have made up for it: I tried afterwards to find comfort in that reflexion. But the comfort of reflexions is thin: the only comfort that counts in life is not to have been a fool. That's a beatitude I shall doubtless never enjoy. 'Why you ought to meet her and talk it over' is what I immediately said. 'Birds of a feather flock together.' I told him who she was and that they were birds of a feather because if he had had in youth a strange adventure she had had about the same time just such another. It was well known to her friends — an incident she was constantly called on to describe. She was charming clever pretty unhappy; but it was none the less the thing to which she had originally owed her reputation.

Being at the age of eighteen somewhere abroad with an aunt she had had a vision of one of her parents at the moment of death. The parent was in England hundreds of miles away and so far as she knew neither dying nor dead. It was by day, in the museum of some great foreign town. She had passed alone, in advance of her companions, into a small room containing some famous work of art and occupied at that moment by two other persons. One of these was an old custodian; the second, before observing him, she took for a stranger, a tourist. She was merely conscious that he was bareheaded and seated on a bench. The instant her eyes rested on him however she beheld to her amazement her father, who, as if he had long waited for her, looked at her in singular distress and an impatience that was akin to reproach. She rushed to him with a bewildered cry, 'Papa, what *is* it?' but this was followed by an exhibition of still livelier feeling when on her movement he simply vanished, leaving the custodian and her relations, who were by that time at her heels, to gather round her in dismay. These persons, the official, the aunt, the cousins, were therefore in a manner witnesses of the fact – the fact at least of the impression made on her; and there was the further testimony of a doctor who was attending one of the party and to whom it was immediately afterwards communicated. He gave her a remedy for hysterics, but said to the aunt privately: 'Wait and see if something doesn't happen at home.' Something *had* happened – the poor father, suddenly and violently seized, had died that morning. The aunt, the mother's sister, received before the day was out a telegram announcing the event and requesting her to prepare her niece for it. Her niece was already prepared, and the girl's sense of this visitation remained of course indelible. We had all, as her friends, had it conveyed to us and had conveyed it creepily to each other. Twelve years had elapsed, and as a woman who had made an unhappy marriage and lived apart from her husband she had become interesting from other sources; but since the name she now bore was a name frequently borne, and since moreover her judicial separation, as things were going, could hardly count as a distinction, it was usual to qualify her as 'the one, you know, who saw her father's ghost'.

As for him, dear man, he had seen his mother's – so there you are! I had never heard of that till this occasion on which our closer, our pleasanter acquaintance led him, through some turn of the subject of our talk, to mention it and to inspire me in so doing with the impulse to let him know that he had a rival in the field – a person with whom he could compare notes. Later on his story became for him, perhaps because of my unduly repeating it, likewise a convenient worldly label; but it hadn't a year before been the ground on which he was introduced to me. He had other merits, just as she, poor thing, had others. I can honestly say that I was quite aware of them from the first – I discovered them sooner than he discovered mine. I remember how it struck me even at the time that his sense of mine was quickened by my having been able to match, though not indeed straight from my own experience, his curious anecdote. It dated, this anecdote, as hers did, from some dozen years before – a year in which, at Oxford, he had for some reason of his own been staying on into the 'Long'. He had been in the August afternoon on the river. Coming back into his room while it was still distinct daylight he found his mother standing there as if her eyes had been fixed on the door. He had had a letter from her that morning out of Wales, where she was staying with her father. At the sight of him she smiled with extraordinary radiance and extended her arms to him, and then as he sprang forward and joyfully opened his own she vanished from the place. He wrote to her that night, telling her what had happened; the letter had been carefully preserved. The next morning he heard of her death. He was through this chance of our talk extremely struck with the little prodigy I was able to produce for him. He had never encountered another case. Certainly they ought to meet, my friend and he; certainly they would have something in common. I would arrange this, wouldn't I? — if *she* didn't mind; for himself he didn't mind in the least. I had promised to speak to her of the matter as soon as possible, and within the week I was able to do so. She 'minded' as little as he; she was perfectly willing to see him. And yet no meeting was to occur — as meetings are commonly understood.

II

THAT'S JUST half my tale — the extraordinary way it was hindered. This was the fault of a series of accidents; but the accidents, persisting for years, became, to me and to others, a subject of mirth with either party. They were droll enough at first, then they grew rather a bore. The odd thing was that both parties were amenable: it wasn't a case of their being indifferent, much less of their being indisposed. It was one of the caprices of chance, aided I suppose by some rather settled opposition of their interests and habits. His were centred in his office, his eternal inspectorship, which left him small leisure, constantly calling him away and making him break engagements. He liked society, but he found it everywhere and took it at a run. I never knew at a given moment where he was, and there were times when for months together I never saw him. She was on her side practically suburban: she lived at Richmond and never went 'out'. She was a woman of distinction, but not of fashion, and felt, as people said, her situation. Decidedly proud and rather whimsical, she lived her life as she had planned it. There were things one could do with her, but one couldn't make her come to one's parties. One went indeed a little more than seemed quite convenient to hers, which consisted of her cousin, a cup of tea and the view. The tea was good; but the view was familiar, though perhaps not, like the cousin – a disagreeable old maid who had been of the group at the museum and with whom she now lived – offensively so. This connexion with an inferior relative, which had partly an economic motive – she proclaimed her companion a marvellous manager – was one of the little perversities we had to forgive her. Another was her estimate of the proprieties created by her rupture with her husband. That was extreme – many persons called it even morbid. She made no advances; she cultivated scruples; she suspected, or I should perhaps rather say she remembered, slights: she was one of the few women I've known whom that particular predicament had rendered modest rather than bold. Dear thing, she had some delicacy! Especially marked were the limits she had set to possible attentions from men: it was always her thought that her husband only waited to pounce on her. She discouraged if she didn't forbid the visits of male persons not senile: she said she could never be too careful.

When I first mentioned to her that I had a friend whom fate had distinguished in the same weird way as herself I put her quite at liberty to say 'Oh bring him out to see me!' I should probably have been able to bring him, and a situation perfectly innocent or at any rate comparatively simple would have been created. But she uttered no such word; she only said: 'I must meet him certainly; yes, I shall look out for him!' That caused the first delay, and meanwhile various things happened. One of them was that as time went on she made, charming as she was, more and more friends, and that it regularly befell that these friends were sufficiently also friends of his to bring him up in conversation. It was odd that without belonging, as it were, to the same world or, according to the horrid term, the same set, my baffled pair should have happened in so many cases to fall in with the same people and make them join in the droll chorus. She had friends who didn't know each other but who inevitably and punctually recommended *him*. She had also the sort of originality, the intrinsic interest, that led her to be kept by each of us as a private resource, cultivated jealously, more or less in secret, as a person whom one didn't meet in society, whom it was not for everyone – whom it was not for the vulgar – to approach, and with whom therefore acquaintance was particularly difficult and particularly precious. We saw her separately, with appointments and conditions, and found it made on the whole for harmony not to tell each other. Somebody had always had a note from her still later than somebody else. There was some silly woman who for a long time, among the unprivileged, owed to three simple visits to Richmond a reputation for being intimate with 'lots of awfully clever out-of-the-way people'.

Everyone has had friends it has seemed a happy thought to bring together, and everyone remembers that his happiest thoughts have not been his greatest successes; but I doubt if there was ever a case in which the failure was in such direct proportion to the quantity of influence set in motion. It's really perhaps here the quantity of influence that was most remarkable. My lady and my gentleman each pronounced it to me and others quite a subject for a roaring farce. The reason first given had with time dropped out of sight and fifty better ones flourished on top of it. They were so awfully alike: they had the same ideas and tricks and tastes, the same prejudices and superstitions and heresies; they said the same things and sometimes did them; they liked and disliked the same persons and places, the same books, authors and styles; there were touches of resemblance even in their looks and features. It established much of a propriety that they were in common parlance equally 'nice' and almost equally handsome. But the great sameness, for wonder and chatter, was their rare perversity in regard to being photographed. They were the only persons ever heard of who had never been 'taken' and who had a passionate objection to it. They just *wouldn't* be — no, not for anything anyone could say. I had loudly complained of this; him in particular I had so vainly desired to be able to show on my drawing-room chimney-piece in a Bond Street frame. It was at any rate the very liveliest of all the reasons why they ought to know each other — all the lively reasons reduced to naught by the strange law that had made them bang so many doors in each other's face, made them the buckets in the well, the two ends of the see-saw, the two parties in the State, so that when one was up the other was down, when one was out the other was in; neither by any possibility entering a house till the other had left it or leaving it all unawares till the other was at hand. They only arrived when they had been given up, which was precisely also when they departed. They were in a word alternate and incompatible; they missed each other with an inveteracy that could be explained only by its being preconcerted. It was however so far from preconcerted that it had ended — literally after several years — by disappointing and annoying them. I don't think their curiosity was lively till it had been proved utterly vain. A great deal was of course done to help them, but it merely laid wires for them to trip. To give examples I should have to have taken notes; but I happen to remember that neither had ever been able to dine on the right occasion. The right occasion for each was the occasion that would be wrong for the other. On the wrong one they were most punctual, and there were never any but wrong ones. The very elements conspired and the constitution of man re-enforced them. A cold, a headache, a bereavement, a storm, a fog, an earthquake, a cataclysm, infallibly intervened. The whole business was beyond a joke.

Yet as a joke it had still to be taken, though one couldn't help feeling that the joke had made the situation serious, had produced on the part of each a consciousness, an awkwardness, a positive dread of the last accident of all, the only one with any freshness left, the accident that *would* bring them together. The final effect of its predecessors had been to kindle this instinct. They were quite ashamed – perhaps even a little of each other. So much preparation, so much frustration: what indeed could be good enough for it all to lead up to? A mere meeting would be mere flatness. Did I see them at the end of years, they often asked, just stupidly confronted? If they were bored by the joke they might be worse bored by something else. They made exactly the same reflexions, and each in some manner was sure to hear of the other's. I really think it was this peculiar diffidence that finally controlled the situation. I mean that if they had failed for the first year or two because they couldn't help it, they kept up the habit because they had – what shall I call it? – grown nervous. It really took some lurking volition to account for anything both so regular and so ridiculous.

III

WHEN TO crown our long acquaintance I accepted his renewed offer of marriage it was humorously said, I know, that I had made the gift of his photograph a condition.

This was so far true that I had refused to give him mine without it. At any rate I had him at last, in his high distinction, on the chimney-piece, where the day she called to congratulate me she came nearer than she had ever done to seeing him. He had in being taken set her an example that I invited her to follow; he had sacrificed his perversity – wouldn't she sacrifice hers? She too must give me something on my engagement – wouldn't she give me the companion-piece? She laughed and shook her head; she had headshakes whose impulse seemed to come from as far away as the breeze that stirs a flower. The companion-piece to the portrait of my future husband was the portrait of his future wife. She had taken her stand – she could depart from it as little as she could explain it. It was a prejudice, an *entêtement*, a vow – she would live and die unphotographed. Now too she was alone in that state: this was what she liked; it made her so much more original. She rejoiced in the fall of her late associate and looked a long time at his picture, about which she made no memorable remark, though she even turned it over to see the back. About our engagement she was charming – full of cordiality and sympathy. 'You've known him even longer than I've *not*,' she said, 'and that seems a very long time.' She understood how we had jogged together over hill and dale and how inevitable it was that we should now rest together. I'm definite about all this because what followed is so strange that it's a kind of relief to me to mark the point up to which our relations were as natural as ever. It was I myself who in a sudden madness altered and destroyed them. I see now that she gave me no pretext and that I only found one in the way she looked at the fine face in the Bond Street frame. How then would I have had her look at it? What I had wanted from the first was to make her care for him. Well, that was what I still wanted – up to the moment of her having promised me she would on this occasion really aid me to break the silly spell that had kept them asunder. I had arranged with him to do his part if she would as triumphantly do hers. I was on a different footing now – I was on a footing to answer for him. I would positively engage that at five on the following Saturday he should be on that spot. He was out of town on pressing business, but, pledged to keep his promise to the letter, would return on purpose and in abundant time. 'Are you perfectly sure?' I remember she asked, looking grave and considering: I thought she had turned a little pale. She was tired, she was indisposed: it was a pity he was to see her after all at so poor a moment. If he only *could* have seen her five years before! However, I replied that this time I was sure and that success therefore depended simply on herself. At five o'clock on the Saturday she would find him in a particular chair I pointed out, the one in which he usually sat and in which – though this I didn't mention – he had been sitting when, the week before, he put the question of our future to me in the way that had brought me round. She looked at it in silence, just as she had looked at the photograph, while I repeated for the twentieth time that it was too preposterous one shouldn't somehow succeed in introducing to one's dearest friend one's second self. '*Am* I your dearest friend?' she asked with a smile that for a moment brought back her beauty. I replied by pressing her to my bosom; after which she said: 'Well, I'll come. I'm extraordinarily afraid, but you may count on me.'

When she had left me I began to wonder what she was afraid of, for she had spoken as if she fully meant it. The next day, late in the afternoon, I had three lines from her: she had found on getting home the announcement of her husband's death. She hadn't seen him for seven years, but she wished me to know it in this way before I should hear of it in another. It made however in her life, strange and sad to say, so little difference that she would scrupulously keep her appointment. I rejoiced for

her – I supposed it would make at least the difference of her having more money; but even in this diversion, far from forgetting
she had said she was afraid, I seemed to catch sight of a reason
for her being so. Her fear, as the evening went on, became con-
tagious, and the contagion took in my breast the form of a
sudden panic. It wasn't jealousy – it just was the dread of jealousy. I called myself a fool for not having been quiet till we were
man and wife. After that I should somehow feel secure. It was
only a question of waiting another month – a trifle surely for
people who had waited so long. It had been plain enough she
was nervous, and now she was free her nervousness wouldn't be
less. What was it therefore but a sharp foreboding? She had been
hitherto the victim of interference, but it was quite possible she
would henceforth be the source of it. The victim in that case
would be my simple self. What had the interference been but the
finger of Providence pointing out a danger? The danger was of
course for poor *me*. It had been kept at bay by a series of accidents unexampled in their frequency; but the reign of accident
was now visibly at an end. I had an intimate conviction that both
parties would keep the tryst. It was more and more impressed on
me that they were approaching, converging. They were like the
seekers for the hidden object in the game of blindfold; they had
one and the other begun to 'burn'. We had talked about breaking the spell; well, it would be effectually broken – unless indeed
it should merely take another form and overdo their encounters
as it had overdone their escapes. This was something I couldn't
sit still for thinking of; it kept me awake – at midnight I was full
of unrest. At last I felt there was only one way of laying the
ghost. If the reign of accident was over I must just take up the
succession. I sat down and wrote a hurried note which would
meet him on his return and which as the servants had gone to
bed I sallied forth bareheaded into the empty gusty street to

drop into the nearest pillar-box. It was to tell him that I shouldn't be able to be at home in the afternoon as I had hoped and that he must postpone his visit till dinner-time. This was an implication that he would find me alone.

IV

WHEN ACCORDINGLY at five she presented herself I naturally felt false and base. My act had been a momentary madness, but I had at least, as they say, to live up to it. She remained an hour; he of course never came; and I could only persist in my perfidy. I had thought it best to let her come; singular as this now seems to me I held it diminished my guilt. Yet as she sat there so visibly white and weary, stricken with a sense of everything her husband's death had opened up, I felt a really piercing pang of pity and remorse. If I didn't tell her on the spot what I had done it was because I was too ashamed. I feigned astonishment – I feigned it to the end; I protested that if ever I had had confidence I had had it that day. I blush as I tell my story – I take it as my penance. There was nothing indignant I didn't say about him; I invented suppositions, attenuations; I admitted in stupefaction, as the hands of the clock travelled, that their luck hadn't turned. She smiled at this vision of their 'luck', but she looked anxious – she looked unusual: the only thing that kept me up was the fact that, oddly enough, she wore mourning – no great depths of crape, but simple and scrupulous black. She had in her bonnet three small black feathers. She carried a little muff of astrachan. This put me, by the aid of some acute reflexion, a little in the right. She had written to me that the sudden event made no difference for her, but apparently it made as much difference as that. If she was inclined to the usual forms why didn't she observe that of not going the first day or two out to tea? There was someone she wanted so much to see that she couldn't wait till her husband was buried. Such a betrayal of eagerness made me hard and cruel enough to practise my odious deceit, though at the same time, as the hour waxed and waned, I suspected in her something deeper still than disappointment and somewhat less successfully concealed. I mean a strange underlying relief, the soft low emission of the breath that comes when a danger is past. What happened as she spent her barren hour with me was that at last she gave him up. She let him go for ever. She made the most graceful joke of it that I've ever seen made of anything; but it was for all that a great date in her life. She spoke with her mild gaiety of all the other vain times, the long game of hide-and-seek, the unprecedented queerness of such a relation. For it *was,* or had been, a relation, wasn't it, hadn't it? That was just the absurd part of it. When she got up to go I said to her that it was more a relation than ever, but that I hadn't the face after what had occurred to propose to her for the present another opportunity. It was plain that the only valid opportunity would be my accomplished marriage. Of course she would be at my wedding? It was even to be hoped that *he* would.

'If *I* am, he won't be!' – I remember the high quaver and the little break of her laugh. I admitted there might be something in that. The thing was therefore to get us safely married first. 'That won't help us. Nothing will help us!' she said as she kissed me farewell. 'I shall never, never see him!' It was with those words she left me.

I could bear her disappointment as I've called it; but when a couple of hours later I received him at dinner I discovered I couldn't bear his. The way my manoeuvre might have affected him hadn't been particularly present to me; but the result of it was the first word of reproach that had ever yet dropped from him. I say 'reproach' because that expression is scarcely too strong for the terms in which he conveyed to me his surprise that under the extraordinary circumstances I shouldn't have found some means not to deprive him of such an occasion. I might really have managed either not to be obliged to go out or to let their meeting take place all the same. They would probably have got on, in my drawing-room, well enough without me. At this I quite broke down – I confessed my iniquity and the miserable reason of it. I hadn't put her off and I hadn't gone out; she had been there and, after waiting for him an hour, had departed in the belief that he had been absent by his own fault.

'She must think me a precious brute!' he exclaimed. 'Did she say of me' – and I remember the just perceptible catch of breath in his pause – 'What she had a right to say?'

'I assure you she said nothing that showed the least feeling. She looked at your photograph, she even turned round the back of it, on which your address happens to be inscribed. Yet it provoked her to no demonstration. She doesn't care so much as all that.'

'Then why are you afraid of her?'

'It wasn't of her I was afraid. It was of you.'

'Did you think I'd be so sure to fall in love with her? You never alluded to such a possibility before,' he went on as I remained silent. 'Admirable person as you pronounced her, that wasn't the light in which you showed her to me.'

'Do you mean that if it *had* been you'd have managed by this time to catch a glimpse of her? I didn't fear things then,' I added. 'I hadn't the same reason.'

He kissed me at this, and when I remembered that she had done so an hour or two before I felt for an instant as if he were taking from my lips the very pressure of hers. In spite of kisses the incident had shed a certain chill, and I suffered horribly from the sense that he had seen me guilty of a fraud. He had seen it only through my frank avowal, but I was as unhappy as if I had a stain to efface. I couldn't get over the manner of his looking at me when I spoke of her apparent indifference to his not having come. For the first time since I had known him he seemed to have expressed a doubt of my word. Before we parted I told him that I'd un-deceive her – start the first thing in the morning for Richmond and there let her know he had been blameless. At this he kissed me again. I'd expiate my sin, I said; I'd humble myself in the dust; I'd confess and ask to be forgiven. At this he kissed me once more.

V

IN THE TRAIN the next day this struck me as a good deal for him to have consented to; but my purpose was firm enough to carry me on. I mounted the long hill to where the view begins, and then I knocked at her door. I was a trifle mystified by the fact that her blinds were still drawn, reflecting that if in the stress of my compunction I had come early I had certainly yet allowed people time to get up.

'At home, mum? She has left home for ever.'

I was extraordinarily startled by this announcement of the elderly parlour-maid. 'She has gone away?'

'She's dead, mum, please.' Then as I gasped at the horrible word: 'She died last night.'

The loud cry that escaped me sounded even in my own ears like some harsh violation of the hour. I felt for the moment as if I had killed her; I turned faint and saw through a vagueness the woman hold out her arms to me. Of what next happened I've no recollection, nor of anything but my friend's poor stupid cousin, in a darkened room, after an interval that I suppose very brief, sobbing at me in a smothered accusatory way. I can't say how long it took me to understand, to believe and then to press back with an immense effort that pang of responsibility which, super-stitiously, insanely, had been at first almost all I was conscious of. The doctor, after the fact, had been superlatively wise and clear: he was satisfied of a long-latent weakness of the heart, determined probably years before by the agitations and terrors to which her marriage had introduced her. She had had in those days cruel scenes with her husband, she had been in fear of her life. All emotion, everything in the nature of anxiety and sus-pense had been after that to be strongly deprecated, as in her marked cultivation of a quiet life she was evidently well aware; but who could say that anyone, especially a 'real lady', might be successfully protected from *every* little rub? She had had one a day or two before in the news of her husband's death – since there were shocks of all kinds, not only those of grief and sur-prise. For that matter she had never dreamed of so near a release: it had looked uncommonly as if he would live as long as herself. Then in the evening, in town, she had manifestly had some mis-adventure: something must have happened there that it would be imperative to clear up. She had come back very late – it was past eleven o'clock, and on being met in the hall by her cousin, who was extremely anxious, had allowed she was tired and must rest a moment before mounting the stairs. They had passed together into the dining-room, her companion proposing a glass of wine and bustling to the sideboard to pour it out. This took but a moment, and when my informant turned round our poor friend had not had time to seat herself. Suddenly, with a small moan that was barely audible, she dropped upon the sofa. She was dead. What unknown 'little rub' had dealt her the blow? What concussion, in the name of wonder, *had* awaited her in town? I mentioned immediately the one thinkable ground of disturbance – her having failed to meet at my house, to which by invitation for the purpose she had come at five o'clock, the gentleman I was to be married to, who had been accidentally kept away and with whom she had no acquaintance whatever. This obviously counted for little; but something else might easily have occurred: nothing in the London streets was more possible than an accident, especially an accident in those desperate cabs. What had she done, where had she gone on leaving my house? I had taken for granted she had gone straight home. We both presently remembered that in her excursions to town she sometimes, for convenience, for refreshment, spent an hour or two at the 'Gentlewomen', the quiet little ladies' club, and I promised that it should be my first care to make at that establishment an earnest appeal. Then we entered the dim and dreadful chamber where she lay locked up in death and where, asking after a little to be left alone with her, I remained for half an hour. Death had made her, had kept her beautiful; but I felt above all, as I kneeled at her bed, that it had made her, had kept her silent. It had turned the key on something I was concerned to know.

On my return from Richmond and after another duty had been performed I drove to his chambers. It was the first time, but I had often wanted to see them. On the staircase, which, as the house contained twenty sets of rooms, was unrestrictedly public, I met his servant, who went back with me and ushered

me in. At the sound of my entrance he appeared in the doorway
of a further room, and the instant we were alone I produced my
news: 'She's dead!'

'Dead?' He was tremendously struck, and I noticed he had no
need to ask whom, in this abruptness, I meant.

'She died last evening – just after leaving me.'

He stared with the strangest expression, his eyes searching
mine as for a trap. 'Last evening – after leaving you?' He
repeated my words in stupefaction. Then he brought out, so that
it was in stupefaction I heard, 'Impossible! I saw her.'

'You "saw" her?'

'On that spot – where you stand.'

This called back to me after an instant, as if to help me to take
it in, the great wonder of the warning of his youth. 'In the hour
of death – I understand: as you so beautifully saw your mother.'

'Ah *not* as I saw my mother – not that way, not that way!' He
was deeply moved by my news – far more moved, it was plain,
than he would have been the day before: it gave me a vivid sense
that, as I had then said to myself, there was indeed a relation
between them and that he had actually been face to face with
her. Such an idea, by its reassertion of his extraordinary privilege, would have suddenly presented him as painfully abnormal
hadn't he vehemently insisted on the difference. 'I saw her living. I saw her to speak to her. I saw her as I see you now.'

It's remarkable that for a moment, though only for a moment,
I found relief in the more personal, as it were, but also the more
natural, of the two odd facts. The next, as I embraced this image
of her having come to him on leaving me and of just what it
accounted for in the disposal of her time, I demanded with a
shade of harshness of which I was aware: 'What on earth did she
come for?'

He had now had a minute to think – to recover himself and

judge of effects, so that if it was still with excited eyes he spoke he showed a conscious redness and made an inconsequent attempt to smile away the gravity of his words. 'She came just to see me. She came – after what had passed at your house – so that we *should*, nevertheless at last meet. The impulse seemed to me exquisite, and that was the way I took it.'

I looked round the room where she had been – where *she* had been and I never had till now. 'And was the way you took it the way she expressed it?'

'She only expressed it by being here and by letting me look at her. That was enough!' he cried with an extraordinary laugh.

I wondered more and more. 'You mean she didn't speak to you?'

'She said nothing. She only looked at me as I looked at her.'

'And you didn't speak either?'

He gave me again his painful smile. 'I thought of *you*. The situation was every way delicate. I used the finest tact. But she saw she had pleased me.' He even repeated his dissonant laugh.

'She evidently "pleased" you!' Then I thought a moment. 'How long did she stay?'

'How can I say? It seemed twenty minutes, but it was probably a good deal less.'

'Twenty minutes of silence!' I began to have my definite view and now in fact quite to clutch at it. 'Do you know you're telling me a thing positively monstrous?'

He had been standing with his back to the fire; at this, with a pleading look, he came to me. 'I beseech you, dearest, to take it kindly.'

I could take it kindly, and I signified as much; but I couldn't somehow, as he rather awkwardly opened his arms, let him draw me to him. So there fell between us for an appreciable time the discomfort of a great silence.

VI

H E BROKE it by presently saying: 'There's absolutely no doubt of her death?'

'Unfortunately none. I've just risen from my knees by the bed where they've laid her out.'

He fixed his eyes hard on the floor; then he raised them to mine.'How does she look?'

'She looks — at peace.'

He turned away again while I watched him; but after a moment he began: 'At what hour then —?'

'It must have been near midnight. She dropped as she reached her house — from an affection of the heart which she knew herself and her physician knew her to have, but of which, patiently, bravely, she had never spoken to me.'

He listened intently and for a minute was unable to speak. At last he broke out with an accent of which the almost boyish confidence, the really sublime simplicity, rings in my ears as I write: 'Wasn't she *wonderful*!' Even at the time I was able to do it justice enough to answer that I had always told him so; but the next minute, as if after speaking he had caught a glimpse of what he might have made me feel, he went on quickly: 'You can easily understand that if she didn't get home till midnight —'

I instantly took him up. 'There was plenty of time for you to have seen her? How so,' I asked, 'when you didn't leave my house till late? I don't remember the very moment — I was preoccupied. But you know that though you said you had lots to do you sat for some time after dinner. She, on her side, was all the evening at the "Gentlewomen", I've just come from there – I've ascertained. She had tea there; she remained a long long time?'

'What was she doing all the long long time?'

I saw him eager to challenge at every step my account of the matter; and the more he showed this the more I was moved to emphasise that version, to prefer with apparent perversity an explanation which only deepened the marvel and the mystery, but which, of the two prodigies it had to choose from, my reviving jealously found easiest to accept. He stood there pleading with a candour that now seems to me beautiful for the privilege of having in spite of supreme defeat known the living woman; while I, with a passion I wonder at today, though it still smoulders in a manner in its ashes, could only reply that, through a strange gift shared by her with his mother and on her own side likewise hereditary, the miracle of his youth had been renewed for him, the miracle of hers for her. She had been to him – yes, and by an impulse as charming as he liked; but oh she hadn't been in the body! It was a simple question of evidence. I had had, I maintained, a definite statement of what she had done – most of the time – at the little club. The place was almost empty, but the servants had noticed her. She had sat motionless in a deep chair by the drawing-room fire; she had leaned back her head, she had closed her eyes, she had seemed softly to sleep.

'I see. But till what o'clock?'

'There', I was obliged to answer, 'the servants fail me a little. The portress in particular is unfortunately a fool, even though she too is supposed to be a Gentlewoman. She was evidently at that period of the evening, without a substitute and against regulations, absent for some little time from the cage in which it's her business to watch the comings and goings. She's muddled, she palpably prevaricates; so I can't positively, from her observation, give you an hour. But it was remarked toward half-past ten that our poor friend was no longer in the club.'

It suited him down to the ground. 'She came straight here, and from here she went straight to the train.'

'She couldn't have run it so close,' I declared. 'That was a thing she particularly never did.'

'There was no need of running it close, my dear – she had plenty of time. Your memory's at fault about my having left you late: I left you, as it happens, unusually early. I'm sorry my stay with you seemed long, for I was back here by ten.'

'To put yourself into your slippers', I retorted, 'and fall asleep in your chair. You slept till morning – you saw her in a dream!' He looked at me in silence and with sombre eyes – eyes that showed me he had some irritation to repress. Presently I went on: 'You had a visit, at an extraordinary hour, from a lady – *soit*: nothing in the world's more probable. But there are ladies and ladies. How in the name of goodness, if she was unannounced and dumb and you had into the bargain never seen the least portrait of her – how could you identify the person we're talking of?'

'Haven't I to absolute satiety heard her described? I'll describe her for you in every particular.'

'Don't!' I cried with a promptness that made him laugh once more. I coloured at this, but I continued: 'Did your servant introduce her?'

'He wasn't here – he's always away when he's wanted. One of the features of this big house is that from the street-door the different floors are accessible practically without challenge. My servant makes love to a young person employed in the rooms above these, and he had a long bout of it last evening. When he's out on that job he leaves my outer door, on the staircase, so much ajar as to enable him to slip back without a sound. The door then only requires a push. She pushed it — that simply took a little courage.'

'A little? It took tons! And it took all sorts of impossible calculations.'

'Well, she had them — she made them. Mind you, I don't deny for a moment', he added, 'that it was very very wonderful!'

Something in his tone kept me a time from trusting myself to speak. At last I said: 'How did she come to know where you live?'

'By remembering the address on the little label the shop-people happily left sticking to the frame I had had made for my photograph.'

'And how was she dressed?'

'In mourning, my own dear. No great depths of crape, but simple and scrupulous black. She had in her bonnet three small black feathers. She carried a little muff of astrachan. She has near the left eye', he continued, 'a tiny vertical scar —'

I stopped him short. 'The mark of a caress from her husband.' Then I added: 'How close you must have been to her!' He made no answer to this, and I thought he blushed, observing which I broke straight off. 'Well, goodbye.'

'You won't stay a little?' He came to me again tenderly, and this time I suffered him. 'Her visit had its beauty,' he murmured as he held me, 'but yours has a greater one.'

I let him kiss me, but I remembered, as I had remembered the day before, that the last kiss she had given, as I supposed, in this world had been for the lips he touched. 'I'm life, you see,' I answered. 'What you saw last night was death.'

'It was life — it was life!'

He spoke with a soft stubbornness — I disengaged myself. We stood looking at each other hard. 'You describe the scene — so far as you describe it at all – in terms that are incomprehensible. She was in the room before you knew it?'

'I looked up from my letter-writing – at that table under the lamp I had been wholly absorbed in it – and she stood before me.'

'Then what did you do?'

'I sprang up with an ejaculation, and she, with a smile, laid her finger, ever so warningly, yet with a sort of delicate dignity, to her lips. I knew it meant silence, but the strange thing was that it seemed immediately to explain and to justify her. We at any rate stood for a time that, as I've told you, I can't calculate, face to face. It was just as you and I stand now.'

'Simply staring?'

He shook an impatient head. 'Ah! *we're* not staring!'

'Yes, but we're talking.'

'Well, *we* were – after a fashion.' He lost himself in the memory of it. 'It was as friendly as this.' I had on my tongue's end to ask if that was saying much for it, but I made the point instead that what they had evidently done was to gaze in mutual admiration. Then I asked if his recognition of her had been immediate. 'Not quite,' he replied, 'for of course I didn't expect her; but it came to me long before she went who she was – who only she could be.'

I thought a little. 'And how did she at last go?'

'Just as she arrived. The door was open behind her and she passed out.'

'Was she rapid – slow?'

'Rather quick. But looking behind her,' he smiled to add. 'I let her go, for I perfectly knew I was to take it as she wished.'

I was conscious of exhaling a long vague sigh. 'Well, you must take it now as I wish – you must let *me* go.'

At this he drew near me again, detaining and persuading me, declaring with all due gallantry that I was a very different matter. I'd have given anything to have been able to ask him if he had touched her, but the words refused to form themselves: I knew to the last tenth of a tone how horrid and vulgar they'd sound. I said something else – I forget exactly what; it was feebly tortuous and intended, meanly enough, to make him tell me without my putting the question. But he didn't tell me; he only repeated, as from a glimpse of the propriety of soothing and consoling me, the sense of his declaration of some minutes before – the assurance that she was indeed exquisite, as I had always insisted, but that I was his 'real' friend and his very own for ever. This led me to reassert, in the spirit of my previous rejoinder, that I had at least the merit of being alive; which in turn drew from him again the flash of contradiction I dreaded. 'Oh *she* was live! She was, she was!'

'She was dead, she was dead!' I asseverated with an energy, a determination it should *be* so, which comes back to me now almost as grotesque. But the sound of the word as it rang out filled me suddenly with horror, and all the natural emotion the meaning of it might have evoked in other conditions gathered and broke in a flood. It rolled over me that here was a great affection quenched and how much I had loved and trusted her. I had a vision at the same time of the lonely beauty of her end. 'She's gone – she's lost to us for ever!' I burst into sobs.

'That's exactly what I feel,' he exclaimed, speaking with extreme kindness and pressing me to him for comfort. 'She's gone; she's lost to us for ever: so what does it matter now?' He bent over me, and when his face had touched mine I scarcely knew if it were wet with my tears or with his own.

VII

I T WAS my theory, my conviction, it became, as I may say, my attitude, that they had still never 'met'; and it was just on this ground I felt it generous to ask him to stand with me at her grave. He did so very modestly and tenderly, and I assumed, though he himself clearly cared nothing for the danger, that the solemnity of the occasion, largely made up of persons who had known them both and had a sense of the long joke, would sufficiently deprive his presence of all light association. On the question of what had happened the evening of her death little more passed between us; I had been taken by a horror of the element of evidence. On either hypothesis it was gross and prying. He on his side lacked producible corroboration – everything, that is, but a statement of his house-porter, on his own admission a most casual and intermittent personage – that between the hours of ten o'clock and midnight no less than three ladies in deep black had flitted in and out of the place. This proved far too much; we had neither of us any use for three. He knew I considered I had accounted for every fragment of her time, and we dropped the matter as settled; we abstained from further discussion. What *I* knew however was that he abstained to please me rather than because he yielded to my reasons. He didn't yield – he was only indulgent; he clung to his interpretation because he liked it better. He liked it better, I held, because it had more to say to his vanity. That, in a similar position, wouldn't have been its effect on me, though I had doubtless quite as much; but these are things of individual humour and as to which no person can judge for another. I should have supposed it more gratifying to be the subject of one of those inexplicable occurrences that are chronicled in thrilling books and disputed about at learned meetings; I could conceive, on the part of a being just engulfed in the infinite and still vibrating with human emotion, of nothing more fine and pure, more high and august, than such an impulse of reparation, of admonition, or even of curiosity. *That* was beautiful, if one would, and I should in his place have thought more of myself for being so distinguished and so selected. It was public that he had already, that he had long figured in that light, and what was such a fact in itself but almost a proof? Each of the strange visitations contributed to establish the other. He had a different feeling; but he had also, I hasten to add, an unmistakeable desire not to make a stand or, as they say, a fuss about it. I might believe what I liked – the more so that the whole thing was in a manner a mystery of my producing. It was an event of my history, a puzzle of my consciousness, not of his; therefore he would take about it any tone that struck me as convenient. We had both at all events other business on hand; we were pressed with preparations for our marriage.

Mine were assuredly urgent, but I found as the days went on that to believe what I 'liked' was to believe what I was more and more intimately convinced of. I found also that I didn't like it so much as that came to, or that the pleasure at all events was far from being the cause of my conviction. My obsession, as I may really call it and as I began to perceive, refused to be elbowed away, as I had hoped, by my sense of paramount duties. If I had a great deal to do I had still more to think of, and the moment came when my occupations were gravely menaced by my thoughts. I see it all now, I feel it, I live it over. It's terribly void of joy, it's full indeed to overflowing of bitterness; and yet I must do myself justice – I couldn't have been other than I was. The same strange impressions, had I to meet them again, would produce the same deep anguish, the same sharp doubts, the same still sharper certainties. Oh it's all easier to remember than to write, but even could I retrace the business hour by hour, could I find terms for the inexpressible, the ugliness and the pain would quickly stay my hand. Let me then note very simply and briefly that a week before our wedding-day, three weeks after her death, I knew in all my fibres that I had something very serious to look in the face and that if I was to make this effort I must make it on the spot and before another hour should elapse. My unextinguished jealousy — that was the Medusa-mask. It hadn't died with her death, it had lividly survived, and it was fed by suspicions unspeakable. They *would* be unspeakable today, that is, if I hadn't felt the sharp need of uttering them at the time. This need took possession of me — to save me, as it seemed, from my fate. When once it had done so I saw — in the urgency of the case, the diminishing hours and shrinking interval — only one issue, that of absolute promptness and frankness. I could at least not do him the wrong of delaying another day; I could at least treat my difficulty as too fine for a subterfuge. Therefore very quietly, but none the less abruptly and hideously, I put it before him on a certain evening that we must reconsider our situation and recognise that it had completely altered.

He stared bravely. 'How in the world altered?'

'Another person has come between us.'

He took but an instant to think. 'I won't pretend not to know whom you mean.' He smiled in pity for my aberration, but he meant to be kind. 'A woman dead and buried!'

'She's buried, but she's not dead. She's dead for the world — she's dead for me. But she's not dead for you.'

'You hark back to the different construction we put on her appearance that evening?'

'No,' I answered, 'I hark back to nothing. I've no need of it. I've more than enough with what's before me.'

'And pray, darling, what may that be?'

'You're completely changed.'

'By that absurdity?' he laughed.

'Not so much by that one as by other absurdities that have followed it.'

'And what may *they* have been?'

We had faced each other fairly, with eyes that didn't flinch; but his had a dim strange light, and my certitude triumphed in his perceptible paleness. 'Do you really pretend', I asked, 'not to know what they are?'

'My dear child,' he replied, 'you describe them too sketchily!'

I considered a moment. 'One may well be embarrassed to finish the picture! But from that point of view – and from the beginning – what was ever more embarrassing than your idiosyncrasy?'

He invoked his vagueness – a thing he always did beautifully. 'My idiosyncrasy?'

'Your notorious, your peculiar power.'

He gave a great shrug of impatience, a groan of overdone disdain. 'Oh my peculiar power!'

'Your accessibility to forms of life,' I coldly went on, 'your command of impressions, appearances, contacts, closed – for our gain or our loss – to the rest of us. That was originally a part of the deep interest with which you inspired me – one of the reasons I was amused, I was indeed positively proud, to know you. It was a magnificent distinction; it's a magnificent distinction still. But of course I had no prevision then of the way it would operate now; and even had that been the case I should have had none of the extraordinary way in which its action would affect me.'

'To what in the name of goodness', he pleadingly enquired, 'are you fantastically alluding?' Then as I remained silent, gathering a tone for my charge, 'How in the world *does* it operate?' he went on; 'and how in the world are you affected?'

'She missed you for five years,' I said, 'but she never misses you now. You're making it up!'

'Making it up?' He had begun to turn from white to red.

'You see her – you see her: you see her every night!' He gave a loud sound of derision, but I felt it ring false. 'She comes to you as she came that evening,' I declared; 'having tried it she found she liked it!' I was able, with God's help, to speak without blind passion or vulgar violence; but those were the exact words – and far from 'sketchy' they then appeared to me – that I uttered. He had turned away in his laughter, clapping his hands at my folly, but in an instant he faced me again with a change of expression that struck me. 'Do you dare to deny', I then asked, 'that you habitually see her?'

He had taken the line of indulgence, of meeting me halfway and kindly humouring me. At all events he to my astonishment suddenly said: 'Well, my dear, what if I do?'

'It's your natural right: it belongs to your constitution and to your wonderful if not perhaps quite enviable fortune. But you'll easily understand that it separates us. I unconditionally release you.'

'Release me?'

'You must choose between me and her.'

He looked at me hard. 'I see.' Then he walked away a little, as if grasping what I had said and thinking how he had best treat it. At last he turned on me afresh. 'How on earth do you know such an awfully private thing?'

'You mean because you've tried so hard to hide it? It *is* awfully private, and you may believe I shall never betray you. You've

done your best, you've acted your part, you've behaved, poor dear! loyally and admirably. Therefore I've watched you in silence, playing my part too; I've noted every drop in your voice, every absence in your eyes, every effort in your indifferent hand: I've waited till I was utterly sure and miserably unhappy. How *can* you hide it when you're abjectly in love with her, when you're sick almost to death with the joy of what she gives you?'
I checked his quick protest with a quicker gesture. 'You love her as you've *never* loved, and, passion for passion, she gives it straight back! She rules you, she holds you, she has you all! A woman, in such a case as mine, divines and feels and sees; she's not a dull dunce who has to be "credibly informed". You come to me mechanically, compunctiously, with the dregs of your tenderness and the remnant of your life. I can renounce you, but I can't share you: the best of you is hers, I know what it is and freely give you up to her for ever!'

He made a gallant fight, but it couldn't be patched up; he repeated his denial, he retracted his admission, he ridiculed my charge, of which I freely granted him moreover the indefensible extravagance. I didn't pretend for a moment that we were talking of common things; I didn't pretend for a moment that he and she were common people. Pray, if they *had* been, how should I ever have cared for them? They had enjoyed a rare extension of being and they had caught me up in their flight; only I couldn't breathe in such air and I promptly asked to be set down. Everything in the facts was monstrous, and most of all my lucid perception of them; the only thing allied to nature and truth was my having to act on that perception. I felt after I had spoken in this sense that my assurance was complete; nothing had been wanting to it but the sight of my effect on him. He disguised indeed the effect in a cloud of chaff, a diversion that gained him time and covered his retreat. He challenged my sincerity, my sanity, almost my humanity, and that of course widened our breach and confirmed our rupture. He did everything in short but convince me either that I was wrong or that he was unhappy: we separated and I left him to his inconceivable communion.

He never married, any more than I've done. When six years later, in solitude and silence, I heard of his death I hailed it as a direct contribution to my theory. It was sudden, it was never properly accounted for, it was surrounded by circumstances in which — for oh I took them to pieces! — I distinctly read an intention, the mark of his own hidden hand. It was the result of a long necessity, of an unquenchable desire. To say exactly what I mean, it was a response to an irresistible call.

THE RED ROOM *BY* H.G. WELLS

H.G. Wells was born in Bromley, Kent in 1866. After an education repeatedly interrupted by his family's financial problems, he eventually found work as a teacher at a succession of schools, where he began to write his first stories. Wells became a prolific writer with a diverse output, of which the famous works are his science fiction novels. These are some of the earliest and most influential examples of the genre, and include classics such as *The Time Machine* and *The War of the Worlds*. Wells also wrote many popular non-fiction books, and used his writing to support the wide range of political and social causes in which he had an interest. H.G. Wells died in London in 1946.

'I CAN ASSURE you,' said I, 'that it will take a very tangible ghost to frighten me.' And I stood up before the fire with my glass in my hand.

'It is your own choosing,' said the man with the withered arm, and glanced at me askance.

'Eight-and-twenty years,' said I, 'I have lived, and never a ghost have I seen as yet.'

The old woman sat staring hard into the fire, her pale eyes wide open. 'Ay,' she broke in; 'and eight-and-twenty years you have lived and never seen the likes of this house, I reckon. There's a many things to see, when one's still but eight-and-twenty.' She swayed her head slowly from side to side. 'A many things to see and sorrow for.'

I half suspected the old people were trying to enhance the spiritual terrors of their house by their droning insistence. I put down my empty glass on the table and looked about the room, and caught a glimpse of myself, abbreviated and broadened to an impossible sturdiness, in the queer old mirror at the end of the room. 'Well,' I said, 'if I see anything tonight, I shall be so much the wiser. For I come to the business with an open mind.'

'It's your own choosing,' said the man, with the withered arm, once more.

I heard the sound of a stick and a shambling step on the flags in the passage outside, and the door creaked on its hinges as a second old man entered, more bent, more wrinkled, more aged even than the first. He supported himself by a single crutch, his eyes were covered by a shade, and his lower lip, half averted, hung pale and pink from his decaying yellow teeth. He made straight for an arm-chair on the opposite side of the table, sat down clumsily, and began to cough. The man with the withered arm gave this new-comer a short glance of positive dislike; the old woman took no notice of his arrival, but remained with her eyes fixed steadily on the fire.

'I said – it's your own choosing,' said the man with the withered arm, when the coughing had ceased for a while.

'It's my own choosing,' I answered.

The man with the shade became aware of my presence for the first time, and threw his head back for a moment and sideways, to see me. I caught a momentary glimpse of his eyes, small and bright and inflamed. Then he began to cough and splutter again.

'Why don't you drink?' said the man with the withered arm, pushing the beer towards him. The man with the shade poured out a glassful with a shaky arm that splashed half as much again on the deal table. A monstrous shadow of him crouched upon the wall and mocked his action as he poured and drank. I must confess I had scarce expected these grotesque custodians. There is to my mind something inhuman in senility, something crouching and atavistic; the human qualities seem to drop from old people insensibly day by day. The three of them made me feel uncomfortable, with their gaunt silences, their bent carriage, their evident unfriendliness to me and to one another.

'If,' said I, 'you will show me to this haunted room of yours, I will make myself comfortable there.'

The old man with the cough jerked his head back so suddenly that it startled me, and shot another glance of his red eyes at me from under the shade; but no one answered me. I waited a minute, glancing from one to the other.

'If,' I said a little louder, 'if you will show me to this haunted room of yours, I will relieve you from the task of entertaining me.'

'There's a candle on the slab outside the door,' said the man with the withered arm, looking at my feet as he addressed me. 'But if you go to the red room tonight –'

('This night of all nights!' said the old woman.)

'You go alone.'

'Very well,' I answered. 'And which way do I go?'

'You go along the passage for a bit,' said he, 'until you come to a door, and through that is a spiral staircase, and halfway up that is a landing and another door covered with baize. Go through that and down the long corridor to the end, and the red room is on your left up the steps.'

'Have I got that right?' I said, and repeated his directions. He corrected me in one particular.

'And are you really going?' said the man with the shade, looking at me again for the third time, with that queer, unnatural tilting of the face.

('This night of all nights!' said the old woman.)

'It is what I came for,' I said, and moved towards the door. As I did so, the old man with the shade rose and staggered round the table, so as to be closer to the others and to the fire. At the door I turned and looked at them, and saw they were all close together, dark against the firelight, staring at me over their shoulders, with an intent expression on their ancient faces.

'Good-night,' I said, setting the door open.

'It's your own choosing,' said the man with the withered arm.

I left the door wide open until the candle was well alight,

and then I shut them in and walked down the chilly, echoing passage.

I must confess that the oddness of these three old pensioners in whose charge her ladyship had left the castle, and the deep-toned, old-fashioned furniture of the housekeeper's room in which they foregathered, affected me in spite of my efforts to keep myself at a matter-of-fact phase. They seemed to belong to another age, an older age, an age when things spiritual were different from this of ours, less certain; an age when omens and witches were credible, and ghosts beyond denying. Their very existence was spectral; the cut of their clothing, fashions born in dead brains. The ornaments and conveniences of the room about them were ghostly – the thoughts of vanished men, which still haunted, rather than participated in the world of today. But with an effort I sent such thoughts to the right-about. The long, draughty subterranean passage was chilly and dusty, and my candle flared and made the shadows cower and quiver. The echoes rang up and down the spiral staircase, and a shadow came sweeping up after me, and one fled before me into the darkness overhead. I came to the landing and stopped there for a moment, listening to a rustling that I fancied I heard; then, satisfied of the absolute silence, I pushed open the baize-covered door and stood in the corridor.

The effect was scarcely what I expected, for the moonlight, coming in by the great window on the grand staircase, picked out everything in vivid black shadow or silvery illumination. Everything was in its place: the house might have been deserted on the yesterday instead of eighteen months ago. There were candles in the sockets of the sconces, and whatever dust had gathered on the carpets or upon the polished flooring was dis-tributed so evenly as to be invisible in the moonlight. I was about to advance, and stopped abruptly. A bronze group stood upon the landing, hidden from me by the corner of the wall, but its shadow fell with marvellous distinctness upon the white panelling, and gave me the impression of someone crouching to waylay me. I stood rigid for half a minute perhaps. Then, with my hand in the pocket that held my revolver, I advanced, only to discover a Ganymede and Eagle glistening in the moonlight. That incident for at time restored my nerve, and a porcelain Chinaman on a buhl table, whose head rocked silently as I passed him, scarcely startled me.

The door to the red room and the steps up to it were in a shadowy corner. I moved my candle from side to side, in order to see clearly the nature of the recess in which I stood before opening the door. Here it was, thought I, that my predecessor was found, and the memory of that story gave me a sudden twinge of apprehension. I glanced over my shoulder at the Ganymede in the moonlight, and opened the door of the red room rather hastily, with my face half turned to the pallid silence of the landing.

I entered, closed the door behind me at once, turned the key I found in the lock within, and stood with the candle held aloft, surveying the scene of my vigil, the great red room of Lorraine Castle, in which the young duke had died. Or rather, in which he had begun his dying, for he had opened the door and fallen headlong down the steps I had just ascended. That had been the end of his vigil, of his gallant attempt to conquer the ghostly tradition of the place; and never, I thought, had apoplexy better served the ends of superstition. And there were other and older stories that clung to the room, back to the half-credible beginning of it all, the tale of a timid wife and the tragic end that came to her husband's jest of frightening her. And looking around that large shadowy room, with its shadowy window bays, its recesses and alcoves, one could well understand the legends that had sprouted in its black corners, its germinating darkness. My candle was a little tongue of flame in its vastness, that failed to pierce the opposite end of the room, and left an ocean of mystery and suggestion beyond its island of light.

I resolved to make a systematic examination of the place at once, and dispel the fanciful suggestions of its obscurity before they obtained a hold upon me. After satisfying myself of the fastening of the door, I began to walk about the room, peering round each article of furniture, tucking up the valances of the bed, and opening its curtains wide. I pulled up the blinds and examined the fastenings of the several windows before closing the shutters, leant forward and looked up the blackness of the wide chimney, and tapped the dark oak panelling for any secret opening. There were two big mirrors in the room, each with a pair of sconces bearing candles, and on the mantelshelf too, were more candles in china candlesticks. All these I lit one after the other. The fire was laid – an unexpected consideration from the old housekeeper – and I lit it, to keep down any disposition to shiver, and when it was burning well, I stood round with my back to it and regarded the room again. I had pulled up a chintz-covered armchair and a table, to form a kind of barricade before me, and on this lay my revolver ready to hand. My precise examination had done me good, but I still found the remoter darkness of the place, and its perfect stillness, too stimulating for the imagination. The echoing of the stir and crackling of the fire was no sort of comfort to me. The shadow in the alcove at the end in particular had that undefinable quality of a presence, that odd suggestion of a lurking, living thing, that comes so easily in silence and solitude. At last, to reassure myself, I walked with a candle into it, and satisfied myself that there was nothing tangible there. I stood that candle upon the floor of the alcove, and left it in that position.

By this time I was in a state of considerable nervous tension, although to my reason there was no adequate cause for the condition. My mind, however, was perfectly clear. I postulated quite unreservedly that nothing supernatural could happen, and to pass the time I began to string some rhymes together, Ingoldsby fashion, of the original legend of the place. A few I spoke aloud, but the echoes were not pleasant. For the same reason I also abandoned, after a time, a conversation with myself upon the impossibility of ghosts and haunting. My mind reverted to the three old and distorted people downstairs, and I tried to keep it upon that topic.

The sombre reds and blacks of the room troubled me; even with seven candles the place was merely dim. The one in the alcove flared in a draught, and the fire-flickering kept the shadows and penumbra perpetually shifting and stirring. Casting about for a remedy, I recalled the candles I had seen in the passage, and, with a slight effort, walked out into the moonlight, carrying a candle and leaving the door open, and presently returned with as many as ten. These I put in various knick-knacks of china with which the room was sparsely adorned, lit and placed where the shadows had lain deepest, some on the floor, some in the window recesses, until at last my seventeen candles were so arranged that not an inch of the room darkened, but had the direct light of at least one of them. It occurred to me that when the ghost came, I could warn him not to trip over them. The room was now quite brightly illuminated. There was something very cheery and reassuring in these little streaming flames, and snuffing them gave me an occupation, and afforded a helpful sense of the passage of time.

Even with that, however, the brooding expectation of the vigil weighed heavily upon me. It was after midnight that the candle in the alcove suddenly went out, and the black shadow sprang back to its place. I did not see the candle go out; I simply turned and saw that the darkness was there, as one might start and see the unexpected presence of a stranger. 'By Jove!' said

I aloud. 'That draught's a strong one!' and taking the matches from the table, I walked across the room in a leisurely manner to relight the corner again. My first match would not strike, and as I succeeded with the second, something seemed to blink on the wall before me. I turned my head involuntarily, and saw that the two candles on the little table by the fireplace were extinguished. I rose at once to my feet.

'Odd!' I said. 'Did I do that myself in a flash of absent-mindedness?'

I walked back, relit one, and as I did so, I saw the candle in the right sconce of one of the mirrors wink and go right out, and almost immediately its companion followed it. There was no mistake about it. The flame vanished, as if the wicks had been suddenly nipped between a finger and thumb, leaving the wick neither glowing nor smoking, but black. While I stood gaping, the candle at the foot of the bed went out, and the shadows seemed to take another step towards me.

'This won't do!' said I, and first one and then another candle on the mantelshelf followed. 'What's up?' I cried, with a queer high note getting into my voice somehow. At that the candle on the wardrobe went out, and the one I had relit in the alcove followed.

'Steady on!' I said. 'These candles are wanted,' speaking with a half-hysterical facetiousness, and scratching away at a match, all the while, for the mantel candlesticks. My hands trembled so much that twice I missed the rough paper of the matchbox. As the mantel emerged from darkness again, two candles in the remoter end of the window were eclipsed. But with the same match I also relit the larger mirror candles, and those on the floor near the doorway, so that for the moment I seemed to gain on the extinctions. But then in a volley there vanished four lights at once in different corners of the room, and I struck another match in quivering haste, and stood hesitating whither to take it.

As I stood undecided, an invisible hand seemed to sweep out the two candles on the table. With a cry of terror, I dashed at the alcove, then into the corner, and then into the window, relighting three, as two more vanished by the fireplace; then, perceiving a better way, I dropped the matches on the iron-bound deed-box in the corner, and caught up the bedroom candlestick. With this I avoided the delay of striking matches; but for all that the steady process of extinction went on, and the shadows I feared and fought against returned, and crept in upon me, first a step gained on this side of me and then on that. It was like a ragged storm-cloud sweeping out of the stars. Now and then one returned for a minute, and was lost again. I was now almost frantic with the horror of the coming darkness, and my self-possession deserted me. I leaped panting and dishevelled from candle to candle in a vain struggle against that remorseless advance.

I bruised myself on the thigh against the table, I sent a chair headlong, I stumbled and fell and whisked the cloth from the table in my fall. My candle rolled away from me, and I snatched another as I rose. Abruptly this was blown out, as I swung it off the table, by the wind of my sudden movement, and immediately the two remaining candles followed. But there was light still in the room, a red light that stayed off the shadows from me. The fire! Of course I could still thrust my candle between the bars and relight it!

I turned to where the flames were still dancing between the glowing coals, and splashing red reflections upon the furniture, made two steps towards the grate, and incontinently the flames dwindled and vanished, the glow vanished, the reflections rushed together and vanished, and as I thrust the candle between the bars darkness closed upon me like the shutting of an eye, wrapped about me in a stifling embrace, sealed my vision, and crushed the last vestiges of reason from my brain. The candle fell from my hand. I flung out my arms in a vain effort to thrust that ponderous blackness away from me, and, lifting up my voice, screamed with all my might – once, twice, thrice. Then I think I must have staggered to my feet. I know I thought suddenly of the moonlit corridor and, with my head bowed and my arms over my face, made a run for the door.

But I had forgotten the exact position of the door, and struck myself heavily against the corner of the bed. I staggered back, turned, and was either struck or struck myself against some other bulky furniture. I have a vague memory of battering myself thus, to and fro in the darkness, of a cramped struggle, and of my own wild crying as I darted to and fro, of a heavy blow at last upon my forehead, a horrible sensation of falling that lasted an age, of my last frantic effort to keep my footing, and then I remember no more.

I opened my eyes in daylight. My head was roughly bandaged, and the man with the withered arm was watching my face. I looked about me, trying to remember what had happened, and for a space I could not recollect. I turned to the corner, and saw the old woman, no longer abstracted, pouring out some drops of medicine from a little blue phial into a glass. 'Where am I?' I asked; 'I seem to remember you, and yet I cannot remember who you are.'

They told me then, and I heard of the haunted red room as one who hears a tale. 'We found you at dawn,' said he, 'and there was blood on your forehead and lips.'

It was very slowly I recovered my memory of my experience. 'You believe now,' said the old man, 'that the room is haunted?' He spoke no longer as one who greets an intruder, but as one who grieves for a broken friend.

'Yes,' said I; 'the room is haunted.'

'And you have seen it. And we, who have lived here all our

lives, have never set eyes upon it. Because we have never dared . . . Tell us, is it truly the old earl who –'

'No,' said I; 'it is not.'

'I told you so,' said the old lady, with the glass in her hand. 'It is his poor young countess who was frightened –'

'It is not,' I said. 'There is neither ghost of earl nor ghost of countess in that room, there is no ghost there at all; but worse, far worse –'

'Well?' they said.

'The worst of all the things that haunt poor mortal man,' said I; 'and that is, in all its nakedness – Fear! Fear that will not have light nor sound, that will not bear with reason, that deafens and darkens and overwhelms. It followed me through the corridor, it fought against me in the room –'

I stopped abruptly. There was an interval of silence. My hand went up to my bandages.

Then the man with the shade sighed and spoke. 'That is it,' said he. 'I knew that was it. A power of darkness. To put such a curse upon a woman! It lurks there always. You can feel it even in the daytime, even of a bright summer's day, in the hangings, in the curtains, keeping behind you however you face about. In the dusk it creeps along the corridor and follows you, so that you dare not turn. There is Fear in that room of hers – black Fear, and there will be – so long as this house of sin endures.'

NIGHTMARE-TOUCH
BY LAFCADIO HEARN

Lafcadio Hearn was born in Lefkada, one of the Greek Ionian Islands, in 1850, the son of an Irish surgeon-soldier and a Greek aristocrat. He was educated in England, and lost the sight of one eye in a childhood accident. He lived in Cincinnati and New Orleans in the USA, where he defied anti-miscegenation laws by marrying an African American woman, and in Martinique, making his living as a journalist and translator. In 1850 he travelled to Japan, where he married for the second time and taught English Literature. He published numerous books about Japan, including several collections of Japanese myths and ghost stories, and died there in 1904.

W HAT *IS* the fear of ghosts among those who believe in
ghosts?

All fear is the result of experience, — experience of the individual or of the race, — experience either of the present life or of lives forgotten. Even the fear of the unknown can have no other origin. And the fear of ghosts must be a product of past pain.

Probably the fear of ghosts, as well as the belief in them, had its beginning in dreams. It is a peculiar fear. No other fear is so intense; yet none is so vague. Feelings thus voluminous and dim are super-individual mostly, — feelings inherited, — feelings made within us by the experience of the dead.

What experience?

Nowhere do I remember reading a plain statement of the reason why ghosts are feared. Ask any ten intelligent persons of your acquaintance, who remember having once been afraid of ghosts, to tell you exactly why they were afraid, — to define the fancy behind the fear; — and I doubt whether even one will be able to answer the question. The literature of folk-lore — oral and written — throws no clear light upon the subject. We find, indeed, various legends of men torn asunder by phantoms; but such gross imaginings could not explain the peculiar quality of ghostly fear. It is not a fear of bodily violence. It is not even a reasoning fear, – not a fear that can readily explain itself, – which would not be the case if it were founded upon definite ideas of physical danger. Furthermore, although primitive ghosts may have been imagined as capable of tearing and devouring, the common idea of a ghost is certainly that of a being intangible and imponderable.*

Now I venture to state boldly that the common fear of ghosts is *the fear of being touched by ghosts*, – or, in other words, that the imagined Supernatural is dreaded mainly because of its imagined power to touch. Only to *touch*, remember – not to wound or to kill.

But this dread of the touch would itself be the result of experience, – chiefly, I think, of prenatal experience stored up in the individual by inheritance, like the child's fear of darkness. And who can ever have had the sensation of being touched by ghosts? The answer is simple: – *Everybody who has been seized by phantoms in a dream*.

Elements of primeval fears – fears older than humanity – doubtless enter into the child-terror of darkness. But the more definite fear of ghosts may very possibly be composed with inherited results of dream – pain, – ancestral experience of nightmare. And the intuitive terror of supernatural touch can thus be evolutionally explained.

Let me now try to illustrate my theory by relating some typical experiences.

---

* I may remark here that in many old Japanese legends and ballads, ghosts are represented as having power to *pull off* people's heads. But so far as the origin of the fear of ghosts is concerned, such stories explain nothing, – since the experiences that evolved the fear must have been real, not imaginary, experiences.

II

WHEN ABOUT five years old I was condemned to sleep by myself in a certain isolated room, thereafter always called the Child's Room. (At that time I was scarcely ever mentioned by name, but only referred to as 'the Child.') The room was narrow, but very high, and, in spite of one tall window, very gloomy. It contained a fire-place wherein no fire was ever kindled; and the Child suspected that the chimney was haunted.

A law was made that no light should be left in the Child's Room at night, – simply because the Child was afraid of the dark. His fear of the dark was judged to be a mental disorder requiring severe treatment. But the treatment aggravated the disorder. Previously I had been accustomed to sleep in a well-lighted room, with a nurse to take care of me. I thought that I should die of fright when sentenced to lie alone in the dark, and – what seemed to me then abominably cruel – actually *locked* into my room, the most dismal room of the house. Night after night when I had been warmly tucked into bed, the lamp was removed; the key clicked in the lock; the protecting light and the footsteps of my guardian receded together. Then an agony of fear would come upon me. Something in the black air would seem to gather and grow – (I thought that I could even *hear* it grow) – till I had to scream. Screaming regularly brought punishment; but it also brought back the light, which more than consoled for the punishment. This fact being at last found out, orders were given to pay no further heed to the screams of the Child.

Why was I thus insanely afraid? Partly because the dark had always been peopled for me with shapes of terror. So far back as memory extended, I had suffered from ugly dreams; and when aroused from them I could always *see* the forms dreamed of, lurking in the shadows of the room. They would soon fade out; but for several moments they would appear like tangible realities. And they were always the same figures. . . . Sometimes, without any preface of dreams, I used to see them at twilight-time, — following me about from room to room, or reaching long dim hands after me, from story to story, up through the interspaces of the deep stairways.

I had complained of these haunters only to be told that I must never speak of them, and that they did not exist. I had complained to everybody in the house; and everybody in the house had told me the very same thing. But there was the evidence of my eyes! The denial of that evidence I could explain only in two ways: — Either the shapes were afraid of big people, and showed themselves to me alone, because I was little and weak; or else the entire household had agreed, for some ghastly reason, to say what was not true. This latter theory seemed to me the more probable one, because I had several times perceived the shapes when I was not unattended; — and the consequent appearance of secrecy frightened me scarcely less than the visions did. Why was I forbidden to talk about what I saw, and even heard, — on creaking stairways, — behind wavering curtains?

'Nothing will hurt you,' — this was the merciless answer to all my pleadings not to be left alone at night. But the haunters *did* hurt me. Only — they would wait until after I had fallen asleep, and so into their power, — for they possessed occult means of preventing me from rising or moving or crying out.

Needless to comment upon the policy of locking me up alone

with these fears in a black room. Unutterably was I tormented in that room — for years! Therefore I felt relatively happy when sent away at last to a children's boarding-school, where the haunters very seldom ventured to show themselves.

They were not like any people that I had ever known. They were shadowy dark-robed figures, capable of atrocious self-distortion, — capable, for instance, of growing up to the ceiling, and then across it, and then lengthening themselves, head-downwards, along the opposite wall. Only their faces were distinct; and I tried not to look at their faces. I tried also in my dreams — or thought that I tried — to awaken myself from the sight of them by pulling at my eyelids with my fingers; but the eyelids would remain closed, as if sealed. . . . Many years afterwards, the frightful plates in Orfila's *Traité des Exhumés*, beheld for the first time, recalled to me with a sickening start the dream-terrors of childhood. But to understand the Child's experience, you must imagine Orfila's drawings intensely alive, and continually elongating or distorting, as in some monstrous anamorphosis.

Nevertheless the mere sight of those nightmare-faces was not the worst of the experiences in the Child's Room. The dreams always began with a suspicion, or sensation of something heavy in the air, — slowly quenching will, — slowly numbing my power to move. At such times I usually found myself alone in a large unlighted apartment; and, almost simultaneously with the first sensation of fear, the atmosphere of the room would become suffused, half-way to the ceiling, with a sombre yellowish glow, making objects dimly visible, — though the ceiling itself remained pitch-black. This was not a true appearance of light: rather it seemed as if the black air were changing colour from beneath. . . . Certain terrible aspects of sunset, on the eve of storm, offer like

effects of sinister colour. . . . Forthwith I would try to escape, —
(feeling at every step a sensation *as of wading*), — and would
sometimes succeed in struggling half-way across the room; — but
there I would always find myself brought to a stand-
still, — paralysed by some innominable opposition. Happy voices
I could hear in the next room; — I could see light through the
transom over the door that I had vainly endeavoured to reach; — I
knew that one loud cry would save me. But not even by the most
frantic effort could I raise my voice above a whisper. . . . And all
this signified only that the Nameless was coming, — was nearing, — was mounting the stairs. I could hear the step, — booming
like the sound of a muffled drum, and I wondered why nobody
else heard it. A long, long time the haunter would take to
come, — malevolently pausing after each ghastly footfall. Then,
without a creak, the bolted door would open, — slowly,
slowly, — and the thing would enter, gibbering soundlessly, — and
put out hands, — and clutch me, — and toss me to the black ceiling, — and catch me descending to toss me up again, and again,
and again. . . . In those moments the feeling was not fear: fear
itself had been torpified by the first seizure. It was a sensation
that has no name in the language of the living. For every touch
brought a shock of something infinitely worse than
pain, — something that thrilled into the innermost secret being of
me, — a sort of abominable electricity, discovering unimagined
capacities of suffering in totally unfamiliar regions of sen-
tiency. . . . This was commonly the work of a single tormentor;
but I can also remember having been caught by a group,
and tossed from one to another, — seemingly for a time of
many minutes.

*

III

WHENCE THE FANCY of those shapes? I do not know. Possibly from some impression of fear in earliest infancy; possibly from some experience of fear in other lives than mine. That mystery is forever insoluble. But the mystery of the shock of the touch admits of a definite hypothesis.

First, allow me to observe that the experience of the sensation itself cannot be dismissed as 'mere imagination.' Imagination means cerebral activity: its pains and its pleasures are alike inseparable from nervous operation, and their physical importance is sufficiently proved by their physiological effects. Dream-fear may kill as well as other fear; and no emotion thus powerful can be reasonably deemed undeserving of study.

One remarkable fact in the problem to be considered is that the sensation of seizure in dreams differs totally from all sensations familiar to ordinary waking life. Why this differentiation? How interpret the extraordinary massiveness and depth of the thrill?

I have already suggested that the dreamer's fear is most probably not a reflection of relative experience, but represents the incalculable total of ancestral experience of dream-fear. If the sum of the experience of active life be transmitted by inheritance, so must likewise be transmitted the summed experience of the life of sleep. And in normal heredity either class of transmissions would probably remain distinct.

Now, granting this hypothesis, the sensation of dream-seizure would have had its beginnings in the earliest phases of dream-consciousness, – long prior to the apparition of man. The first creatures capable of thought and fear must often have dreamed of being caught by their natural enemies. There could not have been much imagining of pain in these primal dreams. But higher nervous development in later forms of being would have been accompanied with larger susceptibility to dream-pain. Still later, with the growth of reasoning-power, ideas of the supernatural would have changed and intensified the character of dream-fear. Furthermore, through all the course of evolution, heredity would have been accumulating the experience of such feeling. Under those forms of imaginative pain evolved through reaction of religious beliefs, there would persist some dim survival of savage primitive fears, and again, under this, a dimmer but incomparably deeper substratum of ancient animal-terrors. In the dreams of the modern child all these latencies might quicken, – one below another, – unfathomably, – with the coming and the growing of nightmare.

It may be doubted whether the phantasms of any particular nightmare have a history older than the brain in which they move. But the shock of the touch would seem to indicate *some point of dream-contact with the total race-experience of shadowy seizure*. It may be that profundities of Self, – abysses never reached by any ray from the life of sun, – are strangely stirred in slumber, and that out of their blackness immediately responds a shuddering of memory, measureless even by millions of years.

THE GHOST *BY* CATHERINE WELLS

Amy Catherine Robbins was born in 1872. Aged 20, she met the novelist and historian H.G. Wells, and lived with him from 1892 until he divorced his first wife in 1895, whereupon they married and had two sons. She published a few short stories during her lifetime, but H.G. Wells published the majority of her literary work as *The Book of Catherine Wells* after her death from cancer in 1927.

S HE WAS a girl of fourteen, and she sat propped up with pillows in an old four-poster bed, coughing a little with the feverish cold that kept her there. She was tired of reading by lamplight, and she lay and listened to the few sounds that she could hear, and looked into the fire. From downstairs, down the wide, rather dark, oak-panelled corridor hung with brown ochre pictures of tremendous naval engagements exploding fierily in their centres, down the broad stone stairs that ended in a heavy, creaking, nail-studded door, there blew in to her remoteness sometimes a gust of dance music. Cousins and cousins and cousins were down there, and Uncle Timothy, as host, leading the fun. Several of them had danced into her room during the day, and said that her illness was a 'perfect shame,' told her that the skating in the park was 'too heavenly,' and danced out again. Uncle Timothy had been as kind as kind could be. But — Downstairs all the full cup of happiness the lonely child had looked forward to so eagerly for a month, was running away like liquid gold.

She watched the flames of the big wood fire in the open grate flicker and fall. She had sometimes to clench her hands to prevent herself from crying. She had discovered – so early was she beginning to collect her little stock of feminine lore – that if you swallowed hard and rapidly as the tears gathered, that you could prevent your eyes brimming over. She wished some one would come. There was a bell within her reach, but she could think of no plausible excuse for ringing it. She wished there was more light in the room. The big fire lit it up cheerfully when the logs flared high; but when they only glowed, the dark shadows crept down from the ceiling and gathered in the corners against the panelling. She turned from the scrutiny of the room to the bright circle of light under the lamp on the table beside her, and the companionable suggestiveness of the currant jelly and spoon, grapes and lemonade and little pile of books and kindly fuss that shone warmly and comfortingly there. Perhaps it would not be long before Mrs Bunting, her uncle's housekeeper, would come in again and sit down and talk to her.

Mrs Bunting, very probably, was more occupied than usual that evening. There were several extra guests, another house-party had motored over for the evening, and they had brought with them a romantic figure, a celebrity, no less a personage than the actor Percival East. The girl had indeed broken down from her fortitude that afternoon when Uncle Timothy had told her of this visitor. Uncle Timothy was surprised; it was only another schoolgirl who would have understood fully what it meant to be denied by a mere cold the chance of meeting face to face that chivalrous hero of drama; another girl who had glowed at his daring, wept at his noble renunciations, been made happy, albeit enviously and vicariously, by his final embrace with the lady of his love.

'There, there, dear child,' Uncle Timothy had said, patting her shoulder and greatly distressed. 'Never mind, never mind. If you can't get up I'll bring him in to see you here. I promise I will. . . . But the *pull* these chaps have over you little women,' he went on, half to himself. . . .

The panelling creaked. Of course, it always did in these old houses. She was of that order of apprehensive, slightly nervous people who do not believe in ghosts, but all the same hope devoutly they may never see one. Surely it was a long time since any one had visited her; it would be hours, she supposed, before the girl who had the room next her own, into which a communicating door comfortingly led, came up to bed. If she rang it took a minute or two before any one reached her from the remote servants' quarters. There ought soon, she thought, to be a housemaid about the corridor outside, tidying up the bedrooms, putting coal on the fires, and making suchlike companionable noises. That would be pleasant. How bored one got in bed anyhow, and how dreadful it was, how unbearably dreadful it was that she should be stuck in bed now, missing everything, missing every bit of the glorious glowing time that was slipping away down there. At that she had to begin swallowing her tears again.

With a sudden burst of sound, a storm of clapping and laughter, the heavy door at the foot of the big stairs swung open and closed. Footsteps came upstairs, and she heard men's voices approaching. Uncle Timothy. He knocked at the door ajar. 'Come in,' she cried gladly. With him was a quiet-faced greyish-haired man of middle age. Then uncle had sent for the doctor after all!

'Here is another of your young worshippers, Mr East,' said Uncle Timothy.

Mr East! She realised in a flash that she had expected him in purple brocade, powdered hair, and ruffles of fine lace. Her uncle smiled at her disconcerted face.

'She doesn't seem to recognise you, Mr East,' said Uncle Timothy.

'Of course I do,' she declared bravely, and sat up, flushed with excitement and her feverishness, bright-eyed and with ruffled hair. Indeed she began to see the stage hero she remembered and the kindly-faced man before her flow together like a composite portrait. There was the little nod of the head, there was the chin, yes! And the eyes, now she came to look at them. 'Why were they all clapping you?' she asked.

'Because I had just promised to frighten them out of their wits,' replied Mr East.

'Oh, how?'

'Mr East,' said Uncle Timothy, 'is going to dress up as our long-lost ghost, and give us a really shuddering time of it downstairs.'

'*Are* you?' cried the girl with all the fierce desire that only a girl can utter in her voice. 'Oh, why am I ill like this, Uncle Timothy? I'm not ill really. Can't you see I'm better? I've been in bed all day. I'm perfectly well. Can't I come down, Uncle *dear* — can't I?'

In her excitement she was half out of bed. 'There, there, child,' soothed Uncle Timothy, hastily smoothing the bed-clothes and trying to tuck her in.

'But *can't* I?'

'Of course, if you want to be thoroughly frightened, frightened out of your wits, mind you,' began Percival East.

'I do, I *do*,' she cried, bouncing up and down in her bed.

'I'll come and show myself when I'm dressed up, before I go down.'

'Oh please, please,' she cried back radiantly. A private performance all to herself! 'Will you be perfectly *awful*?' she laughed exultantly.

'As ever I can,' smiled Mr East, and turned to follow Uncle

Timothy out of the room. 'You know,' he said, holding the door and looking back at her with mock seriousness, 'I shall look rather horrid, I expect. Are you sure you won't mind?'

'*Mind* – when it's you?' laughed the girl.

He went out of the room, shutting the door.

'Rum-ti-tum, ti-tum, ti-ty,' she hummed gaily, and wriggled down into her bed-clothes again, straightened the sheet over her chest, and prepared to wait.

She lay quietly for some time, with a smile on her face, think-ing of Percival East and fitting his grave, kindly face back into its various dramatic settings. She was quite satisfied with him. She began to go over in her mind in detail the last play in which she had seen him act. How splendid he had looked when he fought the duel! She couldn't imagine him gruesome, she thought. What would he do with himself?

Whatever he did, she wasn't going to be frightened. He shouldn't be able to boast he had frightened *her*. Uncle Timothy would be there too, she supposed. Would he?

Footsteps went past her door outside, along the corridor, and died away. The big door at the end of the stairs opened and clanged shut.

Uncle Timothy had gone down.

She waited on.

A log, burnt through the middle to a ruddy thread, fell sud-denly in two tumbling pieces on the hearth. She started at the sound. How quiet everything was. How much longer would he be, she wondered. The fire wanted making up, the pieces of wood collecting together. Should she ring? But he might come in just when the servant was mending the fire, and that would spoil his entry. The fire could wait. . . .

The room was very still, and, with the fallen fire, darker. She heard no more any sound at all from downstairs. That was because her door was shut. All day it had been open, but now the last slender link that held her to downstairs was broken.

The lamp flame gave a sudden fitful leap. Why? Was it going out? Was it? – No.

She hoped he wouldn't jump out at her, but of course he wouldn't. Anyhow, whatever he did she wouldn't be frightened – really frightened. Forewarned is forearmed.

Was that a sound? She started up, her eyes on the door. Nothing.

But surely, the door had minutely moved, it did not sit back quite so close into its frame! Perhaps it— She was sure it had moved. Yes, it had moved – opened an inch, and slowly, as she watched, she saw a thread of light grow between the edge of the door and its frame, grow almost imperceptibly wider, and stop.

He could never come through that? It must have yawned open of its own accord. Her heart began to beat rather quickly. She could see only the upper part of the door, the foot of her bed hid the lower third. . . .

Her attention tightened. Suddenly, as suddenly as a pistol shot, she saw that there was a little figure like a dwarf near the wall, between the door and the fireplace. It was a little cloaked figure, no higher than the table. How *did* he do it? It was moving slowly, very slowly, towards the fire, as if it was quite unconscious of her; it was wrapped about in a cloak that trailed, with a slouched hat on its head bent down to its shoulders. She gripped the clothes with her hands, it was so queer, so unexpected; she gave a little gasping laugh to break the tension of the silence – to show she appreciated him.

The dwarf stopped dead at the sound, and turned its face round to her.

Oh! But she was frightened! It was a dead white face, a long pointed face hunched between its shoulders, there was no colour in the eyes that stared at her! How did he do it, how *did* he do it? It was too good. She laughed again nervously, and with a clutch of terror that she could not control she saw the creature move out of the shadow and come towards her. She braced herself with all her might, she mustn't be frightened by a bit of acting – he was coming nearer, it was horrible, horrible – right up to her bed. . . .

She flung her head beneath her bed-clothes. Whether she screamed or not she never knew. . . .

Some one was rapping at her door, speaking cheerily. She took her head out of the clothes with a revulsion of shame at her fright. The horrible little creature was gone! Mr East was speaking at her door. What was it he was saying? *What?*

'*I'm ready now,*' he said. '*Shall I come in, and begin?*'

THURNLEY ABBEY
BY PERCEVAL LANDON

Perceval Landon was born in 1868 and educated at Oxford. He trained as a lawyer, but became a war correspondent in South Africa during the Boer War, and went on to work as a special correspondent for various publications, travelling constantly and widely to China, Siberia, Tibet, India, Scandinavia and Palestine, among many other places. A close lifelong friend of Rudyard Kipling, Landon published several books about his travels, but is best known for the ghost story 'Thurnley Abbey'. Perceval Landon died in January 1927.

THREE YEARS ago I was on my way out to the East, and as an extra day in London was of some importance, I took the Friday evening mail-train to Brindisi instead of the usual Thursday morning Marseilles express. Many people shrink from the long forty-eight-hour train journey through Europe, and the subsequent rush across the Mediterranean on the nineteen-knot *Isis* or *Osiris*; but there is really very little discomfort on either the train or the mail-boat, and unless there is actually nothing for me to do, I always like to save the extra day and a half in London before I say goodbye to her for one of my longer tramps. This time – it was early, I remember, in the shipping season, probably about the beginning of September – there were few passengers, and I had a compartment in the P & O Indian express to myself all the way from Calais. All Sunday I watched the blue waves dimpling the Adriatic, and the pale rosemary along the cuttings; the plain white towns, with their flat roofs and their bold 'duomos', and the grey-green gnarled olive orchards of Apulia. The journey was just like any other. We ate in the dining-car as often and as long as we decently could. We slept after luncheon; we dawdled the afternoon away with yellow-backed novels; sometimes we exchanged platitudes in the smoking-room, and it was there that I met Alastair Colvin.

Colvin was a man of middle height, with a resolute, well-cut jaw; his hair was turning grey; his moustache was sun-whitened, otherwise he was clean-shaven — obviously a gentleman, and obviously also a preoccupied man. He had no great wit. When spoken to, he made the usual remarks in the right way, and I dare say he refrained from banalities only because he spoke less than the rest of us; most of the time he buried himself in the Wagon-lit Company's time-table, but seemed unable to concentrate his attention on any one page of it. He found that I had been over the Siberian railway, and for a quarter of an hour he discussed it with me. Then he lost interest in it, and rose to go to his compartment. But he came back again very soon, and seemed glad to pick up the conversation again.

Of course this did not seem to me to be of any importance. Most travellers by train become a trifle infirm of purpose after thirty-six hours' rattling. But Colvin's restless way I noticed in somewhat marked contrast with the man's personal importance and dignity; especially ill suited was it to his finely made large hand with strong, broad, regular nails and its few lines. As I looked at his hand I noticed a long, deep, and recent scar of ragged shape. However, it is absurd to pretend that I thought anything was unusual. I went off at five o'clock on Sunday afternoon to sleep away the hour or two that had still to be got through before we arrived at Brindisi.

Once there, we few passengers transhipped our hand baggage, verified our berths — there were only a score of us in all — and then, after an aimless ramble of half an hour in Brindisi, we returned to dinner at the Hôtel International, not wholly surprised that the town had been the death of Virgil. If I remember rightly, there is a gaily painted hall at the International — I do not

wish to advertise anything, but there is no other place in Brindisi
at which to await the coming of the mails – and after dinner I
was looking with awe at a trellis overgrown with blue vines,
when Colvin moved across the room to my table. He picked up
Il Secolo, but almost immediately gave up the pretence of reading
it. He turned squarely to me and said:

'Would you do me a favour?'

One doesn't do favours to stray acquaintances on Continental
expresses without knowing something more of them than I
knew of Colvin. But I smiled in a noncommittal way, and asked
him what he wanted. I wasn't wrong in part of my estimate of
him; he said bluntly:

'Will you let me sleep in your cabin on the *Osiris*?' And he
coloured a little as he said it.

Now, there is nothing more tiresome than having to put up
with a stable-companion at sea, and I asked him rather
pointedly:

'Surely there is room for all of us?' I thought that perhaps he
had been partnered off with some mangy Levantine, and wanted
to escape from him at all hazards.

Colvin, still somewhat confused, said: 'Yes; I am in a cabin
by myself. But you would do me the greatest favour if you would
allow me to share yours.'

This was all very well, but, besides the fact that I always sleep
better when alone, there had been some recent thefts on board
English liners, and I hesitated, frank and honest and self-
conscious as Colvin was. Just then the mail-train came in with a
clatter and a rush of escaping steam, and I asked him to see me
again about it on the boat when we started. He answered me
curtly – I suppose he saw the mistrust in my manner – 'I am a
member of White's.' I smiled to myself as he said it, but I remembered in a moment that the man – if he were really what he

claimed to be, and I make no doubt that he was – must have been sorely put to it before he urged the fact as a guarantee of his respectability to a total stranger at a Brindisi hotel.

That evening, as we cleared the red and green harbour-lights of Brindisi, Colvin explained. This is his story in his own words.

'When I was travelling in India some years ago, I made the acquaintance of a youngish man in the Woods and Forests. We camped out together for a week, and I found him a pleasant companion. John Broughton was a light-hearted soul when off duty, but a steady and capable man in any of the small emergencies that continually arise in that department. He was liked and trusted by the natives, and though a trifle over-pleased with himself when he escaped to civilisation at Simla or Calcutta, Broughton's future was well assured in Government service, when a fair-sized estate was unexpectedly left to him, and he joyfully shook the dust of the Indian plains from his feet and returned to England. For five years he drifted about London. I saw him now and then. We dined together about every eighteen months, and I could trace pretty exactly the gradual sickening of Broughton with a merely idle life. He then set out on a couple of long voyages, returned as restless as before, and at last told me that he had decided to marry and settle down at his place, Thurnley Abbey, which had long been empty. He spoke about looking after the property and standing for his constituency in the usual way. Vivien Wilde, his fiancée, had, I suppose, begun to take him in hand. She was a pretty girl with a deal of fair hair and rather an exclusive manner; deeply religious in a narrow school, she was still kindly and high-spirited, and I thought that Broughton was in luck. He was quite happy and full of information about his future.

'Among other things, I asked him about Thurnley Abbey. He confessed that he hardly knew the place. The last tenant, a man called Clarke, had lived in one wing for fifteen years and seen no one. He had been a miser and a hermit. It was the rarest thing for a light to be seen at the Abbey after dark. Only the barest necessities of life were ordered, and the tenant himself received them at the side-door. His one half-caste manservant, after a month's stay in the house, had abruptly left without warning, and had returned to the Southern States. One thing Broughton complained bitterly about: Clarke had wilfully spread the rumour among the villagers that the Abbey was haunted, and had even condescended to play childish tricks with spirit-lamps and salt in order to scare trespassers away at night. He had been detected in the act of this tomfoolery, but the story spread, and no one, said Broughton, would venture near the house except in broad daylight. The hauntedness of Thurnley Abbey was now, he said with a grin, part of the gospel of the countryside, but he and his young wife were going to change all that. Would I propose myself any time I liked? I, of course, said I would, and equally, of course, intended to do nothing of the sort without a definite invitation.

'The house was put in thorough repair, though not a stick of the old furniture and tapestry were removed. Floors and ceilings were relaid: the roof was made watertight again, and the dust of half a century was scoured out. He showed me some photographs of the place. It was called an Abbey, though as a matter of fact it had been only the infirmary of the long-vanished Abbey of Closter some five miles away. The larger part of this building remained as it had been in pre-Reformation days, but a wing had been added in Jacobean times, and that part of the house had been kept in something like repair by Mr Clarke. He had in both the ground and first floors set a heavy timber door, strongly barred with iron, in the passage between the earlier and the Jacobean parts of the house, and had entirely neglected the former. So there had been a good deal of work to be done.

'Broughton, whom I saw in London two or three times about this period, made a deal of fun over the positive refusal of the workmen to remain after sundown. Even after the electric light had been put into every room, nothing would induce them to remain, though, as Broughton observed, electric light was death on ghosts. The legend of the Abbey's ghosts had gone far and wide, and the men would take no risks. They went home in batches of five and six, and even during the daylight hours there was an inordinate amount of talking between one and another, if either happened to be out of sight of his companion. On the whole, though nothing of any sort or kind had been conjured up even by their heated imaginations during their five months' work upon the Abbey, the belief in the ghosts was rather strengthened than otherwise in Thurnley because of the men's confessed nervousness, and local tradition declared itself in favour of the ghost of an immured nun.

' "Good old nun!" said Broughton.

'I asked him whether in general he believed in the possibility of ghosts, and, rather to my surprise, he said that he couldn't say he entirely disbelieved in them. A man in India had told him one morning in camp that he believed that his mother was dead in England, as her vision had come to his tent the night before. He had not been alarmed, but had said nothing, and the figure vanished again. As a matter of fact, the next possible dak-walla brought on a telegram announcing the mother's death. "There the thing was," said Broughton. But at Thurnley he was practical enough. He roundly cursed the idiotic selfishness of Clarke, whose silly antics had caused all the inconvenience. At the same time, he couldn't refuse to sympathise to some extent with the ignorant workmen. "My own idea," said he, "is that if a ghost ever does come in one's way, one ought to speak to it."

'I agreed. Little as I knew of the ghost world and its conventions, I had always remembered that a spook was in honour bound to wait to be spoken to. It didn't seem much to do, and I felt that the sound of one's own voice would at any rate reassure oneself as to one's wakefulness. But there are few ghosts outside Europe – few, that is, that a white man can see – and I had never been troubled with any. However, as I have said, I told Broughton that I agreed.

'So the wedding took place, and I went to it in a tall hat which I bought for the occasion, and the new Mrs Broughton smiled very nicely at me afterwards. As it had to happen, I took the Orient Express that evening and was not in England again for nearly six months. Just before I came back I got a letter from Broughton. He asked if I could see him in London or come to Thurnley, as he thought I should be better able to help him than anyone else he knew. His wife sent a nice message to me at the end, so I was reassured about at least one thing. I wrote from Budapest that I would come and see him at Thurnley two days after my arrival in London, and as I sauntered out of the Pannonia into the Kerepesi Utcza to post my letters, I wondered of what earthly service I could be to Broughton. I had been out with him after tiger on foot, and I could imagine few men better able at a pinch to manage their own business. However, I had nothing to do, so after dealing with some small accumulations of business during my absence, I packed a kit-bag and departed to Euston.

'I was met by Broughton's great limousine at Thurnley Road station, and after a drive of nearly seven miles we echoed through the sleepy streets of Thurnley village, into which the main gates of the park thrust themselves, splendid with pillars and spreadeagles and tom-cats rampant atop of them. I never was a herald, but I know that the Broughtons have the right to supporters – Heaven knows why! From the gates a quadruple avenue of beech-trees led inwards for a quarter of a mile. Beneath them a neat strip of fine turf edged the road and ran back until the poison of the dead beech-leaves killed it under the trees. There were many wheel-tracks on the road, and a comfortable little pony trap jogged past me laden with a country parson and his wife and daughter. Evidently there was some garden party going on at the Abbey. The road dropped away to the right at the end of the avenue, and I could see the Abbey across a wide pasturage and a broad lawn thickly dotted with guests.

'The end of the building was plain. It must have been almost mercilessly austere when it was first built, but time had crumbled the edges and toned the stone down to an orange-lichened grey wherever it showed behind its curtain of magnolia, jasmine, and ivy. Further on was the three-storied Jacobean house, tall and handsome. There had not been the slightest attempt to adapt the one to the other, but the kindly ivy had glossed over the touching-point. There was a tall flèche in the middle of the building, surmounting a small bell tower. Behind the house there rose the mountainous verdure of Spanish chestnuts all the way up the hill.

'Broughton had seen me coming from afar, and walked across from his other guests to welcome me before turning me over to the butler's care. This man was sandy-haired and rather inclined to be talkative. He could, however, answer hardly any questions about the house; he had, he said, only been there three weeks. Mindful of what Broughton had told me, I made no enquiries about ghosts, though the room into which I was shown might have justified anything. It was a very large low room with oak beams projecting from the white ceiling. Every inch of the walls, including the doors, was covered with tapestry, and a remarkably fine Italian fourpost bedstead, heavily draped, added to the darkness and dignity of the place. All the furniture was old, well made, and dark. Underfoot there was a plain green pile carpet, the only new thing about the room except the electric light fittings and the jugs and basins. Even the looking-glass on the dressing-table was an old pyramidal Venetian glass set in heavy repoussé frame of tarnished silver.

'After a few minutes' cleaning up, I went downstairs and out upon the lawn, where I greeted my hostess. The people gathered there were of the usual country type, all anxious to be pleased and roundly curious as to the new master of the Abbey. Rather to my surprise, and quite to my pleasure, I rediscovered Glenham, whom I had known well in old days in Barotseland: he lived quite close, as, he remarked with a grin, I ought to have known. "But," he added, "I don't live in a place like this." He swept his hand to the long, low lines of the Abbey in obvious admiration, and then, to my intense interest, muttered beneath his breath, "Thank God!" He saw that I had overheard him, and turning to me said decidedly, "Yes, 'thank God' I said, and I meant it. I wouldn't live at the Abbey for all Broughton's money."

' "But surely," I demurred, "you know that old Clarke was discovered in the very act of setting light to his bug-a-boos?"

'Glenham shrugged his shoulders. "Yes, I know about that. But there is something wrong with the place still. All I can say is that Broughton is a different man since he has lived here. I don't believe that he will remain much longer. But — you're staying here? — well, you'll hear all about it tonight. There's a big dinner, I understand." The conversation turned off to old reminiscences, and Glenham soon after had to go.

'Before I went to dress that evening I had twenty minutes' talk with Broughton in his library. There was no doubt that the man was altered, gravely altered. He was nervous and fidgety, and I found him looking at me only when my eye was off him. I naturally asked him what he wanted of me. I told him I would do anything I could, but that I couldn't conceive what he lacked that I could provide. He said with a lustreless smile that there was, however, something, and that he would tell me the following morning. It struck me that he was somehow ashamed of himself, and perhaps ashamed of the part he was asking me to play. However, I dismissed the subject from my mind and went up to dress in my palatial room. As I shut the door a draught blew out the Queen of Sheba from the wall, and I noticed that the tapestries were not fastened to the wall at the bottom. I have always held very practical views about spooks, and it has often seemed to me that the slow waving in firelight of loose tapestry upon a wall would account for ninety-nine per cent of the stories one hears. Certainly the dignified undulation of this lady with her attendants and huntsmen – one of whom was untidily cutting the throat of a fallow deer upon the very steps on which King Solomon, a grey-faced Flemish nobleman with the order of the Golden Fleece, awaited his fair visitor – gave colour to my hypothesis.

'Nothing much happened at dinner. The people were very much like those of the garden party. A young woman next to me seemed anxious to know what was being read in London. As she was far more familiar than I with the most recent magazines and literary supplements, I found salvation in being myself instructed in the tendencies of modern fiction. All true art, she said, was shot through and through with melancholy. How vulgar were the attempts at wit that marked so many modern books! From the beginning of literature it had always been tragedy that embodied the highest attainment of every age. To call such works morbid merely begged the question. No thoughtful man – she looked sternly at me through the steel rim of her glasses – could fail to agree with me. Of course, as one would, I immediately and properly said that I slept with Pett Ridge and Jacobs under my pillow at night, and that if *Jorrocks* weren't quite so large and cornery, I would add him to the company. She hadn't read any of them, so I was saved – for a time. But I remember grimly that she said that the dearest wish of her life was to be in some awful and soul-freezing situation of horror, and I remember that she dealt hardly with the hero of Nat Paynter's vampire story, between nibbles at her brown-bread ice. She was a cheerless soul, and I couldn't help thinking that if there were many such in the neighbourhood, it was not surprising that old Glenham had been stuffed with some nonsense or other about the Abbey. Yet nothing could well have been less creepy than the glitter of silver and glass, and the subdued lights and cackle of conversation all round the dinner-table.

'After the ladies had gone I found myself talking to the rural dean. He was a thin, earnest man, who at once turned the conversation to old Clarke's buffooneries. But, he said, Mr Broughton had introduced such a new and cheerful spirit, not only into the Abbey, but, he might say, into the whole neighbourhood, that he had great hopes that the ignorant superstitions of the past were from henceforth destined to oblivion. Thereupon his other neighbour, a portly gentleman of independent means and position, audibly remarked "Amen", which damped the rural dean, and we talked of partridges past, partridges present, and pheasants to come. At the other end of the table Broughton sat with a couple of his friends, red-faced hunting men. Once I noticed that they were discussing me, but I paid no attention to it at the time. I remembered it a few hours later.

'By eleven all the guests were gone, and Broughton, his wife, and I were alone together under the fine plaster ceiling of the Jacobean drawing-room. Mrs Broughton talked about one or two of the neighbours, and then, with a smile, said that she knew I would excuse her, shook hands with me, and went off to bed. I am not very good at analysing things, but I felt that she talked a little uncomfortably and with a suspicion of effort, smiled rather conventionally, and was obviously glad to go. These things seem trifling enough to repeat, but I had throughout the faint feeling that everything was not square. Under the circumstances, this was enough to set me wondering what on earth the service could be that I was to render – wondering also whether the whole business were not some ill-advised jest in order to make me come down from London for a mere shooting-party.

'Broughton said little after she had gone. But he was evidently labouring to bring the conversation round to the so-called haunting of the Abbey. As soon as I saw this, of course I asked him directly about it. He then seemed at once to lose interest in the matter. There was no doubt about it: Broughton was somehow a changed man, and to my mind he had changed in no way for the better. Mrs Broughton seemed no sufficient cause. He was clearly very fond of her, and she of him. I reminded him that he was going to tell me what I could do for him in the morning, pleaded my journey, lighted a candle, and went upstairs with him. At the end of the passage leading into the old house he grinned weakly and said, "Mind, if you see a ghost, do talk to it; you said you would." He stood irresolutely a moment and then turned away. At the door of his dressing-room he paused once more: "I'm here," he called out, "if you should want anything. Good night," and he shut his door.

'I went along the passage to my room, undressed, switched on a lamp beside my bed, read a few pages of *The Jungle Book*, and then, more than ready for sleep, turned the light off and went fast asleep.

*

'Three hours later I woke up. There was not a breath of wind outside. There was not even a flicker of light from the fireplace. As I lay there, an ash tinkled slightly as it cooled, but there was hardly a gleam of the dullest red in the grate. An owl cried among the silent Spanish chestnuts on the slope outside. I idly reviewed the events of the day, hoping that I should fall off to sleep again before I reached dinner. But at the end I seemed as wakeful as ever. There was no help for it. I must read my *Jungle Book* again till I felt ready to go off, so I fumbled for the pear at the end of the cord that hung down inside the bed, and I switched on the bedside lamp. The sudden glory dazzled me for a moment. I felt under my pillow for my book with half-shut eyes. Then, growing used to the light, I happened to look down to the foot of my bed.

'I can never tell you really what happened then. Nothing I could ever confess in the most abject words could even faintly picture to you what I felt. I know that my heart stopped dead, and my throat shut automatically. In one instinctive movement I crouched back up against the head-boards of the bed, staring at the horror. The movement set my heart going again, and the sweat dripped from every pore. I am not a particularly religious man, but I had always believed that God would never allow any supernatural appearance to present itself to man in such a guise and in such circumstances that harm, either bodily or mental, could result to him. I can only tell you that at that moment both my life and my reason rocked unsteadily on their seats.'

The other *Osiris* passengers had gone to bed. Only he and I remained leaning over the starboard railing, which rattled uneasily now and then under the fierce vibration of the over-engined mail-boat. Far over, there were the lights of a few fishing-smacks riding out the night, and a great rush of white combing and seething water fell out and away from us overside.

At last Colvin went on:

'Leaning over the foot of my bed, looking at me, was a figure swathed in a rotten and tattered veiling. This shroud passed over the head, but left both eyes and the right side of the face bare. It then followed the line of the arm down to where the hand grasped the bed-end. The face was not entirely that of a skull, though the eyes and the flesh of the face were totally gone. There was a thin, dry skin drawn tightly over the features, and there was some skin left on the hand. One wisp of hair crossed the forehead. It was perfectly still. I looked at it, and it looked at me, and my brains turned dry and hot in my head. I had still got the pear of the electric lamp in my hand, and I played idly with it; only I dared not turn the light out again. I shut my eyes, only to open them in a hideous terror the same second. The thing had not moved. My heart was thumping, and the sweat cooled me as it evaporated. Another cinder tinkled in the grate, and a panel creaked in the wall.

'My reason failed me. For twenty minutes, or twenty seconds, I was able to think of nothing else but this awful figure, till there came, hurtling through the empty channels of my senses, the remembrance that Broughton and his friends had discussed me furtively at dinner. The dim possibility of its being a hoax stole gratefully into my unhappy mind, and once there, one's pluck came creeping back along a thousand tiny veins. My first sensation was one of blind unreasoning thankfulness that my brain was going to stand the trial. I am not a timid man, but the best of us needs some human handle to steady him in time of extremity, and in this faint but growing hope that after all it might be only a brutal hoax, I found the fulcrum that I needed. At last I moved.

'How I managed to do it I cannot tell you, but with one spring towards the foot of the bed I got within arm's-length and struck out one fearful blow with my fist at the thing. It crumbled under it, and my hand was cut to the bone. With a sickening revulsion after my terror, I dropped half-fainting across the end of the bed. So it was merely a foul trick after all. No doubt the trick had been played many a time before: no doubt Broughton and his friends had had some large bet among themselves as to what I should do when I discovered the gruesome thing. From my state of abject terror I found myself transported into an insensate anger. I shouted curses upon Broughton. I dived rather than climbed over the bed-end on to the sofa. I tore at the robed skeleton – how well the whole thing had been carried out, I thought – I broke the skull against the floor, and stamped upon its dry bones. I flung the head away under the bed, and rent the brittle bones of the trunk in pieces. I snapped the thin thigh-bones across my knee, and flung them in different directions. The shin-bones I set up against a stool and broke with my heel. I raged like a Berserker against the loathly thing, and stripped the ribs from the backbone and slung the breastbone against the cupboard. My fury increased as the work of destruction went on. I tore the frail rotten veil into twenty pieces, and the dust went up over everything, over the clean blotting-paper and the silver inkstand. At last my work was done. There was but a raffle of broken bones and strips of parchment and crumbling wool. Then, picking up a piece of the skull – it was the cheek and temple bone of the right side, I remember – I opened the door and went down the passage to Broughton's dressing-room. I remember still how my sweat-dripping pyjamas clung to me as I walked. At the door I kicked and entered.

'Broughton was in bed. He had already turned the light on and seemed shrunken and horrified. For a moment he could hardly pull himself together. Then I spoke. I don't know what I said. Only I know that from a heart full and over-full with hatred and contempt, spurred on by shame of my own recent cowardice, I let my tongue run on. He answered nothing. I was amazed at my own fluency. My hair still clung lankily to my wet temples, my hand was bleeding profusely, and I must have looked a strange sight. Broughton huddled himself up at the head of the bed just as I had. Still he made no answer, no defence. He seemed preoccupied with something besides my reproaches, and once or twice moistened his lips with his tongue. But he could say nothing though he moved his hands now and then, just as a baby who cannot speak moves its hands.

'At last the door into Mrs Broughton's room opened and she came in, white and terrified. "What is it? What is it? Oh, in God's name! what is it?" she cried again and again, and then she went up to her husband and sat on the bed in her night-dress, and the two faced me. I told her what the matter was. I spared her husband not a word for her presence there. Yet he seemed hardly to understand. I told the pair that I had spoiled their cowardly joke for them. Broughton looked up.

' "I have smashed the foul thing into a hundred pieces," I said. Broughton licked his lips again and his mouth worked. "By God!" I shouted, "it would serve you right if I thrashed you within an inch of your life. I will take care that not a decent man or woman of my acquaintance ever speaks to you again. And there," I added, throwing the broken piece of the skull upon the floor beside his bed, "there is a souvenir for you, of your damned work tonight!"

'Broughton saw the bone, and in a moment it was his turn to frighten me. He squealed like a hare caught in a trap. He screamed and screamed till Mrs Broughton, almost as bewildered as myself, held on to him and coaxed him like a child to be quiet. But Broughton – and as he moved I thought that ten minutes ago I perhaps looked as terribly ill as he did – thrust her from him, and scrambled out of the bed on to the floor, and still screaming put out his hand to the bone. It had blood on it from my hand. He paid no attention to me whatever. In truth I said nothing. This was a new turn indeed to the horrors of the evening. He rose from the floor with the bone in his hand and stood silent. He seemed to be listening. "Time, time, perhaps," he muttered, and almost at the same moment fell at full length on the carpet, cutting his head against the fender. The bone flew from his hand and came to rest near the door. I picked Broughton up, haggard and broken, with blood over his face. He whispered hoarsely and quickly, "Listen, listen!" We listened.

'After ten seconds' utter quiet, I seemed to hear something. I could not be sure, but at last there was no doubt. There was a quiet sound as of one moving along the passage. Little regular steps came towards us over the hard oak flooring. Broughton moved to where his wife sat, white and speechless, on the bed, and pressed her face into his shoulder.

'Then, the last thing that I could see as he turned the light out, he fell forward with his own head pressed into the pillow of the bed. Something in their company, something in their cowardice, helped me, and I faced the open doorway of the room, which was outlined fairly clearly against the dimly lighted passage. I put out one hand and touched Mrs Broughton's shoulder in the darkness. But at the last moment I too failed. I sank on my knees and put my face in the bed. Only we all heard. The footsteps came to the door, and there they stopped. The piece of bone was lying a yard inside the door. There was a rustle of moving stuff, and the thing was in the room. Mrs Broughton was silent: I could hear Broughton's voice praying, muffled in the pillow: I was cursing my own cowardice. Then the steps moved out again on the oak boards of the passage, and I heard the sounds dying away. In a flash of remorse I went to the door and looked out. At the end of the corridor I thought I saw something that moved away. A moment later the passage was empty. I stood with my forehead against the jamb of the door almost physically sick.

' "You can turn the light on," I said, and there was an answering flare. There was no bone at my feet. Mrs Broughton had fainted. Broughton was almost useless, and it took me ten minutes to bring her to. Broughton only said one thing worth remembering. For the most part he went on muttering prayers. But I was glad afterwards to recollect that he had said that thing. He said in a colourless voice, half as a question, half as a reproach, "You didn't speak to her."

'We spent the remainder of the night together. Mrs Broughton actually fell off into a kind of sleep before dawn, but she suffered so horribly in her dreams that I shook her into consciousness again. Never was dawn so long in coming. Three or four times Broughton spoke to himself. Mrs Broughton would then just tighten her hold on his arm, but she could say nothing. As for me, I can honestly say that I grew worse as the hours passed and the light strengthened. The two violent reactions had battered down my steadiness of view, and I felt that the foundations of my life had been built upon the sand. I said nothing, and after binding up my hand with a towel, I did not move. It was better so. They helped me and I helped them, and we all three knew that our reason had gone very near to ruin that night. At last, when the light came in pretty strongly, and the birds outside were chattering and singing, we felt that we must do something. Yet we never moved. You might have thought that we should particularly dislike being found as we were by the servants: yet nothing of that kind mattered a straw, and an overpowering listlessness bound us as we sat, until Chapman, Broughton's man, actually knocked and opened the door. None of us moved. Broughton, speaking hardly and stiffly, said, "Chapman you can come back in five minutes." Chapman was a discreet man, but it would have made no difference to us if he had carried his news to the "room" at once.

'We looked at each other and I said I must go back. I meant to wait outside till Chapman returned. I simply dared not re-enter my bedroom alone. Broughton roused himself and said that he would come with me. Mrs Broughton agreed to remain in her own room for five minutes if the blinds were drawn up and all the doors left open.

'So Broughton and I, leaning stiffly one against the other, went down to my room. By the morning light that filtered past the blinds we could see our way, and I released the blinds. There was nothing wrong in the room from end to end, except smears of my own blood on the end of the bed, on the sofa, and on the carpet where I had torn the thing to pieces.'

Colvin had finished his story. There was nothing to say. Seven bells stuttered out from the fo'c'sle, and the answering cry wailed through the darkness. I took him downstairs.

'Of course I am much better now, but it is a kindness of you to let me sleep in your cabin.'

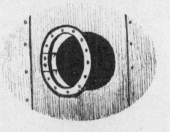

THE UPPER BERTH
BY FRANCIS MARION CRAWFORD

Francis Marion Crawford was born in 1854 in Italy, the son of an American sculptor. He studied at various universities in Europe and the USA, and lived in India for a period in the 1880s where he studied Sanskrit. India provided the inspiration for his first book, *Uncle Isaacs*, published in 1882. Numerous works of both history and fiction followed, but he is best known today for his ghost stories, which were mainly collected in the posthumously published *Uncanny Tales* (1911). Crawford died in Italy, his adopted home for most of his lifetime, in 1909.

I

S OMEBODY ASKED for the cigars. We had talked long, and the conversation was beginning to languish; the tobacco smoke had got into the heavy curtains, the wine had got into those brains which were liable to become heavy, and it was already perfectly evident that, unless somebody did something to rouse our oppressed spirits, the meeting would soon come to its natural conclusion, and we, the guests, would speedily go home to bed, and most certainly to sleep. No one had said anything very remarkable; it may be that no one had anything very remarkable to say. Jones had given us every particular of his last hunting adventure in Yorkshire. Mr Tompkins, of Boston, had explained at elaborate length those working principles, by the due and careful maintenance of which the Atchison, Topeka, and Santa Fé Railroad not only extended its territory, increased its departmental influence, and transported live stock without starving them to death before the day of actual delivery, but, also, had for years succeeded in deceiving those passengers who bought its tickets into the fallacious belief that the corporation aforesaid was really able to transport human life without destroying it. Signor Tombola had endeavoured to persuade us, by arguments which we took no trouble to oppose, that the unity of his country in no way resembled the average modern torpedo, carefully planned, constructed with all the skill of the greatest European arsenals, but, when constructed, destined to be directed by feeble hands into a region where it must undoubtedly explode, unseen, unfeared, and unheard, into the illimitable wastes of political chaos.

It is unnecessary to go into further details. The conversation had assumed proportions which would have bored Prometheus on his rock, which would have driven Tantalus to distraction, and which would have impelled Ixion to seek relaxation in the simple but instructive dialogues of Herr Ollendorff, rather than submit to the greater evil of listening to our talk. We had sat at table for hours; we were bored, we were tired, and nobody showed signs of moving.

Somebody called for cigars. We all instinctively looked towards the speaker. Brisbane was a man of five-and-thirty years of age, and remarkable for those gifts which chiefly attract the attention of men. He was a strong man. The external proportions of his figure presented nothing extraordinary to the common eye, though his size was above the average. He was a little over six feet in height, and moderately broad in the shoulder; he did not appear to be stout, but, on the other hand, he was certainly not thin; his small head was supported by a strong and sinewy neck; his broad, muscular hands appeared to possess a peculiar skill in breaking walnuts without the assistance of the ordinary cracker, and, seeing him in profile, one could not help remarking the extraordinary breadth of his sleeves, and the unusual thickness of his chest. He was one of those men who are commonly spoken of among men as deceptive; that is to say, that though he looked exceedingly strong he was in reality very much stronger than he looked. Of his features I need say little.

His head was small, his hair is thin, his eyes are blue, his nose is large, he has a small moustache, and a square jaw. Everybody knows Brisbane, and when he asked for a cigar everybody looked at him.

'It is a very singular thing,' said Brisbane.

Everybody stopped talking. Brisbane's voice was not loud, but possessed a peculiar quality of penetrating general conversation, and cutting it like a knife. Everybody listened. Brisbane, perceiving that he had attracted their general attention, lit his cigar with great equanimity.

'It is very singular,' he continued, 'that thing about ghosts. People are always asking whether anybody has seen a ghost. I have.'

'Bosh! What, you? You don't mean to say so, Brisbane? Well, for a man of his intelligence!'

A chorus of exclamations greeted Brisbane's remarkable statement. Everybody called for cigars, and Stubbs, the butler, suddenly appeared from the depths of nowhere with a fresh bottle of dry champagne. The situation was saved; Brisbane was going to tell a story.

I am an old sailor, said Brisbane, and as I have to cross the Atlantic pretty often, I have my favourites. Most men have their favourites. I have seen a man wait in a Broadway bar for three-quarters of an hour for a particular car which he liked. I believe the bar-keeper made at least one-third of his living by that man's preference. I have a habit of waiting for certain ships when I am obliged to cross that duck-pond. It may be a prejudice, but I was never cheated out of a good passage but once in my life. I remember it very well; it was a warm morning in June, and the Custom House officials, who were hanging about waiting for a steamer already on her way up from the Quarantine, presented a peculiarly hazy and thoughtful appearance. I had not much luggage – I never have. I mingled with the crowd of passengers, porters, and officious individuals in blue coats and brass buttons, who seemed to spring up like mushrooms from the deck of a moored steamer to obtrude their unnecessary services upon the independent passenger. I have often noticed with a certain interest the spontaneous evolution of these fellows. They are not there when you arrive; five minutes after the pilot has called 'Go ahead!' they, or at least their blue coats and brass buttons, have disappeared from deck and gangway as completely as though they had been consigned to that locker which tradition ascribes to Davy Jones. But, at the moment of starting, they are there, clean-shaved, blue-coated, and ravenous for fees. I hastened on board. The *Kamtschatka* was one of my favourite ships. I say was, because she emphatically no longer is. I cannot conceive of any inducement which could entice me to make another voyage in her. Yes, I know what you are going to say. She is uncommonly clean in the run aft, she has enough bluffing off in the bows to keep her dry, and the lower berths are most of them double. She has a lot of advantages, but I won't cross in her again. Excuse the digression. I got on board. I hailed a steward, whose red nose and redder whiskers were equally familiar to me.

'One hundred and five, lower berth,' said I, in the businesslike tone peculiar to men who think no more of crossing the Atlantic than taking a whisky cocktail at down-town Delmonico's.

The steward took my portmanteau, greatcoat, and rug. I shall never forget the expression on his face. Not that he turned pale. It is maintained by the most eminent divines that even miracles cannot change the course of nature. I have no hesitation in saying that he did not turn pale; but, from his expression, I judged that he was either about to shed tears, to sneeze, or to drop my portmanteau. As the latter contained two bottles of particularly fine old sherry presented to me for my voyage by my old friend Snigginson van Pickyns, I felt extremely nervous. But the steward did none of these things.

'Well, I'm d——d!' said he in a low voice, and led the way.

I supposed my Hermes, as he led me to the lower regions, had had a little grog, but I said nothing, and followed him. One hundred and five was on the port side, well aft. There was nothing remarkable about the state-room. The lower berth, like most of those upon the *Kamtschatka*, was double. There was plenty of room; there was the usual washing apparatus, calculated to convey an idea of luxury to the mind of a North American Indian; there were the usual inefficient racks of brown wood, in which it is more easy to hand a large-sized umbrella than the common tooth-brush of commerce. Upon the uninviting mattresses were carefully bolded together those blankets which a great modern humorist has aptly compared to cold buckwheat cakes. The question of towels was left entirely to the imagination. The glass decanters were filled with a transparent liquid faintly tinged with brown, but from which an odour less faint, but not more pleasing, ascended to the nostrils, like a far-off sea-sick reminiscence of oily machinery. Sad-coloured curtains half-closed the upper berth. The hazy June daylight shed a faint illumination upon the desolate little scene. Ugh! how I hate that state-room!

The steward deposited my traps and looked at me, as though he wanted to get away – probably in search of more passengers and more fees. It is always a good plan to start in favour with those functionaries, and I accordingly gave him certain coins there and then.

'I'll try and make yer comfortable all I can,' he remarked, as he put the coins in his pocket. Nevertheless, there was a doubtful intonation in his voice which surprised me. Possibly his scale of fees had gone up, and he was not satisfied; but on the whole

I was inclined to think that, as he himself would have expressed it, he was 'the better for a glass'. I was wrong, however, and did the man injustice.

II

NOTHING ESPECIALLY worthy of mention occurred during that day. We left the pier punctually, and it was very pleasant to be fairly under way, for the weather was warm and sultry, and the motion of the steamer produced a refreshing breeze. Everybody knows what the first day at sea is like. People pace the decks and stare at each other, and occasionally meet acquaintances whom they did not know to be on board. There is the usual uncertainty as to whether the food will be good, bad, or indifferent, until the first two meals have put the matter beyond a doubt; there is the usual uncertainty about the weather, until the ship is fairly off Fire Island. The tables are crowded at first, and then suddenly thinned. Pale-faced people spring from their seats and precipitate themselves towards the door, and each old sailor breathes more freely as his sea-sick neighbour rushes from his side, leaving him plenty of elbow-room and an unlimited command over the mustard.

One passage across the Atlantic is very much like another, and we who cross very often do not make the voyage for the sake of novelty. Whales and icebergs are indeed always objects of interest, but, after all, one whale is very much like another whale, and one rarely sees an iceberg at close quarters. To the majority of us the most delightful moment of the day on board an ocean steamer is when we have taken our last turn on deck, have smoked our last cigar, and having succeeded in tiring ourselves, feel at liberty to turn in with a clear conscience. On that first night of the voyage I felt particularly lazy, and went to bed in one hundred and five rather earlier than I usually do. As I turned in, I was amazed to see that I was to have a companion. A portmanteau, very like my own, lay in the opposite corner, and in the upper berth had been deposited a neatly-folded rug, with a stick and umbrella. I had hoped to be alone, and I was disappointed; but I wondered who my room-mate was to be, and I determined to have a look at him.

Before I had been long in bed he entered. He was, as far as I could see, a very tall man, very thin, very pale, with sandy hair and whiskers and colourless grey eyes. He had about him, I thought, an air of rather dubious fashion; the sort of man you might see in Wall Street, without being able precisely to say what he was doing there – the sort of man who frequents the Café Anglais, who always seems to be alone and who drinks champagne; you might meet him on a racecourse, but he would never appear to be doing anything there either. A little over-dressed – a little odd. There are three or four of his kind on every ocean steamer. I made up my mind that I did not care to make his acquaintance, and I went to sleep saying to myself that I would study his habits in order to avoid him. If he rose early, I would rise late; if he went to bed late, I would go to bed early. I did not care to know him. If you once know people of that kind they are always turning up. Poor fellow! I need not have taken the trouble to come to so many decisions about him, for I never saw him again after that first night in one hundred and five.

I was sleeping soundly when I was suddenly waked by a loud noise. To judge from the sound, my room-mate must have sprung with a single leap from the upper berth to the floor. I heard him fumbling with the latch and bolt of the door, which opened almost immediately, and then I heard his footsteps as he ran at full speed down the passage, leaving the door open behind him. The ship was rolling a little, and I expected to hear him stumble or fall, but he ran as though he were running for his life. The door swung on its hinges with the motion of the vessel, and the sound annoyed me. I got up and shut it, and groped my way back to my berth in the darkness. I went to sleep again; but I have no idea how long I slept.

When I awoke it was still quite dark, but I felt a disagreeable sensation of cold, and it seemed to me that the air was damp. You know the peculiar smell of a cabin which has been wet with sea-water. I covered myself up as well as I could and dozed off again, framing complaints to be made the next day, and selecting the most powerful epithets in the language. I could hear my room-mate turn over in the upper berth. He had probably returned while I was asleep. Once I thought I heard him groan, and I argued that he was sea-sick. That is particularly unpleasant when one is below. Nevertheless I dozed off and slept till early daylight.

The ship was rolling heavily, much more than on the previous evening, and the grey light which came in through the porthole changed in tint with every movement according as the angle of the vessel's side turned the glass seawards or skywards. It was very cold – unaccountably so for the month of June. I turned my head and looked at the porthole, and saw to my surprise that it was wide open and hooked back. I believe I swore audibly. Then I got up and shut it. As I turned back I glanced at the upper berth. The curtains were drawn close together; my companion had probably felt cold as well as I. It struck me that I had slept enough. The state-room was uncomfortable, though, strange to say, I could not smell the dampness which had annoyed me in the night. My room-mate was still asleep – excellent opportunity for avoiding him, so I dressed at once and went on deck. The day was warm and cloudy, with an oily smell on the water. It was seven o'clock as I came out – much later than I had imagined. I came across the doctor, who was taking his first sniff of the morning air. He was a young man from the West of Ireland – a tremendous fellow, with black hair and blue eyes, already inclined to be stout; he had a happy-go-lucky, healthy look about him which was rather attractive.

'Fine morning,' I remarked, by way of introduction.

'Well,' said he, eyeing me with an air of ready interest, 'it's a fine morning and it's not a fine morning. I don't think it's much of a morning.'

'Well, no – it is not so very fine,' said I.

'It's just what I call fuggly weather,' replied the doctor.

'It was very cold last night, I thought,' I remarked. 'However, when I looked about, I found that the porthole was wide open. I had not noticed it when I went to bed. And the state-room was damp, too.'

'Damp!' said he. 'Whereabouts are you?'

'One hundred and five –'

To my surprise the doctor started visibly, and stared at me.

'What is the matter?' I asked.

'Oh – nothing,' he answered; 'only everybody has complained of that state-room for the last three trips.'

'I shall complain too,' I said. 'It has certainly not been properly aired. It is a shame!'

'I don't believe it can be helped,' answered the doctor. 'I believe there is something – well, it is not my business to frighten passengers.'

'You need not be afraid of frightening me,' I replied. 'I can stand any amount of damp. If I should get a bad cold I will come to you.'

I offered the doctor a cigar, which he took and examined very critically.

'It is not so much the damp,' he remarked. 'However, I dare say you will get on very well. Have you a room-mate?'

'Yes; a deuce of a fellow, who bolts out in the middle of the night, and leaves the door open.'

Again the doctor glanced curiously at me. Then he lit the cigar and looked grave.

'Did he come back?' he asked presently.

'Yes. I was asleep, but I waked up, and heard him moving. Then I felt cold and went to sleep again. This morning I found the porthole open.'

'Look here,' said the doctor quietly, 'I don't care much for this ship. I don't care a rap for her reputation. I tell you what I will do. I have a good-sized place up here. I will share it with you, though I don't know you from Adam.'

I was very much surprised at the proposition. I could not imagine why he should take such a sudden interest in my welfare. However, his manner as he spoke of the ship was peculiar.

'You are very good, doctor,' I said. 'But, really, I believe even now the cabin could be aired, or cleaned out, or something. Why do you not care for the ship?'

'We are not superstitious in our profession, sir,' replied the doctor, 'but the sea makes people so. I don't want to prejudice you, and I don't want to frighten you, but if you will take my advice you will move in here. I would as soon see you overboard,' he added earnestly, 'as know that you or any other man was to sleep in one hundred and five.'

'Good gracious! Why?' I asked.

'Just because on the last three trips the people who have slept there actually have gone overboard,' he answered gravely.

The intelligence was startling and exceedingly unpleasant, I confess. I looked hard at the doctor to see whether he was making game of me, but he looked perfectly serious. I thanked him warmly for his offer, but told him I intended to be the exception to the rule by which every one who slept in that particular state-room went overboard. He did not say much, but looked as grave as ever, and hinted that, before we got across, I should probably reconsider his proposal. In the course of time we went to breakfast, at which only an inconsiderable number of passengers assembled. I noticed that one or two of the officers who breakfasted with us looked grave. After breakfast I went into my state-room in order to get a book. The curtains of the upper berth were still closely drawn. Not a word was to be heard. My room-mate was probably still asleep.

As I came out I met the steward whose business it was to look after me. He whispered that the captain wanted to see me, and then scuttled away down the passage as if very anxious to avoid any questions. I went toward the captain's cabin, and found him waiting for me.

'Sir,' said he, 'I want to ask a favour of you.'

I answered that I would do anything to oblige him.

'Your room-mate had disappeared,' he said. 'He is known to have turned in early last night. Did you notice anything extraordinary in his manner?'

The question coming, as it did, in exact confirmation of the fears the doctor had expressed half an hour earlier, staggered me.

'You don't mean to say he has gone overboard?' I asked.

'I fear he has,' answered the captain.

'This is the most extraordinary thing –' I began.

'Why?' he asked.

'He is the fourth, then?' I exclaimed. In answer to another question from the captain, I explained, without mentioning the doctor, that I had heard the story concerning one hundred and five. He seemed very much annoyed at hearing that I knew of it. I told him what had occurred in the night.

'What you say,' he replied, 'coincides almost exactly with what was told me by the room-mates of two of the other three. They bolt out of bed and run down the passage. Two of them were seen to go overboard by the watch; we stopped and lowered boats, but they were not found. Nobody, however, saw or heard the man who was lost last night — if he is really lost. The steward, who is a superstitious fellow, perhaps, and expected something to go wrong, went to look for him, this morning, and found his berth empty, but his clothes lying about, just as he had left them. The steward was the only man on board who knew him by sight, and he has been searching everywhere for him. He has disappeared! Now, sir, I want to beg you not to mention the circumstance to any of the passengers; I don't want the ship to get a bad name, and nothing hangs about an ocean-goer like stories of suicides. You shall have your choice of any one of the officers' cabins you like, including my own, for the rest of the passage. Is that a fair bargain?'

'Very,' said I; 'and I am much obliged to you. But since I am alone, and have the state-room to myself, I would rather not move. If the steward will take out that unfortunate man's things, I would as leave stay where I am. I will not say anything about the matter, and I think I can promise you that I will not follow my room-mate.'

The captain tried to dissuade me from my intention, but I preferred having a state-room alone to being the chum of any officer on board. I do not know whether I acted foolishly, but if I had taken his advice I should have had nothing more to tell. There would have remained the disagreeable coincidence of several suicides occurring among men who had slept in the same cabin, but that would have been all.

That was not the end of the matter, however, by any means. I obstinately made up my mind that I would not be disturbed by such tales, and I even went so far as to argue the question with the captain. There was something wrong about the state-room, I said. It was rather damp. The porthole had been left open last night. My room-mate might have been ill when he came on board, and he might have become delirious after he went to bed. He might even now be hiding somewhere on board, and might be found later. The place ought to be aired and the fastening on the port looked to. If the captain would give me leave, I would see that what I thought necessary were done immediately.

'Of course you have a right to stay where you are if you please,' he replied, rather petulantly; 'but I wish you would turn out and let me lock the place up, and be done with it.'

I did not see it in the same light, and left the captain, after promising to be silent concerning the disappearance of my companion. The latter had had no acquaintances on board, and was not missed in the course of the day. Towards evening I met the doctor again, and he asked me whether I had changed my mind. I told him I had not.

'Then you will before long,' he said, very gravely.

III

WE PLAYED whist in the evening, and I went to bed late. I will confess now that I felt a disagreeable sensation when I entered my state-room. I could not help thinking of the tall man I had seen on the previous night, who was now dead, drowned, tossing about in the long swell, two or three hundred miles astern. His face rose very distinctly before me as I undressed, and I even went so far as to draw back the curtains of the upper berth, as though to persuade myself that he was actually gone. I also bolted the door of the state-room. Suddenly I became aware that the porthole was open, and fastened back. This was more than I could stand. I hastily threw on my dressing-gown and went in search of Robert, the steward of my passage. I was very angry, I remember, and when I found him I dragged him roughly to the door of one hundred and five, and pushed him towards the open porthole.

'What the deuce do you mean, you scoundrel, by leaving that port open every night? Don't you know it is against the regulations? Don't you know that if the ship heeled and the water began to come in, ten men could not shut it? I will report you to the captain, you blackguard, for endangering the ship!'

I was exceedingly wroth. The man trembled and turned pale, and then began to shut the round glass plate with the heavy brass fittings.

'Why don't you answer me?' I said roughly.

'If you please, sir,' faltered Robert, 'there's nobody on board as can keep this 'ere port shut at night. You can try it yourself, sir. I ain't a-going to stop hany longer on board o' this vessel, sir; I ain't, indeed. But if I was you, sir, I'd just clear out and go and sleep with the surgeon, or something, I would. Look 'ere, sir, is that fastened what you may call securely, or not, sir? Try it, sir, see if it will move a hinch.'

I tried the port, and found it perfectly tight.

'Well, sir,' continued Robert triumphantly, 'I wager my reputation as a A1 steward that in 'arf an hour it will be open again; fastened back, too, sir, that's the horful thing – fastened back!'

I examined the great screw and the looped nut that ran on it.

'If I find it open in the night, Robert, I will give you a sovereign. It is not possible. You may go.'

'Soverin' did you say, sir? Very good, sir. Thank ye, sir. Goodnight, sir. Pleasant reepose, sir, and all manner of hinchantin' dreams, sir.'

Robert scuttled away, delighted at being released. Of course, I thought he was trying to account for his negligence by a silly story, intended to frighten me, and I disbelieved him. The consequence was that he got his sovereign, and I spent a very peculiarly unpleasant night.

I went to bed, and five minutes after I had rolled myself up in my blankets the inexorable Robert extinguished the light that burned steadily behind the ground-glass pane near the door. I lay quite still in the dark trying to go to sleep, but I soon found that impossible. It had been some satisfaction to be angry with the steward, and the diversion had banished that unpleasant sensation I had at first experienced when I thought of the drowned man who had been my chum; but I was no longer sleepy, and I lay awake for some time, occasionally glancing at the porthole, which I could just see from where I lay, and which, in the darkness, looked like a faintly-luminous soup-plate suspended in blackness. I believe I must have lain there for an hour, and, as I remember, I was just dozing into sleep when I was roused by a draught of cold air, and by distinctly feeling the spray of the sea blown upon my face. I started to my feet, and not having allowed in the dark for the motion of the ship, I was instantly thrown violently across the state-room upon the couch which was placed beneath the porthole. I recovered myself immediately, however, and climbed upon my knees. The porthole was again wide open and fastened back!

Now these things are facts. I was wide awake when I got up,

and I should certainly have been waked by the fall had I still been dozing. Moreover, I bruised my elbows and knees badly, and the bruises were there on the following morning to testify to the fact, if I myself had doubted it. The porthole was wide open and fastened back – a thing so unaccountable that I remember very well feeling astonishment rather that fear when I discovered it. I at once closed the plate again, and screwed down the loop nut with all my strength. It was very dark in the state-room. I reflected that the port had certainly been opened within an hour after Robert had at first shut it in my presence, and I determined to watch it, and see whether it would open again. Those brass fittings are very heavy and by no means easy to move; I could not believe that the clamp had been turned by the shaking of the screw. I stood peering out through the thick glass at the alternate white and grey streaks of the sea that foamed beneath the ship's side. I must have remained there a quarter of an hour.

Suddenly, as I stood, I distinctly heard something moving behind me in one of the berths, and a moment afterwards, just as I turned instinctively to look – though I could, of course, see nothing in the darkness – I heard a very faint groan. I sprang across the state-room, and tore the curtains of the upper berth aside, thrusting in my hands to discover if there were any one there. There was some one.

I remember that the sensation as I put my hands forward was as though I were plunging them into the air of a damp cellar, and from behind the curtains came a gust of wind that smelled horribly of stagnant sea-water. I laid hold of something that had the shape of a man's arm, but was smooth, and wet, and icy cold. But suddenly, as I pulled, the creature sprang violently forward against me, a clammy oozy mass, as it seemed to me, heavy and wet, yet endowed with a sort of supernatural strength. I reeled across the state-room, and in an instant the door opened and the thing rushed out. I had not had time to be frightened, and quickly recovering myself, I sprang through the door and gave chase at the top of my speed, but I was too late. Ten yards before me I could see – I am sure I saw it – a dark shadow moving in the dimly lighted passage, quickly as the shadow of a fast horse thrown before a dog-cart by the lamp on a dark night. But in a moment it had disappeared, and I found myself holding on to the polished rail that ran along the bulkhead where the passage turned towards the companion. My hair stood on end, and the cold perspiration rolled down my face. I am not ashamed of it in the least: I was very badly frightened.

Still I doubted my senses, and pulled myself together. It was absurd, I thought. The Welsh rarebit I had eaten had disagreed with me. I had been in a nightmare. I made my way back to my state-room, and entered it with an effort. The whole place smelled of stagnant sea-water, as it had when I had waked on the previous evening. It required my utmost strength to go in, and grope among my things for a box of wax lights. As I lighted a railway reading lantern which I always carry in case I want to read after the lamps are out, I perceived that the porthole was again open, and a sort of creeping horror began to take possession of me which I never felt before, nor wish to feel again. But I got a light and proceeded to examine the upper berth, expecting to find it drenched with sea-water.

But I was disappointed. The bed had been slept in, and the smell of the sea was strong; but the bedding was as dry as a bone. I fancied that Robert had not had the courage to make the bed after the accident of the previous night – it had all been a hideous dream. I drew the curtains back as far as I could and examined the place very carefully. It was perfectly dry. But the porthole was open again. With a sort of dull bewilderment of horror I closed it and screwed it down, and thrusting my heavy stick through the brass loop, wrenched it with all my might, till the thick metal began to bend under the pressure. Then I hooked my reading lantern into the red velvet at the head of the couch, and sat down to recover my senses if I could. I sat there all night, unable to think of rest – hardly able to think at all. But the port-hole remained closed, and I did not believe it would now open again without the application of a considerable force.

The morning dawned at last, and I dressed myself slowly, thinking over all that had happened in the night. It was a beautiful day and I went on deck, glad to get out into the early, pure sunshine, and to smell the breeze from the blue water, so different from the noisome, stagnant odour of my state-room. Instinctively I turned aft, towards the surgeon's cabin. There he stood, with a pipe in his mouth, taking his morning airing precisely as on the preceding day.

'Good-morning,' said he quietly, but looking at me with evident curiosity.

'Doctor, you were quite right,' said I. 'There is something wrong about that place.'

'I thought you would change your mind,' he answered, rather triumphantly. 'You have had a bad night, eh? Shall I make you a pick-me-up? I have a capital recipe.'

'No, thanks,' I cried. 'But I would like to tell you what happened.'

I then tried to explain as clearly as possible precisely what had occurred, not omitting to state that I had been scared as I had never been scared in my whole life before. I dwelt particularly on the phenomenon of the porthole, which was a fact to which I could testify, even if the rest had been an illusion. I had closed it twice in the night, and the second time I had actually bent the brass in wrenching it with my stick. I believe I insisted a good deal on this point.

'You seem to think I am likely to doubt the story,' said the doctor, smiling at my detailed account of the state of the porthole. 'I do not doubt in the least. I renew my invitation to you. Bring your traps here, and take half my cabin.'

'Come and take half of mine for one night,' I said. 'Help me to get at the bottom of this thing.'

'You will get to the bottom of something else if you try,' answered the doctor.

'What?' I asked.

'The bottom of the sea. I am going to leave this ship. It is not canny.'

'Then you will not help me to find out —'

'Not I,' said the doctor quickly. 'It is my business to keep my wits about me — not to go fiddling about with ghosts and things.'

'Do you really believe it is a ghost?' I enquired, rather contemptuously. But as I spoke I remembered very well the horrible sensation of the supernatural which had got possession of me during the night. The doctor turned sharply on me —

'Have you any reasonable explanation of these things to offer?' he asked. 'No; you have not. Well, you say you will find an explanation. I say that you won't, sir, simply because there is not any.'

'But, my dear sir,' I retorted, 'do you, a man of science, mean to tell me that such things cannot be explained?'

'I do,' he answered stoutly. 'And, if they could, I would not be concerned in the explanation.'

I did not care to spend another night alone in the state-room, and yet I was obstinately determined to get at the root of the disturbances. I do not believe there are many men who would have slept there alone, after passing two such nights. But I made up my mind to try it, if I could not get any one to share a watch with me. The doctor was evidently not inclined for such an experiment. He said he was a surgeon, and that in case any accident occurred on board he must be always in readiness. He could not afford to have his nerves unsettled. Perhaps he was quite right, but I am inclined to think that his precaution was prompted by his inclination. On enquiry, he informed me that there was no one on board who would be likely to join me in my investigations, and after a little more conversation I left him. A little later I met the captain, and told him my story. I said that, if no one would spend the night with me, I would ask leave to have the light burning all night, and would try it alone.

'Look here,' said he, 'I will tell you what I will do. I will share your watch myself, and we will see what happens. It is my belief that we can find out between us. There may be some fellow skulking on board, who steals a passage by frightening the passengers. It is just possible that there may be something queer in the carpentering of that berth.'

I suggested taking the ship's carpenter below and examining the place; but I was overjoyed at the captain's offer to spend the night with me. He accordingly sent for the workman and ordered him to do anything I required. We went below at once. I had all the bedding cleared out of the upper berth, and we examined the place thoroughly to see if there was a board loose anywhere, or a panel which could be opened or pushed aside. We tried the planks everywhere, tapped the flooring, unscrewed the fittings of the lower berth and took it to pieces – in short, there was not a square inch of the state-room which was not searched and tested. Everything was in perfect order, and we put everything back in its place. As we were finishing our work, Robert came to the door and looked in.

'Well, sir – find anything, sir?' he asked, with a ghastly grin.

'You were right about the porthole, Robert,' I said, and I gave him the promised sovereign. The carpenter did his work silently and skilfully, following my directions. When he had done he spoke.

'I'm a plain man, sir,' he said. 'But it's my belief you had better just turn out your things, and let me run half a dozen four-inch screws through the door of this cabin. There's no good never came o' this cabin yet, sir, and that's all about it. There's been four lives lost out o' here to my own remembrance, and that is four trips. Better give it up, sir – better give it up!'

'I will try it for one night more,' I said.

'Better give it up, sir – better give it up! It's a precious bad job,' repeated the workman, putting his tools in his bag and leaving the cabin.

But my spirits had risen considerably at the prospect of having the captain's company, and I made up my mind not to be prevented from going to the end of this strange business. I abstained from Welsh rarebits and grog that evening, and did not even join in the customary game of whist. I wanted to be quite sure of my nerves, and my vanity made me anxious to make a good figure in the captain's eyes.

IV

THE CAPTAIN was one of those splendidly tough and cheerful specimens of seafaring humanity whose combined courage, hardihood, and calmness in difficulty leads them naturally into high posiitons of trust. He was not the man to be led away by an idle tale, and the mere fact that he was willing to join me in the investigation was proof that he thought there was something seriously wrong, which could not be accounted for on ordinary theories, nor laughed down as a common superstition. To some extent, too, his reputation was at stake, as well as the reputation of the ship. It is no light thing to lose passengers overboard, and he knew it.

About ten o'clock that evening, as I was smoking a last cigar, he came up to me, and drew me aside from the beat of the other passengers who were patrolling the deck in the warm darkness.

'This is a serious matter, Mr Brisbane,' he said. 'We must make up our minds either way – to be disappointed or to have a pretty rough time of it. You see I cannot afford to laugh at the affair, and I will ask you to sign your name to a statement of whatever occurs. If nothing happens tonight we will try it again tomorrow and next day. Are you ready?'

So we went below, and entered the state-room. As we went in I could see Robert the steward, who stood a little further down the passage, watching us, with his usual grin, as though certain that something dreadful was about to happen. The captain closed the door behind us and bolted it.

'Supposing we put your portmanteau before the door,' he suggested. 'One of us can sit on it. Nothing can get out then. Is the port screwed down?'

I found it as I had left it in the morning. Indeed, without using a lever, as I had done, no one could have opened it. I drew back the curtains of the upper berth so that I could see well into it. By the captain's advice I lighted my reading lantern, and placed it so that it shone upon the white sheets above. He insisted upon sitting on the portmanteau, declaring that he wished to be able to swear that he had sat before the door.

Then he requested me to search the state-room thoroughly,

an operation very soon accomplished, as it consisted merely in looking beneath the lower berth and under the couch below the porthole. The spaces were quite empty.

'It is impossible for any human being to get in,' I said, 'or for any human being to open the port.'

'Very good,' said the captain calmly. 'If we see anything now, it must be either imagination or something supernatural.'

I sat down on the edge of the lower berth.

'The first time it happened,' said the captain, crossing his legs and leaning back against the door, 'was in March. The passenger who slept here, in the upper berth, turned out to have been a lunatic – at all events, he was known to have been a little touched, and he had taken his passage without the knowledge of his friends. He rushed out in the middle of the night, and threw himself overboard, before the officer who had the watch could stop him. We stopped and lowered a boat; it was a quiet night, just before that heavy weather came on; but we could not find him. Of course his suicide was afterwards accounted for on the ground of his insanity.'

'I suppose that often happens?' I remarked, rather absently.

'Not often – no,' said the captain; 'never before in my experience, though I have heard of it happening on board of other ships. Well, as I was saying, that occurred in March. On the very next trip—What are you looking at?' he asked, stopping suddenly in his narration.

I believe I gave no answer. My eyes were riveted upon the porthole. It seemed to me that the brass loop-nut was beginning to turn very slowly upon the screw – so slowly, however, that I was not sure it moved at all. I watched it intently, fixing its position in my mind, and trying to ascertain whether it changed. Seeing where I was looking, the captain looked too.

'It moves!' he exclaimed, in a tone of conviction. 'No, it does not,' he added, after a minute.

'If it were the jarring of the screw,' said I, 'it would have opened during the day; but I found it this evening jammed tight as I left it this morning.'

I rose and tried the nut. It was certainly loosened, for by an effort I could move it with my hands.

'The queer thing,' said the captain, 'is that the second man who was lost is supposed to have got through that very port. We had a terrible time over it. It was in the middle of the night, and the weather was very heavy; there was an alarm that one of the ports was open and the sea running in. I came below and found everything flooded, the water pouring in every time she rolled, and the whole port swinging from the top bolts – not the port-hole in the middle. Well, we managed to shut it, but the water did some damage. Ever since that the place smells of sea-water from time to time. We supposed the passenger had thrown himself out, though the Lord only knows how he did it. The steward kept telling me that he cannot keep anything shut here. Upon my word – I can smell it now, cannot you?' he enquired, sniffing the air suspiciously.

'Yes – distinctly,' I said, and I shuddered as that same odour of stagnant sea-water grew stronger in the cabin. 'Now, to smell like this, the place must be damp,' I continued, 'and yet when I examined it with the carpenter this morning everything was perfectly dry. It is most extraordinary – hallo!'

My reading lantern, which had been placed in the upper berth, was suddenly extinguished. There was still a good deal of light from the pane of ground glass near the door, behind which loomed the regulation lamp. The ship rolled heavily, and the curtain of the upper berth swung far out into the state-room and back again. I rose quickly from my seat on the edge of the bed, and the captain at the same moment started to his feet with a loud cry of surprise. I had turned with the intention of taking down the lantern to examine it, when I heard his exclamation, and immediately afterwards his call for help. I sprang towards him. He was wrestling with all his might with the brass loop of the port. It seemed to turn against his hands in spite of all his efforts. I caught up my cane, a heavy oak stick I always used to carry, and thrust it through the ring and bore on it with all my strength. But the strong wood snapped suddenly and I fell upon the couch. When I rose again the port was wide open, and the captain was standing with his back against the door, pale to the lips.

'There is something in that berth!' he cried, in a strange voice, his eyes almost starting from his head. 'Hold the door, while I look – it shall not escape us, whatever it is!'

But instead of taking his place, I sprang upon the lower bed, and seized something which lay in the upper berth.

It was something ghostly, horrible beyond words, and it moved in my grip. It was like the body of a man long drowned, and yet it moved, and had the strength of ten men living; but I gripped it with all my might – the slippery, oozy, horrible thing – the dead white eyes seemed to stare at me out of the dusk; the putrid odour of rank sea-water was about it, and its shiny hair hung in foul wet curls over its dead face. I wrestled with the dead thing; it thrust itself upon me and forced me back and nearly broke my arms; it wound its corpse's arms about my neck, the living death, and overpowered me, so that I, at last, cried aloud and fell, and left my hold.

As I fell the thing sprang across me, and seemed to throw itself upon the captain. When I last saw him on his feet his face was white and his lips set. It seemed to me that he struck a violent blow at the dead being, and then he, too, fell forward upon his face, with an inarticulate cry of horror.

The thing paused an instant, seeming to hover over his

prostrate body, and I could have screamed again for very fright, but I had no voice left. The thing vanished suddenly, and it seemed to my disturbed senses that it made its exit through the open port, though how that was possible, considering the smallness of the aperture, is more than any one can tell. I lay a long time on the floor, and the captain lay beside me. At last I partially recovered my senses and moved, and instantly I knew that my arm was broken – the small bone of my left forearm near the wrist.

I got upon my feet somehow, and with my remaining hand I tried to raise the captain. He groaned and moved, and at last came to himself. He was not hurt, but he seemed badly stunned.

Well, do you want to hear any more? There is nothing more. That is the end of my story. The carpenter carried out his scheme of running half a dozen four-inch screws through the door of one hundred and five; and if ever you take a passage in the *Kamtschatka*, you may ask for a berth in that state-room. You will be told that it is engaged – yes – it is engaged by that dead thing.

I finished the trip in the surgeon's cabin. He doctored my broken arm, and advised me not to 'fiddle about with ghosts and things' any more. The captain was very silent, and never sailed again in that ship, though it is still running. And I will not sail in her either. It was a very disagreeable experience, and I was very badly frightened, which is a thing I do not like. That is all. That is how I saw a ghost – if it was a ghost. It was dead, anyhow.

THE AUTHENTIC NARRATIVE
OF THE GHOST OF A HAND
BY JOSEPH SHERIDAN LE FANU

Joseph Sheridan Le Fanu was born in 1814 in Dublin. He
trained as a lawyer, but began publishing stories in 1838 in
Trinity College student magazine. He worked as a journalist and newspaper proprietor, but enjoyed a period of great
popularity in the middle part of the century, following the
publication of his best-known mystery novels, *The House
by the Churchyard* (1863), *Uncle Silas* (1864) and *Carmilla*
(1872). Long after Le Fanu's death in 1873, M.R. James
edited a collection of supernatural tales, *Madam Crowl's
Ghost and Other Tales of Mystery* (1923), which helped to
consolidate Le Fanu's reputation as a master of the Victorian
ghost story.

MISS REBECCA Chattesworth, in a letter dated late in the autumn of 1753, gives a minute and curious relation of occurrences in the Tiled House, which, it is plain, although at starting she protests against all such fooleries, she has heard with a peculiar sort of interest, and relates it certainly with an awful sort of particularity.

I was for printing the entire letter, which is really very singular as well as characteristic. But my publisher meets me with his *veto*; and I believe he is right. The worthy old lady's letter *is*, perhaps, too long; and I must rest content with a few hungry notes of its tenor.

That year, and somewhere about the 24th October, there broke out a strange dispute between Mr Alderman Harper, of High Street, Dublin, and my Lord Castlemallard, who, in virtue of his cousinship to the young heir's mother, had undertaken for him the management of the tiny estate on which the Tiled or Tyled House – for I find it spelt both ways – stood.

This Alderman Harper had agreed for a lease of the house for his daughter, who was married to a gentleman named Prosser. He furnished it, and put up hangings, and otherwise went to

considerable expense. Mr and Mrs Prosser came there some time
in June, and after having parted with a good many servants in
the interval, she made up her mind that she could not live in the
house, and her father waited on Lord Castlemallard, and told
him plainly that he would not take out the lease because the
house was subjected to annoyances which he could not explain.
In plain terms, he said it was haunted, and that no servants
would live there more than a few weeks, and that after what his
son-in-law's family had suffered there, not only should he be
excused from taking a lease of it, but that the house itself ought
to be pulled down as a nuisance and the habitual haunt of something worse than human malefactors.

Lord Castlemallard filed a bill in the Equity side of the
Exchequer to compel Mr Alderman Harper to perform his con-
tract, by taking out the lease. But the Alderman drew an answer,
supported by no less than seven long affidavits, copies of all
which were furnished to his lordship, and with the desired effect;
for rather than compel him to place them upon the file of the
court, his lordship struck, and consented to release him.

I am sorry the cause did not proceed at least far enough to place
upon the files of the court the very authentic and unaccountable
story which Miss Rebecca relates.

The annoyances described did not begin till the end of
August, when, one evening, Mrs Prosser, quite alone, was sitting in the twilight at the back parlour window, which was open,
looking out into the orchard, and plainly saw a hand stealthily
placed upon the stone window-sill outside, as if by someone
beneath the window, at her right side, intending to climb up.
There was nothing but the hand, which was rather short but
handsomely formed, and white and plump, laid on the edge of
the window-sill; and it was not a very young hand, but one aged,
somewhere about forty, as she conjectured. It was only a few

weeks before that the horrible robbery at Clondalkin had taken place, and the lady fancied that the hand was that of one of the miscreants who was now about to scale the windows of the Tiled House. She uttered a loud scream and an ejaculation of terror, and at the same moment the hand was quietly withdrawn.

Search was made in the orchard, but no indications of any person's having been under the window, beneath which, ranged along the wall, stood a great column of flower-pots, which it seemed must have prevented any one's coming within reach of it.

The same night there came a hasty tapping, every now and then, at the window of the kitchen. The women grew frightened, and the servant-man, taking firearms with him, opened the back-door, but discovered nothing. As he shut it, however, he said, 'a thump came on it', and a pressure as of somebody striving to force his way in, which frightened *him*; and though the tapping went on upon the kitchen window panes, he made no further explorations.

About six o'clock on the Saturday evening following, the cook, 'an honest, sober woman, now aged nigh sixty years', being alone in the kitchen, saw, on looking up, it is supposed, the same fat but aristocratic-looking hand, laid with its palm against the glass, near the side of the window, and this time moving slowly up and down, pressed all the while against the glass, as if feeling carefully for some inequality in its surface. She cried out, and said something like a prayer on seeing it. But it was not withdrawn for several seconds after.

After this, for a great many nights, there came at first a low, and afterwards an angry rapping, as it seemed with a set of clenched knuckles, at the back-door. And the servant-man would not open it, but called to know who was there; and there came no answer, only a sound as if the palm of the hand was placed against it, and drawn slowly from side to side with a sort of soft, groping motion.

All this time, sitting in the back parlour, which, for the time, they used as a drawing-room, Mr and Mrs Prosser were disturbed by rappings at the window, sometimes very low and furtive, like a clandestine signal, and at others sudden, and so loud as to threaten the breaking of the pane.

This was all at the back of the house, which looked upon the orchard as you know. But on a Tuesday night, at about half-past nine, there came precisely the same rapping at the hall-door, and went on, to the great annoyance of the master and terror of his wife, at intervals, for nearly two hours.

After this, for several days and nights, they had no annoyance whatsoever, and began to think that nuisance had expended itself. But on the night of the 13th September, Jane Easterbrook, an English maid, having gone into the pantry for the small silver bowl in which her mistress's posset was served, happening to look up at the little window of only four panes, observed through an auger-hole which was drilled through the window frame, for the admission of a bolt to secure the shutter, a white pudgy finger—first the tip, and then the two first joints introduced, and turned about this way and that, crooked against the inside, as if in search of a fastening which its owner designed to push aside. When the maid got back into the kitchen we are told 'she fell into "a swounde", and was all the next day very weak'.

Mr Prosser being, I've heard, a hard-headed and conceited sort of fellow, scouted the ghost, and sneered at the fears of his family. He was privately of opinion that the whole affair was a practical joke or a fraud, and waited an opportunity of catching the rogue *flagrante delicto*. He did not long keep this theory to himself, but let it out by degrees with no stint of oaths and threats, believing that some domestic traitor held the thread of the conspiracy.

Indeed it was time something were done; for not only his servants, but good Mrs Prosser herself, had grown to look unhappy and anxious. They kept at home from the hour of sunset, and would not venture about the house after nightfall, except in couples.

The knocking had ceased for about a week, when one night, Mrs Prosser being in the nursery, her husband, who was in the parlour, heard it begin very softly at the hall-door. The air was quite still, which favoured his hearing distinctly. This was the first time there had been any disturbance at that side of the house, and the character of the summons was changed.

Mr Prosser, leaving the parlour-door open, it seems, went quietly into the hall. The sound was that of beating on the outside of the stout door, softly and regularly, 'with the flat of the hand'. He was going to open it suddenly, but changed his mind; and went back very quietly, and on to the head of the kitchen stair, where there was a 'strong closet' over the pantry, in which he kept his firearms, swords, and canes.

Here he called his manservant, whom he believed to be honest, and, with a pair of loaded pistols in his own coat-pockets, and giving another pair to him, he went as lightly as he could, followed by the man, and with a stout walking-cane in his hand, forward to the door.

Everything went as Mr Prosser wished. The besieger of his house, so far from taking fright at their approach, grew more impatient; and the sort of patting which had aroused his attention at first assumed the rhythm and emphasis of a series of double-knocks.

Mr Prosser, angry, opened the door with his right arm across, cane in hand. Looking, he saw nothing; but his arm was jerked up oddly, as it might be with the hollow of a hand, and something passed under it, with a kind of gentle squeeze. The servant neither saw nor felt anything, and did not know why his master looked back so hastily, cutting with his cane, and shutting the door with so sudden a slam.

From that time Mr Prosser discontinued his angry talk and swearing about it, and seemed nearly as averse from the subject as the rest of his family. He grew, in fact, very uncomfortable, feeling an inward persuasion that when, in answer to the summons, he had opened the hall-door, he had actually given admission to the besieger.

He said nothing to Mrs Prosser, but went up earlier to his bedroom, 'where he read a while in his Bible, and said his prayers'. I hope the particular relation of this circumstance does not indicate its singularity. He lay awake a good while, it appears; and, as he supposed, about a quarter past twelve he heard the soft palm of a hand patting on the outside of the bedroom door, and then brushed slowly along it.

Up bounced Mr Prosser, very much frightened, and locked the door, crying, 'Who's there?' but receiving no answer but the same brushing sound of a soft hand drawn over the panels, which he knew only too well.

In the morning the housemaid was terrified by the impression of a hand in the dust of the 'little parlour' table, where they had been unpacking delft and other things the day before. The print of the naked foot in the sea-sand did not frighten Robinson Crusoe half so much. They were by this time all nervous, and some of them half-crazed, about the hand.

Mr Prosser went to examine the mark, and made light of it, but as he swore afterwards, rather to quiet his servants than from any comfortable feeling about it in his own mind; however, he had them all, one by one, into the room, and made each place his or her hand, palm downward, on the same table, thus taking a similar impression from every person in the house, including himself and his wife; and his 'affidavit' deposed that the formation of the hand so impressed differed altogether from those of the living inhabitants of the house, and corresponded with that of the hand seen by Mrs Prosser and by the cook.

Whoever or whatever the owner of that hand might be, they all felt this subtle demonstration to mean that it was declared he was no longer out of doors, but had established himself in the house.

And now Mrs Prosser began to be troubled with strange and horrible dreams, some of which as set out in detail, in Aunt Rebecca's long letter, are really very appalling nightmares. But one night, as Mr Prosser closed his bedchamber-door, he was struck somewhat by the utter silence of the room, there being no sound of breathing, which seemed unaccountable to him, as he knew his wife was in bed, and his ears were particularly sharp.

There was a candle burning on a small table at the foot of the bed, beside the one he held in one hand, a heavy ledger, connected with his father-in-law's business being under his arm. He drew the curtain at the side of the bed, and saw Mrs Prosser lying, as for a few seconds he mortally feared, dead, her face being motionless, white, and covered with a cold dew; and on the pillow, close beside her head, and just within the curtains, was, as he first thought, a toad – but really the same fattish hand, the wrist resting on the pillow, and the fingers extended towards her temple.

Mr Prosser, with a horrified jerk, pitched the ledger right at the curtains, behind which the owner of the hand might be supposed to stand. The hand was instantaneously and smoothly snatched away, the curtains made a great wave, and Mr Prosser got round the bed in time to see the closet-door, which was at the other side, pulled to by the same white, puffy hand, as he believed.

He drew the door open with a fling, and stared in: but the closet was empty, except for the clothes hanging from the pegs on the wall, and the dressing-table and looking-glass facing the windows. He shut it sharply, and locked it, and felt for a minute, he says, 'as if he were like to lose his wits'; then, ringing at the bell, he brought the servants, and with much ado they recovered Mrs Prosser from a sort of 'trance', in which, he says, from her looks, she seemed to have suffered 'the pains of death': and Aunt Rebecca adds, 'from what she told me of her visions, with her own lips, he might have added, "and of hell also" '.

But the occurrence which seems to have determined the crisis was the strange sickness of their eldest child, a little boy aged between two and three years. He lay awake, seemingly in paroxysms of terror, and the doctors who were called in, set down the symptoms to incipient water on the brain. Mrs Prosser used to sit up with the nurse by the nursery fire, much troubled in mind about the condition of her child.

His bed was placed sideways along the wall, with its head against the door of a press or cupboard, which, however, did not shut quite close. There was a little valance, about a foot deep, round the top of the child's bed, and this descended within some ten or twelve inches of the pillow on which it lay.

They observed that the little creature was quieter whenever they took it up and held it on their laps. They had just replaced him, as he seemed to have grown quite sleepy and tranquil, but he was not five minutes in his bed when he began to scream in one of his frenzies of terror; at the same moment the nurse, for the first time, detected, and Mrs Prosser equally plainly saw, following the direction of *her* eyes, the real cause of the child's sufferings.

Protruding through the aperture of the press, and shrouded in the shade of the valance, they plainly saw the white fat hand, palm downwards, presented towards the head of the child. The mother uttered a scream, and snatched the child from its little bed, and she and the nurse ran down to the lady's sleeping-room, where Mr Prosser was in bed, shutting the door as they entered; and they had hardly done so, when a gentle tap came to it from the outside.

There is a great deal more, but this will suffice. The singularity of the narrative seems to me to be this, that it describes the ghost of a hand, and no more. The person to whom that hand belonged never once appeared: nor was it a hand separated from a body, but only a hand so manifested and introduced that its owner was always, by some crafty accident, hidden from view.

In the year 1819, at a college breakfast, I met a Mr Prosser – a thin, grave, but rather chatty old gentleman, with very white hair drawn back into a pigtail – and he told us all, with a concise particularity, a story of his cousin, James Prosser, who, when an infant, had slept for some time in what his mother said was a haunted nursery in an old house near Chapelizod, and who, whenever he was ill, over-fatigued, or in any wise feverish, suffered all through his life as he had done from a time he could scarce remember, from a vision of a certain gentleman, fat and pale, every curl of whose wig, every button and fold of whose laced clothes, and every feature and line of whose sensual, benignant, and unwholesome face, was as minutely engraven upon his memory as the dress and lineaments of his own grandfather's portrait, which hung before him every day at breakfast, dinner, and supper.

Mr Prosser mentioned this as an instance of a curiously monotonous, individualised, and persistent nightmare, and hinted the extreme horror and anxiety with which his cousin, of whom he spoke in the past tense as 'poor Jemmie', was at any time induced to mention it.

I hope the reader will pardon me for loitering so long in the Tiled House, but this sort of lore has always had a charm for me; and people, you know, especially old people, will talk of what most interests themselves, too often forgetting that others may have had more than enough of it.

A PAIR OF HANDS
BY ARTHUR QUILLER-COUCH

Sir Arthur Thomas Quiller-Couch was born in Cornwall in 1863 and educated at Oxford. He published his first novel, *Dead Man's Rock*, in 1887, the beginning of a formidable literary output which included works of literary criticism and journalism as well as novels, stories and poetry. He edited several anthologies, including the influential *Oxford Book of English Verse* (1900). He was knighted in 1910, and appointed a Professor of English Literature at the University of Cambridge in 1912 – his inaugural lectures were published in two volumes, *On the Art of Writing* and *On the Art of Reading*, in 1916 and 1920. Quiller-Couch died at his home in Cornwall in May 1944.

I T HAPPENED when I lived down in Cornwall. Tresillack was the name of the house, which stood quite alone at the head of a coombe, within sound of the sea but without sight of it; for though the coombe led down to a wide open beach it wound and twisted on its way, and its overlapping sides closed the view from the house, which was advertised as 'secluded'. I was very poor in those days, but I was young enough to be romantic and wise enough to like independence, and the word 'secluded' took my fancy.

'The misfortune was that it had taken the fancy of several previous tenants. You know, I dare say, the kind of person who rents a secluded house in the country? "Shady" is the word, is it not? Well, the previous tenants of Tresillack had been shady with a vengeance.

'I knew nothing of this when I first made application to the landlord, who lived in a farm at the foot of the coombe, on a cliff overlooking the beach.

'To him I presented myself fearlessly as a spinster of decent family and small but assured income, intending a rural life of seemliness and economy. He met my advances politely, but with an air of suspicion. I began by disliking him for it; afterwards I set it down as an unpleasant feature in the local character. I was doubly mistaken. Farmer Hosking was slow-witted, but as honest a man as ever stood up against hard times; and a more open and hospitable race than the people on that coast I never wish to meet. It was the caution of a child who had burnt his fingers, not once but many times. Had I known what I afterwards learned of Farmer Hosking's tribulations as landlord of a "secluded country residence", I should have faltered as I undertook to prove the bright exception in a long line of painful experiences. He had bought the Tresillack estate twenty years before because the land adjoined his own, but the house was a nuisance and had been so from the beginning.

' "Well, miss," he said, "you're welcome to look over it; a pretty enough place, inside and out. There's no trouble about keys, because I've put in a housekeeper, a widow-woman, and she'll show you round. With your leave I'll step up the coombe so far with you, and put you in your way." As I thanked him he paused and rubbed his chin. "There's one thing I must tell you, though. Whoever takes the house must take Mrs Carkeek along with it."

' "Mrs Carkeek?" I echoed dolefully. "Is that the housekeeper?"

' "Yes. I'm sorry, miss," he added, my face telling him no doubt what sort of woman I expected Mrs Carkeek to be; "but I had to make it a rule after — after some things had happened. And I dare say you won't find her so bad. Mary Carkeek's a sensible, comfortable woman, and knows the place. She was in service there to Squire Kendall when he sold up and went: her first place it was."

' "I may as well see the house, anyhow," said I dejectedly. So we started to walk up the coombe. The path, which ran beside a little chattering stream, was narrow for the most part, and

Farmer Hosking, with an apology, strode on ahead to beat aside the brambles. But whenever its width allowed us to walk side by side I caught him from time to time stealing a shy inquisitive glance under his rough eyebrows. It was clear that he could not sum me up to his satisfaction.

'I don't know what foolish fancy prompted it, but about half-way up the coombe I stopped short and asked:

' "There are no ghosts, I suppose?"

'It struck me, a moment after I had uttered it, as a supremely silly question; but he took it quite seriously. "No: I never heard tell of any ghosts." He laid a queer sort of stress on the word. "There's always been trouble with servants, and maids' tongues will be runnin'. But Mary Carkeek lives up there alone, and she seems comfortable enough."

'We walked on. By and by he pointed with his stick. "It don't look like a place for ghosts, now, do it?"

'Certainly it did not. Above an untrimmed orchard rose a terrace of turf scattered with thorn bushes, and above this a terrace of stone, upon which stood the prettiest cottage I had ever seen. It was long and low and thatched; a deep verandah ran from end to end. Clematis, banksia roses and honeysuckle climbed the posts of this verandah and clustered along its roof, beneath the lattices of the bedroom windows. The house was small enough to be called a cottage, and rare enough in features and in situation to confer distinction on any tenant. It suggested what in those days we should have called "elegant" living. And I could have clapped my hands for joy.

'My spirits mounted still higher when Mrs Carkeek opened the door. A healthy middle-aged woman with a thoughtful, but contented, face, and a smile, she was comfortable; and while we walked through the rooms together (for Mr Hosking waited outside) I "took to" Mrs Carkeek. Her speech was direct and practical; the rooms, in spite of their faded furniture, were bright and exquisitely clean; and somehow the very atmosphere of the house gave me a sense of feeling at home and cared for; yes, of being loved. Don't laugh, my dears; for when I've done you may not think this fancy altogether foolish.

'I stepped out onto the verandah, and Farmer Hosking pocketed the pruning-knife which he had been using on a bush of jasmine.

' "This is better than anything I had dreamed of," said I.

' "Well, miss, that's not a wise way of beginning a bargain, if you'll excuse me."

'He took no advantage, however, and we struck the bargain as we returned down the coombe to his farm. I had meant to engage a maid of my own, but now it occurred to me that I might do very well with Mrs Carkeek. Within the week I have moved into my new home.

'I can hardly describe to you the happiness of my first month at Tresillack, because if I take the reasons which I had for being happy, one by one, there remains over something which I cannot account for. I was young, healthy; I felt myself independent and adventurous; the season was high summer, the weather glorious, the garden in all the pomp of June, yet sufficiently unkempt to keep me busy, give me a sharp appetite for meals, and send me to bed in that drowsy stupor which comes of the odours of earth. I spent the most of my time out of doors, winding up the day's work with a walk down the cool valley, along the beach and back.

'I soon found that all housework could be safely left to Mrs Carkeek. She did not talk much; indeed, her only fault (a rare one in housekeepers) was that she talked too little, and even when I addressed her seemed at times unable to give me her attention. It was as though her mind strayed off to some small job she had forgotten, and her eyes wore a listening look, as though she waited for the neglected task to speak and remind her. But, as a matter of fact, she forgot nothing. Indeed, my dears, I was never so well attended to in my life.

'Well, that is what I'm coming to. That is just it. The woman not only had the rooms swept and dusted and my meals prepared to the moment.

'In a hundred odd little ways this orderliness, these preparations, seemed to read my desires. Did I wish the roses renewed in a bowl upon the dining-table, sure enough at the next meal they would be replaced by fresh ones. And how on earth had she guessed the very roses, the very shapes and colours I had lightly wished for? Every day, and from morning to night, I happened on others, each slight, but all bearing witness to a ministering intelligence as subtle as it was untiring.

'I am a light sleeper, with an uncomfortable knack of waking with the sun and roaming early. No matter how early I rose at Tresillack, Mrs Carkeek seemed to have preceded me. Finally I had to conclude that she arose and dusted and tidied as soon as she judged me safely a-bed. For once, finding the drawing-room (where I had been sitting late) "redded up" at four in the morning, and no trace of a plate of raspberries which I had carried thither after dinner and left overnight, I determined to test her, and walked through to the kitchen, calling her by name.

'I found the kitchen as clean as a pin, and the fire laid, but no trace of Mrs Carkeek. I walked upstairs and knocked at her door. At the second knock, a sleepy voice cried out, and presently the good woman stood before me in her nightgown, looking (I thought) very badly scared.

' "No," I said, "it's not a burglar. But I've found out what I wanted, that you do your morning's work overnight. And now go back to your bed like a good soul, whilst I take a run down to the beach."

'She stood blinking in the dawn. Her face was still white.

' "O, miss," she gasped, "I was so sure you must have seen something!"

' "And so I have," I answered, "but it was neither burglars nor ghosts."

' "Thank God!" I heard her say as she turned her back to me in her grey bedroom — which faced the north. And I took this for a carelessly pious expression and ran downstairs thinking no more of it.

'A few days later I began to understand.

'The plan of Tresillack house (I must explain) was simplicity itself. To the left of the hall as you entered was the dining-room; to the right the drawing-room. The foot of the stairs faced the front door, and beside it, passing a glazed inner door, you found two others right and left, the left opening on the kitchen, the right on a passage which ran under the stairs to a neat pantry with the usual shelves and linen-press, and under the window a porcelain basin and brass tap. On the first morning of my tenancy I had visited this pantry and turned the tap, but no water ran. I supposed this to be accidental. Mrs Carkeek had to wash up, and no doubt Mrs Carkeek would complain of any failure in the water supply.

'But the day after I had picked a basketful of roses, and carried them into the pantry as a handy place to arrange them in. I chose a china bowl and went to fill it at the tap. Again the water would not run.

'I called Mrs Carkeek. "What is wrong with this tap?" I asked. "The rest of the house is well enough supplied."

' "I don't know, miss. I never use it."

' "But there must be a reason; and you must find it a great nuisance washing up the plates and glasses in the kitchen. Come around to the back with me, and we'll have a look at the cisterns."

' "The cisterns'll be all right, miss. I assure you I don't find it a trouble."

'But I was not to be put off. The back of the house stood but ten feet from a wall which was really but a stone face built against the cliff. Above the cliff rose the kitchen garden, and from its lower path we looked over the wall's parapet upon the cisterns. There were two – a very large one, supplying the kitchen and the bathroom above the kitchen; and a small one, fed by the other, obviously leading by a pipe which I could trace, to the pantry. Now the big cistern stood almost full, and yet the small one, though on a lower level, was empty.

' "It's as plain as daylight," said I. "The pipe between the two is choked." And I clambered on to the parapet.

' "I wouldn't, miss. The pantry tap is only cold water, and no use to me. From the kitchen boiler I get it hot, you see."

' "But I want the pantry water for my flowers." I bent over and groped. "I thought as much!" said I, as I wrenched out a thick plug of cork, and immediately the water began to flow. I turned triumphantly on Mrs Carkeek, who had grown suddenly red in the face. Her eyes were fixed on the cork in my hand. To keep it more firmly wedged in its place somebody had wrapped it round with a rag of calico print; and discoloured though the rag was, I seemed to recall the pattern (a lilac sprig). Then, as our eyes met, it occurred to me that only two mornings before Mrs Carkeek had worn a print gown of that same sprigged pattern.

'I had the presence of mind to hide this very small discovery, and presently Mrs Carkeek regained her composure. But I felt disappointed in her. She had deliberately acted a fib before me; and why? Merely because she preferred the kitchen to the pantry tap. It was childish. "But servants are all the same," I told myself. "I must take Mrs Carkeek as she is; and, after all, she is a treasure."

'On the second night after this, I was lying in bed and reading myself sleepy over a novel, when a small sound disturbed me. I listened. The sound was clearly that of water trickling. A shower (I told myself) had filled the water-pipes which drained the roof. Somehow I could not fix the sound. I rose and drew up the blind.

'To my astonishment no rain was falling; no rain had fallen. There was no wind, no cloud; only a still moon high over the eastern slope of the coombe, the distant splash of waves, and the fragrance of many roses. I went back to bed and listened again. Yes, the trickling sound continued, quite distinct in the silence of the house, not to be confused for a moment with the dull murmur of the beach. After a while it began to grate on my nerves. I caught up my candle, flung my dressing-gown about me, and stole softly downstairs.

'Then it was simple. I traced the sound to the pantry. "Mrs Carkeek has left the tap running," said I: and, sure I found it so – a thin trickle steadily running to waste in the porcelain basin. I turned off the tap, went contentedly back to my bed, and slept –

'– for some hours. I opened my eyes in darkness and at once knew what had awakened me. The tap was running again. Now, it had shut easily in my hand, but not so easily that I could believe it had slipped open again of its own accord. "This is Mrs Carkeek's doing," said I; and I am afraid I added "Drat Mrs Carkeek!"

'Well there was no help for it: so I struck a light, looked at my watch, saw that the hour was just three o'clock, and I descended the stairs again. At the pantry door I paused. I was not afraid – not one little bit. In fact the notion that anything might be wrong had never crossed my mind. But I remember thinking, with my hand on the door, that if Mrs Carkeek were in the pantry I might happen to give her a severe fright.

'I pushed the door open briskly. Mrs Carkeek was not there.

But something was there, by the porcelain basin. My heart seemed to stand still — so still! And in the stillness I remember setting down the brass candlestick on a tall nest of drawers beside me.

'Over the porcelain basin and beneath the water trickling from the tap I saw two hands.

'That was all — two small hands, a child's hands. I cannot tell how they ended.

'No; they were not cut off. I saw them quite distinctly; just a pair of small hands and the wrists, and after that — nothing. They were moving briskly — washing themselves clean. I saw the water trickle and splash over them — not through them — but just as it would on real hands. They were the hands of a little girl, too. Oh, yes, I was sure of that at once. Boys and girls wash their hands differently. I can't just tell you what the difference is, but it's unmistakable.

'I saw all this before my candle slipped and fell with a crash. I had set it down without looking — for my eyes were fixed on the basin — and had balanced it on the edge of the nest of drawers. After the crash, in the darkness there, with the water running, I suffered some bad moments.

'Oddly enough, the thought uppermost with me was that I must shut off that tap before escaping. I had to. And after a while I picked up all my courage, and with a little sob thrust out my hand and did it. Then I fled.

'The dawn was close upon me: and as soon as the sky reddened I took my bath, dressed and went downstairs. And there at the pantry door I found Mrs Carkeek, also dressed, with my candlestick in her hand.

' "Ah"; said I, "you picked it up."

'Our eyes met. Clearly Mrs Carkeek wished me to begin, and I determined at once to have it out with her.

' "And you knew all about it. That's what accounts for your plugging up the cistern."

' "You saw . . . ?" she began.

' "Yes, yes. And you must tell me all about it – never mind how bad. Is – is it – murder?"

' "Law bless you, miss, whatever put such horrors in your head?"

' "She was washing her hands."

' "Ah, so she does, poor dear! But – murder! And dear little Miss Margaret, that wouldn't hurt a fly!"

' "Miss Margaret?"

' "Eh, she died at seven. Squire Kendall's only daughter; and that's over twenty years ago. I was her nurse, miss, and I know – diphtheria it was; she took it down in the village."

' "But how do you know it is Margaret?"

' "Those hands – why, how could I mistake, that used to be her nurse?"

' "But why does she wash them?"

' "Well, miss, being always a dainty child – and the house-work, you see –"

'I took a long breath. "Do you mean to tell me that all this tidying and dusting –" I broke off. "Is it she who has been tak-ing this care of me?"

'Mrs Carkeek met my look steadily.

' "Who else, miss?"

' "Poor little soul!"

' "Well now" – Mrs Carkeek rubbed my candlestick with the edge of her apron – "I'm so glad you take it like this. For there isn't really nothing to be afraid of – is there?" She eyed me wist-fully. "It's my belief she loves you, miss. But only to think what a time she must have had with the others!"

' "Were they bad?"

' "They was awful. Didn't Farmer Hosking tell you? They carried on fearful – one after another, and each one worse than the last."

' "What was the matter with them? Drink?"

' "Drink, miss, with some of 'em. There was the Major – he used to go mad with it, and run about the coombe in his night-shirt. Oh, scandalous! And his wife drank too – that is, if she ever was his wife. Just think of that tender child washing up after their nasty doings!

' "But that wasn't the worst, miss – not by a long way. There was a pair here with two children, a boy and gel, the eldest scarce six. Poor mites!

' "They beat those children, miss – your blood would boil! And starved, and tortured 'em, it's my belief. You could hear their screams, I've been told, away back in the high-road, and that's the best part of half a mile.

' "Sometimes they was locked up without food for days together. But it's my belief that little Miss Margaret managed to feed them somehow. Oh, I can see her creeping to the door and comforting!"

' "But perhaps she never showed herself when these awful people were here, but took to flight until they left."

' "You didn't never know her, miss. How brave she was! She'd have stood up to lions. She'd've been here all the while: and only to think what her innocent eyes and ears must have took in! There was another couple –" Mrs Carkeek sunk her voice.

' "Oh, hush!" said I, "if I'm to have any peace of mind in this house!"

' "But you won't go, miss? She loves you, I know she do. And think what you might be leaving her to – what sort of tenant might come next. For she can't go. She've been here ever since her father sold the place. He died soon after. You mustn't go!"

'Now I had resolved to go, but all of a sudden I felt how mean this resolution was.

' "After all," said I, "there's nothing to be afraid of."

' "That's it, miss; nothing at all. I don't even believe it's so very uncommon. Why, I've heard my mother tell of farmhouses where the rooms were swept every night as regular as clockwork, and the floors sanded, and the pots and pans scoured, and all while the maids slept. They put it down to the piskies; but we know better, miss, and now we've got the secret between us we can lie easy in our beds, and if we hear anything, say, "God bless the child!" and go to sleep.'

'I spent three years at Tresillack, and all that while Mrs Carkeek lived with me and shared the secret. Few women, I dare to say, were ever so completely wrapped around with love as we were during those three years.

'It ran through my waking life like a song: it smoothed my pillow, touched and made my table comely, in summer lifted the heads of the flowers as I passed, and in winter watched the fire with me and kept it bright.

' "Why did I ever leave Tresillack?" Because one day, at the end of five years, Farmer Hosking brought me word that he had sold the house. There was no avoiding it, at any rate; the purchaser being a Colonel Kendall, a brother of the old Squire.

' "A married man?" I asked.

' "Yes, miss; with a family of eight. As pretty children as ever you see, and the mother a good lady. It's the old home to Colonel Kendall."

' "I see. And that is why you feel bound to sell."

' "It's a good price, too, that he offers. You mustn't think but I'm sorry enough –"

' "To turn me out? I thank you, Mr Hosking; but you are doing the right thing."

' "She – Margaret – will be happy," I said; "with her cousins, you know."

' "Oh, yes, miss, she will be happy, sure enough," Mrs Carkeek agreed.

'So when the time came I packed up my boxes and tried to be cheerful. But on the last morning, when they stood in the hall, I sent Mrs Carkeek upstairs upon some poor excuse, and stepped alone into the pantry.

' "Margaret!" I whispered.

'There was no answer at all. I had scarcely dared to hope for one. Yet I tried again, and, shutting my eyes this time, stretched out both hands and whispered:

' "Margaret!"

'And I will swear to my dying day that two little hands stole and rested – for a moment only – in mine.'

THE OPEN DOOR
BY MARGARET OLIPHANT

Margaret Oliphant, née Wilson, was born on 4 April 1828 in East Lothian. She married her cousin Francis Oliphant in 1852, but was widowed just seven years later. Having earlier found success with her first novel in 1849, Oliphant began writing full time to support her own and, later, her brother's family. She published over a hundred books, including historical and romantic fiction, biography and literary history, the best known and most popular of which being the 'Chronicles of Carlingford' series. Towards the end of her life she wrote several works of supernatural fiction, including *A Beleaguered City* (1880). Margaret Oliphant died in 1897 aged 69, having survived all three of her children.

I TOOK THE house of Brentwood on my return from India in 18 –, for the temporary accommodation of my family, until I could find a permanent home for them. It had many advantages which made it peculiarly appropriate. It was within reach of Edinburgh, and my boy Roland, whose education had been considerably neglected, could go in and out to school, which was thought to be better for him than either leaving home altogether or staying there always with a tutor. The first of these expedients would have seemed preferable to me, the second commended itself to his mother. The doctor, like a judicious man, took the midway between. 'Put him on his pony, and let him ride into the High School every morning; it will do him all the good in the world,' Dr Simson said; 'and when it is bad weather there is the train.' His mother accepted this solution of the difficulty more easily than I could have hoped; and our pale-faced boy, who had never known anything more invigorating than Simla, began to encounter the brisk breezes of the North in the subdued severity of the month of May. Before the time of the vacation in July we had the satisfaction of seeing him begin to acquire something of the brown and ruddy complexion of his school-fellows.

The English system did not commend itself to Scotland in these days. There was no little Eton at Fettes; nor do I think, if there had been, that a genteel exotic of that class would have tempted either my wife or me. The lad was doubly precious to us, being the only one left us of many; and he was fragile in body, we believed, and deeply sensitive in mind. To keep him at home, and yet to send him to school – to combine the advantages of the two systems – seemed to be everything that could be desired. The two girls also found at Brentwood everything they wanted. They were near enough to Edinburgh to have masters and lessons as many as they required for completing that never-ending education which the young people seem to require nowadays. Their mother married me when she was younger than Agatha, and I should like to see them improve upon their mother! I myself was then no more than twenty-five – an age at which I see the young fellows now groping about them, with no notion what they are going to do with their lives. However, I suppose every generation has a conceit of itself which elevates it, in its own opinion, above that which comes after it.

Brentwood stands on that fine and wealthy slope of country, one of the richest in Scotland, which lies between the Pentland Hills and the Firth. In clear weather you could see the blue gleam – like a bent bow, embracing the wealthy fields and scattered houses – of the great estuary on one side of you; and on the other the blue heights, not gigantic like those we had been used to, but just high enough for all the glories of the atmosphere, the play of clouds, and sweet reflections, which give to a hilly country an interest and a charm which nothing else can emulate. Edinburgh, with its two lesser heights – the Castle and the Calton Hill – its spires and towers piercing through the smoke, and Arthur's Seat, lying crouched behind, like a guardian no longer very needful, taking his repose beside the well-beloved charge, which is now, so to speak, able to take care of itself without him – lay at our right hand. From the lawn and drawing-room windows we could see all these varieties of landscape. The colour was sometimes a little chilly, but sometimes, also, as animated and full of vicissitude as a drama. I was never tired of it. Its colour and freshness revived the eyes which had grown weary of arid plains and blazing skies. It was always cheery, and fresh, and full of repose.

The village of Brentwood lay almost under the house, on the other side of the deep little ravine, down which a stream – which ought to have been a lovely, wild, and frolicsome little river – flowed between its rocks and trees. The river, like so many in that district, had, however, if its earlier life been sacrificed to trade, and was grimy with paper-making. But this did not affect our pleasure in it so much as I have known it to affect other streams. Perhaps our water was more rapid – perhaps less clogged with dirt and refuse. Our side of the dell was charmingly *accidenté*, and clothed with fine trees, through which various paths wound down to the river-side and to the village bridge which crossed the stream. The village lay in the hollow, and climbed, with very prosaic houses, the other side. Village architecture does not flourish in Scotland. The blue slates and the grey stone are sworn foes to the picturesque; and though I do not, for my own part, dislike the interior of an old-fashioned pewed and galleried church, with its little family settlements on all sides, the square box outside, with its bit of a spire like a handle to lift it by, is not an improvement to the landscape. Still a cluster of houses on differing elevations – with scraps of garden coming in between, a hedgerow with clothes laid out to dry, the opening of a street with its rural sociability, the women at their doors, the slow waggon lumbering along – gives a centre to the landscape. It was cheerful to look at, and convenient in a hundred ways. Within ourselves we had walks in plenty, the glen being always beautiful in all its phases, whether the woods were green in the spring or ruddy in the autumn. In the park which surrounded the house were the ruins of the former mansion of Brentwood, a much smaller and less important house than the solid Georgian edifice which we inhabited. The ruins were picturesque, however, and gave importance to the place. Even we, who were but temporary tenants, felt a vague pride in them, as if they somehow reflected a certain consequence upon ourselves. The old building had the remains of a tower, an indistinguishable mass of mason-work, overgrown with ivy, and the shells of walls attached to this were half filled up with soil. I had never examined it closely, I am ashamed to say. There was a large room, or what had been a large room, with the lower part of the windows still existing, on the principal floor, and underneath other windows, which were perfect, though half filled up with fallen soil, and waving with a wild growth of brambles and chance growths of all kinds. This was the oldest part of all. At a little distance were some very commonplace and disjointed fragments of building, one of them suggesting a certain pathos by its very commonness and the complete wreck which it showed. This was the end of a low gable, a bit of grey wall, all encrusted with lichens, in which was a common doorway. Probably it had been a servants' entrance, a back-door, or opening into what are called 'the offices' in Scotland. No offices remained to be entered – pantry and kitchen had all been swept out of being; but there stood the doorway open and vacant, free to all the winds, to the rabbits, and every wild creature. It struck my eye, the first time I went to Brentwood, like a melancholy comment upon a life that was over. A door that led to nothing – closed once, perhaps, with anxious care, bolted and guarded, now void of any meaning. It impressed me, I remember, from the first; so perhaps it may be said that my mind was prepared to attach to it an importance which nothing justified.

The summer was a very happy period of repose for us all. The warmth of Indian suns was still in our veins. It seemed to us that we could never have enough of the greenness, the dewiness, the freshness of the northern landscape. Even its mists were pleasant to us, taking all the fever out of us, and pouring in vigour and refreshment. In autumn we followed the fashion of the time, and went away for change which we did not in the least require. It was when the family had settled down for the winter, when the days were short and dark, and the rigorous reign of frost upon us, that the incidents occurred which alone could justify me in intruding upon the world my private affairs. These incidents were, however, of so curious a character, that I hope my inevitable references to my own family and pressing personal interests will meet with a general pardon.

I was absent in London when these events began. In London an old Indian plunges back into the interests with which all his previous life has been associated, and meets old friends at every step. I had been circulating among some half-dozen of these — enjoying the return to my former life in shadow, though I had been so thankful in substance to throw it aside — and had missed some of my home letters, what with going down from Friday to Monday to old Benbow's place in the country, and stopping on the way back to dine and sleep at Sellar's and to take a look into Cross's stables, which occupied another day. It is never safe to miss one's letters. In this transitory life, as the Prayer-book says, how can one ever be certain what is going to happen? All was well at home. I knew exactly (I thought) what they would have to say to me: 'The weather has been so fine, that Roland has not once gone by train, and he enjoys the ride beyond anything.' 'Dear papa, be sure that you don't forget anything, but bring us so-and-so, and so-and-so' – a list as long as my arm. Dear girls and dearer mother! I would not for the world have forgotten their commissions, or lost their little letters, for all the Benbows and Crosses in the world.

But I was confident in my home-comfort and peacefulness. When I got back to my club, however, three or four letters were lying for me, upon some of which I noticed the 'immediate,' 'urgent,' which old-fashioned people and anxious people still believe will influence the post-office and quicken the speed of the mails. I was about to open one of these, when the club porter brought me two telegrams, one of which, he said, had arrived the night before. I opened, as was to be expected, the last first, and this was what I read: 'Why don't you come or answer? For God's sake, come. He is much worse.' This was a thunderbolt to fall upon a man's head who had one only son, and he the light of his eyes! The other telegram, which I opened with hands trembling so much that I lost time by my haste, was to much the same purport: 'No better; doctor afraid of brain-fever. Calls for you day and night. Let nothing detain you.' The first thing I did was to look up the time-tables to see if there was any way of getting off sooner than by the night train, though I knew well enough there was not; and then I read the letters, which furnished, alas! too clearly, all the details. They told me that the boy had been pale for some time, with a scared look. His mother had noticed it before I left home, but would not say anything to alarm me. This look had increased day by day; and soon it was observed that Roland came home at a wild gallop through the park, his pony panting and in foam, himself 'as white as a sheet,' but with the perspiration streaming from his forehead. For a long time he had resisted all questioning, but at length had developed such strange changes of mood, showing a reluctance to go to school, a desire to be fetched in the carriage at night – which was a ridiculous piece of luxury – an unwillingness to go out into the grounds, and nervous start at every sound, that his mother had insisted upon an explanation. When the boy – our boy Roland, who had never known what fear was – began to talk to her of voices he had heard in the park, and shadows that had appeared to him among the ruins, my wife promptly put him to bed and sent for Dr Simson – which, of course, was the only thing to do.

I hurried off that evening, as may be supposed, with an anxious heart. How I got through the hours before the starting of the train, I cannot tell. We must all be thankful for the quickness of the railway when in anxiety; but to have thrown myself into a post-chaise as soon as horses could be put to, would have been a relief. I got to Edinburgh very early in the blackness of the winter morning, and scarcely dared look the man in the face, at whom I gasped 'What news?' My wife had sent the brougham for me, which I concluded, before the man spoke, was a bad sign. His answer was that stereotyped answer which leaves the imagination so wildly free – 'Just the same.' Just the same! What might that mean? The horses seemed to me to creep along the long dark country road. As we dashed through the park, I thought I heard some one moaning among the trees, and clenched my fist at him (whoever he might be) with fury. Why had the fool of a woman at the gate allowed any one to come in to disturb the quiet of the place? If I had not been in such hot haste to get home, I think I should have stopped the carriage and got out to see what tramp it was that had made an entrance, and chosen my grounds, of all places in the world, – when my boy was ill! – to grumble and groan in. But I had no reason to complain of our slow pace here. The horses flew like lightning along the intervening path, and drew up at the door all panting, as if they had run a race. My wife stood waiting to receive me with a pale face, and a candle in her hand, which made her look paler still as the wind blew the flame about. 'He is sleeping,' she said in a whisper, as if her voice might wake him. And I replied, when I could find my voice, also in a whisper, as though the jingling of the horses' furniture and the sound of their hoofs must not have been more dangerous. I stood on the steps with her a moment, almost afraid to go in, now that I was here; and it seemed to me that I saw without observing, if I may say so, that the horses were unwilling to turn round, though their stables lay that way, or that the men were unwilling. These things occurred to me afterwards, though at the moment I was not capable of anything but to ask questions and to hear of the condition of the boy.

I looked at him from the door of his room, for we were afraid to go near, lest we should disturb that blessed sleep. It looked like actual sleep – not the lethargy into which my wife told me he would sometimes fall. She told me everything in the next room, which communicated with his, rising now and then and going to the door of communication; and in this there was much that was very startling and confusing to the mind. It appeared that ever since the winter began, since it was early dark, and night had fallen before his return from school, he had been hearing voices among the ruins – at first only a groaning, he said, at which his pony was as much alarmed as he was, but by degrees a voice. The tears ran down my wife's cheeks as she described to me how he would start up in the night and cry out, 'Oh, mother, let me in! oh, mother, let me in!' with a pathos which rent her heart. And she sitting there all the time, only longing to do everything his heart could desire! But though she would try to soothe him, crying, 'You are at home, my darling. I am here. Don't you know me? Your mother is here!' he would only stare at her, and after a while spring up again with the same cry. At other times he would be quite reasonable, she said, asking eagerly when I was coming, but declaring that he must go with

me as soon as I did so, 'to let them in.' 'The doctor thinks his
nervous system must have received a shock,' my wife said. 'Oh,
Henry, can it be that we have pushed him on too much with his
work — a delicate boy like Roland? — and what is this work in
comparison with his health? Even you would think little of hon-
ours or prizes if it hurt the boy's health.' Even I! as if I were an
inhuman father sacrificing my child to my ambition. But I would
not increase her trouble by taking any notice. After a while they
persuaded me to lie down, to rest, and to eat — none of which
things had been possible since I received their letters. The mere
fact of being on the spot, of course, in itself was a great thing;
and when I knew that I could be called in a moment, as soon as
he was awake and wanted me, I felt capable, even in the dark,
chill morning twilight, to snatch an hour or two's sleep. As it
happened, I was so worn out with the strain of anxiety, and he so
quieted and consoled by knowing I had come, that I was not disturbed till the afternoon, when the twilight had again settled
down. There was just daylight enough to see his face when I
went to him; and what a change in a fortnight! He was paler and
more worn, I thought, than even in those dreadful days in the
plains before we left India. His hair seemed to me to have grown
long and lank; his eyes were like blazing lights projecting out of
his white face. He got hold of my hand in a cold and tremulous
clutch, and waved to everybody to go away. 'Go away — even
mother,' he said, —'go away.' This went to her heart, for she did
not like that even I should have more of the boy's confidence
than herself; but my wife has never been a woman to think of
herself; and she left us alone. 'Are they all gone?' he said, eagerly.
'They would not let me speak. The doctor treated me as if I were
a fool. You know I am not a fool, papa.'

'Yes, yes, my boy, I know; but you are ill, and quiet is so necessary. You are not only not a fool, Roland, but you are reasonable

and understand. When you are ill you must deny yourself; you must not do everything that you might do being well.'

He waved his thin hand with a sort of indignation. 'Then, father, I am not ill,' he cried. 'Oh, I thought when you came you would not stop me, – you would see the sense of it! What do you think is the matter with me, all of you? Simson is well enough, but he is only a doctor. What do you think is the matter with me? I am no more ill than you are. A doctor, of course, he thinks you are ill the moment he looks at you – that's what he's there for – and claps you into bed.'

'Which is the best place for you at present, my dear boy.'

'I made up my mind,' cried the little fellow, 'that I would stand it till you came home. I said to myself, I won't frighten mother and the girls. But now, father,' he cried, half jumping out of bed, 'it's not illness, – it's a secret.'

His eyes shone so wildly, his face was so swept with strong feeling, that my heart sank within me. It could be nothing but fever that did it, and fever had been so fatal. I got him into my arms to put him back into bed. 'Roland,' I said, humouring the poor child, which I knew was the only way, 'if you are going to tell me this secret to do any good, you know you must be quite quiet, and not excite yourself. If you excite yourself, I must not let you speak.'

'Yes, father,' said the boy. He was quiet directly, like a man, as if he quite understood. When I had laid him back on his pillow, he looked up at me with that grateful sweet look with which children, when they are ill, break one's heart, the water coming into his eyes in his weakness. 'I was sure as soon as you were here you would know what to do,' he said.

'To be sure, my boy. Now keep quiet, and tell it all out like a man.' To think I was telling lies to my own child! for I did it only to humour him, thinking, poor little fellow, his brain was wrong.

'Yes, father. Father, there is some one in the park, – some one that has been badly used.'

'Hush, my dear; you remember, there is to be no excitement. Well, who is this somebody, and who has been ill-using him? We will soon put a stop to that.'

'Ah,' cried Roland, 'but it is not so easy as you think. I don't know who it is. It is just a cry. Oh, if you could hear it! It gets into my head in my sleep. I heard it as clear – as clear; – and they think that I am dreaming – or raving perhaps,' the boy said, with a sort of disdainful smile.

This look of his perplexed me; it was less like fever than I thought. 'Are you quite sure you have not dreamt it, Roland?' I said.

'Dream? – that!' He was springing up again when he suddenly bethought himself, and lay down flat with the same sort of smile on his face. 'The pony heard it too,' he said. 'She jumped as if she had been shot. If I had not grasped at the reius, – for I was frightened, father—'

'No shame to you, my boy,' said I, though I scarcely knew why.

'If I hadn't held to her like a leech, she'd have pitched me over her head, and never drew breath till we were at the door. Did the pony dream it?' he said, with a soft disdain, yet indulgence for my foolishness. Then he added slowly: 'It was only a cry the first time, and all the time before you went away. I wouldn't tell you, for it was so wretched to be frightened. I thought it might be a hare or a rabbit snared, and I went in the morning and looked, but there was nothing. It was after you went I heard it really first, and this is what he says.' He raised himself on his elbow close to me, and looked me in the face. ' "Oh, mother, let me in! oh, mother, let me in!" ' As he said the words a mist came over his face, the mouth quivered, the soft features all melted and changed, and when he had ended these pitiful words, dissolved in a shower of heavy tears.

Was it a hallucination? Was it the fever of the brain? Was it the disordered fancy caused by great bodily weakness? How could I tell? I thought it wisest to accept it as if it were all true.

'This is very touching, Roland,' I said.

'Oh, if you had just heard it, father! I said to myself, if father heard it he would do something; but mamma, you know, she's given over to Simson, and that fellow's a doctor, and never thinks of anything but clapping you into bed.'

'We must not blame Simson for being a doctor, Roland.'

'No, no,' said my boy, with delightful toleration and indulgence; 'oh no; that's the good of him – that's what he's for; I know that. But you – you are different; you are just father: and you'll do something, – directly, papa, directly, – this very night.'

'Surely,' I said. 'No doubt it is some little lost child.'

He gave me a sudden, swift look, investigating my face as though to see whether, after all, this was everything my eminence as 'father' came to, – no more than that? Then he got hold of my shoulder, clutching it with his thin hand: 'Look here,' he said, with a quiver in his voice; 'suppose it wasn't – living at all!'

'My dear boy, how then could you have heard it?' I said.

He turned away from me with a pettish exclamation – 'As if you didn't know better than that!'

'Do you want to tell me it is a ghost?' I said.

Roland withdrew his hand; his countenance assumed an aspect of great dignity and gravity; a slight quiver remained about his lips. 'Whatever it was – you always said we were not to call names. It was something – in trouble. Oh, father, in terrible trouble!'

'But, my boy,' I said – I was at my wits' end – 'if it was a child that was lost, or any poor human creature — but, Roland, what do you want me to do?'

'I should know if I was you,' said the child, eagerly. 'That is what I always said to myself – Father will know. Oh, papa, papa, to have to face it night after night, in such terrible, terrible trouble! and never to be able to do it any good. I don't want to cry; it's like a baby, I know; but what can I do else? – out there all by itself in the ruin, and nobody to help it. I can't bear it, I can't bear it!' cried my generous boy. And in his weakness he burst out, after many attempts to restrain it, into a great childish fit of sobbing and tears.

I do not know that I ever was in a greater perplexity in my life; and afterwards, when I thought of it, there was something comic in it too. It is bad enough to find your child's mind possessed with the conviction that he has seen – or heard – a ghost. But that he should require you to go instantly and help that ghost, was the most bewildering experience that had ever come my way. I am a sober man myself, and not superstitious – at least any more than everybody is superstitious. Of course I do not believe in ghosts; but I don't deny, any more than other people, that there are stories, which I cannot pretend to understand. My blood got a sort of chill in my veins at the idea that Roland should be a ghost-seer; for that generally means a hysterical temperament and weak health, and all that men most hate and fear for their children. But that I should take up his ghost and right its wrongs, and save it from its trouble, was such a mission as was enough to confuse any man. I did my best to console my boy without giving any promise of this astonishing kind; but he was too sharp for me. He would have none of my caresses. With sobs breaking in at intervals upon his voice, and the rain-drops hanging on his eyelids, he yet returned to the charge.

'It will be there now – it will be there all the night. Oh think, papa, think, if it was me! I can't rest for thinking of it. Don't!' he cried, putting away my hand – 'don't! You go and help it, and mother can take care of me.'

'But, Roland, what can I do?'

My boy opened his eyes, which were large with weakness and fever, and gave me a smile such, I think, as sick children only know the secret of. 'I was sure you would know as soon as you came. I always said – Father will know: and mother,' he cried, with a softening of repose upon his face, his limbs relaxing, his form sinking with a luxurious ease in his bed – 'mother can come and take care of me.'

I called her, and saw him turn to her with the complete dependence of a child, and then I went away and left them, as perplexed a man as any in Scotland. I must say, however, I had this consolation, that my mind was greatly eased about Roland. He might be under a hallucination, but his head was clear enough, and I did not think him so ill as everybody else did. The girls were astonished even at the ease with which I took it. 'How do you think he is?' they said in a breath, coming round me, laying hold of me. 'Not half so ill as I expected,' I said; 'not very bad at all.' 'Oh, papa, you are a darling!' cried Agatha, kissing me, and crying upon my shoulder; while little Jeanie, who was as pale as Roland, clasped both her arms round mine, and could not speak at all. I knew nothing about it, not half so much as Simson: but they believed in me; they had a feeling that all would go right now. God is very good to you when your children look to you like that. It makes one humble, not proud. I was not worthy of it; and then I recollected that I had to act the part of a father to Roland's ghost, which made me almost laugh, though I might just as well have cried. It was the strangest mission that ever was intrusted to mortal man.

It was then I remembered suddenly the looks of the men when

they turned to take the brougham to the stables in the dark that morning: they had not liked it, and the horses had not liked it. I remembered that even in my anxiety about Roland I had heard them tearing along the avenue back to the stables, and had made a memorandum mentally that I must speak of it. It seemed to me that the best thing I could do was to go to the stables now and make a few inquiries. It is impossible to fathom the minds of rustics; there might be some devilry of practical joking, for anything I knew; or they might have some interest in getting up a bad reputation for the Brentwood avenue. It was getting dark by the time I went out, and nobody who knows the country will need to be told how black is the darkness of a November night under high laurel-bushes and yew-trees. I walked into the heart of the shrubberies two or three times, not seeing a step before me, till I came out upon the broader carriage-road, where the trees opened a little, and there was a faint grey glimmer of sky visible, under which the great limes and elms stood darkling like ghosts; but it grew black again as I approached the corner where the ruins lay. Both eyes and ears were on the alert, as may be supposed; but I could see nothing in the absolute gloom, and, so far as I can recollect, I heard nothing. Nevertheless there came a strong impression upon me that somebody was there. It is a sensation which most people have felt. I have seen when it has been strong enough to awake me out of sleep, the sense of some one looking at me. I suppose my imagination had been affected by Roland's story; and the mystery of the darkness is always full of suggestions. I stamped my feet violently on the gravel to rouse myself, and called out sharply, 'Who's there?' Nobody answered, nor did I expect any one to answer, but the impression had been made. I was so foolish that I did not like to look back, but went sideways, keeping an eye on the gloom behind. It was with great relief that I spied the light in the stables, making a sort of oasis in the darkness. I walked very quickly into the midst of that lighted and cheerful place, and thought the clank of the groom's pail one of the pleasantest sounds I had ever heard. The coachman was the head of this little colony, and it was to his house I went to pursue my investigations. He was a native of the district, and had taken care of the place in the absence of the family for years; it was impossible but that he must know everything that was going on, and all the traditions of the place. The men, I could see, eyed me anxiously when I thus appeared at such an hour among them, and followed me with their eyes to Jarvis's house, where he lived alone with his old wife, their children being all married and out in the world. Mrs Jarvis met me with anxious questions. How was the poor young gentleman? but the others knew, I could see by their faces, that not even this was the foremost thing in my mind.

'Noises? – ou ay, there'll be noises – the wind in the trees, and the water soughing down the glen. As for tramps, Cornel, no, there's little o' that kind o' cattle about here; and Merran at the gate's a careful body.' Jarvis moved about with some embarrassment from one leg to another as he spoke. He kept in the shade, and did not look at me more than he could help. Evidently his mind was perturbed, and he had reasons for keeping his own counsel. His wife sat by, giving him a quick look now and then, but saying nothing. The kitchen was very snug, and warm, and bright – as different as could be from the chill and mystery of the night outside.

'I think you are trifling with me, Jarvis,' I said.

'Triflin', Cornel? no me. What would I trifle for? If the deevil himsel was in the auld hoose, I have no interest in't one way or another—'

'Sandy, hold your peace!' cried his wife, imperatively.

'And what am I to hold my peace for, wi' the Cornel standing there asking a' thae questions? I'm saying, if the deevil himsel—'

'And I'm telling ye hold your peace!' cried the woman, in great excitement. 'Dark November weather and lang nichts, and us that ken a' we ken. How daur ye name – a name that shouldna be spoken?' She threw down her stocking and got up, also in great agitation. 'I tell't ye you never could keep it. It's no a thing that will hide; and the haill toun kens as weel as you or me. Tell the Cornel straight out – or see, I'll do it. I dinna hold wi' your secrets: and a secret that the haill toun kens!' She snapped her fingers with an air of large disdain. As for Jarvis, ruddy and big as he was, he shrank to nothing before this decided woman. He repeated to her two or three times her own adjuration, 'Hold your peace!' then, suddenly changing his tone, cried out, 'Tell him then, confound ye! I'll wash my hands o't. If a' the ghosts in Scotland were in the auld hoose, is that ony concern o' mine?'

After this I elicited without much difficulty the whole story. In the opinion of the Jarvises, and of everybody about, the certainty that the place was haunted was beyond all doubt. As Sandy and his wife warmed to the tale, one tripping up another in their eagerness to tell everything, it gradually developed as distinct a superstition as I ever heard, and not without poetry and pathos. How long it was since the voice had been heard first, nobody could tell with certainty. Jarvis's opinion was that his father, who had been coachman at Brentwood before him, had never heard anything about it, and that the whole thing had arisen within the last ten years, since the complete dismantling of the old house: which was a wonderfully modern date for a tale so well authenticated. According to these witnesses, and to several whom I questioned afterwards, and who were all in perfect agreement, it was only in the months of November and

December that 'the visitation' occurred. During these months, the darkest of the year, scarcely a night passed without the recurrence of these inexplicable cries. Nothing, it was said, had ever been seen – at least nothing that could be identified. Some people, bolder or more imaginative than the others, had seen the darkness moving, Mrs Jarvis said, with unconscious poetry. It began when night fell, and continued, at intervals, till day broke. Very often it was only an inarticulate cry and moaning, but sometimes the words which had taken possession of my poor boy's fancy had been distinctly audible – 'Oh, mother, let me in!' The Jarvises were not aware that there had ever been any investigation into it. The estate of Brentwood had lapsed into the hands of a distant branch of the family, who had lived but little there; and of the many people who had taken it, as I had done, few had remained through two Decembers. And nobody had taken the trouble to make a very close examination into the facts. 'No, no,' Jarvis said, shaking his head. 'No, no, Cornel. Wha wad set themsels up for a laughin'-stock to a' the country-side, making a wark about a ghost? Naebody believes in ghosts. It bid to be the wind in the trees, the last gentleman said, or some effec' o' the water wrastlin' among the rocks. He said it was a' quite easy explained: but he gave up the hoose. And when you cam, Cornel, we were awfu' anxious you should never hear. What for should I have spoiled the bargain and hairmed the property for no-thing?'

'Do you call my child's life nothing?' I said in the trouble of the moment, unable to restrain myself. 'And instead of telling this all to me, you have told it to him – to a delicate boy, a child unable to sift evidence, or judge for himself, a tender-hearted young creature—'

I was walking about the room with an anger all the hotter that I felt it to be most likely quite unjust. My heart was full of bitterness against the stolid retainers of a family who were content to risk other people's children and comfort rather than let a house lie empty. If I had been warned I might have taken precautions, or left the place, or sent Roland away, a hundred things which now I could not do; and here I was with my boy in a brain-fever, and his life, the most precious life on earth, hanging in the balance, dependent on whether or not I could get to the reason of a commonplace ghost-story! I paced about in high wrath, not seeing what I was to do; for, to take Roland away, even if he were able to travel, would not settle his agitated mind; and I feared even that a scientific explanation of refracted sound, or reverberation, or any other of the easy certainties with which we elder men are silenced, would have very little effect upon the boy.

'Cornel,' said Jarvis, solemnly, 'and *she'll* bear me witness – the young gentleman never heard a word from me – no, nor from either groom or gardener; I'll gie ye my word for that. In the first place, he's no a lad that invites ye to talk. There are some that are, and some that are na. Some will draw ye on, till ye've tellt them a' the clatter of the toun, and a' ye ken, and whiles mair. But Maister Roland, his mind's fu' of his books. He's aye civil and kind, and a fine lad; but no that sort. And ye see it's for a' our interest, Cornel, that you should stay at Brentwood. I took it upon me mysel to pass the word – "No a syllable to Maister Roland, nor to the young leddies – no a syllable." The women-servants, that have little reason to be out at night, ken little or nothing about it. And some think it grand to have a ghost so long as they're no in the way of coming across it. If you had been tellt the story to begin with maybe ye would have thought so yourself.'

This was true enough, though it did not throw any light upon my perplexity. If we had heard of it to start with, it is possible that all the family would have considered the possession of a ghost a distinct advantage. It is the fashion of the times. We never think what a risk it is to play with young imaginations, but cry out, in the fashionable jargon, 'A ghost! – nothing else was wanted to make it perfect.' I should not have been above this myself. I should have smiled, of course, at the idea of the ghost at all, but then to feel that it was mine would have pleased my vanity. Oh yes, I claim no exemption. The girls would have been delighted. I could fancy their eagerness, their interest, and excitement. No; if we had been told, it would have done no good – we should have made the bargain all the more eagerly, the fools that we are. 'And there has been no attempt to investigate it,' I said, 'to see what it really is?'

'Eh, Cornel,' said the coachman's wife, 'wha would investigate, as ye call it, a thing that nobody believes in? Ye would be the laughin'-stock of a' the country-side, as my man says.'

'But you believe in it,' I said, turning upon her hastily. The woman was taken by surprise. She made a step backward out of my way.

'Lord, Cornel, how ye frichten a body! Me! – there's awfu' strange things in this world. An unlearned person doesna ken what to think. But the minister and the gentry they just laugh in your face. Inquire into the thing that is not! Na, na, we just let it be.'

'Come with me, Jarvis,' I said, hastily, 'and we'll make an attempt at least. Say nothing to the men or to anybody. I'll come back after dinner, and we'll make a serious attempt to see what it is, if it is anything. If I hear it – which I doubt – you may be sure I shall never rest till I make it out. Be ready for me about ten o'clock.'

'Me, Cornel!' Jarvis said, in a faint voice. I had not been looking at him in my own preoccupation, but when I did so, I found that the greatest change had come over the fat and ruddy coachman. 'Me, Cornel!' he repeated, wiping the perspiration from his brow. His ruddy face hung in flabby folds, his knees knocked together, his voice seemed half extinguished in his throat. Then he began to rub his hands and smile upon me in a deprecating, imbecile way. 'There's nothing I wouldna do to pleasure ye, Cornel,' taking a step further back. 'I'm sure, *she* kens I've aye said I never had to do with a mair fair, weel-spoken gentleman—' Here Jarvis came to a pause, again looking at me, rubbing his hands.

'Well?' I said.

'But eh, sir!' he went on, with the same imbecile yet insinuating smile, 'if ye'll reflect that I am no used to my feet. With a horse atween my legs, or the reins in my hand, I'm maybe nae worse than other men; but on fit, Cornel— It's no the – bogles;— but I've been cavalry, ye see,' with a little hoarse laugh, 'a' my life. To face a thing ye didna understan' – on your feet, Cornel.'

'Well, sir, if *I* do it,' said I tartly, 'why shouldn't you?'

'Eh, Cornel, there's an awfu' difference. In the first place, ye tramp about the haill country-side, and think naething of it; but a walk tires me mair than a hunard miles' drive: and then ye're a gentleman, and do your ain pleasure; and you're no so auld as me; and it's for your ain bairn, ye see, Cornel; and then—'

'He believes in it, Cornel, and you dinna believe in it,' the woman said.

'Will you come with me?' I said, turning to her.

She jumped back, upsetting her chair in her bewilderment. 'Me!' with a scream, and then fell into a sort of hysterical laugh. 'I wouldna say but what I would go; but what would the folk say to hear of Cornel Mortimer with an auld silly woman at his heels?'

The suggestion made me laugh too, though I had little inclination for it. 'I'm sorry you have so little spirit, Jarvis,' I said. 'I must find some one else, I suppose.'

Jarvis, touched by this, began to remonstrate, but I cut him short. My butler was a soldier who had been with me in India, and was not supposed to fear anything – man or devil, – certainly not the former; and I felt that I was losing time. The Jarvises were too thankful to get rid of me. They attended me to the door with the most anxious courtesies. Outside, the two grooms stood close by, a little confused by my sudden exit. I don't know if perhaps they had been listening – at least standing as near as possible, to catch any scrap of the conversation. I waved my hand to them as I went past, in answer to their salutations, and it was very apparent to me that they also were glad to see me go.

And it will be thought very strange, but it would be weak not to add, that I myself, though bent on the investigation I have spoken of, pledged to Roland to carry it out, and feeling that my boy's health, perhaps his life, depended on the result of my inquiry, – I felt the most unaccountable reluctance to pass these ruins on my way home. My curiosity was intense; and yet it was all my mind could do to pull my body along. I daresay the scientific people would describe it the other way, and attribute my cowardice to the state of my stomach. I went on; but if I had followed my impulse, I should have turned and bolted. Everything in me seemed to cry out against it; my heart thumped, my pulses all began, like sledge-hammers, beating against my ears and every sensitive part. It was very dark, as I have said; the old house, with its shapeless tower, loomed a heavy mass through the darkness, which was only not entirely so solid as itself. On the other hand, the great dark cedars of which we were so proud seemed to fill up the night. My foot strayed out of the path in my confusion and the gloom together, and I brought myself up with a cry as I felt myself knock against something solid. What was it? The contact with hard stone and lime and prickly bramble-bushes restored me a little to myself. 'Oh, it's only the old gable,' I said aloud, with a little laugh to reassure myself. The rough feeling of the stones reconciled me. As I groped about thus, I shook off my visionary folly. What so easily explained as that I should have strayed from the path in the darkness? This brought me back to common existence, as if I had been shaken by a wise hand out of all the silliness of superstition. How silly it was, after all! What did it matter which path I took? I laughed again, this time with better heart – when suddenly, in a moment, the blood was chilled in my veins, a shiver stole along my spine, my faculties seemed to forsake me. Close by me at my side, at my feet, there was a sigh. No, not a groan, not a moaning, not anything so tangible – a perfectly soft, faint, inarticulate sigh. I sprang back, and my heart stopped beating. Mistaken! no, mistake was impossible. I heard it as clearly as I hear myself speak; a long, soft, weary sigh, as if drawn to the utmost, and emptying out a load of sadness that filled the breast. To hear this in the solitude, in the dark, in the night (though it was still early), had an effect which I cannot describe. I feel it now – something cold creeping over me, up into my hair, and down to my feet, which refused to move. I cried out, with a trembling voice, 'Who is there?' as I had done before – but there was no reply.

I got home I don't quite know how; but in my mind there was no longer any indifference as to the thing, whatever it was, that haunted these ruins. My scepticism disappeared like a mist. I was as firmly determined that there was something as Roland was. I did not for a moment pretend to myself that it was possible I could be deceived; there were movements and noises which I understood all about, cracklings of small branches in the frost, and little rolls of gravel on the path, such as have a very eerie sound sometimes, and perplex you with wonder as to who has done it, *when there is no real mystery*; but I assure you all these little movements of nature don't affect you one bit *when there is something*. I understood *them*. I did not understand the sigh. That was not simple nature; there was meaning in it – feeling, the soul of a creature invisible. This is the thing that human nature trembles at – a creature invisible, yet with sensations, feelings, a power somehow of expressing itself. I had not the same sense of unwillingness to turn my back upon the scene of the mystery which I had experienced in going to the stables; but I almost ran home, impelled by eagerness to get everything done that had to be done, in order to apply myself to finding it out. Bagley was in the hall as usual when I went in. He was always there in the afternoon, always with the appearance of perfect occupation, yet, so far as I know, never doing anything. The door was open, so that I hurried in without any pause, breathless; but the sight of his calm regard, as he came to help me off with my overcoat, subdued me in a moment. Anything out of the way, anything incomprehensible, faded to nothing in the presence of Bagley. You saw and wondered how *he* was made: the parting of his hair, the tie of his white neckcloth, the fit of his trousers, all perfect as works of art; but you could see how they were done, which makes all the difference. I flung myself upon him, so to speak, without waiting to note the extreme unlikeness of the man to anything of the kind I meant. 'Bagley,' I said, 'I want you to come out with me tonight to watch for—'

'Poachers, Colonel,' he said, a gleam of pleasure running all over him.

'No, Bagley; a great deal worse,' I cried.

'Yes, Colonel; at what hour, sir?' the man said; but then I had not told him what it was.

It was ten o'clock when we set out. All was perfectly quiet indoors. My wife was with Roland, who had been quite calm, she said, and who (though, no doubt, the fever must run its course) had been better ever since I came. I told Bagley to put on a thick greatcoat over his evening coat, and did the same myself – with strong boots; for the soil was like a sponge, or worse. Talking to him, I almost forgot what we were going to do. It was darker even than it had been before, and Bagley kept very close to me as we went along. I had a small lantern in my hand, which gave us a partial guidance. We had come to the corner where the path turns. On one side was the bowling-green, which the girls had taken possession of for their croquet-ground – a wonderful enclosure surrounded by high hedges of holly, three hundred years old and more: on the other, the ruins. Both were black as night; but before we got so far, there was a little opening in which we could just discern the trees and the lighter line of the road. I thought it best to pause there and take breath. 'Bagley,' I said, 'there is something about these ruins I don't understand. It is there I am going. Keep your eyes open and your wits about you. Be ready to pounce upon any stranger you see – anything, man or woman. Don't hurt, but seize – anything you see.' 'Colonel,' said Bagley, with a little tremor in his breath, 'they do say there's things there – as is neither man nor woman.' There was no time for words. 'Are you game to follow me, my man? that's the question,' I said. Bagley fell in without a word, and saluted. I knew then I had nothing to fear.

We went, so far as I could guess, exactly as I had come, when I heard that sigh. The darkness, however, was so complete that all marks, as of trees or paths, disappeared. One moment we felt our feet on the gravel, another sinking noiselessly into the slippery grass, that was all. I had shut up my lantern, not wishing to scare any one, whoever it might be. Bagley followed, it seemed to me, exactly in my footsteps as I made my way, as I supposed, towards the mass of the ruined house. We seemed to take a long time groping along seeking this; the squash of the wet soil under our feet was the only thing that marked our progress. After a while I stood still to see, or rather feel, where we were. The darkness was very still, but no stiller than is usual in a winter's night. The sounds I have mentioned – the crackling of twigs, the roll of a pebble, the sound of some rustle in the dead leaves, or creeping creature on the grass – were audible when you listened, all mysterious enough when your mind is disengaged, but to me cheering now as signs of the livingness of nature, even in the death of the frost. As we stood still there came up from the trees in the glen the prolonged hoot of an owl. Bagley started with alarm, being in a state of general nervousness, and not knowing what he was afraid of. But to me the sound was encouraging and pleasant, being so comprehensible. 'An owl,' I said, under my breath. 'Y – es, Colonel,' said Bagley, his teeth chattering. We stood still about five minutes, while it broke into the still brooding of the air, the sound widening out in circles, dying upon the darkness. This sound, which is not a cheerful one, made me almost gay. It was natural, and relieved the tension of the mind. I moved on with new courage, my nervous excitement calming down.

When all at once, quite suddenly, close to us, at our feet, there broke out a cry. I made a spring backwards in the first moment of surprise and horror, and in doing so came sharply against the same rough masonry and brambles that had struck me before. This new sound came upwards from the ground – a low, moaning, wailing voice, full of suffering and pain. The contrast between it and the hoot of the owl was indescribable; the one with a wholesome wildness and naturalness that hurt nobody – the other, a sound that made one's blood curdle, full of human misery. With a great deal of fumbling – for in spite of everything I could do to keep up my courage my hands shook – I managed to remove the slide of my lantern. The light leaped out like something living, and made the place visible in a moment. We were what would have been inside the ruined building had anything remained but the gable-wall which I have described. It was close to us, the vacant doorway in it going out straight into the blackness outside. The light showed the bit of wall, the ivy glistening upon it in clouds of dark green, the bramble-branches waving, and below, the open door – a door that led to nothing. It was from this the voice came which died out just as the light flashed upon this strange scene. There was a moment's silence, and then it broke forth again. The sound was so near, so penetrating, so pitiful, that, in the nervous start I gave, the light fell out of my hand. As I groped for it in the dark my hand was clutched by Bagley, who I think must have dropped upon his knees; but I was too much perturbed myself to think much of this. He clutched at me in the confusion of his terror, forgetting all his usual decorum. 'For God's sake, what is it, sir?' he gasped. If I yielded, there was evidently an end of both of us. 'I can't tell,' I said, 'any more than you; that's what we've got to find out: up, man, up!' I pulled him to his feet. 'Will you go round and examine the other side, or will you stay here with the lantern?' Bagley gasped at me with a face of horror. 'Can't we stay together, Colonel?' he said – his knees were trembling under him. I pushed him against the corner of the wall, and put the light into his hands. 'Stand fast till I come back; shake yourself together, man; let nothing pass you,' I said. The voice was within two or three feet of us, of that there could be no doubt.

I went myself to the other side of the wall, keeping close to it. The light shook in Bagley's hand, but, tremulous though it was, shone out through the vacant door, one oblong block of light marking all the crumbling corners and hanging masses of foliage. Was that something dark huddled in a heap by the side of it?

I pushed forward across the light in the doorway, and fell upon it with my hands; but it was only a juniper-bush growing close against the wall. Meanwhile, the sight of my figure crossing the doorway had brought Bagley's nervous excitement to a height: he flew at me, gripping my shoulder. 'I've got him, Colonel! I've got him!' he cried, with a voice of sudden exultation. He thought it was a man, and was at once relieved. But at that moment the voice burst forth again between us, at our feet — more close to us than any separate being could be. He dropped off from me, and fell against the wall, his jaw dropping as if he were dying. I suppose, at the same moment, he saw that it was me whom he had clutched. I, for my part, had scarcely more command of myself. I snatched the light out of his hand, and flashed it all about me wildly. Nothing, — the juniper-bush which I thought I had never seen before, the heavy growth of the glistening ivy, the brambles waving. It was close to my ears now, crying, crying, pleading as if for life. Either I heard the same words Roland had heard, or else, in my excitement, his imagination got possession of mine. The voice went on, growing into distinct articulation, but wavering about, now from one point, now from another, as if the owner of it were moving slowly back and forward. 'Mother! mother!' and then an outburst of wailing. As my mind steadied, getting accustomed (as one's mind gets accustomed to anything), it seemed to me as if some uneasy, miserable creature was pacing up and down before a closed door. Sometimes — but that must have been excitement — I thought I heard a sound like knocking, and then another burst, 'Oh, mother! mother!' All this close, close to the space where I was standing with my lantern — now before me, now behind me: a creature restless, unhappy, moaning, crying, before the vacant doorway, which no one could either shut or open more.

'Do you hear it, Bagley? do you hear what it is saying?' I

cried, stepping in through the doorway. He was lying against the wall – his eyes glazed, half dead with terror. He made a motion of his lips as if to answer me, but no sounds came; then lifted his hand with a curious imperative movement as if ordering me to be silent and listen. And how long I did so I cannot tell. It began to have an interest, an exciting hold upon me, which I could not describe. It seemed to call up visibly a scene any one could understand – a something shut out, restlessly wandering to and fro; sometimes the voice dropped, as if throwing itself down – sometimes wandered off a lew paces, growing sharp and clear. 'Oh, mother, let me in! oh, mother, mother, let me in! oh, let me in!' every word was clear to me. No wonder the boy had gone wild with pity. I tried to steady my mind upon Roland, upon his conviction that I could do something, but my head swam with the excitement, even when I partially overcame the terror. At last the words died away, and there was a sound of sobs and moaning. I cried out, 'In the name of God who are you?' with a kind of feeling in my mind that to use the name of God was profane, seeing that I did not believe in ghosts or anything supernatural; but I did it all the same, and waited, my heart giving a leap of terror lest there should be a reply. Why this should have been I cannot tell, but I had a feeling that if there was an answer it would be more than I could bear. But there was no answer; the moaning went on, and then, as if it had been real, the voice rose a little higher again, the words recommenced, 'Oh, mother, let me in! oh, mother, let me in!' with an expression that was heart-breaking to hear.

As if it had been real! What do I mean by that? I suppose I got less alarmed as the thing went on. I began to recover the use of my senses – I seemed to explain it all to myself by saying that this had once happened, that it was a recollection of a real scene. Why there should have seemed something quite satisfactory and composing in this explanation I cannot tell, but so it was. I began to listen almost as if it had been a play, forgetting Bagley, who, I almost think, had fainted, leaning against the wall. I was startled out of this strange spectatorship that had fallen upon me by the sudden rush of something which made my heart jump once more, a large black figure in the doorway waving its arms. 'Come in! come in! come in!' it shouted out hoarsely at the top of a deep bass voice, and then poor Bagley fell down senseless across the threshold. He was less sophisticated than I, – he had not been able to bear it any longer. I took him for something supernatural, as he took me, and it was some time before I awoke to the necessities of the moment. I remembered only after, that from the time I began to give my attention to the man, I heard the other voice no more. It was some time before I brought him to. It must have been a strange scene: the lantern making a luminous spot in the darkness, the man's white face lying on the black earth, I over him, doing what I could for him. Probably I should have been thought to be murdering him had any one seen us. When at last I succeeded in pouring a little brandy down his throat, he sat up and looked about him wildly. 'What's up?' he said; then recognising me, tried to struggle to his feet with a faint 'Beg your pardon, Colonel.' I got him home as best I could, making him lean upon my arm. The great fellow was as weak as a child. Fortunately he did not for some time remember what had happened. From the time Bagley fell the voice had stopped, and all was still.

'You've got an epidemic in your house, Colonel,' Simson said to me next morning. 'What's the meaning of it all? Here's your butler raving about a voice. This will never do, you know; and so far as I can make out, you are in it too.'

'Yes, I am in it, doctor. I thought I had better speak to you. Of course you are treating Roland all right – but the boy is not raving, he is as sane as you or me. It's all true.'

'As sane as – I – or you. I never thought the boy insane. He's got cerebral excitement, fever. I don't know what you've got. There's something very queer about the look of your eyes.'

'Come,' said I, 'you can't put us all to bed, you know. You had better listen and hear the symptoms in full.'

The doctor shrugged his shoulders, but he listened to me patiently. He did not believe a word of the story, that was clear; but he heard it all from beginning to end. 'My dear fellow,' he said, 'the boy told me just the same. It's an epidemic. When one person falls a victim to this sort of thing, it's as safe as can be – there's always two or three.'

'Then how do you account for it?' I said.

'Oh, account for it! – that's a different matter; there's no accounting for the freaks our brains are subject to. If it's delusion; if it's some trick of the echoes or the winds – some phonetic disturbance or other—'

'Come with me tonight, and judge for yourself,' I said.

Upon this he laughed aloud, then said, 'That's not such a bad idea; but it would ruin me for ever if it were known that John Simson was ghost-hunting.'

'There it is,' said I; 'you dart down on us who are unlearned with your phonetic disturbances, but you daren't examine what the thing really is for fear of being laughed at. That's science!'

'It's not science – it's common-sense,' said the doctor. 'The thing has delusion on the front of it. It is encouraging an unwholesome tendency even to examine. What good could come of it? Even if I am convinced, I shouldn't believe.'

'I should have said so yesterday; and I don't want you to be convinced or to believe,' said I. 'If you prove it to be a delusion, I shall be very much obliged to you for one. Come; somebody must go with me.'

'You are cool,' said the doctor. 'You've disabled this poor fellow of yours, and made him – on that point – a lunatic for life; and now you want to disable me. But for once, I'll do it. To save appearance, if you'll give me a bed, I'll come over after my last rounds.'

It was agreed that I should meet him at the gate, and that we should visit the scene of last night's occurrences before we came to the house, so that nobody might be the wiser. It was scarcely possible to hope that the cause of Bagley's sudden illness should not somehow steal into the knowledge of the servants at least, and it was better that all should be done as quietly as possible. The day seemed to me a very long one. I had to spend a certain part of it with Roland, which was a terrible ordeal for me – for what could I say to the boy? The improvement continued, but he was still in a very precarious state, and the trembling vehemence with which he turned to me when his mother left the room filled me with alarm. 'Father?' he said, quietly. 'Yes, my boy; I am giving my best attention to it – all is being done that I can do. I have not come to any conclusion – yet. I am neglecting nothing you said,' I cried. What I could not do was to give his active mind any encouragement to dwell upon the mystery. It was a hard predicament, for some satisfaction had to be given him. He looked at me very wistfully, with the great blue eyes which shone so large and brilliant out of his white and worn face. 'You must trust me,' I said. 'Yes, father. Father understands,' he said to himself, as if to soothe some inward doubt. I left him as soon as I could. He was about the most precious thing I had on earth, and his health my first thought; but yet somehow, in the excitement of this other subject, I put that aside, and preferred not to dwell upon Roland, which was the most curious part of it all.

That night at eleven I met Simson at the gate. He had come by train, and I let him in gently myself. I had been so much absorbed in the coming experiment that I passed the ruins in going to meet him, almost without thought, if you can understand that. I had my lantern; and he showed me a coil of taper which he had ready for use. 'There is nothing like light,' he said, in his scoffing tone. It was a very still night, scarcely a sound, but not so dark. We could keep the path without difficulty as we went along. As we approached the spot we could hear a low moaning, broken occasionally by a bitter cry. 'Perhaps that is your voice,' said the doctor; 'I thought it must be something of the kind. That's a poor brute caught in some of these infernal traps of yours; you'll find it among the bushes somewhere.' I said nothing. I felt no particular fear, but a triumphant satisfaction in what was to follow. I led him to the spot where Bagley and I had stood on the previous night. All was silent as a winter night could be – so silent that we heard far off the sound of the horses in the stables, the shutting of a window at the house. Simson lighted his taper and went peering about, poking into all the corners. We looked like two conspirators lying in wait for some unfortunate traveller; but not a sound broke the quiet. The moaning had stopped before we came up; a star or two shone over us in the sky, looking down as if surprised at our strange proceedings. Dr Simson did nothing but utter subdued laughs under his breath. 'I thought as much,' he said. 'It is just the same with tables and all other kinds of ghostly apparatus; a sceptic's presence stops everything. When I am present nothing ever comes off. How long do you think it will be necessary to stay here? Oh, I don't complain; only, when *you* are satisfied, *I* am – quite.'

I will not deny that I was disappointed beyond measure by this result. It made me look like a credulous fool. It gave the doctor such a pull over me as nothing else could. I should point all his morals for years to come, and his materialism, his scepticism, would be increased beyond endurance. 'It seems, indeed,' I said, 'that there is to be no—' 'Manifestation,' he said, laughing; 'that is what all the mediums say. No manifestations, in consequence of the presence of an unbeliever.' His laugh sounded very uncomfortable to me in the silence; and it was now near midnight. But that laugh seemed the signal; before it died away the moaning we had heard before was resumed. It started from some distance off, and came towards us, nearer and nearer, like some one walking along and moaning to himself. There could be no idea now that it was a hare caught in a trap. The approach was slow, like that of a weak person with little halts and pauses. We heard it coming along the grass straight towards the vacant doorway. Simson had been a little startled by the first sound. He said hastily, 'That child has no business to be out so late.' But he felt, as well as I, that this was no child's voice. As it came nearer, he grew silent, and, going to the doorway with his taper, stood looking out towards the sound. The taper being unprotected blew about in the night air, though there was scarcely any wind. I threw the light of my lantern steady and white across the same space. It was in a blaze of light in the midst of the blackness. A little icy thrill had gone over me at the first sound, but as it came close, I confess that my only feeling was satisfaction. The scoffer could scoff no more. The light touched his own face, and showed a very perplexed countenance. If he was afraid, he concealed it with great success, but he was perplexed. And then all that had happened on the previous night was enacted once more. It fell strangely upon me with a sense of repetition. Every cry, every sob seemed the same as before. I listened almost without any emotion at all in my own person, thinking of its effect upon Simson. He maintained a very bold front on the whole. All that coming and going of the voice was, if our ears could be trusted, exactly in front of the vacant, blank doorway, blazing full of light, which caught and shone in the glistening leaves of the great hollies at a little distance. Not a rabbit could have crossed the turf without being seen; – but there was nothing. After a time. Simson, with a certain caution and bodily reluctance, as it seemed to me, went out with his roll of taper into this space. His figure showed against the holly in full outline. Just at this moment the voice sank, as was its custom, and seemed to fling itself down at the door. Simson recoiled violently, as if some one had come up against him, then turned, and held his taper low as if examining something. 'Do you see anybody?' I cried in a whisper, feeling the chill of nervous panic steal over me at this action. 'It's nothing but a— confounded juniper-bush,' he said. This I knew very well to be nonsense, for the juniper-bush was on the other side. He went about after this round and round, poking his taper everywhere, then returned to me on the inner side of the wall. He scoffed no longer; his face was contracted and pale. 'How long does this go on?' he whispered to me, like a man who does not wish to interrupt some one who is speaking. I had become too much perturbed myself to remark whether the successions and changes of the voice were the same as last night. It suddenly went out in the air almost as he was speaking, with a soft reiterated sob dying away. If there had been anything to be seen, I should have said that the person was at that moment crouching on the ground close to the door.

We walked home very silent afterwards. It was only when we were in sight of the house that I said, 'What do you think of it?' 'I can't tell what to think of it,' he said, quickly. He took – though he was a very temperate man – not the claret I was going to offer him, but some brandy from the tray, and swallowed it almost undiluted. 'Mind you, I don't believe a word of it,' he said, when he had lighted his candle; 'but I can't tell what to think,' he turned round to add, when he was half-way upstairs.

All of this, however, did me no good with the solution of my problem. I was to help this weeping, sobbing thing, which was already to me as distinct a personality as anything I knew – or what should I say to Roland? It was on my heart that my boy would die if I could not find some way of helping this creature. You may be surprised that I should speak of it in this way. I did not know if it was man or woman; but I no more doubted that it was a soul in pain than I doubted my own being; and it was my business to soothe this pain – to deliver it, if that was possible. Was ever such a task given to an anxious father trembling for his only boy? I felt in my heart, fantastic as it may appear, that I must fulfil this somehow, or part with my child; and you may conceive that rather than do that I was ready to die. But even my dying would not have advanced me – unless by bringing me into the same world with that seeker at the door.

Next morning Simson was out before breakfast, and came in with evident signs of the damp grass on his boots, and a look of worry and weariness, which did not say much for the night he had passed. He improved a little after breakfast, and visited his two patients, for Bagley was still an invalid. I went out with him on his way to the train, to hear what he had to say about the boy. 'He is going on very well,' he said; 'there are no complications as yet. But mind you, that's not a boy to be trifled with, Mortimer. Not a word to him about last night.' I had to tell him then of my last interview with Roland, and of the impossible demand he had made upon me – by which, though he tried to laugh, he was much discomposed, as I could see. 'We must just perjure ourselves all round,' he said, 'and swear you exorcised it'; but the man was too kind-hearted to be satisfied with that. 'It's frightfully serious for you, Mortimer. I can't laugh as I should like to. I wish I saw a way out of it, for your sake. By the way,' he added shortly, 'didn't you notice that juniper-bush on the left-hand side?' 'There was one on the right hand of the door. I noticed you made that mistake last night.' 'Mistake!' he cried, with a curious low laugh, pulling up the collar of his coat as though he felt the cold, – 'there's no juniper there this morning, left or right. Just go and see.' As he stepped into the train a few minutes after, he looked back upon me and beckoned me for a parting word. 'I'm coming back tonight,' he said.

I don't think I had any feeling about this as I turned away from that common bustle of the railway which made my private preoccupations feel so strangely out of date. There had been a distinct satisfaction in my mind before that his scepticism had been so entirely defeated. But the more serious part of the matter pressed upon me now. I went straight from the railway to the manse, which stood on a little plateau on the side of the river opposite to the woods of Brentwood. The minister was one of a class which is not so common in Scotland as it used to be. He was a man of good family, well educated in the Scotch way, strong in philosophy, not so strong in Greek, strongest of all in experience, – a man who had 'come across,' in the course of his life, most people of note that had ever been in Scotland – and who was said to be very sound in doctrine, without infringing the toleration with which old men, who are good men, are generally endowed. He was old-fashioned; perhaps he did not think so much about the troublous problems of theology as many of the young men, nor ask himself any hard questions about the Confession of Faith – but he understood human nature, which is perhaps better. He received me with a cordial welcome. 'Come away, Colonel Mortimer,' he said; 'I'm all the more glad to see you, that I feel it's a good sign for the boy. He's doing well? — God be praised — and the Lord bless him and keep him. He has many a poor body's prayers — and that can do nobody harm.'

'He will need them all, Dr Moncrieff,' I said, 'and your counsel too.' And I told him the story — more than I had told Simson. The old clergyman listened to me with many suppressed exclamations, and at the end the water stood in his eyes.

'That's just beautiful,' he said. 'I do not mind to have heard anything like it; it's as fine as Burns when he wished deliverance to one — that is prayed for in no kirk. Ay, ay! so he would have you console the poor lost spirit? God bless the boy! There's something more than common in that, Colonel Mortimer. And also the faith of him in his father! — I would like to put that into a sermon.' Then the old gentleman gave me an alarmed look, and said, 'No, no; I was not meaning a sermon; but I must write it down for the "Children's Record."' I saw the thought that passed through his mind. Either he thought, or he feared I would think, of a funeral sermon. You may believe this did not make me more cheerful.

I can scarcely say that Dr Moncrieff gave me any advice. How could any one advise on such a subject? But he said, 'I think I'll come too. I'm an old man; I'm less liable to be frighted than those that are further off the world unseen. It behoves me to think of my own journey there. I've no cut-and-dry beliefs on the subject. I'll come too: and maybe at the moment the Lord will put into our heads what to do.'

This gave me a little comfort — more than Simson had given me. To be clear about the cause of it was not my grand desire. It was another thing that was in my mind — my boy. As for the poor soul at the open door, I had no more doubt, as I have said, of its existence than I had of my own. It was no ghost to me. I knew the creature, and it was in trouble. That was my feeling about it, as it was Roland's. To hear it first was a great shock to my nerves, but not now; a man will get accustomed to anything. But to do something for it was the great problem; how was I to be serviceable to a being that was invisible, that was mortal no longer? 'Maybe at the moment the Lord will put it into our heads.' This is very old-fashioned phraseology, and a week before, most likely, I should have smiled (though always with kindness) at Dr Moncrieff's credulity; but there was a great comfort, whether rational or otherwise I cannot say, in the mere sound of the words.

The road to the station and the village lay through the glen – not by the ruins; but though the sunshine and the fresh air, and the beauty of the trees, and the sound of the water were all very soothing to the spirits, my mind was so full of my own subject that I could not refrain from turning to the right hand as I got to the top of the glen, and going straight to the place which I may call the scene of all my thoughts. It was lying full in the sunshine, like all the rest of the world. The ruined gable looked due east, and in the present aspect of the sun the light streamed down through the doorway as our lantern had done, throwing a flood of light upon the damp grass beyond. There was a strange suggestion in the open door – so futile, a kind of emblem of vanity – all free around, so that you could go where you pleased, and yet that semblance of an enclosure – that way of entrance, unnecessary, leading to nothing. And why any creature should pray and weep to get in – to nothing: or be kept out – by nothing! You could not dwell upon it, or it made your brain go round. I remembered, however, what Simson said about the juniper, with a little smile on my own mind as to the inaccuracy of recollection, which even a scientific man will be guilty of. I could see now the light of my lantern gleaming upon the wet glistening surface of the spiky leaves at the right hand – and he ready to go

to the stake for it that it was the left! I went round to make sure.
And then I saw what he had said. Right or left there was no juniper at all. I was confounded by this, though it was entirely a
matter of detail: nothing at all: a bush of brambles waving, the
grass growing up to the very walls. But after all, though it gave
me a shock for a moment, what did that matter? There were
marks as if a number of footsteps had been up and down in front
of the door; but these might have been our steps; and all was
bright, and peaceful, and still. I poked about the other ruin – the
larger ruins of the old house – for some time, as I had done
before. There were marks upon the grass here and there, I could
not call them footsteps, all about; but that told for nothing one
way or another. I had examined the ruined rooms closely the
first day. They were half filled up with soil and *débris*, withered
brackens and bramble – no refuge for any one there. It vexed me
that Jarvis should see me coming from that spot when he came
up to me for his orders. I don't know whether my nocturnal
expeditions had got wind among the servants. But there was a
significant look in his face. Something in it I felt was like my
own sensation when Simson in the midst of his scepticism was
struck dumb. Jarvis felt satisfied that his veracity had been put
beyond question. I never spoke to a servant of mine in such a
peremptory tone before. I sent him away 'with a flea in his lug,'
as the man described it afterwards. Interference of any kind was
intolerable to me at such a moment.

But what was strangest of all was, that I could not face Roland.
I did not go up to his room as I would have naturally done at
once. This the girls could not understand. They saw there was
some mystery in it. 'Mother has gone to lie down,' Agatha said;
'he has had such a good night.' 'But he wants you so, papa!'
cried little Jeanie, always with her two arms embracing mine in
a pretty way she had. I was obliged to go at last – but what could

I say? I could only kiss him, and tell him to keep still – that I was doing all I could. There is something mystical about the patience of a child. 'It will come all right, won't it, father?' he said. 'God grant it may! I hope so, Roland.' 'Oh yes, it will come all right.' Perhaps he understood that in the midst of my anxiety I could not stay with him as I should have done otherwise. But the girls were more surprised than it is possible to describe. They looked at me with wondering eyes. 'If I were ill, papa, and you only stayed with me a moment, I should break my heart,' said Agatha. But the boy had a sympathetic feeling. He knew that of my own will I would not have done it. I shut myself up in the library, where I could not rest, but kept pacing up and down like a caged beast. What could I do? and if I could do nothing, what would become of my boy? These were the questions that, without ceasing, pursued each other through my mind.

Simson came out to dinner, and when the house was all still, and most of the servants in bed, we went out and met Dr Moncrieff, as we had appointed, at the head of the glen. Simson, for his part, was disposed to scoff at the Doctor. 'If there are to be any spells, you know, I'll cut the whole concern,' he said. I did not make him any reply. I had not invited him; he could go or come as he pleased. He was very talkative, far more so than suited my humour, as we went on. 'One thing is certain, you know, there must be some human agency,' he said. 'It is all bosh about apparitions. I never have investigated the laws of sound to any great extent, and there's a great deal in ventriloquism that we don't know much about.' 'If it's the same to you,' I said, 'I wish you'd keep all that to yourself, Simson. It doesn't suit my state of mind.' 'Oh, I hope I know how to respect idiosyncrasy,' he said. The very tone of his voice irritated me beyond measure. These scientific fellows, I wonder people put up with them as they do, when you have no mind for their cold-blooded confidence. Dr Moncrieff met us about eleven o'clock, the same time as on the previous night. He was a large man, with a venerable countenance and white hair – old, but in full vigour, and thinking less of a cold night walk than many a younger man. He had his lantern as I had. We were fully provided with means of lighting the place, and we were all of us resolute men. We had a rapid consultation as we went up, and the result was that we divided to different posts. Dr Moncrieff remained inside the wall – if you can call that inside where there was no wall but one. Simson placed himself on the side next the ruins, so as to intercept any communication with the old house, which was what his mind was fixed upon. I was posted on the other side. To say that nothing could come near without being seen was self-evident. It had been so also on the previous night. Now, with our three lights in the midst of the darkness, the whole place seemed illuminated. Dr Moncrieff's lantern, which was a large one, without any means of shutting up – an old-fashioned lantern with a pierced and ornamental top – shone steadily, the rays shooting out of it upward into the gloom. He placed it on the grass, where the middle of the room, if this had been a room, would have been. The usual effect of the light streaming out of the doorway was prevented by the illumination which Simson and I on either side supplied. With these differences, everything seemed as on the previous night.

And what occurred was exactly the same, with the same air of repetition, point for point, as I had formerly remarked. I declare that it seemed to me as if I were pushed against, put aside, by the owner of the voice as he paced up and down in his trouble, – though these are perfectly futile words, seeing that the stream of light from my lantern, and that from Simson's taper, lay broad and clear, without a shadow, without the smallest break, across the entire breadth of the grass. I had ceased even to be alarmed, for my part. My heart was rent with pity and trouble – pity for the poor suffering human creature that moaned and pleaded so, and trouble for myself and my boy. God! if I could not find any help – and what help could I find? – Roland would die.

We were all perfectly still till the first outburst was exhausted, as I knew (by experience) it would be. Dr Moncrieff, to whom it was new, was quite motionless on the other side of the wall, as we were in our places. My heart had remained almost at its usual beating during the voice. I was used to it; it did not rouse all my pulses as it did at first. But just as it threw itself sobbing at the door (I cannot use other words), there suddenly came something which sent the blood coursing through my veins and my heart into my mouth. It was a voice inside the wall – the minister's well-known voice. I would have been prepared for it in any kind of adjuration, but I was not prepared for what I heard. It came out with a sort of stammering, as if too much moved for utterance. 'Willie, Willie! Oh, God preserve us! is it you?'

These simple words had an effect upon me that the voice of the invisible creature had ceased to have. I thought the old man, whom I had brought into this danger, had gone mad with terror. I made a dash round to the other side of the wall, half crazed myself with the thought. He was standing where I had left him, his shadow thrown vague and large upon the grass by the lantern which stood at his feet. I lifted my own light to see his face as I rushed forward. He was very pale, his eyes wet and glistening, his mouth quivering with parted lips. He neither saw nor heard me. We that had gone through this experience before, had crouched towards each other to get a little strength to bear it. But he was not even aware that I was there. His whole being seemed absorbed in anxiety and tenderness. He held out his hands, which trembled, but it seemed to me with eagerness, not fear. He went on speaking all the time. 'Willie, if it is you – and it's you, if it is not a delusion of Satan, – Willie, lad! why come ye here frighting them that know you not? Why came ye not to me?'

He seemed to wait for an answer. When his voice ceased, his countenance, every line moving, continued to speak. Simson gave me another terrible shock, stealing into the open doorway with his light, as much awe-stricken, as wildly curious, as I. But the minister resumed, without seeing Simson, speaking to some one else. His voice took a tone of expostulation –

'Is this right to come here? Your mother's gone with your name on her lips. Do you think she would ever close her door on her own lad? Do ye think the Lord will close the door, ye faint-hearted creature? No! – I forbid ye! I forbid ye!' cried the old man. The sobbing voice had begun to resume its cries. He made a step forward, calling out the last words in a voice of command. 'I forbid ye! Cry out no more to man. Go home, ye wandering spirit! go home! Do you hear me? – me that christened ye, that have struggled with ye, that have wrestled for ye with the Lord!' Here the loud tones of his voice sank into tenderness. 'And her too, poor woman! poor woman! her you are calling upon. She's no here. You'll find her with the Lord. Go there and seek her, not here. Do you hear me, lad? go after her there. He'll let you in, though it's late. Man, take heart! if you will lie and sob and greet, let it be at heaven's gate, and no your poor mother's ruined door.'

He stopped to get his breath: and the voice had stopped, not as it had done before, when its time was exhausted and all its repetitions said, but with a sobbing catch in the breath as if over-ruled. Then the minister spoke again, 'Are you hearing me, Will? Oh, laddie, you've liked the beggarly elements all your days. Be done with them now. Go home to the Father – the Father! Are you hearing me?' Here the old man sank down upon his knees, his face raised upwards, his hands held up with a tremble in them, all white in the light in the midst of the darkness. I resisted as long as I could, though I cannot tell why, – then I, too, dropped upon my knees. Simson all the time stood in the doorway, with an expression in his face such as words could not tell, his under lip dropped, his eyes wild, staring. It seemed to be to him, that image of blank ignorance and wonder, that we were praying. All the time the voice, with a low arrested sobbing, lay just where he was standing, as I thought.

'Lord,' the minister said – 'Lord, take him into Thy everlasting habitations. The mother he cries to is with Thee. Who can open to him but Thee? Lord, when is it too late for Thee, or what is too hard for Thee? Lord, let that woman there draw him inower! Let her draw him inower!'

I sprang forward to catch something in my arms that flung itself wildly within the door. The illusion was so strong, that I never paused till I felt my forehead graze against the wall and my hands clutch the ground – for there was nobody there to save from falling, as in my foolishness I thought. Simson held out his hand to me to help me up. He was trembling and cold, his lower lip hanging, his speech almost inarticulate. 'It's gone,' he said, stammering, – 'it's gone!' We leant upon each other for a moment, trembling so much both of us that the whole scene trembled as if it were going to dissolve and disappear; and yet as long as I live I will never forget it – the shining of the strange lights, the blackness all round, the kneeling figure with all the whiteness of the light concentrated on its white venerable head and uplifted hands. A strange solemn stillness seemed to close all round us. By intervals a single syllable, 'Lord! Lord!' came from the old minister's lips. He saw none of us, nor thought of us. I never knew how long we stood, like sentinels guarding him at his prayers, holding our lights in a confused dazed way, not knowing what we did. But at last he rose from his knees, and

standing up at his full height, raised his arms, as the Scotch manner is at the end of a religious service, and solemnly gave the
apostolical benediction – to what? to the silent earth, the dark
woods, the wide breathing atmosphere – for we were but specta-
tors gasping an Amen!

It seemed to me that it must be the middle of the night, as we
all walked back. It was in reality very late. Dr Moncrieff put his
arm into mine. He walked slowly, with an air of exhaustion. It
was as if we were coming from a deathbed. Something hushed
and solemnised the very air. There was that sense of relief in it
which there always is at the end of a death-struggle. And nature,
persistent, never daunted, came back in all of us, as we returned
into the ways of life. We said nothing to each other, indeed, for
a time; but when we got clear of the trees and reached the opening near the house, where we could see the sky, Dr Moncrieff
himself was the first to speak. 'I must be going,' he said; 'it's
very late, I'm afraid. I will go down the glen, as I came.'

'But not alone. I am going with you, Doctor.'

'Well, I will not oppose it. I am an old man, and agitation
wearies more than work. Yes; I'll be thankful of your arm.
Tonight, Colonel, you've done me more good turns than one.'

I pressed his hand on my arm, not feeling able to speak. But
Simson, who turned with us, and who had gone along all this
time with his taper flaring, in entire unconsciousness, came to
himself, apparently at the sound of our voices, and put out that
wild little torch with a quick movement, as if of shame. 'Let me
carry your lantern,' he said; 'it is heavy.' He recovered with a
spring, and in a moment, from the awe-stricken spectator he had
been, became himself, sceptical and cynical. 'I should like to ask
you a question,' he said. 'Do you believe in Purgatory, Doctor?
It's not in the tenets of the Church, so far as I know.'

'Sir,' said Dr Moncrieff, 'an old man like me is sometimes not very sure what he believes. There is just one thing I am certain of – and that is the loving kindness of God.'

'But I thought that was in this life. I am no theologian—'

'Sir,' said the old man again, with a tremor in him which I could feel going over all his frame, 'if I saw a friend of mine within the gates of hell, I would not despair but his Father would take him by the hand still – if he cried like *you*.'

'I allow it is very strange – very strange. I cannot see through it. That there must be human agency, I feel sure. Doctor, what made you decide upon the person and the name?'

The minister put out his hand with the impatience which a man might show if he were asked how he recognised his brother. 'Tuts!' he said, in familiar speech – then more solemnly, 'how should I not recognise a person that I know better – far better – than I know you?'

'Then you saw the man?'

Dr Moncrieff made no reply. He moved his hand again with a little impatient movement, and walked on, leaning heavily on my arm. And we went on for a long time without another word, threading the dark paths, which were steep and slippery with the damp of the winter. The air was very still – not more than enough to make a faint sighing in the branches, which mingled with the sound of the water to which we were descending. When we spoke again, it was about indifferent matters – about the height of the river, and the recent rains. We parted with the minister at his own door, where his old housekeeper appeared in great perturbation, waiting for him. 'Eh me, minister! the young gentleman will be worse?' she cried.

'Far from that – better. God bless him!' Dr Moncrieff said.

I think if Simson had begun again to me with his questions, I should have pitched him over the rocks as we returned up the glen; but he was silent, by a good inspiration. And the sky was clearer than it had been for many nights, shining high over the trees, with here and there a star faintly gleaming through the wilderness of dark and bare branches. The air, as I have said, was very soft in them, with a subdued and peaceful cadence. It was real, like every natural sound, and came to us like a hush of peace and relief. I thought there was a sound in it as of the breath of a sleeper, and it seemed clear to me that Roland must be sleeping, satisfied and calm. We went up to his room when we went in. There we found the complete hush of rest. My wife looked up out of a doze, and gave me a smile: 'I think he is a great deal better; but you are very late,' she said in a whisper, shading the light with her hand that the doctor might see his patient. The boy had got back something like his own colour. He woke as we stood all round his bed. His eyes had the happy half-awakened look of childhood, glad to shut again, yet pleased with the interruption and glimmer of the light. I stooped over him and kissed his forehead, which was moist and cool. 'All is well, Roland,' I said. He looked up at me with a glance of pleasure, and took my hand and laid his cheek upon it, and so went to sleep.

For some nights after, I watched among the ruins, spending all the dark hours up to midnight patrolling about the bit of wall which was associated with so many emotions; but I heard nothing, and saw nothing beyond the quiet course of nature: nor so far as I am aware, has anything been heard again. Dr Moncrieff gave me the history of the youth, whom he never hesitated to name. I did not ask, as Simson did, how he recognised him. He had been a prodigal – weak, foolish, easily imposed upon, and 'led away,' as people say. All that we had heard had passed actually in life, the Doctor said. The young man had come home thus a day or two after his mother died – who was no more than the housekeeper in the old house – and distracted with the news, had thrown himself down at the door and called upon her to let him in. The old man could scarcely speak of it for tears. To me it seemed as if – heaven help us, how little do we know about anything! – a scene like that might impress itself somehow upon the hidden heart of nature. I do not pretend to know how, but the repetition had struck me at the time as, in its terrible strangeness and incomprehensibility, almost mechanical – as if the unseen actor could not exceed or vary, but was bound to re-enact the whole. One thing that struck me, however, greatly, was the likeness between the old minister and my boy in the manner of regarding these strange phenomena. Dr Moncrieff was not terrified, as I had been myself, and all the rest of us. It was no 'ghost,' as I fear we all vulgarly considered it, to him – but a poor creature whom he knew under these conditions, just as he had known him in the flesh, having no doubt of his identity. And to Roland it was the same. This spirit in pain – if it was a spirit – this voice out of the unseen – was a poor fellow-creature in misery, to be succoured and helped out of his trouble, to my boy. He spoke to me quite frankly about it when he got better. 'I knew father would find out some way,' he said. And this was when he was strong and well, and all idea that he would turn hysterical or become a seer of visions had happily passed away.

I must add one curious fact which does not seem to me to have any relation to the above, but which Simson made great use of, as the human agency which he was determined to find somehow. We had examined the ruins very closely at the time of these occurrences; but afterwards, when all was over, as we went casually about them one Sunday afternoon in the idleness of that unemployed day, Simson with his stick penetrated an old window which had been entirely blocked up with fallen soil. He jumped down into it in great excitement, and called me to follow. There we found a little hole – for it was more a hole than a room – entirely hidden under the ivy and ruins, in which there was a quantity of straw laid in a corner, as if some one had made a bed there, and some remains of crusts about the floor. Some one had lodged there, and not very long before, he made out; and that this unknown being was the author of all the mysterious sounds we heard he is convinced. 'I told you it was human agency,' he said, triumphantly. He forgets, I suppose, how he and I stood with our lights seeing nothing, while the space between us was audibly traversed by something that could speak, and sob, and suffer. There is no argument with men of this kind. He is ready to get up a laugh against me on this slender ground. 'I was puzzled myself – I could not make it out – but I always felt convinced human agency was at the bottom of it. And here it is – and a clever fellow he must have been,' the Doctor says.

Bagley left my service as soon as he got well. He assured me it was no want of respect; but he could not stand 'them kind of things,' and the man was so shaken and ghastly that I was glad to give him a present and let him go. For my own part, I made a point of staying out the time, two years, for which I had taken Brentwood; but I did not renew my tenancy. By that time we had settled, and found for ourselves a pleasant home of our own.

I must add that when the doctor defies me, I can always bring back gravity to his countenance, and a pause in his railing, when I remind him of the juniper-bush. To me that was a matter of little importance. I could believe I was mistaken. I did not care about it one way or other; but on his mind the effect was different. The miserable voice, the spirit in pain, he could think of as the result of ventriloquism, or reverberation, or – anything you please: an elaborate prolonged hoax executed somehow by the tramp that had found a lodging in the old tower. But the juniper-bush staggered him. Things have effects so different on the minds of different men.

THE NURSE'S TALE
BY ELIZABETH GASKELL

Elizabeth Gaskell was born on 29 September 1810 in London. She was brought up in Knutsford, Cheshire by her aunt after her mother died when she was two years old. In 1832 she married William Gaskell, who was a Unitarian minister like her father. After their marriage they lived in Manchester with their children. Elizabeth Gaskell published her first novel, *Mary Barton*, in 1848 to great success. She went on to publish much of her work in Charles Dickens's magazines, *Household Words* and *All the Year Round*. Along with short stories and a biography of Charlotte Brontë, she published five more novels including *North and South* (1855) and *Wives and Daughters* (1866). Elizabeth Gaskell died on 12 November 1865.

YOU KNOW, my dears, that your mother was an orphan, and an only child; and I dare say you have heard that your grandfather was a clergyman up in Westmoreland, where I come from. I was just a girl in the village school, when, one day, your grandmother came in to ask the mistress if there was any scholar there who would do for a nurse-maid; and mighty proud I was, I can tell ye, when the mistress called me up, and spoke of me being a good girl at my needle, and a steady, honest girl, and one whose parents were very respectable, though they might be poor. I thought I should like nothing better than to serve the pretty young lady, who was blushing as deep as I was, as she spoke of the coming baby, and what I should have to do with it. However, I see you don't care so much for this part of my story, as for what you think is to come, so I'll tell you at once. I was engaged and settled at the parsonage before Miss Rosamond (that was the baby, who is now your mother) was born. To be sure, I had little enough to do with her when she came, for she was never out of her mother's arms, and slept by her all night long; and proud enough was I sometimes when missis trusted her to me. There never was such a baby before or since, though you've all of you been fine enough in your turns; but for sweet, winning ways, you've none of you come up to your mother. She took after her mother, who was a real lady born; a Miss Furnivall, a grand-daughter of Lord Furnivall's, in Northumberland. I believe she had neither brother nor sister, and had been brought up in my lord's family till she had married your grandfather, who was just a curate, son to a shopkeeper in Carlisle – but a clever, fine gentleman as ever was – and one who was a right-down hard worker in his parish, which was very wide, and scattered all abroad over the Westmoreland Fells. When your mother, little Miss Rosamond, was about four or five years old, both her parents died in a fortnight – one after the other. Ah! that was a sad time. My pretty young mistress and me was looking for another baby, when my master came home from one of his long rides, wet and tired, and took the fever he died of; and then she never held up her head again, but just lived to see her dead baby, and have it laid on her breast, before she sighed away her life. My mistress had asked me, on her death-bed, never to leave Miss Rosamond; but if she had never spoken a word, I would have gone with the little child to the end of the world.

The next thing, and before we had well stilled our sobs, the executors and guardians came to settle the affairs. They were my poor young mistress's own cousin, Lord Furnivall, and Mr Esthwaite, my master's brother, a shopkeeper in Manchester; not so well to do then as he was afterwards, and with a large family rising about him. Well! I don't know if it were their settling, or because of a letter my mistress wrote on her death-bed to her cousin, my lord; but somehow it was settled that Miss Rosamond and me were to go to Furnivall Manor House, in Northumberland, and my lord spoke as if it had been her mother's wish that she should live with his family, and as if he had no objections, for that one or two more or less could make no difference in so grand a household. So, though that was not the way in which I should have wished the coming of my bright and pretty pet to have been looked at – who was like a sunbeam in any family, be it never so grand – I was well pleased that all the folks in the Dale should stare and admire, when they heard I was going to be young lady's maid at my Lord Furnivall's at Furnivall Manor.

But I made a mistake in thinking we were to go and live where my lord did. It turned out that the family had left Furnivall Manor House fifty years or more. I could not hear that my poor young mistress had ever been there, though she had been brought up in the family; and I was sorry for that, for I should have liked Miss Rosamond's youth to have passed where her mother's had been.

My lord's gentleman, from whom I asked as many questions as I durst, said that the Manor House was at the foot of the Cumberland Fells, and a very grand place; that an old Miss Furnivall, a great-aunt of my lord's, lived there, with only a few servants; but that it was a very healthy place, and my lord had thought that it would suit Miss Rosamond very well for a few years, and that her being there might perhaps amuse his old aunt.

I was bidden by my lord to have Miss Rosamond's things ready by a certain day. He was a stern, proud man, as they say all the Lords Furnivall were; and he never spoke a word more than was necessary. Folk did say he had loved my young mistress; but that, because she knew that his father would object, she would never listen to him, and married Mr Esthwaite; but I don't know. He never married, at any rate. But he never took much notice of Miss Rosamond; which I thought he might have done if he had cared for her dead mother. He sent his gentleman with us to the Manor House, telling him to join him at Newcastle that same evening; so there was no great length of time for him to make us known to all the strangers before he, too, shook us off; and we were left, two lonely young things (I was not eighteen) in the great old Manor House. It seems like yesterday that we drove there. We had left our own dear parsonage very early, and we had both cried as if our hearts would break, though we were travelling in my lord's carriage, which I thought so much of once. And now it was long past noon on a September day, and we stopped to change horses for the last time at a little smoky town, all full of colliers and miners. Miss Rosamond had fallen asleep, but Mr Henry told me to waken her, that she might see the park and the Manor House as we drove up. I thought it rather a pity; but I did what he bade me, for fear he should complain of me to my lord. We had left all signs of a town, or even a village, and were then inside the gates of a large wild park – not like the parks here in the south, but with rocks, and the noise of running water, and gnarled thorn-trees, and old oaks, all white and peeled with age.

The road went up about two miles, and then we saw a great and stately house, with many trees close around it, so close that in some places their branches dragged against the walls when the wind blew; and some hung broken down; for no-one seemed to take much charge of the place – to lop the wood, or to keep the moss-covered carriage-way in order. Only in front of the house all was clear. The great oval drive was without a weed; and neither tree nor creeper was allowed to grow over the long, many-windowed front; at both sides of which a wing projected, which were each the ends of other side fronts; for the house, although it was so desolate, was even grander than I expected. Behind it rose the Fells, which seemed unenclosed and bare enough; and on the left hand of the house, as you stood facing it, was a little, old-fashioned flower-garden, as I found out afterwards. A door opened out upon it from the west front;

it had been scooped out of the thick, dark wood for some old Lady Furnivall; but the branches of the great forest-trees had grown and over-shadowed it again, and there were very few flowers that would live there at that time.

When we drove up to the great front entrance, and went into the hall, I thought we would be lost – it was so large, and vast and grand. There was a chandelier all of bronze, hung down from the middle of the ceiling; and I had never seen one before, and looked at it all in amaze. Then, at one end of the hall, was a great fire-place, as large as the sides of the houses in my country, with massy andirons and dogs to hold the wood; and by it were heavy, old-fashioned sofas. At the opposite end of the hall, to the left as you went in – on the western side – was an organ built into the wall, and so large that it filled up the best part of that end. Beyond it, on the same side, was a door; and opposite, on each side of the fire-place, were also doors leading to the east front; but those I never went through as long as I stayed in the house, so I can't tell you what lay beyond.

The afternoon was closing in, and the hall, which had no fire lighted in it, looked dark and gloomy, but we did not stay there a moment. The old servant, who had opened the door for us, bowed to Mr Henry, and took us in through the door at the further side of the great organ, and led us through several smaller halls and passages into the west drawing-room, where he said that Miss Furnivall was sitting. Poor little Miss Rosamond held very tight to me, as if she were scared and lost in that great place; and as for myself, I was not much better. The west drawing-room was very cheerful-looking, with a warm fire in it, and plenty of good, comfortable furniture about. Miss Furnivall was an old lady not far from eighty, I should think, but I do not know. She was thin and tall, and had a face as full of fine wrinkles as if they had been drawn all over it with a needle's point. Her eyes were very watchful, to make up, I suppose, for her being so deaf as to be obliged to use a trumpet. Sitting with her, working at the same great piece of tapestry, was Mrs Stark, her maid and companion, and almost as old as she was. She had lived with Miss Furnivall ever since they both were young, and now she seemed more like a friend than a servant; she looked so cold, and grey, and stony, as if she had never loved or cared for anyone; and I don't suppose she did care for anyone, except her mistress; and, owing to the great deafness of the latter, Mrs Stark treated her very much as if she were a child. Mr Henry gave some message from my lord, and then he bowed goodbye to us all – taking no notice of my sweet little Miss Rosamond's outstretched hand – and left us standing there, being looked at by the two old ladies through their spectacles.

I was right glad when they rung for the old footman who had shown us in at first, and told him to take us to our rooms. So we went out of that great drawing-room and into another sitting-room, and out of that, and then up a great flight of stairs, and along a broad gallery – which was something like a library, having books all down one side, and windows and writing-tables all down the other – till we came to our rooms, which I was not sorry to hear were just over the kitchens; for I began to think I should be lost in that wilderness of a house. There was an old nursery, that had been used for all the little lords and ladies long ago, with a pleasant fire burning in the grate, and the kettle boiling on the hob, and tea-things spread out on the table; and out of that room was the night-nursery, with a little crib for Miss Rosamond close to my bed. And old James called up Dorothy, his wife, to bid us welcome; and both he and she were so hospitable and kind, that by-and-by Miss Rosamond and me felt quite at home; and by the time tea was over, she was sitting on Dorothy's knee, and chattering away as fast as her little tongue could go. I soon found out that Dorothy was from Westmoreland, and that bound her and me together, as it were; and I would never wish to meet with kinder people than were old James and his wife. James had lived pretty nearly all his life in my lord's family, and thought there was no-one so grand as they. He even looked down a little on his wife; because, till he had married her, she had never lived in any but a farmer's household. But he was very fond of her, as well he might be. They had one servant under them, to do all the rough work. Agnes they called her; and she and me, and James and Dorothy, with Miss Furnivall and Mrs Stark, made up the family; always remembering my sweet little Miss Rosamond! I used to wonder what they had done before she came, they thought so much of her now. Kitchen and drawing-room, it was all the same. The hard, sad Miss Furnivall, and the cold Mrs Stark, looked pleased when she came fluttering in like a bird, playing and pranking hither and thither, with a continual murmur, and pretty prattle of gladness. I am sure, they were sorry many a time when she flitted away into the kitchen, though they were too proud to ask her to stay with them, and were a little surprised at her taste; though to be sure, as Mrs Stark said, it was not to be wondered at, remembering what stock her father had come of. The great, old rambling house was a famous place for little Miss Rosamond. She made expeditions all over it, with me at her heels; all, except the east wing, which was never opened, and whither we never thought of going. But in the western and northern part was many a pleasant room; full of things that were curiosities to us, though they might not have been to people who had seen more. The windows were darkened by the sweeping boughs of the trees, and the ivy which had overgrown them; but, in the green gloom, we could manage to see old china jars and carved ivory boxes, and great heavy books, and, above all, the old pictures!

Once, I remember, my darling would have Dorothy go with us to tell us who they all were; for they were all portraits of some of my lord's family, though Dorothy could not tell us the names of everyone. We had gone through most of the rooms, when we came to the old state drawing-room over the hall, and there was a picture of Miss Furnivall; or, as she was called in those days, Miss Grace, for she was the younger sister. Such a beauty she must have been! but with such a set, proud look, and such scorn looking out of her handsome eyes, with her eyebrows just a little raised, as if she wondered how anyone could have the impertinence to look at her, and her lip curled at us, as we stood there gazing. She had a dress on, the like of which I had never seen before, but it was all the fashion when she was young; a hat of some soft white stuff like beaver, pulled a little over her brows, and a beautiful plume of feathers sweeping round it on one side; and her gown of blue satin was open in front to a quilted white stomacher.

'Well, to be sure!' said I, when I had gazed my fill. 'Flesh is grass, they do say; but who would have thought that Miss Furnivall had been such an out-and-out beauty, to see her now.'

'Yes,' said Dorothy. 'Folks change sadly. But if what my master's father used to say was true, Miss Furnivall, the elder sister, was handsomer than Miss Grace. Her picture is here somewhere; but, if I show it you, you must never let on, even to James, that you have seen it. Can the little lady hold her tongue, think you?' asked she.

I was not so sure, for she was such a little sweet, bold, open-spoken child, so I set her to hide herself; and then I helped Dorothy to turn a great picture, that leaned with its face towards the wall, and was not hung up as the others were. To be sure, it beat Miss Grace for beauty; and, I think, for scornful pride, too, though in that matter it might be hard to choose. I could have looked at it an hour, but Dorothy seemed half frightened at having shown it to me, and hurried it back again, and bade me run and find Miss Rosamond, for that there were some ugly places about the house, where she should like ill for the child to go. I was a brave, high-spirited girl, and thought little of what the old woman said, for I liked hide-and-seek as well as any child in the parish; so off I ran to find my little one.

As winter drew on, and the days grew shorter, I was sometimes almost certain that I heard a noise as if someone was playing on the great organ in the hall. I did not hear it every evening; but, certainly, I did very often, usually when I was sitting with Miss Rosamond, after I had put her to bed, and keeping quite still and silent in the bedroom. Then I used to hear it booming and swelling away in the distance. The first night, when I went down to my supper, I asked Dorothy who had been playing music, and James said very shortly that I was a gowk to take the wind soughing among the trees for music; but I saw Dorothy look at him very fearfully, and Bessy, the kitchen-maid, said something beneath her breath, and went quite white. I saw they did not like my question, so I held my peace till I was with Dorothy alone, when I knew I could get a good deal out of her. So, the next day, I watched my time, and I coaxed and asked her who it was that played the organ; for I knew that it was the organ and not the wind well enough, for all I had kept silence before James. But Dorothy had had her lesson, I'll warrant, and never a word could I get from her. So then I tried Bessy, though I had always held my head rather above her, as I was evened to James and Dorothy, and she was little better than their servant. So she said I must never, never tell; and if ever I told, I was never to say *she* had told me; but it was a very strange noise, and she had heard it many a time, but most of all on winter nights, and before storms; and folks did say it was the old lord playing on the great organ in the hall, just as he used to do when he was alive; but who the old lord was, or why he played, and why he played on stormy winter evenings in particular, she either could not or would not tell me. Well! I told you I had a brave heart; and I thought it was rather pleasant to have that grand music rolling about the house, let who would be the player; for now it rose above the great gusts of wind, and wailed and triumphed just like a living creature, and then it fell to a softness most complete, only it was always music, and tunes, so it was nonsense to call it the wind. I thought at first, that it might be Miss Furnivall who played, unknown to Bessy; but one day, when I was in the hall by myself, I opened the organ and peeped all about it and around it, as I had done to the organ in Crosthwaite church once before, and I saw it was all broken and destroyed inside, though it looked so brave and fine; and then, though it was noonday, my flesh began to creep a little, and I shut it up, and ran away pretty quickly to my own bright nursery; and I did not like hearing the music for some time after that, any more than James and Dorothy did. All this time Miss Rosamond was making herself more and more beloved. The old ladies liked her to dine with them at their early dinner. James stood behind Miss Furnivall's chair, and I behind Miss Rosamond's all in state; and after dinner, she would play about in a corner of the great drawing-room as still as any mouse, while Miss Furnivall slept, and I had my dinner in the kitchen. But she was glad enough to come to me in the nur-sery afterwards; for, as she said, Miss Furnivall was so sad, and Mrs Stark so dull; but she and I were merry enough; and by-and-by, I got not to care for that weird rolling music, which did one no harm, if we did not know where it came from.

That winter was very cold. In the middle of October the frosts began, and lasted many, many weeks. I remember one day, at dinner, Miss Furnivall lifted up her sad, heavy eyes, and said to

Mrs Stark, 'I am afraid we shall have a terrible winter,' in a strange kind of meaning way. But Mrs Stark pretended not to hear, and talked very loud of something else. My little lady and I did not care for the frost; not we! As long as it was dry, we climbed up the steep brows behind the house, and went up on the Fells, which were bleak and bare enough, and there we ran races in the fresh, sharp air; and once we came down by a new path, that took us past the two old gnarled holly-trees, which grew about half-way down by the east side of the house. But the days grew shorter and shorter, and the old lord, if it was he, played away, more and more stormily and sadly, on the great organ. One Sunday afternoon — it must have been towards the end of November — I asked Dorothy to take charge of little missy when she came out of the drawing-room, after Miss Fur-nivall had had her nap; for it was too cold to take her with me to church, and yet I wanted to go. And Dorothy was glad enough to promise, and was so fond of the child, that all seemed well; and Bessy and I set off very briskly, though the sky hung heavy and black over the white earth, as if the night had never fully gone away, and the air, though still, was very biting and keen.

'We shall have a fall of snow,' said Bessy to me. And sure enough, even while we were in church, it came down thick, in great large flakes — so thick, it almost darkened the windows. It had stopped snowing before we came out, but it lay soft, thick and deep beneath our feet, as we tramped home. Before we got to the hall, the moon rose, and I think it was lighter then — what with the moon, and what with the white dazzling snow — than it had been when we went to church, between two and three o'clock. I have not told you that Miss Furnivall and Mrs Stark never went to church; they used to read the prayers together, in their quiet, gloomy way; they seemed to feel the Sunday very long without their tapestry-work to be busy at. So when I went to Dorothy in the kitchen, to fetch Miss Rosamond and take her upstairs with me, I did not much wonder when the old woman told me that the ladies had kept the child with them, and that she had never come to the kitchen, as I had bidden her, when she was tired of behaving pretty in the drawing-room. So I took off my things and went to find her, and bring her to her supper in the nursery. But when I went into the best drawing-room, there sat the two old ladies, very still and quiet, dropping out a word now and then, but looking as if nothing so bright and merry as Miss Rosamond had ever been near them. Still I thought she might be hiding from me; it was one of her pretty ways – and that she had persuaded them to look as if they knew nothing about her; so I went softly peeping under this sofa, and behind that chair, making believe I was sadly frightened at not finding her.

'What's the matter, Hester?' said Mrs Stark, sharply. I don't know if Miss Furnivall had seen me, for, as I told you, she was very deaf, and she sat quite still, idly staring into the fire, with her hopeless face. 'I'm only looking for my little Rosy Posy,' replied I, still thinking that the child was there, and near me, though I could not see her.

'Miss Rosamond is not here,' said Mrs Stark. 'She went away, more than an hour ago, to find Dorothy.' And she, too, turned and went on looking into the fire.

My heart sank at this, and I began to wish I had never left my darling. I went back to Dorothy and told her. James was gone out for the day, but she, and me, and Bessy took lights, and went up into the nursery first; and then we roamed over the great, large house, calling and entreating Miss Rosamond to come out of her hiding-place, and not frighten us to death in that way. But there was no answer; no sound.

'Oh!' said I, at last, 'can she have got into the east wing and hidden there?'

But Dorothy said it was not possible, for that she herself had never been in there; that the doors were always locked, and my lord's steward had the keys, she believed; at any rate, neither she nor James had ever seen them: so I said I would go back, and see if, after all, she was not hidden in the drawing-room, unknown to the old ladies; and if I found her there, I said, I would whip her well for the fright she had given me; but I never meant to do it. Well, I went back to the west drawing-room, and I told Mrs Stark we could not find her anywhere, and asked for leave to look all about the furniture there, for I thought now that she might have fallen asleep in some warm, hidden corner; but no! we looked – Miss Furnivall got up and looked, trembling all over – and she was nowhere there; then we set off again, every-one in the house, and looked in all the places we had searched before, but we could not find her. Miss Furnivall shivered and shook so much, that Mrs Stark took her back into the warm drawing-room; but not before they had made me promise to bring her to them when she was found. Well-a-day! I began to think she never would be found, when I bethought me to look into the great front court, all covered with snow. I was upstairs when I looked out; but, it was such clear moonlight, I could see, quite plain, two little footprints, which might be traced from the hall-door and round the corner of the east wing. I don't know how I got down, but I tugged open the great stiff hall-door, and, throwing the skirt of my gown over my head for a cloak, I ran out. I turned the east corner, and there a black shadow fell on the snow; but when I came again into the moonlight, there were the little foot-marks going up – up to the Fells. It was bitter cold; so cold, that the air almost took the skin off my face as I ran; but I ran on, crying to think how my poor little darling must be per-ished and frightened. I was within sight of the holly-trees, when I saw a shepherd coming down the hill, bearing something in his arms wrapped in his maud. He shouted to me, and asked me if I had lost a bairn; and, when I could not speak for crying, he bore towards me, and I saw my wee bairnie, lying still, and white, and stiff in his arms, as if she had been dead. He told me he had been up the Fells to gather in his sheep, before the deep cold of night came on, and that under the holly-trees (black marks on the hill-side, where no other bush was for miles around) he had found my little lady – my lamb – my queen – my darling – stiff and cold in the terrible sleep which is frost-begotten, Oh! the joy and the tears of having her in my arms once again! for I would not let him carry her; but took her, maud and all, into my own arms, and held her near my own warm neck and heart, and felt the life stealing slowly back again into her little gentle limbs. But she was still insensible when we reached the hall, and I had no breath for speech. We went in by the kitchen-door.

'Bring me the warming-pan,' said I; and I carried her upstairs and began undressing her by the nursery fire, which Bessy had kept up. I called my little lammie all the sweet and playful names I could think of – even while my eyes were blinded by my tears; and at last, oh! at length she opened her large blue eyes. Then I put her into her warm bed, and sent Dorothy down to tell Miss Furnivall that all was well; and I made up my mind to sit by my darling's bedside the live-long night. She fell away into a soft sleep as soon as her pretty head had touched the pillow, and I watched by her till morning light; when she wakened up bright and clear – or so I thought at first – and, my dears, so I think now.

She said, that she had fancied that she should like to go to Dorothy, for that both the old ladies were asleep, and it was very dull in the drawing-room; and that, as she was going through the west lobby, she saw the snow through the high window falling – falling – soft and steady; but she wanted to see it lying pretty and white on the ground; so she made her way into the great hall; and then, going to the window, she saw it bright and soft upon the drive; but while she stood there, she saw a little girl, not so old as she was, 'but so pretty,' said my darling, 'and this little girl beckoned to me to come out; and oh, she was so pretty and so sweet, I could not choose but go.' And then this other little girl had taken her by the hand, and side by side the two had gone round the east corner.

'Now you are a naughty little girl, and telling stories,' said I. 'What would your good mamma, that is in heaven, and never told a story in her life, say to her little Rosamond, if she heard her – and I dare say she does – telling stories!'

'Indeed, Hester,' sobbed out my child, 'I'm telling you true. Indeed I am.'

'Don't tell me!' said I, very stern. 'I tracked you by your foot-marks through the snow; there were only yours to be seen: and if you had had a little girl to go hand in hand with you up the hill, don't you think the footprints would have gone along with yours?'

'I can't help it, dear, dear Hester,' said she, crying, 'if they did not; I never looked at her feet, but she held my hand fast and tight in her little one, and it was very, very cold. She took me up the Fell-path, up to the holly-trees; and there I saw a lady weeping and crying; but when she saw me, she hushed her weeping, and smiled very proud and grand, and took me on her knee, and began to lull me to sleep; and that's all, Hester – but that is true; and my dear mamma knows it is,' said she, crying. So I thought the child was in a fever, and pretended to believe her, as she went over her story – over and over again, and always the same. At last Dorothy knocked at the door with Miss Rosamond's breakfast; and she told me the old ladies were down in the eating parlour, and that they wanted to speak to me. They had both been into the night-nursery the evening before, but it was after Miss Rosamond was asleep; so they had only looked at her – not asked me any questions.

'I shall catch it,' thought I to myself, as I went along the north gallery. 'And yet,' I thought, taking courage, 'it was in their charge I left her; and it's they that's to blame for letting her steal away unknown and unwatched.' So I went in boldly, and told my story. I told it all to Miss Furnivall, shouting it close to her ear; but when I came to the mention of the other little girl out in the snow, coaxing and tempting her out, and willing her up to the grand and beautiful lady by the holly-tree, she threw her arms up – her old and withered arms – and cried aloud, 'Oh! Heaven forgive! Have mercy!'

Mrs Stark took hold of her; roughly enough, I thought; but she was past Mrs Stark's management, and spoke to me, in a kind of wild warning and authority.

'Hester! keep her from that child! It will lure her to her death! That evil child! Tell her it is a wicked, naughty child.' Then, Mrs Stark hurried me out of the room; where, indeed, I was glad enough to go; but Miss Furnivall kept shrieking out, 'Oh, have mercy! Wilt Thou never forgive! It is many a long year ago –'

I was very uneasy in my mind after that. I durst never leave Miss Rosamond, night or day, for fear lest she might slip off again, after some fancy or other; and all the more, because I thought I could make out that Miss Furnivall was crazy, from their odd ways about her; and I was afraid lest something of the same kind (which might be in the family, you know) hung over my darling. And the great frost never ceased all this time; and, whenever it was a more stormy night than usual, between the gusts, and through the wind, we heard the old lord playing on the great organ. But, old lord, or not, wherever Miss Rosamond went, there I followed; for my love for her, pretty, helpless orphan, was stronger than my fear for the grand and terrible sound. Besides, it rested with me to keep her cheerful and merry, as beseemed her age. So we played together, and wandered together, here and there, and everywhere; for I never dared to lose sight of her again in that large and rambling house. And so it happened, that one afternoon, not long before Christmas-day, we were playing together on the billiard-table in the great hall (not that we knew the right way of playing, but she liked to roll the smooth ivory balls with her pretty hands, and I liked to do whatever she did); and, by-and-by, without our noticing it, it grew dusk indoors, though it was still light in the open air, and I was thinking of taking her back into the nursery, when, all of a sudden, she cried out, 'Look, Hester! look! there is my poor little girl out in the snow!'

I turned towards the long narrow windows, and there, sure enough, I saw a little girl, less than my Miss Rosamond – dressed all unfit to be out-of-doors on such a bitter night – crying, and beating against the window-panes, as if she wanted to be let in. She seemed to sob and wail, till Miss Rosamond could bear it no longer, and was flying to the door to open it, when, all of a sudden, and close upon us, the great organ pealed out so loud and thundering, it fairly made me tremble; and all the more, when I remembered me that, even in the stillness of that dead-cold weather, I had heard no sound of little battering hands upon the windowglass, although the phantom child had seemed to put forth all its force; and, although I had seen it wail and cry, no faintest touch of sound had fallen upon my ears. Whether I remembered all this at the very moment, I do not know; the great organ sound had so stunned me into terror; but this I know, I caught up Miss Rosamond before she got the hall-door opened, and clutched her, and carried her away, kicking and screaming, into the large, bright kitchen, where Dorothy and Agnes were busy with their mince-pies.

'What is the matter with my sweet one?' cried Dorothy, as I bore in Miss Rosamond, who was sobbing as if her heart would break.

'She won't let me open the door for my little girl to come in; and she'll die if she is out on the Fells all night. Cruel, naughty Hester,' she said, slapping me; but she might have struck harder, for I had seen a look of ghastly terror on Dorothy's face, which made my very blood run cold.

'Shut the back-kitchen door fast, and bolt it well,' said she to Agnes. She said no more; she gave me raisins and almonds to quiet Miss Rosamond; but she sobbed about the little girl in the snow, and would not touch any of the good things. I was thankful when she cried herself to sleep in bed. Then I stole down to the kitchen, and told Dorothy I had made up my mind. I would carry my darling back to my father's house in Applethwaite; where, if we lived humbly, we lived at peace. I said I had been frightened enough with the old lord's organ-playing; but now that I had seen for myself this little moaning child, all decked out as no child in the neighbourhood could be, beating and battering to get in, yet always without any sound or noise – with the dark wound on its right shoulder; and that Miss Rosamond had known it again for the phantom that had nearly lured her to her death (which Dorothy knew was true); I would stand it no longer.

I saw Dorothy change colour once or twice. When I had done, she told me she did not think I could take Miss Rosamond with me, for that she was my lord's ward, and I had no right over her; and she asked me would I leave the child that I was so fond of just for sounds and sights that could do me no harm; and that they had all had to get used to in their turns? I was all in a hot, trembling passion; and I said it was very well for her to talk; that knew what these sights and noises betokened, and that had, perhaps, had something to do with the spectre child while it was alive. And I taunted her so, that she told me all she knew at last; and then I wished I had never been told, for it only made me more afraid than ever.

She said she had heard the tale from old neighbours that were alive when she was first married; when folks used to come to the hall sometimes, before it had got such a bad name in the countryside: it might not be true, or it might, what she had been told.

The old lord was Miss Furnivall's father – Miss Grace, as Dorothy called her, for Miss Maude was the elder, and Miss Furnivall by rights. The old lord was eaten up with pride. Such a proud man was never seen or heard of; and his daughters were like him. No-one was good enough to wed them, although they had choice enough; for they were the great beauties of their day, as I had seen by their portraits, where they hung in the state drawing-room. But, as the old saying is, 'Pride will have a fall'; and these two haughty beauties fell in love with the same man, and he no better than a foreign musician, whom their father had down from London to play music with him at the Manor House. For, above all things, next to his pride, the old lord loved music. He could play on nearly every instrument that ever was heard of, and it was a strange thing it did not soften him; but he was a fierce dour old man, and had broken his poor wife's heart with his cruelty, they said. He was mad after music, and would pay any money for it. So he got this foreigner to come; who made such beautiful music, that they said the very birds on the trees stopped their singing to listen. And, by degrees, this foreign gentleman got such a hold over the old lord, that nothing would serve him but that he must come every year; and it was he that had the great organ brought from Holland, and built up in the hall, where it stood now. He taught the old lord to play on it; but many and many a time, when Lord Furnivall was thinking of nothing but his fine organ, and his finer music, the dark foreigner was walking abroad in the woods with one of the young ladies; now Miss Maude, and then Miss Grace.

Miss Maude won the day and carried off the prize, such as it was; and he and she were married, all unknown to anyone; and before he made his next yearly visit, she had been confined of a little girl at a farm-house on the Moors, while her father and Miss Grace thought she was away at Doncaster Races. But though she was a wife and a mother, she was not a bit softened, but as haughty and as passionate as ever; and perhaps more so, for she was jealous of Miss Grace, to whom her foreign husband paid a deal of court – by way of blinding her – as he told his wife. But Miss Grace triumphed over Miss Maude, and Miss Maude grew fiercer and fiercer, both with her husband and with her sister; and the former – who could easily shake off what was disagreeable, and hide himself in foreign countries – went away a month before his usual time that summer, and half-threatened that he would never come back again. Meanwhile, the little girl was left at the farm-house, and her mother used to have her horse saddled and gallop wildly over the hills to see her once every week, at the very least; for where she loved she loved, and where she hated she hated. And the old lord went on playing – playing on his organ; and the servants thought the sweet music he made had soothed down his awful temper, of which (Dorothy said) some terrible tales could be told. He grew infirm too, and had to walk with a crutch; and his son – that was the present Lord Furnivall's father – was with the army in America, and the other son at sea; so Miss Maude had it pretty much her own way, and she and Miss Grace grew colder and bitterer to each other every day; till at last they hardly ever spoke, except when the old lord was by. The foreign musician came again the next summer, but it was for the last time; for they led him such a life with their jealousy and their passions, that he grew weary, and went away, and never was heard of again. And Miss Maude, who had always meant to have her marriage acknowledged when her father should be dead, was left now a deserted wife, whom nobody knew to have been married, with a child that she dared not own, although she loved it to distraction; living with a father whom she feared, and a sister whom she hated. When the next summer passed over, and the dark foreigner never came, both Miss Maude and Miss Grace grew gloomy and sad; they had a haggard look about them, though they looked handsome as ever. But, by-and-by, Maude brightened; for her father grew more and more infirm, and more than ever carried away by his music; and she and Miss Grace lived almost entirely apart, having separate rooms, the one on the west side, Miss Maude on the east – those very rooms which were now shut up. So she thought she might have her little girl with her, and no-one need ever know except those who dared not speak about it, and were bound to believe that it was, as she said, a cottager's child she had taken a fancy to. All this, Dorothy said, was pretty well known; but what came afterwards no-one knew, except Miss Grace and Mrs Stark, who was even then her maid, and much more of a friend to her than ever her sister had been. But the servants supposed, from words that were dropped, that Miss Maude had triumphed over Miss Grace, and told her that all the time the dark foreigner had been mocking her with pretended love – he was her own husband. The colour left Miss Grace's cheek and lips that very day for ever, and she was heard to say many a time that sooner or later she would have her revenge; and Mrs Stark was for ever spying about the east rooms.

One fearful night, just after the New Year had come in, when the snow was lying thick and deep; and the flakes were still falling – fast enough to blind anyone who might be out and abroad — there was a great and violent noise heard, and the old lord's voice above all, cursing and swearing awfully, and the cries of a little child, and the proud defiance of a fierce woman, and the sound of a blow, and a dead stillness, and moans and wailings dying away on the hill-side! Then the old lord summoned all his servants, and told them, with terrible oaths, and words more terrible, that his daughter had disgraced herself, and that he had turned her out of doors — her, and her child — and that if ever they gave her help, or food, or shelter, he prayed that they might never enter heaven. And, all the while, Miss Grace stood by him, white and still as any stone; and, when he had ended, she heaved a great sigh, as much as to say her work was done, and her end was accomplished. But the old lord never touched his organ again, and died within the year; and no wonder! for, on the morrow of that wild and fearful night, the shepherds, coming down the Fell side, found Miss Maude sitting, all crazy and smiling, under the holly-trees, nursing a dead child, with a terrible mark on its right shoulder. 'But that was not what killed it,' said Dorothy: 'it was the frost and the cold. Every wild creature was in its hole, and every beast in its fold, while the child and its mother were turned out to wander on the Fells! And now you know all! and I wonder if you are less frightened now?'

I was more frightened than ever; but I said I was not. I wished Miss Rosamond and myself well out of that dreadful house for ever; but I would not leave her, and I dared not take her away. But oh, how I watched her, and guarded her! We bolted the doors, and shut the window-shutters fast, an hour or more before dark, rather than leave them open five minutes too late. But my little lady still heard the weird child crying and mourning; and not all we could do or say could keep her from wanting to go to her, and let her in from the cruel wind and the snow. All this time I kept away from Miss Furnivall and Mrs Stark, as much as ever I could; for I feared them – I knew no good could be about them, with their grey, hard faces, and their dreamy eyes, looking back into the ghastly years that were gone. But, even in my fear, I had a kind of pity for Miss Furnivall, at least. Those gone down to the pit can hardly have a more hopeless look than that which was ever on her face. At last I even got so sorry for her – who never said a word but what was quite forced from her – that I prayed for her; and I taught Miss Rosamond to pray for one who had done a deadly sin; but often when she came to those words, she would listen, and start up from her knees, and say, 'I hear my little girl plaining and crying very sad – oh, let her in, or she will die!'

One night – just after New Year's Day had come at last, and the long winter had taken a turn, as I hoped – I heard the west drawing-room bell ring three times, which was the signal for me. I would not leave Miss Rosamond alone, for all she was asleep – for the old lord had been playing wilder than ever – and I feared lest my darling should waken to hear the spectre child; see her, I knew she could not. I had fastened the windows too well for that. So I took her out of her bed, and wrapped her up in such outer clothes as were most handy, and carried her down to the drawing-room, where the old ladies sat at their tapestry-work as usual. They looked up when I came in, and Mrs Stark asked, quite astounded, 'Why did I bring Miss Rosamond there, out of her warm bed?' I had begun to whisper, 'Because I was afraid of her being tempted out while I was away, by the wild child in the snow,' when she stopped me short (with a glance at Miss Furnivall), and said Miss Furnivall wanted me to undo some work she had done wrong, and which neither of them could see to unpick. So I laid my pretty dear on the sofa, and sat down on a stool by them, and hardened my heart against them, as I heard the wind rising and howling.

Miss Rosamond slept on sound, for all the wind blew so; and Miss Furnivall said never a word, nor looked round when the gusts shook the windows. All at once she started up to her full height, and put up one hand, as if to bid us to listen.

'I hear voices!' said she. 'I hear terrible screams – I hear my father's voice!'

Just at that moment my darling wakened with a sudden start: 'My little girl is crying, oh, how she is crying!' and she tried to get up and go to her, but she got her feet entangled in the blanket, and I caught her up; for my flesh had begun to creep at these noises, which they heard while we could catch no sound. In a minute or two the noises came, and gathered fast, and filled our ears; we, too, heard voices and screams, and no longer heard the winter's wind that raged abroad. Mrs Stark looked at me, and I at her, but we dared not speak. Suddenly Miss Furnivall went towards the door, out into the anteroom, through the west lobby, and opened the door into the great hall. Mrs Stark followed, and I durst not be left, though my heart almost stopped beating for fear. I wrapped my darling tight in my arms, and went out with them. In the hall the screams were louder than ever; they seemed to come from the east wing – nearer and nearer – close on the other side of the locked-up doors – close behind them. Then I noticed that the great bronze chandelier seemed all alight, though the hall was dim, and that a fire was blazing in the vast hearth-place, though it gave no heat; and I shuddered up with terror, and folded my darling closer to me. But as I did so the east door shook, and she, suddenly struggling to get free from me, cried, 'Hester! I must go. My little girl is there! I hear her; she is coming! Hester, I must go!'

I held her tight with all my strength; with a set will, I held her. If I had died, my hands would have grasped her still, I was so resolved in my mind. Miss Furnivall stood listening, and paid no regard to my darling, who had got down to the ground, and whom I, upon my knees now, was holding with both my arms clasped round her neck; she still striving and crying to get free.

All at once, the east door gave way with a thundering crash, as if torn open in a violent passion, and there came into that broad and mysterious light, the figure of a tall old man, with grey hair and gleaming eyes. He drove before him, with many a relentless gesture of abhorrence, a stern and beautiful woman, with a little child clinging to her dress.

'Oh, Hester! Hester!' cried Miss Rosamond; 'it's the lady! the lady below the holly-trees; and my little girl is with her. Hester! Hester! let me go to her; they are drawing me to them. I feel them – I feel them. I must go!'

Again she was almost convulsed by her efforts to get away; but I held her tighter and tighter, till I feared I should do her a hurt; but rather that than let her go towards those terrible phantoms. They passed along towards the great hall-door, where the winds howled and ravened for their prey; but before they reached that, the lady turned; and I could see that she defied the old man with a fierce and proud defiance; but then she quailed – and then she threw up her arms wildly and piteously to save her child – her little child – from a blow from his uplifted crutch.

And Miss Rosamond was torn as by a power stronger than mine and writhed in my arms, and sobbed (for by this time the poor darling was growing faint).

'They want me to go with them on to the Fells – they are drawing me to them. Oh, my little girl! I would come, but cruel, wicked Hester holds me very tight.' But when she saw the uplifted crutch, she swooned away, and I thanked God for it. Just at this moment – when the tall old man, his hair streaming as in the blast of a furnace, was going to strike the little shrinking child – Miss Furnivall, the old woman by my side, cried out,

'Oh father! father! spare the little innocent child!' But just then I saw – we all saw – another phantom shape itself, and grow clear out of the blue and misty light that filled the hall; we had not seen her till now, for it was another lady who stood by the old man, with a look of relentless hate and triumphant scorn. That figure was very beautiful to look upon, with a soft, white hat drawn down over the proud brows, and a red and curling lip. It was dressed in an open robe of blue satin. I had seen that figure before. It was the likeness of Miss Furnivall in her youth; and the terrible phantoms moved on, regardless of old Miss Furnivall's wild entreaty – and the uplifted crutch fell on the right shoulder of the little child, and the younger sister looked on, stony, and deadly serene. But at that moment, the dim lights, and the fire that gave no heat, went out of themselves, and Miss Furnivall lay at our feet stricken down by the palsy – death-stricken.

Yes! she was carried to her bed that night never to rise again. She lay with her face to the wall, muttering low, but muttering always: 'Alas! alas! what is done in youth can never be undone in age! What is done in youth can never be undone in age!'

THEY *BY* RUDYARD KIPLING

Rudyard Kipling was born in Bombay in India on 30 December 1865. He was sent back to England when he was seven years old but returned to India in 1882 to work as the assistant editor of the *Civil & Military Gazette* in Lahore. He published poetry and stories in newspapers but it was the publication of *Plain Tales from the Hills* in 1888 that brought him his first major success. His most famous works are *Barrack-room Ballads* (1892), *The Jungle Book* (1894), *Kim* (1901), and *Just So Stories* (1902). Rudyard Kipling died on 18 January 1936.

ONE VIEW called me to another; one hill top to its fellow, half across the county, and since I could answer at no more trouble than the snapping forward of a lever, I let the county flow under my wheels. The orchid-studded flats of the East gave way to the thyme, ilex, and grey grass of the Downs; these again to the rich cornland and fig-trees of the lower coast, where you carry the beat of the tide on your left hand for fifteen level miles; and when at last I turned inland through a huddle of rounded hills and woods I had run myself clean out of my known marks. Beyond that precise hamlet which stands godmother to the capital of the United States, I found hidden villages where bees, the only things awake, boomed in eighty-foot lindens that overhung grey Norman churches; miraculous brooks diving under stone bridges built for heavier traffic than would ever vex them again; tithe-barns larger than their churches, and an old smithy that cried out aloud how it had once been a hall of the Knights of the Temple. Gipsies I found on a common where the gorse, bracken, and heath fought it out together up a mile of Roman road; and a little farther on I disturbed a red fox rolling dog-fashion in the naked sunlight.

As the wooded hills closed about me I stood up in the car to take the bearings of that great Down whose ringed head is a landmark for fifty miles across the low countries. I judged that the lie of the country would bring me across some westward-running road that went to his feet, but I did not allow for the confusing veils of the woods. A quick turn plunged me first into a green cutting brim-full of liquid sunshine, next into a gloomy tunnel where last year's dead leaves whispered and scuffled about my tyres. The strong hazel stuff meeting overhead had not been cut for a couple of generations at least, nor had any axe helped the moss-cankered oak and beech to spring above them. Here the road changed frankly into a carpeted ride on whose brown velvet spent primrose-clumps showed like jade, and a few sickly, white-stalked bluebells nodded together. As the slope favoured I shut off the power and slid over the whirled leaves, expecting every moment to meet a keeper; but I only heard a jay, far off, arguing against the silence under the twilight of the trees.

Still the track descended. I was on the point of reversing and working my way back on the second speed ere I ended in some swamp, when I saw sunshine through the tangle ahead and lifted the brake.

It was down again at once. As the light beat across my face my forewheels took the turf of a great still lawn from which sprang horsemen ten feet high with levelled lances, monstrous peacocks, and sleek round-headed maids of honour – blue, black, and glistening – all of clipped yew. Across the lawn – the marshalled woods besieged it on three sides – stood an ancient house of lichened and weather-worn stone, with mullioned windows and roofs of rose-red tile. It was flanked by semi-circular walls, also rose-red, that closed the lawn on the fourth side, and at their feet a box hedge grew man-high. There were doves on the roof about the slim brick chimneys, and I caught a glimpse of an octagonal dove-house behind the screening wall.

Here, then, I stayed; a horseman's green spear laid at my breast; held by the exceeding beauty of that jewel in that setting.

'If I am not packed off for a trespasser, or if this knight does not ride a wallop at me,' thought I, 'Shakespeare and Queen Elizabeth at least must come out of that half-open garden door and ask me to tea.'

A child appeared at an upper window, and I thought the little thing waved a friendly hand. But it was to call a companion, for presently another bright head showed. Then I heard a laugh among the yew-peacocks, and turning to make sure (till then I had been watching the house only) I saw the silver of a fountain behind a hedge thrown up against the sun. The doves on the roof cooed to the cooing water; but between the two notes I caught the utterly happy chuckle of a child absorbed in some light mischief.

The garden door – heavy oak sunk deep in the thickness of the wall – opened further: a woman in a big garden hat set her foot slowly on the time-hollowed stone step and as slowly walked across the turf. I was forming some apology when she lifted up her head and I saw that she was blind.

'I heard you,' she said. 'Isn't that a motor car?'

'I'm afraid I've made a mistake in my road. I should have turned off up above – never dreamed –' I began.

'But I'm very glad. Fancy a motor car coming into the garden! It will be such a treat –' She turned and made as though looking about her. 'You – you haven't seen anyone, have you – perhaps?'

'No one to speak to, but the children seemed interested at a distance.'

'Which?'

'I saw a couple up at the window just now, and I think I heard a little chap in the grounds.'

'Oh, lucky you!' she cried, and her face brightened. 'I hear them, of course, but that's all. You've seen them and heard them?'

'Yes,' I answered. 'And if I know anything of children, one of them's having a beautiful time by the fountain yonder. Escaped, I should imagine.'

'You're fond of children?'

I gave her one or two reasons why I did not altogether hate them.

'Of course, of course,' she said. 'Then you understand. Then you won't think it foolish if I ask you to take your car through the gardens, once or twice – quite slowly. I'm sure they'd like to see it. They see so little, poor things. One tries to make their life pleasant, but –' she threw out her hands towards the woods. 'We're so out of the world here.'

'That will be splendid,' I said. 'But I can't cut up your grass.'

She faced to the right. 'Wait a minute,' she said. 'We're at the South gate, aren't we? Behind those peacocks there's a flagged path. We call it the Peacocks' Walk. You can't see it from here, they tell me, but if you squeeze along by the edge of the wood you can turn at the first peacock and get on to the flags.'

It was sacrilege to wake that dreaming house-front, with the clatter of machinery, but I swung the car to clear the turf, brushed along the edge of the wood and turned in on the broad stone path where the fountain-basin lay like one star-sapphire.

'May I come too?' she cried. 'No, please don't help me. They'll like it better if they see me.'

She felt her way lightly to the front of the car, and with one foot on the step she called: 'Children, oh, children! Look and see what's going to happen!'

The voice would have drawn lost souls from the Pit, for the yearning that underlay its sweetness, and I was not surprised to hear an answering shout behind the yews. It must have been the child by the fountain, but he fled at our approach, leaving a little toy boat in the water. I saw the glint of his blue blouse among the still horsemen.

Very disposedly we paraded the length of the walk and at her request backed again. This time the child had got the better of his panic, but stood far off and doubting.

'The little fellow's watching us,' I said. 'I wonder if he'd like a ride.'

'They're very shy still. Very shy. But, oh, lucky you to be able to see them! Let's listen.'

I stopped the machine at once, and the humid stillness, heavy with the scent of box, cloaked us deep. Shears I could hear where some gardener was clipping; a mumble of bees and broken voices that might have been the doves.

'Oh, unkind!' she said weariedly.

'Perhaps they're only shy of the motor. The little maid at the window looks tremendously interested.'

'Yes?' She raised her head. 'It was wrong of me to say that. They are really fond of me. It's the only thing that makes life worth living – when they're fond of you, isn't it? I daren't think what the place would be without them. By the way, is it beautiful?'

'I think it is the most beautiful place I have ever seen.'

'So they all tell me. I can feel it, of course, but that isn't quite the same thing.'

'Then have you never –?' I began, but stopped abashed.

'Not since I can remember. It happened when I was only a few months old, they tell me. And yet I must remember something, else how could I dream about colours. I see light in my dreams, and colours, but I never see *them*. I only hear them just as I do when I'm awake.'

'It's difficult to see faces in dreams. Some people can, but most of us haven't the gift,' I went on, looking up at the window where the child stood all but hidden.

'I've heard that too,' she said. 'And they tell me that one never sees a dead person's face in a dream. Is that true?'

'I believe it is – now I come to think of it.'

'But how is it with yourself – yourself?' The blind eyes turned towards me.

'I have never seen the faces of my dead in any dream,' I answered.

'Then it must be as bad as being blind.'

The sun had dipped behind the woods and the long shades were possessing the insolent horsemen one by one. I saw the light die from off the top of a glossy-leaved lance and all the brave hard green turn to soft black. The house, accepting another day at end, as it had accepted an hundred thousand gone, seemed to settle deeper into its rest among the shadows.

'Have you ever wanted to?' she said after the silence.

'Very much sometimes,' I replied. The child had left the window as the shadows closed upon it.

'Ah! So've I, but I don't suppose it's allowed . . . Where d'you live?'

'Quite the other side of the county – sixty miles and more, and I must be going back. I've come without my big lamp.'

'But it's not dark yet. I can feel it.'

'I'm afraid it will be by the time I get home. Could you lend me someone to set me on my road at first? I've utterly lost myself.'

'I'll send Madden with you to the cross-roads. We are so out of the world, I don't wonder you were lost! I'll guide you round to the front of the house; but you will go slowly, won't you, till you're out of the grounds? It isn't foolish, do you think?'

'I promise you I'll go like this,' I said, and let the car start herself down the flagged path.

We skirted the left wing of the house, whose elaborately cast lead guttering alone was worth a day's journey; passed under a great rose-grown gate in the red wall, and so round to the high front of the house which in beauty and stateliness as much excelled the back as that all others I had seen.

'Is it so very beautiful?' she said wistfully when she heard my raptures. 'And you like the lead-figures too? There's the old azalea garden behind. They say that this place must have been made for children. Will you help me out, please? I should like to come with you as far as the cross-roads, but I mustn't leave them. Is that you, Madden? I want you to show this gentleman the way to the cross-roads. He has lost his way but – he has seen them.'

A butler appeared noiselessly at the miracle of old oak that must be called the front door, and slipped aside to put on his hat. She stood looking at me with open blue eyes in which no sight lay, and I saw for the first time that she was beautiful.

'Remember,' she said quietly, 'if you are fond of them you will come again,' and disappeared within the house.

The butler in the car said nothing till we were nearly at the lodge gates, where catching a glimpse of a blue blouse in the shrubbery I swerved amply lest the devil that leads little boys to play should drag me into child-murder.

'Excuse me,' he asked of a sudden, 'but why did you do that, Sir?'

'The child yonder.'

'Our young gentleman in blue?'

'Of course.'

'He runs about a good deal. Did you see him by the fountain, Sir?'

'Oh, yes, several times. Do we turn here?'

'Yes, Sir. And did you 'appen to see them upstairs too?'

'At the upper window? Yes.'

'Was that before the mistress come out to speak to you, Sir?'

'A little before that. Why d'you want to know?'

He paused a little. 'Only to make sure that — that they had seen the car, Sir, because with children running about, though I'm sure you're driving particularly careful, there might be an accident. That was all, Sir. Here are the cross-roads. You can't miss your way from now on. Thank you, Sir, but that isn't *our* custom, not with —'

'I beg your pardon,' I said, and thrust away the British silver.

'Oh, it's quite right with the rest of 'em as a rule. Good-bye, Sir.'

He retired into the armour-plated conning tower of his caste and walked away. Evidently a butler solicitous for the honour of his house and interested, probably through a maid, in the nursery.

Once beyond the signposts at the cross-roads I looked back, but the crumpled hills interlaced so jealously that I could not see where the house had lain. When I asked its name at a cottage along the road the fat woman who sold sweetmeats there gave me to understand that people with motor cars had small right to live — much less to 'go about talking like carriage folk'. They were not a pleasant-mannered community.

When I retraced my route on the map that evening I was little wiser. Hawkin's Old Farm appeared to be the Survey title of the place, and the old County Gazetteer, generally so ample, did not allude to it. The big house of those parts was Hodnington Hall, Georgian with early Victorian embellishments, as an atrocious steel engraving attested. I carried my difficulty to a neighbour – a deep-rooted tree of that soil – and he gave me a name of a family which conveyed no meaning.

A month or so later – I went again, or it may have been that my car took the road of her own volition. She over-ran the fruit-less Downs, threaded every turn of the maze of lanes below the hills, drew through the high-walled woods, impenetrable in their full leaf, came out at the cross-roads where the butler had left me, and a little farther on developed an internal trouble which forced me to turn her in on a grass way-waste that cut into a summer-silent hazel wood. So far as I could make sure by the sun and a six-inch Ordnance map, this should be the road flank of that wood which I had first explored from the heights above. I made a mighty serious business of my repairs and a glittering shop of my repair kit, spanners, pump, and the like, which I spread out orderly upon a rug. It was a trap to catch all child-hood, for on such a day, I argued, the children would not be far off. When I paused in my work I listened, but the wood was so full of the noises of summer (though the birds had mated) that I could not at first distinguish these from the tread of small cau-tious feet stealing across the dead leaves. I rang my bell in an alluring manner, but the feet fled, and I repented, for to a child a sudden noise is very real terror. I must have been at work half an hour when I heard in the wood the voice of the blind woman crying: 'Children, oh, children! Where are you?' and the still-ness made slow to close on the perfection of that cry.

She came towards me, half feeling her way between the tree boles, and though a child it seemed clung to her skirt, it swerved into the leafage like a rabbit as she drew nearer.

'Is that you?' she said, 'from the other side of the county?'

'Yes, it's me from the other side of the county.'

'Then why didn't you come through the upper woods? They were there just now.'

'They were here a few minutes ago. I expect they knew my car had broken down, and came to see the fun.'

'Nothing serious, I hope? How do cars break down?'

'In fifty different ways. Only mine has chosen the fifty-first.'

She laughed merrily at the tiny joke, cooed with delicious laughter, and pushed her hat back.

'Let me hear,' she said.

'Wait a moment,' I cried, 'and I'll get you a cushion.'

She set her foot on the rug all covered with spare parts, and stooped above it eagerly. 'What delightful things!' The hands through which she saw glanced in the chequered sunlight. 'A box here – another box! Why you've arranged them like playing shop!'

'I confess now that I put it out to attract them. I don't need half those things really.'

'How nice of you! I heard your bell in the upper wood. You say they were here before that?'

'I'm sure of it. Why are they so shy? That little fellow in blue who was with you just now ought to have got over his fright. He's been watching me like a Red Indian.'

'It must have been your bell,' she said. 'I heard one of them go past me in trouble when I was coming down. They're shy – so shy even with me.' She turned her face over her shoulder and cried again: 'Children, oh, children! Look and see!'

'They must have gone off together on their own affairs,' I suggested, for there was a murmur behind us of lowered voices broken by the sudden squeaking giggles of childhood. I returned to my tinkerings and she leaned forward, her chin on her hand, listening interestedly.

'How many are they?' I said at last. The work was finished, but I saw no reason to go.

Her forehead puckered a little in thought. 'I don't quite know,' she said simply. 'Sometimes more — sometimes less. They come and stay with me because I love them, you see.'

'That must be very jolly,' I said, replacing a drawer, and as I spoke I heard the inanity of my answer.

'You — you aren't laughing at me,' she cried. 'I — I haven't any of my own. I never married. People laugh at me sometimes about them because — because —'

'Because they're savages,' I returned. 'It's nothing to fret for. That sort laugh at everything that isn't in their own fat lives.'

'I don't know. How should I? I only don't like being laughed at about *them*. It hurts; and when one can't see . . . I don't want to seem silly,' her chin quivered like a child's as she spoke, 'but we blindies have only one skin, I think. Everything outside hits straight at our souls. It's different with you. You've such good defences in your eyes — looking out — before anyone can really pain you in your soul. People forget that with us.'

I was silent reviewing that inexhaustible matter — the more than inherited (since it is also carefully taught) brutality of the Christian peoples, beside which the mere heathendom of the West Coast nigger is clean and restrained. It led me a long distance into myself.

'Don't do that!' she said of a sudden, putting her hands before her eyes.

'What?'

She made a gesture with her hand.

'That! It's — it's all purple and black. Don't! That colour hurts.'

'But, how in the world do you know about colours?' I exclaimed, for here was a revelation indeed.

'Colours as colours?' she asked.

'No. *Those* Colours which you saw just now.'

'You know as well as I do,' she laughed, 'else you wouldn't have asked that question. They aren't in the world at all. They're in *you* – when you went so angry.'

'D'you mean a dull purplish patch, like port wine mixed with ink?' I said.

'I've never seen ink or port wine, but the colours aren't mixed. They are separate – all separate.'

'Do you mean black streaks and jags across the purple?'

She nodded. 'Yes – if they are like this,' and zig-zagged her finger again, 'but it's more red than purple – that bad colour.'

'And what are the colours at the top of the – whatever you see?'

Slowly she leaned forward and traced on the rug the figure of the Egg itself.

'I see them so,' she said, pointing with a grass stem, 'white, green, yellow, red, purple, and when people are angry or bad, black across the red – as you were just now.'

'Who told you anything about it – in the beginning?' I demanded.

'About the Colours? No one. I used to ask what colours were when I was little – in table-covers and curtains and carpets, you see – because some colours hurt me and some made me happy. People told me; and when I got older that was how I saw people.' Again she traced the outline of the Egg which it is given to very few of us to see.

'All by yourself?' I repeated.

'All by myself. There wasn't anyone else. I only found out afterwards that other people did not see the Colours.'

She leaned against the tree bole plaiting and unplaiting chance-plucked grass stems. The children in the wood had drawn nearer. I could see them with the tail of my eye frolicking like squirrels.

'Now I am sure you will never laugh at me,' she went on after a long silence. 'Nor at *them*.'

'Goodness! No!' I cried, jolted out of my train of thought. 'A man who laughs at a child – unless the child is laughing too – is a heathen!'

'I didn't mean that, of course. You'd never laugh *at* children, but I thought – I used to think – that perhaps you might laugh about *them*. So now I beg your pardon . . . What are you going to laugh at?'

I had made no sound, but she knew.

At the notion of your begging my pardon. If you had done your duty as a pillar of the State and a landed proprietress you ought to have summoned me for trespass when I barged through your woods the other day. It was disgraceful of me – inexcusable.'

She looked at me, her head against the tree trunk – long and steadfastly – this woman who could see the naked soul.

'How curious,' she half whispered. 'How very curious.'

'Why, what have I done?'

'You don't understand . . . And yet you understood about the Colours. Don't you understand?'

She spoke with a passion that nothing had justified, and I faced her bewilderedly as she rose. The children had gathered themselves in a roundel behind a bramble bush. One sleek head bent over something smaller, and the set of the little shoulders told me that fingers were on lips. They, too, had some child's tremendous secret. I alone was hopelessly astray there in the broad sunlight.

'No,' I said, and shook my head as though the dead eyes could note. 'Whatever it is, I don't understand yet. Perhaps I shall later – if you'll let me come again.'

'You will come again,' she answered. 'You will surely come again and walk in the wood.'

'Perhaps the children will know me well enough by that time to let me play with them – as a favour. You know what children are like.'

'It isn't a matter of favour but of right,' she replied, and while I wondered what she meant, a dishevelled woman plunged round the bend of the road, loose-haired, purple, almost lowing with agony as she ran. It was my rude, fat friend of the sweetmeat shop. The blind woman heard and stepped forward. 'What is it, Mrs Madehurst?' she asked.

The woman flung her apron over her head and literally grovelled in the dust, crying that her grandchild was sick to death, that the local doctor was away fishing, that Jenny the mother was at her wits' end, and so forth, with repetitions and bellowings.

'Where's the next nearest doctor?' I asked between paroxysms.

'Madden will tell you. Go round to the house and take him with you. I'll attend to this. Be quick!' She half supported the fat woman into the shade. In two minutes I was blowing all the horns of Jericho under the front of the House Beautiful, and Madden, in the pantry, rose to the crisis like a butler and a man.

A quarter of an hour at illegal speeds caught us a doctor five miles away. Within the half-hour we had decanted him, much interested in motors, at the door of the sweetmeat shop, and drew up the road to await the verdict.

'Useful things cars,' said Madden, all man and no butler. 'If I'd had one when mine took sick she wouldn't have died.'

'How was it?' I asked.

'Croup. Mrs Madden was away. No one knew what to do. I drove eight miles in a tax cart for the doctor. She was choked when we came back. This car'd ha' saved her. She'd have been close on ten now.'

I'm sorry,' I said. 'I thought you were rather fond of children from what you told me going to the cross-roads the other day.'

'Have you seen 'em again, Sir – this mornin'?'

'Yes, but they're well broke to cars. I couldn't get any of them within twenty yards of it.'

He looked at me carefully as a scout considers a stranger – not as a menial should lift his eyes to his divinely appointed superior.

'I wonder why,' he said just above the breath that he drew.

We waited on. A light wind from the sea wandered up and down the long lines of the woods, and the wayside grasses, whitened already with summer dust, rose and bowed in sallow waves.

A woman, wiping the suds off her arms, came out of the cottage next the sweetmeat shop.

'I've be'n listenin' in de back-yard,' she said cheerily. 'He says Arthur's unaccountable bad. Did ye hear him shruck just now? Unaccountable bad. I reckon t'will come Jenny's turn to walk in de wood nex' week along, Mr Madden.'

'Excuse me, Sir, but your lap-robe is slipping,' said Madden deferentially. The woman started, dropped a curtsey, and hurried away.

'What does she mean by "walking in the wood"?' I asked.

'It must be some saying they use hereabouts. I'm from Norfolk myself,' said Madden. 'They're an independent lot in this county. She took you for a chauffeur, Sir.'

I saw the Doctor come out of the cottage followed by a draggle-tailed wench who clung to his arm as though he could make treaty for her with Death. 'Dat sort,' she wailed – 'dey're just as much to us dat has 'em as if dey was lawful born. Just as much – just as much! An' God he'd be just as pleased if you saved 'un, Doctor. Don't take it from me. Miss Florence will tell ye de very same. Don't leave 'im, Doctor!'

'I know, I know,' said the man; 'but he'll be quiet for a while

now. We'll get the nurse and the medicine as fast as we can.' He
signalled me to come forward with the car, and I strove not to be
privy to what followed; but I saw the girl's face, blotched and
frozen with grief, and I felt the hand without a ring clutching at
my knees when we moved away.

The Doctor was a man of some humour, for I remember he
claimed my car under the Oath of Aesculapius, and used it and
me without mercy. First we convoyed Mrs Madehurst and the
blind woman to wait by the sick bed till the nurse should come.
Next we invaded a neat county town for prescriptions (the Doctor said the trouble was cerebrospinal meningitis), and when the
County Institute, banked and flanked with scared market cattle,
reported itself out of nurses for the moment we literally flung
ourselves loose upon the county. We conferred with the owners
of great houses – magnates at the ends of overarching avenues
whose big-boned womenfolk strode away from their tea-tables
to listen to the imperious Doctor. At last a white-haired lady sitting under a cedar of Lebanon and surrounded by a court of
magnificent Borzois – all hostile to motors – gave the Doctor,
who received them as from a princess, written orders which we
bore many miles at top speed, through a park, to a French nun-
nery, where we took over in exchange a pallid-faced and
trembling Sister. She knelt at the bottom of the tonneau telling
her beads without pause till, by short cuts of the Doctor's inven-
tion, we had her to the sweetmeat shop once more. It was a long
afternoon crowded with mad episodes that rose and dissolved
like the dust of our wheels; cross-sections of remote and incomprehensible lives through which we raced at right angles; and I
went home in the dusk, wearied out, to dream of the clashing
horns of cattle; round-eyed nuns walking in a garden of graves;
pleasant tea-parties beneath shaded trees; the carbolic-scented,
grey-painted corridors of the County Institute; the steps of shy

children in the wood, and the hands that clung to my knees as the motor began to move.

I had intended to return in a day or two, but it pleased Fate to hold me from that side of the county, on many pretexts, till the elder and the wild rose had fruited. There came at last a brilliant day, swept clear from the south-west, that brought the hills within hand's reach — a day of unstable airs and high filmy clouds. Through no merit of my own I was free, and set the car for the third time on that known road. As I reached the crest of the Downs I felt the soft air change, saw it glaze under the sun; and, looking down at the sea, in that instant beheld the blue of the Channel turn through polished silver and dulled steel to dingy pewter. A laden collier hugging the coast steered outward for deeper water, and, across copper-coloured haze, I saw sails rise one by one on the anchored fishing-fleet. In a deep dene behind me an eddy of sudden wind drummed through sheltered oaks, and spun aloft the first dry sample of autumn leaves. When I reached the beach road the sea-fog fumed over the brickfields, and the tide was telling all the groins of the gale beyond Ushant. In less than an hour summer England vanished in chill grey. We were again the shut island of the North, all the ships of the world bellowing at our perilous gates; and between their outcries ran the piping of bewildered gulls. My cap dripped moisture, the folds of the rug held it in pools or sluiced it away in runnels, and the salt-rime stuck to my lips.

Inland the smell of autumn loaded the thickened fog among the trees, and the drip became a continuous shower. Yet the late flowers — mallow of the wayside, scabious of the field, and dahlia of the garden — showed gay in the mist, and beyond the sea's breath there was little sign of decay in the leaf. Yet in the villages the house doors were all open, and bare-legged, bare-headed children sat at ease on the damp doorsteps to shout 'pip-pip' at the stranger.

I made bold to call at the sweetmeat shop, where Mrs Madehurst met me with a fat woman's hospitable tears. Jenny's child, she said, had died two days after the nun had come. It was, she felt, best out of the way, even though insurance offices, for reasons which she did not pretend to follow, would not willingly insure such stray lives. 'Not but what Jenny didn't tend to Arthur as though he'd come all proper at de end of de first year – like Jenny herself.' Thanks to Miss Florence, the child had been buried with a pomp which, in Mrs Madehurst's opinion, more than covered the small irregularity of its birth. She described the coffin, within and without, the glass hearse, and the evergreen lining of the grave.

'But how's the mother?' I asked.

'Jenny? Oh, she'll get over it. I've felt dat way with one or two o' my own. She'll get over. She's walkin' in de wood now.'

'In this weather?'

Mrs Madehurst looked at me with narrowed eyes across the counter.

'I dunno but it opens de 'eart like. Yes, it opens de 'eart. Dat's where losin' and bearin' comes so alike in de long run, we do say.'

Now the wisdom of the old wives is greater than that of all the Fathers, and this last oracle sent me thinking so extendedly as I went up the road, that I nearly ran over a woman and a child at the wooded corner by the lodge gates of the House Beautiful.

'Awful weather!' I cried, as I slowed dead for the turn.

'Not so bad,' she answered placidly out of the fog. 'Mine's used to 'un. You'll find yours indoors, I reckon.'

Indoors, Madden received me with professional courtesy, and kind inquiries for the health of the motor, which he would put under cover.

I waited in a still, nut-brown hall, pleasant with late flowers and warmed with a delicious wood fire – a place of good influence and great peace. (Men and women may sometimes, after great effort, achieve a creditable lie; but the house, which is their temple, cannot say anything save the truth of those who have lived in it.) A child's cart and a doll lay on the black-and-white floor, where a rug had been kicked back. I felt that the children had only just hurried away – to hide themselves, most like – in the many turns of the great adzed staircase that climbed statelily out of the hall, or to crouch at gaze behind the lions and roses of the carven gallery above. Then I heard her voice above me, singing as the blind sing – from the soul:

> In the pleasant orchard-closes.

And all my early summer came back at the call.

> In the pleasant orchard-closes,
> > God bless all our gains say we –
> But may God bless all our losses,
> > Better suits with our degree.

She dropped the marring fifth line, and repeated –

> Better suits with our degree!

I saw her lean over the gallery, her linked hands white as pearl against the oak.

'Is that you – from the other side of the county?' she called.

'Yes, me – from the other side of the county,' I answered, laughing.

'What a long time before you had to come here again.' She

ran down the stairs, one hand lightly touching the broad rail. 'It's two months and four days. Summer's gone!'

'I meant to come before, but Fate prevented.'

'I knew it. Please do something to that fire. They won't let me play with it, but I can feel it's behaving badly. Hit it!'

I looked on either side of the deep fireplace, and found but a half-charred hedge-stake with which I punched a black log into flame.

'It never goes out, day or night,' she said, as though explaining. 'In case anyone comes in with cold toes, you see.'

'It's even lovelier inside than it was out,' I murmured. The red light poured itself along the age-polished dusky panels till the Tudor roses and lions of the gallery took colour and motion. An old eagle-topped convex mirror gathered the picture into its mysterious heart, distorting afresh the distorted shadows, and curving the gallery lines into the curves of a ship. The day was shutting down in half a gale as the fog turned to stringy scud. Through the uncurtained mullions of the broad window I could see valiant horsemen of the lawn rear and recover against the wind that taunted them with legions of dead leaves.

'Yes, it must be beautiful,' she said. 'Would you like to go over it? There's still light enough upstairs.'

I followed her up the unflinching, wagon-wide staircase to the gallery whence opened the thin fluted Elizabethan doors.

'Feel how they put the latch low down for the sake of the children.' She swung a light door inward.

'By the way, where are they?' I asked. 'I haven't even heard them today.'

She did not answer at once. Then, 'I can only hear them,' she replied softly. 'This is one of their rooms – everything ready, you see.'

She pointed into a heavily timbered room. There were little

low gate tables and children's chairs. A doll's house, its hooked front half open, faced a great dappled rocking-horse, from whose padded saddle it was but a child's scramble to the broad window-seat overlooking the lawn. A toy gun lay in a corner beside a gilt wooden cannon.

'Surely they've only just gone,' I whispered. In the failing light a door creaked cautiously. I heard the rustle of a frock and the patter of feet – quick feet through a room beyond.

'I heard that,' she cried triumphantly. 'Did you? Children, oh, children! Where are you?'

The voice filled the walls that held it lovingly to the last perfect note, but there came no answering shout such as I had heard in the garden. We hurried on from room to oak-floored room; up a step here, down three steps there; among a maze of passages; always mocked by our quarry. One might as well have tried to work an unstopped warren with a single ferret. There were bolt-holes innumerable – recesses in walls, embrasures of deep slitten windows now darkened, whence they could start up behind us; and abandoned fireplaces, six feet deep in the masonry, as well as the tangle of communicating doors. Above all, they had the twilight for their helper in our game. I had caught one or two joyous chuckles of evasion, and once or twice had seen the silhouette of a child's frock against some darkening window at the end of a passage; but we returned empty-handed to the gallery, just as a middle-aged woman was setting a lamp in its niche.

'No, I haven't seen her either this evening, Miss Florence,' I heard her say, 'but that Turpin he says he wants to see you about his shed.'

'Oh, Mr Turpin must want to see me very badly. Tell him to come to the hall, Mrs Madden.'

I looked down into the hall whose only light was the dulled

fire, and deep in the shadow I saw them at last. They must have slipped down while we were in the passages, and now thought themselves perfectly hidden behind an old gilt leather screen. By child's law, my fruitless chase was as good as an introduction, but since I had taken so much trouble I resolved to force them to come forward later by the simple trick, which children detest, of pretending not to notice them. They lay close, in a little huddle, no more than shadows except when a quick flame betrayed an outline.

'And now we'll have some tea,' she said. 'I believe I ought to have offered it you at first, but one doesn't arrive at manners somehow when one lives alone and is considered – h'm – peculiar.' Then with very pretty scorn, 'Would you like a lamp to see to eat by?'

'The firelight's much pleasanter, I think.' We descended into that delicious gloom and Madden brought tea.

I took my chair in the direction of the screen ready to surprise or be surprised as the game should go, and at her permission, since a hearth is always sacred, bent forward to play with the fire.

'Where do you get these beautiful short faggots from?' I asked idly. 'Why, they are tallies!'

'Of course,' she said. 'As I can't read or write I'm driven back on the early English tally for my accounts. Give me one and I'll tell you what it meant.'

I passed her an unburned hazel-tally, about a foot long, and she ran her thumb down the nicks.

'This is the milk-record for the home farm for the month of April last year, in gallons,' said she. 'I don't know what I should have done without tallies. An old forester of mine taught me the system. It's out of date now for everyone else; but my tenants respect it. One of them's coming now to see me. Oh, it doesn't matter. He has no business here out of office hours. He's a greedy, ignorant man – very greedy – or he wouldn't come here after dark.'

'Have you much land then?'

'Only a couple of hundred acres in hand, thank goodness. The other six hundred are nearly all let to folk who knew my folk before me, but this Turpin is quite a new man – and a high-way robber.'

'But are you sure I shan't be –?'

'Certainly not. You have the right. He hasn't any children.'

Ah, the children!' I said, and slid my low chair back till it nearly touched the screen that hid them. 'I wonder whether they'll come out for me.'

There was a murmur of voices – Madden's and a deeper note – at the low, dark side door, and a ginger-headed, canvas-gaitered giant of the unmistakable tenant-farmer type stumbled or was pushed in.

'Come to the fire, Mr Turpin,' she said.

'If – if you please, Miss, I'll – I'll be quite as well by the door.' He clung to the latch as he spoke like a frightened child. Of a sudden I realised that he was in the grip of some almost over-powering fear.

'Well?'

'About that new shed for the young stock – that was all. These first autumn storms settin' in . . . But I'll come again, Miss.' His teeth did not chatter much more than the door latch.

'I think not,' she answered levelly. 'The new shed – m'm. What did my agent write you on the 15th?'

'I – fancied p'raps that if I came to see you – ma – man to man like, Miss. But –'

His eyes rolled into every corner of the room wide with horror. He half opened the door through which he had entered, but I noticed it shut again – from without and firmly.

'He wrote what I told him,' she went on. 'You are overstocked already. Dunnett's Farm never carried more than fifty bullocks – even in Mr Wright's time. And *he* used cake. You've sixty-seven and you don't cake. You've broken the lease in that respect. You're dragging the heart out of the farm.'

'I'm – I'm getting some minerals – superphosphates – next week. I've as good as ordered a truck-load already. I'll go down to the station tomorrow about 'em. Then I can come and see you man to man like, Miss, in the daylight . . . That gentleman's not going away, is he?' He almost shrieked.

I had only slid the chair a little farther back, reaching behind me to tap on the leather of the screen, but he jumped like a rat.

'No. Please attend to me, Mr Turpin.' She turned in her chair and faced him with his back to the door. It was an old and sordid little piece of scheming that she forced from him – his plea for the new cow-shed at his landlady's expense, that he might with the covered manure pay his next year's rent out of the valuation after, as she made clear, he had bled the enriched pastures to the bone. I could not but admire the intensity of his greed, when I saw him out-facing for its sake whatever terror it was that ran wet on his forehead.

I ceased to tap the leather – was, indeed, calculating the cost of the shed – when I felt my relaxed hands taken and turned softly between the soft hands of a child. So at last I had triumphed. In a moment I would turn and acquaint myself with those quick-footed wanderers . . .

The little brushing kiss fell in the centre of my palm – as a gift on which the fingers were, once, expected to close: as the all-faithful half-reproachful signal of a waiting child not used to neglect even when grown-ups were busiest – a fragment of the mute code devised very long ago.

Then I knew. And it was as though I had known from the first day when I looked across the lawn at the high window.

I heard the door shut. The woman turned to me in silence, and I felt that she knew.

What time passed after this I cannot say. I was roused by the fall of a log, and mechanically rose to put it back. Then I returned to my place in the chair very close to the screen.

'Now you understand,' she whispered, across the packed shadows.

'Yes, I understand – now. Thank you.'

'I – I only hear them.' She bowed her head in her hands. 'I have no right, you know – no other right. I have neither borne nor lost – neither borne nor lost!'

'Be very glad then,' said I, for my soul was torn open within me.

'Forgive me!'

She was still, and I went back to my sorrow and my joy.

'It was because I loved them so,' she said at last, brokenly. '*That* was why it was, even from the first – even before I knew that they – they were all I should ever have. And I loved them so!'

She stretched out her arms to the shadows and the shadows within the shadow.

'They came because I loved them – because I needed them. I – I must have made them come. Was that wrong, think you?'

'No – no.'

'I – I grant you that the toys and – and all that sort of thing were nonsense, but – but I used to so hate empty rooms myself when I was little.' She pointed to the gallery. 'And the passages all empty . . . And how could I ever bear the garden door shut? Suppose –'

'Don't! For pity's sake, don't!' I cried. The twilight had brought a cold rain with gusty squalls that plucked at the leaded windows.

'And the same thing with keeping the fire in all night. *I* don't think it so foolish – do you?'

I looked at the broad brick hearth, saw, through tears I believe, that there was no unpassable iron on or near it, and bowed my head.

'I did all that and lots of other things – just to make believe. Then they came. I heard them, but I didn't know that they were not mine by right till Mrs Madden told me –'

'The butler's wife? What?'

'One of them – I heard – she saw. And knew. Hers! *Not* for me. I didn't know at first. Perhaps I was jealous. After-wards, I began to understand that it was only because I loved them, not because – . . . . Oh, you *must* bear or lose,' she said pit-eously. There is no other way – and yet they love me. They must! Don't they?'

There was no sound in the room except the lapping voices of the fire, but we two listened intently, and she at least took com-fort from what she heard. She recovered herself and half rose. I sat still in my chair by the screen.

'Don't think me a wretch to whine about myself like this, but – but I'm all in the dark, you know, and *you* can see.'

In truth I could see, and my vision confirmed me in my resolve, though that was like the very parting of spirit and flesh. Yet a little longer I would stay since it was the last time.

'You think it is wrong, then?' she cried sharply, though I had said nothing.

'Not for you. A thousand times no. For you it is right . . . I am grateful to you beyond words. For me it would be wrong. For me only . . .'

'Why?' she said, but passed her hand before her face as she had done at our second meeting in the wood. 'Oh, I see,' she went on simply as a child. 'For you it would be wrong.' Then with a little indrawn laugh, 'And, d'you remember, I called you lucky – once – at first. You who must never come here again!'

She left me to sit a little longer by the screen, and I heard the sound of her feet die out along the gallery above.

penguin.co.uk/vintage-classics

VINTAGE CLASSICS

Vintage launched in the United Kingdom in 1990, and was originally the paperback home for the Random House Group's literary authors. Now, Vintage is comprised of some of London's oldest and most prestigious literary houses, including Chatto & Windus (1855), Hogarth (1917), Jonathan Cape (1921) and Secker & Warburg (1935), alongside the newer or relaunched hardback and paperback imprints: The Bodley Head, Harvill Secker, Yellow Jersey, Square Peg, Vintage Paperbacks and Vintage Classics.

From Angela Carter, Graham Greene and Aldous Huxley to Toni Morrison, Haruki Murakami and Virginia Woolf, Vintage Classics is renowned for publishing some of the greatest writers and thinkers from around the world and across the ages – all complemented by our beautiful, stylish approach to design. Vintage Classics' authors have won many of the world's most revered literary prizes, including the Nobel, the Man Booker, the Prix Goncourt and the Pulitzer, and through their writing they continue to capture imaginations, inspire new perspectives and incite curiosity.

In 2007 Vintage Classics introduced its distinctive red spine design, and in 2012 Vintage Children's Classics was launched to include the much-loved authors of our childhood. Random House joined forces with the Penguin Group in 2013 to become Penguin Random House, making it the largest trade publisher in the United Kingdom.

@vintagebooks